Nudging Nyame

by

Robert Wright

This is a work of fiction. Certain long-standing institutions, organizations, agencies, places, groups, leadership titles, and the underlying physics are mentioned and described as a backdrop to the story, but their involvement in the events described in this book is entirely fictional. Names of characters and their actions are fictitious and wholly the product of the author's imagination. Any resemblance to actual persons, living or dead, is purely coincidental.

Cover designs: Buzz Erlinger-Ford, buzzgraffix@gmail.com

ISBN: 979-8-218-09264-1

Library of Congress Control Number: 2022919725

Published in the United States of America
by
Robert Philip Wright

Acknowledgements

Many thanks are extended to Buzz Erlinger-Ford for his expertise in converting the main concepts of the story into the cover design, and to Niles Lehman, PhD, for his professional scientific review of the manuscript. Most certainly, my sincere gratitude goes to my wife, Janice, for her patience and encouragement during my writing of this book and for her final editing.

Prologue

"If we can perturb an asteroid out of impact trajectory, it follows that we can also transform one on a benign trajectory into an Earth-impactor."

Carl Sagan and Steven Ostro
Dangers of asteroid deflection
Nature, 1994, Volume 368

***

Gravity's inexorable pull gathered primordial grit left over from the dawn of creation and shaped the gray graveled mass into a sphere. Lifeless, silent, it drifted in the absolute cold of infinite space. Interstellar, it arrived and passed through the outer darkness, across the paths of myriad bodies orbiting their central star, altering the course of one, leaving angst, and opportunity, in its wake.

***

The Agency's supercomputer labored for more than a week, executing trillions of floating-point operations every second. Accurate trajectory computations were insanely complex. In addition to the Sun itself, all the bodies in orbit around it attracted every other body. And there were many.

In his very secure executive office, he copied the result into a flash memory chip, then carefully inserted it into the cap of his silver Montblanc pen. The dangerous values escaped the building and found their way to his home near the nation's capital. The select few in his cellar raised a toast with premium French brandy in fine, cut crystal glasses: "To the future … to a new world order."

The men unleashed their control files, hacked into the Intergovernmental Mission Control Center communications labyrinth. Time and duration values rode the space-communications backbone and arrived at the asteroid just before it disappeared behind the Sun, beyond the orbit of Mars.

The deflection system responded. The velocity vector changed according to the dictates of this clandestine group.

Weeks later, the Sun no longer occulted the line-of-sight to the asteroid. But Earth-bound telescopes could not see it through blue sunlit skies. Close to the limb of the Sun, space telescopes looked away from it, rather than risk damage to sensitive optics.

Finally, the errant asteroid could be seen in the night sky. Ellipsoidal, the slowly-tumbling lump of gray was much too far away for radar astronomy. Legions of ground telescopes turned toward it. Refined trajectory data were loaded into identical orbit models on two supercomputers; one lived secretly at the Agency, the other far across the country at the Jet Propulsion Laboratory.

The tensely-awaited prediction again took over two weeks. It was *not* a wide miss with zero likelihood of catastrophe, as the Center had expected, as they thought they had commanded. The probability of Earth impact increased over twenty-one times! The cross-hairs of the likelihood ellipses changed to a point a few hundred kilometers southwest of a large city, with just 3 years and 66 days before impact.

The warning spewed out with withering effect: panic ensued, suspicions arose, cooperation thinned. The international asteroid defense effort froze in uncertainty. But the countdown could not be stopped. Days decremented to possible ground impact along the now-deadly trajectory.

Elcano and Wākea
[9 Years 325 Days before Impact]

Telescopes rested on the northwest shoulder of the red-rocked rim of the caldera on the Spanish island of La Palma. The road leading there followed creases and contours sculpted over eons. It curved back and forth like a paved mountain snake.

Elazar gripped the door handle. Tomás drove at a youthful speed. They'd been here before; Tomás knew the road. The rented SUV swayed with the curse of nausea. "Tomás! Tomás! Please slow down. I may vomit my airplane lunch."

"Yes, Professor. I'm sorry."

"Tomás, I was young once, always in a hurry to absorb life and learn its secrets. Now I look to the stars."

The accommodations for Gran Telescopio Canarias were comfortable, suitable for visiting astronomers. Their scheduled observing runs did not start until the evening of the next day. The flight from Madrid was short, just three hours. But the old man needed to be well-rested, as his age and declining health required.

The next morning, over a light breakfast, they talked. Hair thin and gray, skin wrinkled with wisdom, Elazar pointed his shaking bony finger to the objectives: the schedule and telescope settings placed before him by Tomás. Professor Etxarte's favorite graduate student was working on his doctoral thesis topic: Blue Stars of the Pleiades.

Elazar Etxarte had come a long way from the town of Getaria on the coast in the far north of Spain. His father had been a fisherman and wanted Elazar to follow in his footsteps over the gangplanks to the boats. But the lure of the stars over a nighttime sea, and chronic seasickness, pulled him in a different direction, through a university education to an esteemed position at the prestigious Universidad Complutense de Madrid. He became a respected professor of astronomy, attracting graduate students to this noble ancient discipline and to his classes.

Elazar flew frequently to La Palma. He did so now with greater interest since Gran Telescopio Canarias had achieved First Light. In flight, he often looked down with pride at the sea surrounding the islands. Five centuries earlier, Magellan's fleet had sailed from Seville to Tenerife, one of the Canary Islands, the first leg of the famous around-the-world voyage. A Basque sailor and navigator, also from Getaria, Juan Sebastián Elcano, had been the master of a ship in Magellan's fleet on that first leg. Despite being in the air over the same sea, and not on a wind-driven sailing ship, Elazar felt strongly connected to Juan Sebastián.

Elazar felt refreshed after his needed mid-day nap. Tomás respectfully opened the passenger-side door for his professor, held Elazar's elbow, and helped him up and in, then took the wheel and drove off at an acceptable speed. Like the day before, the road was curvy, but now it wasn't far to the big telescope. Tomás parked so they could see the western horizon while still comfortably seated inside. Elazar always looked forward to the setting Sun, not only for its beauty as the nearest star, but also for the black clear night that usually followed. They watched as the tops of the white clouds below were swept with a beautiful red-orange hue as the Sun dipped below the ocean's horizon.

Inside the observatory, Tomás worked with the telescope operator who called up the ephemeris for the Seven Sisters, the Pleiades: right ascension and declination versus time for the telescope's location. Their attention turned to the new spectrograph. Elazar looked over his student's shoulder like an expectant father.

The computer now controlled the super-accurate pointing of the optical machine. The physical span of its light-collecting reflecting surface, an inverted geodesic dome of 36 rapidly-adjusted, abutting hexagonal mirrors, was the largest on the planet. On another volcanic island, in another ocean, ultra-sophisticated adaptive optics had been ingeniously engineered into the observing system. The image-correcting technology of the pair of giant Keck telescopes on Mauna Kea had also been designed into Gran Telescopio. While the aperture of the grand telescope was larger, the site was lower with more image-distorting atmosphere above. But, as often cited by Spanish astronomers, oxygen deprivation was not a problem for those at this telescope.

Elazar and Tomás had gone through this same ritual some months earlier at Gran Telescopio, with an older imaging spectrograph. Tomás now confirmed that the new higher-resolution device had been correctly installed and calibrated. In the previous visit's imagery, Elazar had noted a faint point of light amid the dimmer siblings of the Seven Sisters. But it was white, not tinted blue by the nebulae in the intervening line of sight. Maybe the older spectrograph had produced an image error.

Astronomical discovery was always exciting. The massive 400-ton telescope moved slowly, smooth as machined silk, into precise position as the image of the Pleiades rose into view in the clear darkening sky. The Seven Sisters and the fainter stars of this mythological constellation remained fixed in their well-known pattern ... except for the small white one. It was still there and still white, but when compared to the earlier images, it had moved! Professor Etxarte exercised his authority and changed the observing objectives.

Gran Telescopio automatically recorded the observing arc data of the moving white object this night and over the following two weeks. According to international agreement and protocol, Elazar sent the data to the Jet Propulsion Laboratory in California and the International Astronomical Union's Minor Planet Center in Massachusetts. They computed the trajectory of the point of reflected light with sufficient accuracy and applied a huge database of predicted positions of known asteroids to determine if the tiny white one matched any of them. It did not!

Enormous computational power swung into action. The object's predicted trajectory was determined: interstellar. It would slice through the ecliptic, the plane of the Earth's orbit around the Sun, at a slight angle. Its path was open, hyperbolic, taking it on a one-time pass through the solar system, never to return. Its trajectory brought it closer to the Sun than the Earth's orbit, qualifying it as a Near-Earth Object. But it would miss the Earth by a wide margin. If it had been on a collision course, there would have been no time to do anything other than to warn, create panic, and to flee from the area around the computed point of impact.

Upon his return from La Palma, Elazar announced his retirement. That wasn't a surprise, with many years to his credit. But there was more. Test results came back to his doctor while he'd been away with Tomás. Cancer was confirmed. It had spread and was terminal. Elazar elected radiation treatment, but to little avail. His remaining days were numbered as to when his human elliptic orbit would open up to a spiritual hyperbolic trajectory, never to return, to where he would be among the stars forever.

Feeble and gaunt, Elazar entered the crowded office. "I'm sorry to be late."

The president of Universidad Complutense stood and welcomed him. "Professor Etxarte, please do not worry. Your discovery is important, for the university."

Elazar took his seat at the conference table. The radiation treatment had taken longer this time. "I, or rather we, have discovered a celestial body, a special one. I will submit the name Elcano to the IAU. Even though it is not in a closed orbit, its trajectory has been determined."

There was unexpected pushback. "But Elazar, the Spanish del Cano is more appropriate for our university."

Elazar looked around the office, "Tomás. What do you think? You were at my side during the observing runs."

"Professor, what can I say? I am from Madrid. I understand your reasons, but I think del Cano should be its name."

"That's what you Spaniards would say!" Tension built in the suddenly quiet room. Separatism in the north still echoed in their minds. Elazar knew that Basques predated the Castilians by thousands of years. All in the room knew that Elazar had the honor of proposing a name for his discovered space traveler.

In an absolute, authoritative tone, Elazar countered with, "My dear friends, need I remind you that I am from Getaria, the home of the Basque navigator Juan Sebastián Elcano, Juan Sebastián *del Cano*, as you would speak it. As you must know, he was the one who brought the remaining ship of Magellan's fleet, the Victoria, the rest of the way around the world after the catastrophe in the Philippines. Like our passing celestial visitor, Elcano was also a traveler in a new world."

"Why not name it Victoria?"

Elazar stood abruptly. "No! Elcano. It is my choice." With that, the meeting was over.

Back in his office, Elazar sat down at his desk, bending over, wincing from abdominal pain. Recovered, he sat up, sweating, and looked for quite some time at the framed photograph on the wall. It was of the statue of the famous navigator in the town square of Getaria. Many times he had walked around this statue, had touched it, and had read the inscription with proud understanding. Elazar clicked the send icon and slapped his desk. "Elcano it is!"

The IAU agreed.

***

In a mere two months, Elazar and his Elcano impacted the life of another astronomer far away, a student. She gripped the steering wheel, stepped on the gas pedal and left surf, sea, and sand far behind and below. Kayla had rented a four-wheel drive SUV in Hilo, then stopped at the Mauna Kea Observatories office to confirm her reservations on the side of the sleeping apex of the volcano. It was her first visit to Hawai'i, but there was no time to sit on the beach with a Mai Tai and watch an orange disc slip below the edge of the sea. She had a date with a man she'd never met and a very advanced optical machine to observe an asteroid and an interstellar object named by an old astronomer on the other side of the Earth.

She swung into a shopping mall and left with a cheap Styrofoam cooler, bag of ice, cans of Gatorade, and a big stack of her favorite energy bars. She'd read that there would be a little kitchen and a small store at the facility, but Kayla didn't trust that information. She'd been stung before in remote, dark mountainous places, telescopically looking at the heavens without the polluting light from little towns.

Clear green-blue water, sandy beaches, white surf, and palm trees gave way to open scruffy grass fields, red soil, flows of ancient black lava, and occasional thickets of trees. Blue sky changed to dark clouds. Big fat drops poured down. A heavy shower enveloped her. The winding two-lane road became slippery. While she didn't know of him, she drove as Tomás had done at La Palma. Wipers danced across the windshield like fast-paced metronomes. The low roar of pelting rain filled the interior. She couldn't see more than a few car lengths, but didn't slow. She'd never weathered heavy rains on the roads to Palomar. Used to Southern California highways on clear sunlit days, Kayla was driving a bit fast and skidded around a blind curve. Her leather case with laptop computer inside slid across the backseat and hit the door with a resounding thunk. The cooler on the seat beside her tipped over, dumping out cans of Gatorade, energy bars and ice. "Dammit!"

An oncoming car crossed the center line and was coming straight at her. Wide eyed, both drivers swerved. Kayla nearly went off the road. Street language from Watts almost spilled out, but she caught herself. Kayla had come a long way from South Los Angeles.

The heavy rain let up. Hale Pōhaku lay some miles ahead. At over 9,000 feet, the Mid-Level Facility was almost twice as high as Palomar, higher than Gran Telescopio Canarias. Observing runs for Keck II at the summit had been approved for her just a few days before. There was an unhappy research astronomer from the University of Hawai'i; he'd been bumped off the schedule. Time-slot dominoes fell into a reshuffled set of runs in the following days.

His deep space research had been delayed.

Kayla did have dormitory reservations; somebody had to be bumped from one of the rooms to accommodate her. She'd been strongly advised to stay there for a few hours to acclimate before ascending the partially-paved road that evening to start work at the top of Mauna Kea. She planned to stay for more than a day and would stay acclimated with much shorter round-trip travel times. Kayla would be yet another intruder on the Hawai'ians' sacred peak that was occasionally dusted in white. The rusty-red cinders at the summit resembled landscape images from NASA's Mars rover missions: spellbinding views of the surface of the red planet.

She needed to rest and breathe the thin air for a time. Altitude sickness rendered some visiting astronomers ineffective. Fatigue, dizziness, and nausea made them more of a problem than an asset when using giant high-altitude telescopes to probe the universe. Hypoxia impaired their decision-making, mathematical ability, and memory. The Keck II facilities, including an enclosed heated control room, weren't pressurized like the cabin of the big jetliner from Los Angeles which had taken her to the biggest island: Hawai'i.

This was the price she'd have to pay to be above as much of the Earth's optically-turbulent atmosphere as possible, above much of what made stars twinkle and blurred telescope images. At the peak, the effects of scintillation were greatly reduced on light that had travelled unfathomable trillions of kilometers to fall silently on Mauna Kea. Only a space-borne telescope would have a cleaner view of the universe; but with adaptive optics, even that was open to argument. Keck I and Keck II had been super-engineered. Extremely rapid adjustments were applied to each of the abutting 36 hexagonal mirrors that collectively spanned 10 meters.

She neared the access road to Mauna Kea from Saddle Road, which traversed the island east-west from Hilo. Kayla could have continued on to Kamuela on the other side, to the Remote Observing Facility 11,000 feet lower than Keck II. At Kamuela she wouldn't have to contend with dizziness at the top. But Kayla requested, or rather demanded, that she personally direct telescope operations on site. She didn't want to miss this opportunity to see the famous big machine up close, and to make certain everything was done right.

Kayla turned right and passed a cylindrical stack of volcanic rocks, tropical flowers resting on top. They weren't dried out, having very recently been placed there. She suspected that this was one of a number of altars to one of the native Hawai'ians' deities, maybe this one to Pele. She'd done some anthropological research before making the trip.

Kayla slowed to get her bearings as she approached a cluster of buildings. They had been named in honor of Ellison Shoji Onizuka, the Hawai'ian-born astronaut killed in the infamous Challenger shuttle disaster almost four decades earlier. Star-minded tourists were gathering in the Visitor Information Station and gift shop, awaiting the nightly astronomy demonstration with portable telescopes on the outdoor patio, but they were nothing like the ones at the summit.

There was a cluster of people across the road. They weren't tourists. With soft olive skin, they wore traditional green ti leaf headbands. Some women were doing the story-telling hula while chanting ancient words with graceful hand motions pointing toward the mountain peak, then up higher to Wākea, the Sky Father. Their beliefs had been handed down orally through generations, animated with the sign language of the ancient hula. They told of Wākea who had mated with Papahānaumoku, the Earth Mother. Together they had created the Hawai'ian Islands; they were the original ancestors of Hawai'ian chiefs and high priests. The islands had gestated in the womb of the sea. Perhaps Pele, goddess of volcanoes and fire, had also had a hand in the islands' birth by lifting them up out of the deep water, roiling and steaming to life.

Large men with big chests and muscled arms were holding poles with Hawai'ian flags, disrespectfully upside down. The flags were fluttering straight out in the stiff cool breeze. Back at Caltech, Kayla had been told about the protests against TMT, the Thirty Meter Telescope. It would add to the array of 13 telescopes already there. For many Hawai'ians, Mauna Kea was the gateway to the heavens, Wākea's gateway to the Earth. For astronomers, Mauna Kea was a gateway to the same heavens. TMT proponents argued that this would enable peering deep into the very origins of the universe, possibly leading to why we are here. The Hawai'ians against building TMT countered that this was already known: Wākea, the Sky Father, had created everything.

Piercing dark eyes stared at Kayla as she drove slowly past. Some carried the hatred handed down since European explorers had first set foot on the islands. Now, people from afar were still desecrating sacred Hawai'ian land. Her beautiful but unsmiling Black face just stared back. She stopped. A big Hawai'ian man walked over. He thought she'd come to join them. Kayla pressed a button and the window rolled down. He leaned in, thinking she needed directions. He smiled, winked, and said, "Howzit, sista?" He just received her cold blank stare in return. Ignored, he followed up with, "Park there. Join us."

From the depths of Watts, Kayla replied, "Hey! Back off, mister. I'm here to look into the same fuckin' universe that wraps around all of us."

He snapped back, like he'd touched something contaminated. Kayla shrugged, made the universally-known, middle-finger gesture, and drove into the facility's parking lot. The gathering was more peaceful than the protests years earlier back in Los Angeles, when a policeman in Minneapolis had knelt too long on the neck of a Black man during his arrest. As she braked to a stop, Kayla thought to herself, Now *that* was a protest!

The Mid-Level Facility was for visiting astronomers and the staff that operated and maintained the telescopes and the road to get there. She looked up toward the summit and noted small patches of white, then checked in at the main building. The small lobby was impressive. The flags of all the countries involved hung from staffs mounted on a second-floor interior balcony. Kayla did a quick walk around the place, pleased to find a nice little dining room with a self-use kitchen and a small store with edibles that could supplement her stash of Gatorade and energy bars.

Kayla thought that the rotund man behind the desk looked Polynesian. He was. As she signed her registration form, he made a matter-of-fact statement, seemingly serious, as he handed her the keys to her room. "You do know that the summit is *kapu*, taboo unless you're a Hawai'ian royal chieftain or high priest." He broke into a wide grin. He reserved those words for *haoles*, those non-native people that had trod the sacred land since the Islands' discovery by a British naval officer.

A brief flashback brought Kayla back to the neighborhood of her youth. An urge tugged at her. She bit her lip to keep old words, hard street language, from coming out. Instead, she raised a clenched fist, heel of her palm facing toward him. That sign of Black Power wiped the grin from his face. The bullet scar on her left cheek punctuated her intent. Ironically, the British had had something to do with her ancestors as well, having been transported by a sailing slave ship all the way from Ghana. As she turned away, *kapu* did stick in her mind. The people she'd just passed down the road now gave her pause.

Kayla went back out to her rented vehicle to get her stuff. She pulled out her suitcase and heard the chanting of the Hawai'ians. She stopped, looked over, and reflected. Her old Watts neighborhood was still a dangerous place. The Caltech campus and JPL were safe enough, but outside that academic bubble, she was now near some people with serious cultural intent.

On the other side of the globe, a spacefaring nation had regressed and invaded the Ukraine. Fighter jets had invaded the airspace around Taiwan. The American political scene had become increasingly divisive. The coronavirus pandemic had left its scars. Against this sobering backdrop, Kayla felt the sands of the world were shifting under her feet, that everything could be coming apart, that stepping into something held sacred wouldn't be helpful.

Yet, there were some very positive things that would touch her field of research. NASA's Double Asteroid Redirection Test space vehicle was predicted to plunge into an asteroid of a binary pair in two months. Amidst all this was an additional unknown danger, soon to be revealed, as Elcano and QW7, her asteroid, approached each other.

Kayla lugged her belongings down a long set of steps with high sides and hand rails to one of the three dormitory buildings. A person dizzied by the altitude could easily tumble off unprotected stairs, possibly a few had. She shivered in the brisk wind. Her warm jacket was still in her suitcase. It was certainly not warm and balmy like the soft breezes at sea-level. She found her modest dorm room. It wasn't like the luxury hotel rooms in Hilo, but it had a bed, desk and chair, bathroom, and closet. It would do, being much better than the small apartment she'd shared with her widowed mother back in Watts. She turned on the wall heater and rubbed her hands together for warmth. Kayla hefted her suitcase up onto the bed, zipped it open, put clothes on hangers and on shelves in the closet to make the room her own comfy little nest away from her place in Pasadena.

She performed a personal ritual first done when she'd won the state's science fair. Kayla pulled out a hard-cover, dog-eared book and set it on the night stand. It had been her ticket out, to not becoming a drug dealer, or a bitch for the Grape Street Crips, or dead. She patted the cover of a reprint of *Theoria Motus*, a translation from the original German: *Theory of the Motion of the Heavenly Bodies Moving about the Sun in Conic Sections.* She then placed her father's Army commemorative brass challenge coin on it.

Kayla had to get back to business and report before she took a short, hopefully refreshing, nap. She quickly established a link with the facility's Wi-Fi network and sent an email message: "Arrived OK. Getting used to the altitude. It's damn cold, way colder than Palomar. Then it's up the hill tonight. Please feed Tiger and clean his litter box."

She set her cell phone alarm and sat on the edge of the bed. Kayla pulled out a single sheet of paper from her leather case. They'd never met, but she held the impressive biography of Professor Elazar Etxarte and read it again. She knew that if not for him, she'd still be back at Caltech doing asteroid research for her doctoral thesis.

Kayla fell back on the mattress, her head into the fluff of the pillow. Her mind swirled, thinking that she should meet Elazar someday. As she drifted off, Kayla mused that Sky Father may have also sired a cold gray visitor from beyond the solar system, maybe in revenge for what White people were doing to the sacred peak of Mauna Kea. But she was proudly Black. Kayla hoped she'd get a pass. She thought about *kapu* and Elcano as the soft fuzz of sleep lifted her away.

Kayla had downloaded Elcano's ephemeris onto her laptop computer at the Jet Propulsion Laboratory. Over the Internet, she had already communicated it to Keck II operations. But she wanted to be there, to check the files, to be sure. Kayla had also downloaded the ephemeris of a well-known orbiting body, one of many. It was the center of her research, big enough to be considered a minor planet, big enough to be dangerous: asteroid 467317 (2000 QW7).

Tigers
[12 Years 330 Days before Impact]

Cushioned gray folding seats rested on wide tiers that stepped down toward the large blackboard that covered the wall. Laptop computers and narrow-lined notebooks rested on small fold-over tables. Only half of the seats were filled with expectant, somewhat intimidated students. They sat Zen-like in preparation for the complex mental sprint led by the famous astrophysicist on Caltech's faculty.

Tall, stoic, elegant, he walked in and pulled the door shut behind him. Eyes and cheekbones set him apart from most in the class, but not all. He brought out an abacus from his briefcase and set it upright on the lecture podium, on its flat side edge. This ancient digital computer had been with Professor Zhang-Wei Huang since his youngest years in Taiwan. It served as a reminder to his class of the digital states at the very heart of electronic computers: on and off, ones and zeros ... very many ones and zeros. Zhang-Wei was there to help his students sort them out, store them, and manipulate them for immense computational power for the benefit of many: mathematicians, engineers, astronomers, and astrophysicists.

Zhang-Wei, Professor Huang to his students and Zhang to his friends and fellow faculty, flipped open his laptop computer on the podium and reached over to throw a switch on the wall. A white screen unrolled down from the ceiling with the growling sound of a slowly-grinding motor. The first image came to projected life, the lesson: Nonlinear Stochastic Systems. Images danced from one to the next as he described their meaning, their underlying theory. Students scribbled furiously or typed frantically on their laptops. When he reached his full lecturing stride, he rolled the screen back up with the flip of a switch, giving a brief pause for students to catch their mental breaths. Zhang picked up the abacus, quickly multiplied two large numbers. The beads clicked and clacked in rapid staccato, his fingers a blur as he moved them from one value state to the other. He finished the calculation in a couple of seconds and set the abacus, his trophy abacus, back on its flat edge for all to see.

Zhang-Wei took to the blackboard with simple white chalk. He wrote out equations, flow diagrams, and complex relationships that had been on the screen. But they now had his soul as they flowed from his hand while he spoke. The rapid sounds of solid chalk striking the board and the hint of drifting dust reminded him of a small dingy classroom in the working-class section of Taipei.

The eager minds before him were doctoral candidates. They needed Professor Huang's knowledge to complete their research in various disciplines, which they would encapsulate in their accepted theses and use to pass their rigorous oral examinations. One student, Kayla, studying astrophysics, sat in the first row, once again nearest to the unfolding action. She asked the most insightful questions and caught his attention from the very first day. Rapid back-and-forth dialogue on some obscure aspect of stochastic applications to non-linear problems often left obtuse students behind, trying to keep up.

***

For Zhang-Wei Huang, very few things were more complicated than the combined understanding and application of physics, mathematics, computer science, and software engineering. But China's history was one of them. This history had been flavored with his mother's visceral hatred of the Communists that controlled mainland China. Her husband's father, Huang Jing, had been extremely loyal to Chiang Kai-shek during the violent struggle between the Nationalist Kuomintang and the Communists. Jing had also been an instructor at the Chengtu Central Military Academy, the last stronghold where Chiang Kai-shek and his son directed its defense against the forces of Mao Zedong before fleeing to Taiwan across the strait. In the dangerous confusing melee, Huang Jing's family had also managed to flee to Taiwan, leaving nearly all their belongings behind, arriving with very little money and just what they could carry. Huang Jing had not been as fortunate. Eventual reports of his capture, repeated often by Zhang-Wei's mother, rang in his ears. The story was replete with torture and execution by Mao's tiger-hunting teams, armed with execution quotas and encouraged to outdo each other. This family story was liberally laced with his mother's vitriol. Hate had many dimensions, hers the darkest when it came to Communist China. She had imbued this in him since he was old enough to walk, talk, and listen.

The prowess of the tiger, its attributes of ferocity, spirit, and drive, had been embedded in Chinese culture since its earliest writings and paintings, and it was now embedded in the Huang family. Taiwan's capital city of Taipei held many tigers. In the small apartment, Zhang-Wei's mother, Liang, paced back and forth as if caged, nervous, relentless, stalking his future. Zhang-Wei's father worked long hours at the tractor factory, often to exhaustion, driven by his own tiger spirit.

Zhang-Wei learned very well at his mother's knee, under her verbal whip. Far across the Pacific Ocean, American children played baseball, football, basketball, and soccer in supposed balance with classwork and homework for their well-rounded upbringing. In the small Taipei apartment, after intently listening and studying in school, Zhang-Wei buried his head in book after book on science and math and on the puzzling, complex grammar and words of the English language.

Young Zhang-Wei and his parents were quite proud that he could add, subtract, divide, and multiply numbers with an abacus faster than others could enter the same numbers on a desk-top electronic calculator to get the answer. His parents could not afford such electronic luxuries, but they pushed him hard with this simple ancient device. Before his teenage years, he'd won an abacus competition. He beat all the others in the final round by accurately and very quickly determining the product of two large numbers. He never forgot those numbers and how he did the multiplication. On the stage, he proudly received an abacus. It had a polished mahogany frame with brass corners and black beads on narrow wood dowels. The side of the frame had a brass plate inscribed with Mandarin characters, Hànzì, for his name, date, and "Taipei Champion". The framed photograph of Zhang-Wei accepting the award sat in a place of honor on a small table next to an old sepia-toned photograph of Jing in China in happier times.

Zhang-Wei continued in that track of serious study habits, leaning toward orbiting planetary bodies. Top grades, entrance exam scores, and teacher recommendations netted him acceptance at the California Institute of Technology. The administrators were so impressed that they accepted him directly without the need for intermediate study to prove his academic worth. When the letter reached the apartment, he carefully and respectfully mouthed the contraction, "Caltech." The tiger mother was happy, as was his father who now had to work more hours to cover the costs.

Huang Zhang-Wei then got a passport and a student visa for entry into the United States of America. The path to full citizenship would follow, wherein he Americanized his name to Zhang-Wei Huang. His dedication to studying computer science and astrophysics at Caltech was almost beyond belief to his professors and fellow students alike. This was pushed to the limit when news of his father's death reached him, brought down by a heart attack, standing at a metal lathe on the overnight shift. Family funds were scarce, but Zhang-Wei took time away from his classes and flew home for the traditional funeral service and cremation. A white banner had been fastened over the doorway to the small apartment. When he returned to Caltech, he placed a white banner over the door to his dorm room. As he studied into the late hours, his roommate fast asleep, that white cloth drove him on with renewed strength. When asked or kidded about his study habits, he'd reply in Mandarin Chinese, followed by the English translation of a phrase he had coined, and almost believed: eating and sleeping are signs of weakness.

Top honors were bestowed on him when he received his PhD.

His mother and close-knit extended family back in Taipei were very proud of the academic accomplishments that his tiger mother had successfully driven him to achieve.

Zhang-Wei continued with post-doctoral work at the nearby famous Jet Propulsion Laboratory. He learned that in the early days of Caltech, the fledgling laboratory had been moved off campus to the foothills of the San Gabriel Mountains. This had been fostered by the noise and explosions of dangerous rocket-engine testing when little was known about this form of propulsion. The foothills were a safer distance away from the main campus. With the likes of genius Theodore von Kármán from Hungary in its lineage, planetary probes and the Mars Rover missions in its history, JPL was *the* place to be: government funded, Caltech managed.

At JPL, Zhang-Wei applied computer science and software engineering to the prediction of intra-planetary spacecraft trajectories and the determination of the orbits of asteroids, especially those that were predicted to come nervously close to the Earth. Research papers and presentations at conferences flowed out like a torrent and caught the eye of senior NASA officials. They wanted to promote him to a leadership position at JPL. But Caltech academia held sway; he was offered a faculty position as a professor, leading to tenure. This was good for Caltech, plus he could still work cooperatively with the people at JPL whom he'd come to know very well. They gave him his own office, even his own parking space.

Zhang-Wei still loved Taiwan and the memories of his childhood. He was proud of his Chinese ancestry, but had also come to love America. As far as he was concerned, raising his right hand and becoming a naturalized citizen eclipsed his doctoral ceremony. But he couldn't shed his acrid hatred of the Communists in Beijing, exacerbated by how they'd treated the citizens of Hong Kong after the British left, which his mother had been quick to point out, and their threats against Taiwan. Despite being the recipient of occasional racial bigotry, often cloaking jealousy, he was more than determined to make a life in his adopted country, a life that would please his mother and himself. However, she not so quietly wished that her eldest son would return to the island of his birth, apply himself there, maybe meet a nice Taiwanese girl, and start a family. There were a number of very good technology-focused universities in Taipei. Certainly, she thought, they would welcome her son; they would have. But she deferred to his wishes, made somewhat easier considering the history of Taiwan-American relations and the long-standing tension with Communist China across the strait.

***

Professor Huang completed his intense lecture and wrote the study assignment and problem set on the blackboard. He turned and looked across his audience, unsmiling, while reaching back and touching what he'd written. Without having to speak it, his students knew what that meant: work through the coming nights if necessary, but they better come back prepared, one reason the lecture hall was only half-filled. Students filed out, but Kayla lingered behind, noticed by some who glanced back through the doorway.

"Professor Huang, do you have time for coffee? I have some questions about that modified convergence algorithm. I have a suggestion, a different finite differencing method that will yield a more-accurate solution, but with a heavier computational load."

A slight smile appeared, "Yes, the usual place at the long oak table. I have some things to take care of at JPL. I'll see you for coffee, and your ideas, at one o'clock."

"Great!" Kayla walked out the door, long legs striding down the hallway.

Zhang-Wei carefully, reverently, placed his precious abacus back in his black briefcase and headed out the door. At the same time, an older professor came out from the lecture room across the hallway. Their different eyes met. "Hello, Lajos. How's the computer research coming?"

"Good, very good, Zhang. We are making things colder, and controlling light; we are close. I'm sure glad that those covid restrictions have loosened. My laboratory is filled again with bright minds. You got your vaccinations, right?"

"Yes, I did. There were some side effects, sore muscles, fever, but I'm feeling better. Well, good luck. Lajos, you make your own luck; you work very hard."

"When my, I mean Caltech's, quantum computing becomes reality and can host your computationally-intensive algorithms, many doors will open, and long-denied solutions will spill out."

"I hope so. I've been working with JPL, applying stochastic optimization to the N-body problem of asteroid trajectory calculations, using the complete physics of our solar system and the gravitational effects of many of the known larger asteroids. Lajos, like our current dynamics model, it considers everything: the flow of updated position data from ground and space telescopes, radio observatories, and the pressure of the light from the Sun."

"How's that working?"

"Promising, but it took our best computer three days to anneal to a solution, and it only had a partial parameter set. The full physics and dynamics, and more bodies, will take much longer."

Lajos reached up and put his beefy arm around Zhang-Wei's shoulder, "I promise you, quantum computing will do it in a few seconds. We are approaching absolute zero and manipulating light in a new way. We can compare results for validation."

Lajos looked back at his small lecture room. "This was my last class. No more instruction. I must devote my time completely to my research."

"Do you have any promising students?"

"Two or three. One is from India, another from San Diego. My student from China, that I'd advised, is especially promising. I'm bringing him into my laboratory. Others are idiots with wealthy parents. I filter them out. They would never have survived in Budapest. That young Kayla, now in your class, did quite well in mine. She came out of the California State University system, a top graduate with very high recommendations. I got a personal call from the president of the Dominguez Hills campus. She certainly has lived up to her billing."

"Yes, also in my classes. She's not afraid of my assignments or my questions, or the questions of others."

Lajos agreed.

They parted at the end of the hall. Zhang-Wei glanced back over his shoulder at the sulky Lajos Vadja. He was twenty years older, and Zhang-Wei had taken his computer engineering classes when he'd first arrived from Taiwan.

Professor Vadja had black unkempt hair and black bushy eyebrows over dark eyes set in a broad, unsmiling face. They amplified his normally sullen look. Shorter, Lajos had a husky build, similar to the Magyars that rode out of the east from the Urals and molded the land into Hungary. Born and raised in Budapest, he was proud that he'd graduated with degrees in physics and computer engineering from Budapest's University of Technology and Economics, the same university attended by Theodore von Kármán, the recognized father of Caltech's JPL. He often bragged about that obscure fact to his students and fellow professors, just so they'd know his academic blood line, as if they really cared.

Lajos Vadja had a dark brooding personality, like he carried the weight of the world's technical problems on his broad shoulders. Normally, students that were having trouble in his classes approached him with trepidation, but Zhang-Wei had been unafraid. That impressed Lajos.

During the early years, when Zhang-Wei was his student fresh from Taiwan, they were discussing a particularly vexing problem. Lajos leaned back in his office chair, looked up, and threw both hands toward the ceiling. "We Hungarians ... and Chinese, of course ... we'll solve the problems of the world. We are tigers! We are born to it."

"Professor Vadja, that's *Taiwanese*."

"Yes. Yes, I know. I'm sorry, Zhang."

Zhang-Wei had become trusted and respected enough for Lajos to pull him into the depths of his dark family history. Close relatives of Lajos had been killed in the Hungarian Revolution by Russian troops when tanks had rolled into the streets to quell the uprising started by students. With that grisly revelation, Zhang-Wei told Lajos the fate of Jing at the hands of Mao Zedong. Despite the age difference, they became kindred spirits in family suffering, but

Lajos was careful not to outwardly show any favoritism. But now that Zhang-Wei was also a professor, first names were used when they met. And they would meet often, drawn together by the pull of an asteroid.

Absolute Zero
[12 Years 298 Days before Impact]

Lajos entered Caltech's prestigious on-campus Institute for Quantum Information and Matter, IQIM. Brilliant students streamed in and out, crowding the hallways. Probing the ultimate secrets of the universe, at the smallest scale imaginable, was stimulating, challenging. He carried his thick leather briefcase tucked up under his right arm, as a football player would do when running toward the end zone. He stared straight ahead with his locally-famous furrowed black brows, striding with pace and purpose. Students spread apart as he passed, as if being repelled by the anti-magnetism of his reputation and personality. Professor Vadja came up to a black door labeled "Quantum Computing" in large white letters and pressed the entry code on the wall's keypad. The door latch retreated with a deep metallic *thud* that echoed down the hallway. Passing students glanced with interest, some with envy. Lajos entered and closed the heavy door behind him.

He'd demanded a high level of security from Caltech if he were to lead this very important computer research program. Other research and government institutions, not to mention commercial enterprises around the world, were investing heavy sums in quantum computing, attempting to leverage the most fundamental nature of matter. The first to score in quantum computing's end zone would influence and possibly control much of human activity, including fundamental research in science, medicine, and communications security. Lajos had emphatically made this point when he'd slammed his fist on the heavy wood of a large conference room table before Caltech's President and Board of Trustees. He'd stressed that this was more important than when Theodore von Kármán had formed the famous Jet Propulsion Laboratory. He just had to arrogantly state that he and Theodore had gone to the same university in Budapest and were both Jewish ... as was Albert Einstein, he'd added for good measure.

Lajos pulled himself up to a new unapologetic level of arrogance. But he pushed the limit when it came to funding the effort. Laboratory equipment, especially cryogenic systems, and intelligent post-doctoral staff would be expensive, let alone his demanded salary beyond that of other senior department heads. He insisted that his research not be funded nor directed by the government, despite the NASA-JPL and Caltech long-term successful relationship. He convinced the trustees that when, not if, he achieved reliable, sustainable quantum computing, Caltech would own the design and the rights to it outright. If the government wanted it, they would have to pay, as would others. Lajos predicted that the cash flow from quantum computing services and patents could fund the entire institute for decades and enable fundamental breakthroughs across many disciplines, yielding other sources of revenue. They reluctantly agreed. Lajos could be very convincing when required.

His tremendous research success thus far added to his academic prowess, supported by a plethora of peer-reviewed publications, plus his claim to be at the top of his engineering class when he'd received his diploma in Budapest. A suspicious trustee, on a Danube River cruise, had quietly and personally confirmed this. While at Caltech, Lajos was nominated for the Nobel Prize in Physics. Even though not selected for this famous award, Lajos took it upon himself to inform the trustees of his nomination, which they already knew. Like the Magyars that rode out of the Urals, social graces were not his forte.

Lajos carefully selected graduate students, engineers, and post-doctoral staff. They labored in various windowed rooms and corners of the large, partially-compartmented IQIM laboratory space. They ceased talking and stood in unison, almost at attention, in their white lab coats as their famous principal investigator entered. He'd not required this, but to them it just seemed like the right thing to do. As he strode to his private locked office, he gave them all an abrupt hand wave. They quickly returned to their investigative work, huddled around complex equipment on gleaming tables.

Of the two enclosures with locked doors, one was Lajos's office; the other had recently-added, blacked-out glass panels. In a space adjacent to it was a multi-level cryogenic cooling system with warning signs and metal tubes wrapped in dense, thermally-insulating foam rubber that fed into this secretive room. Inside this room was another system. The inverted apex of the conic hyper-cooler sucked the last bit of thermal energy from the processer, almost. At very near Absolute Zero, its molecules and atoms lay motionless, almost, to reveal the mysteries of quantum physics. Squeezed Light bathed the atomic vanishing point where multiple states existed simultaneously in elusive quantum bits. The mind of God, or God's creation, was infinitely complex.

***

Despite his Jewish heritage, Lajos wasn't a particularly religious man when it came to its practice, except on the High Holy Days. He did believe in a god that created all things, not from afar, but creation by just thinking as the Infinite Consciousness. For Lajos, defining, knowing, and understanding God was entirely different than mere belief or blind faith. Lajos thought that understanding the physics of the matter and energy of the universe could help him delve into the mind of God.

With the rabbi at his synagogue, he had privately argued that the universe *is* the mind of God, and that hopefully God would not stop thinking. The rabbi retorted, "Lajos, of all the living things, do you think that Yahweh is thinking of you at this moment, of that fly on the wall? How about the pencil on my desk?"

"Absolutely! He, or She, or What, is even thinking of you ... and that yarmulke on your head."

Lajos strongly felt that God did continuously think about the quantum nature of the universe, and therefore had created superposition, photon polarization, entanglement, coherence, de-coherence, electromagnetic radiation, gravity waves, sub-atomic particles, and other humanly-defined, mind-bending things that have operated in the sub-nanoscale world since the Big Bang. Lajos believed that this indeed happened, the creation from which the human species had evolved ... not the Adam and Eve described in the first book of the Torah, when God placed fully-formed progenitors of the human race into a lovely garden with a mythical tree that bore special fruit offered by the sly entwined serpent: the knowledge of good and evil.

Lajos also believed that the theoretical Higgs boson did exist, well before it was first revealed through the CERN Large Hadron Collider in Switzerland. The world's scientific community had mixed feelings when the Higgs boson had been dubbed the God Particle. However, Lajos thought it was very appropriate, that God had more to reveal ... and hopefully would first reveal it to him. But Lajos often corrected the popular vernacular, saying that it was not the God Particle, but God's Particle, because God thought of it and continues thinking of it. Lajos also clung to something said by Albert Einstein: "God is subtle, but he is not malicious." Having eaten of the fruit of the tree, Lajos would handle the malicious part.

From the time he first set foot on campus, Lajos mentally inhaled and absorbed the writings and research of Caltech's famous Richard Feynman, shared winner of the Nobel Prize in Physics. Feynman died before Lajos arrived, but he strongly felt that Feynman had been probing and understanding the mind of God, through God's thinking of neutrinos, antineutrinos, quarks, and man's mind-stretching mathematics that attempted to describe and predict their behaviors. That Richard Feynman had theorized the feasibility of quantum computing wasn't lost on Lajos. It drove him.

Professor Vadja was a controlling man who trusted no one but himself. Research results on critical matters were reported directly to him, not to be completely shared with others, even with others in the laboratory. If that happened, termination or reassignment happened quickly. Sometimes, unknown to his IQIM staff, obscure important details were cleverly omitted or changed slightly in papers submitted to peer-reviewed journals, to put others in the outside world off-track: maliciousness at work. Through his reins of control, research tasks went directly to small groups who reported back only to him and discussed only in his private office. Research data and reports were filed on a computer server, backed up on another, each layered with security firewalls. The servers couldn't be accessed from outside the room. He added more restrictions. Once reports or data had been electronically stored, they couldn't be deleted and could only be accessed for viewing and further processing in the laboratory, not for transferring to a solid state thumb drive that could be hidden in a pocket. There were no USB ports on any of the laboratory computers ... except for the one in Lajos's locked office.

Red-domed security cameras laced the laboratory. When in his office, a computer monitor to Lajos's left displayed real-time camera imagery. His brilliant mind could easily multi-task as he kept an eye on things in the laboratory and his mind on test results. Unknown to those that worked in the lab, Lajos could watch real-time surveillance video from his expensive home in Pasadena, a home that belied what Caltech paid him, even though that was a very significant sum.

Lajos shared nothing, but did reach out to other corners of Caltech in order to test his quantum computing research. And Zhang-Wei was one who needed Lajos's computing power, in order to untangle and enable accurate N-body asteroid orbit prediction.

***

An expected but unknown visitor was on Lajos's schedule. He arrived and was waiting outside the lab's entry door. In addition to the keypad, there was a button on Lajos's desk that triggered a buzzer and a flashing red light in the laboratory. Research staff knew to quickly cover their equipment, computer monitors, and papers with a white sheet whenever anyone entered.

Lajos went from his office and opened the black door, revealing a red-haired and tall angular man who walked in with a slight limp. National and international scientists and professors visiting

IQIM were nothing unusual. There had been a wide variety of visitors who had passed through the Quantum Computing door, carefully escorted and guarded. But some of them had looks not typically associated with academia. Some wore slick silk suits, drove black Mercedes and silver Audi sedans. They appeared as if they would be more comfortable in the financial halls of banks and investment companies on Wall Street, or in the underground lairs of the modern Mafia. Younger ones fit the modern image of Silicon Valley billionaires. In un-socked feet, deck shoes, jeans, and open-collared shirts, they unfolded themselves out of low, fast vehicles made by Ferrari, Maserati, and Bugatti. All wanted a place to invest their billions with the best possibility of a huge return and, more importantly, more power. Quantum computing was the thing; Lajos Vadja was the man ... and a very good salesman and investment counselor.

With his visitor inside, Lajos closed and locked his office door, then turned a dial on the wall, electrically-stimulating polarizing sheets on his glass windows, silently making them opaque. They sat down and just looked across the desk at each other for a few seconds, each taking the measure of the other. The visitor had a cold icy stare. Lajos noticed that his guest slightly winced in pain as he sat down, then broke the silence with a suspicious, "I am Lajos Vadja. What can I do for you?"

"Everything … and nothing. Please understand. We can shut you down."

"Who in the hell are you!? From the government?"

"That is not relevant. We are more than aware of your important work but have some concerns. And an offer."

That erased the furrows between Lajos's now-raised eyebrows. Lajos regained his stern composure. "And just what might those be? I do not rely on government funding. I do not depend on you, whoever you are."

The visitor leaned to one side and appeared to massage his hip with his hand, as if putting a joint back in place. Snidely he asked, "Do you think that deflects our interest? First, there are too many visitors." Then he accurately rattled off names and organizations, from memory, that Lajos knew very well. Some names were known only to Lajos, or so he had thought.

Astonished at the breach of his under-cover business dealings, Lajos slightly paled. "I see … I see. But I will not be threatened! Do you have an offer that compensates for this restriction?"

"You and Caltech will be well compensated, very well, on one condition."

"And just what might that be, Mister … ?"

The visitor still didn't introduce himself, but gave a carefully-measured reply. "When you make the breakthrough to reliable, sustainable quantum computing, we must have the first and *only* access to it, and absolutely nobody else for a minimum of one year. No publications. No presentations. *Nothing*."

Lajos churned over this new economic business model, weighing the pros and cons, including the implied personal threat. "But what about NASA's Jet Propulsion Laboratory? They have an evolving need that could become urgent if a big space rock is discovered heading our way. Quantum computing will stay within my secure walls, but they'll have access to it."

"No! Not even JPL. They're doing well enough with the supercomputer power they now have." Rather than speaking it, he scribbled a large monetary number on a small square of paper, folded it, and slid it across the desk. "This will be for you. Now, commit it to memory and destroy it in the shredder I see behind your desk."

Lajos's eyebrows arched further as he comprehended the figure, then swung around and turned on the shredder. As its tiny motor wound down, Lajos responded with authority, "I can make this happen. How can I reach you?"

The visitor pulled out a business card and slid it across the desk. It had just a single phone number on one side, nothing else; no name, organization, nor address. "When the phone is answered, ask for the Scott. You must be precise; not Scott, but *the* Scott. Enunciate precisely."

Lajos flipped the card over, looking for more information. All he found was the Masonic symbol of the Freemasons: the compass and square, the instruments of measurement needed to design and build.

But within their arms, the 'G' for the geometry of the universe had been replaced by the all-seeing eye of God as shown at the top of the pyramid on the back of a one dollar bill. Lajos knew of such things and nodded his head slowly, affirming to himself that the mind of God not only thinks, but necessarily sees, and that the compass and square correctly symbolized that God was the architect of the universe. Lajos just stared and absorbed the image. Then, almost as if coming out of a trance, he asked, "What are your concerns?"

"Beyond your personal safety, you have foreign nationals working in your laboratory. We feel that this is an unacceptable risk, especially the one from China. I'm sure you'll know what to do." The visitor let that hang in the air.

Then from his coat, he pulled out some folded, printed sheets and laid them before Lajos.

Lajos asked, "What are these?"

Then the dagger to the heart: "Nothing, really, just documents of your conspiracies, funds transferred to your secret bank account, intercepted and transcribed communications. They break many Federal statutes. You should have been more careful. I suggest you shred them; but never forget that I, and others, have them safely tucked away."

The blunt visitor stood abruptly to leave, his hard business over. Lajos escorted him to the laboratory door. As he did, Liu was coming out from the space with the blackened windows. Their eyes met for the first time in instant primordial communication. The visitor's eyes penetrated like a laser. Liu flinched, turned quickly and went back into the blackened room, but not before the visitor reached up to adjust his collar and squeezed the tiny hidden lapel camera.

At the opened heavy door, the visitor turned to Lajos, "You know what you must do."

One of Lajos's carefully-picked post-doctoral staff included Liu Yang from Shanghai. He was an exceptionally sharp, insightful young man; brilliant, in fact. Lajos had been his thesis advisor. Liu was also a member of the vibrant on-campus Caltech Chinese Association. He was proud that an ancestor of his had immigrated to

America to work in the gold mines around Grass Valley, California, up north, but had died in a mining accident. He bridled when discussing the later racist Chinese Exclusion Act, especially when the rhetoric of the Black Lives Matter movement had been thrust into the conversation. Liu felt that their objectives were too narrowly focused. And he reassured Lajos that, as far as he was concerned, the Exclusion Act was long ago, and that he now would work very hard helping Lajos in a different deep shaft, mining the secrets of the universe.

Liu apparently had a large extended family back in China and needed to visit them often. Unknown to Lajos, the threads of that family reached into the Chinese Communist Party. The visit reasons Liu most often cited were deaths or marriages in the family. Lajos was suspicious by nature, but Liu was his top researcher. Lajos knew some results and methods could be memorized and carried back to China, but the amount of data and the complexities of quantum theory as applied to computing made such a breach difficult without copies. These huge databases were impossible to memorize.

That evening, Lajos was watching live, laboratory security-camera imagery from his home as the microwave oven heated his goulash. He was pondering how to remove Liu without raising a stir and finding a replacement for the important work behind the blackened glass panels. Liu was working late, as he often did, and had called up his latest report on a laboratory computer monitor. He attempted to hide his cell phone from view, hunched over, turning his back to the red dome on the ceiling. He was doing more than reviewing his work. He held the phone next to his chest while taking photographs of screen image after screen image. Then with fingers dancing across the keyboard, he did much more ... hacking into Lajos's sacred secure pair of servers. Liu was not able to retrieve information for downloading, but was able to corrupt it, setting back the laboratory's proprietary work by years.

That did it! The reason for his removal had been given, as if a gift. Lajos vowed to himself to discharge Liu the next day, not quietly, but in front of all the others. Liu would be summarily escorted out, stripped of his position and status. It would be a public disgrace and loss of face, something of the Chinese culture that Lajos understood and had used before as leverage.

But Liu was gone the next day. He rested comfortably halfway across the Pacific on a China Airlines first class flight to Shanghai.

He wouldn't return.

Intellectual property had slipped out of IQIM, leaving behind vandalized, corrupted files. The ultra-thin, one-of-a-kind special crystal wafer at the tip of the cryogenic cooler in the black-glass room was missing. Lajos was unspeakably upset, virtually seething, blood vessels bulging on his broad forehead. Soon, news of this extremely volatile incident reached the President of Caltech. Lajos sat on the other side of his desk, sweating ... not only about this, but also about the shredded papers given to him by his visitor, the Scott.

Skating on Black
[12 Years 271 Days before Impact]

Kayla still lived in South Los Angeles while attending Caltech classes as an undergraduate. Her mother, after a long hard day of cleaning houses, was on the couch watching the Winter Olympics. Kayla thought it was televised meaningless pap for the masses. But ice skating did have a certain beauty. She sat down next to her mother and watched paired skaters: White skaters performing on white ice to classical music written by classical composers. The skaters held each others' hands, circling around and around a common center, their outstretched arms acting like mutual gravitational attraction. Kayla understood the physics in this beauty. It reminded her of a rare asteroid, studied in Zhang-Wei's class, finally revealed as a mated pair of asteroids in orbit around each other. The high-resolution Keck II telescope on the peak of Mauna Kea had enabled this discovery. The program switched to downhill skiing, something out of reach and interest to those in the Watts ghetto. Finally, she'd had enough of televised snow and ice. "Mom, I'm going to take a nap. Wake me in two hours. I have a heavy assignment and computations to check before I head up to Palomar."

"Yes, baby, I will. More slave labor for that Chinese dictator?"

"Mother … don't say that! He's a professor, a U.S. citizen, and the top astrophysicist at Caltech. It's an honor to be in his class. But he does demand a lot."

"Whatever you say, honey. You've worked long and hard to get there. Don't look back. Just look at what you did at Dominguez

Hills: a scholarship, *Summa Cum Laude* graduate, all while busting your ass working part-time to make ends meet."

"Mom, you worked hard, too." Kayla kissed her mother on the forehead and went to her bedroom for a power nap before awakening for deep study and laptop calculations into the early morning. She had been on a dead run since Zhang-Wei had given her the firm assignment: QW7 at Palomar.

She drifted off. In the small dark room, Kayla's eyes moved rapidly under closed lids, driven by a dream. Active parts of her deep subconscious framed moving images across the vision of her sleeping mind. Two ice skaters with gray, featureless faces came out of a gray mist and separated. From opposite ends of the ice, they skated toward each other and attempted to clasp hands to bind them together into a fast, swirling circle, converting momentum from linear to angular. But the centrifugal force was too great. The larger, stronger man, his faced blurred, couldn't hold onto and bring the mere waif of a skater into his orbit. In her hazy dream logic, Kayla became the female skater. Part way through her orbit around him, she slipped away into a different direction, falling to the ice, sliding hard into the wall at the edge. With the sound of her impact, the ice turned from white to black. She and her faceless skating partner attempted the maneuver again, this time skating on black. On the black velvet of the surrounding seating area, spectators turned into twinkling points of light. They tried and failed again, and again she slid into the wall. Her partner skated up to her, his face now a pock-marked, gravelly gray boulder. Bony gray fingers reached down, gripped her hand, and helped her stand, then pointed up. Kayla looked up and saw a small dark-gray circle against a brilliant-blue, sunlit sky; it grew larger and larger. Raw trembling fear gripped her as it expanded into a deathly-gray disc with countless shadowed craters and rocks, eclipsing the Sun. Its gray turned to blood red, then to bright red, then dazzling yellow as bright flames fluttered and streamed from the outer edge, blotting out the sky.

Gunshots from the street shattered the night! Kayla awoke with a start, in a sweat. Wailing sirens approached, familiar neighborhood sounds around the Projects on Grape Street. She stood and started to part the curtains to look outside, but her mother pulled her away from becoming a target.

A long tedious night followed, work spread out on the kitchen table, fingers tapping across her laptop keyboard. She gulped down some Gatorade and munched a chocolate energy bar. She told her mom, "Goodbye. I'm heading out."

"Drive carefully, baby. You already got two speeding tickets."

Kayla jumped in her well-weathered car. The grinding starter motor complained, but brought the engine to life. Kayla would beat the heavy traffic getting out of Los Angeles to get on the interstate highway south toward Palomar Mountain.

The laptop computer in the case on the seat beside her contained the latest updated ephemeris of 467317 (2000 QW7), a rather large asteroid so-named and cataloged according to the necessary but somewhat arcane naming convention used by the global community of astronomers. Kayla had been working closely with Professor Huang on a more-advanced, more-accurate orbit determination method for location prediction. Time was the enemy. The further out in time for the prediction, the greater the uncertainty that surrounded it. As if it had a bipolar disorder, time was also a friend, as Professor Vadja had emphasized and mathematically proved to her: the further out in time an Earth-saving deflection was applied to an asteroid, the less energy required.

Kayla had more than a passing affinity for this cold hunk of gathered space rock. In one of her early Caltech classes, students had been asked to select an asteroid that could pass near the Earth and report on it. She went down the long list and stopped at QW7. Its official discovery date was August 26, 2000: her birthday. Earlier observations, the first one, on the third day of that month, had been used with others for the initial calculations during its period of confirmation gestation. But for Kayla, they formally shared the same birthday: she in a Los Angeles hospital, QW7 atop Haleakalā on the island of Maui by a telescope that was part of the Near-Earth Asteroid Tracking program. She felt that they were somehow sisters. Kayla knew virtually everything about QW7's physical parameters and computed orbit: perihelion and aphelion distances, angle with respect to the ecliptic plane, sidereal orbital period, and other orbital elements computed to the 15th decimal place. Even these accuracies were insufficient to accurately warn in enough time to actually prepare for an Earth impact, in order to take defensive measures many years in advance. But QW7 was not a threat. She did wonder why the International Astronomical Union, with its headquarters in Paris, had not yet seen fit to approve a name for QW7 as had been done for other asteroids. Maybe none had been proposed because it had been discovered by an automatic machine process and not by human intervention and personal inspection.

In a few days, this slowly-tumbling asteroid, estimated to be about twice the size of the Empire State Building, would pass relatively close to the Earth. At its closest point of approach, it was predicted by JPL to pass within 0.036 astronomical units of the Earth, or roughly 5.3 million kilometers, or slightly less than 14 times the distance between the Earth and the Moon. A comfortable miss for those worried about such things. And there were those that did worry for many other detected and tracked large asteroids: Near-Earth Objects (NEO) due to their orbits and Potentially Hazardous Asteroids (PHA) due to their size.

Kayla would be working with a small team at the Palomar Observatory to track QW7 using the Hale 200-inch-diameter solid Pyrex 14.5-ton mirror. There were much larger telescopes on the planet, by mirror diameter, but they had been scheduled for higher priority tasks. The Hale telescope was considered as a more-than-capable antique in the timescale of scientific advancement. As part of her doctoral research, she'd compare the predicted track, using Zhang-Wei's computationally-intensive method, with the actual track using the pointing data from Palomar's analogue-controlled telescope. Due to its proximity to the Earth during its closest passage, the accuracy of its computed actual track would be at its optimum, a good benchmark upon which to compare with her professor's predictions.

Under United Nations charter, JPL was an important part of the International Asteroid Warning Network that had been established just a few years earlier. Zhang-Wei was leading an effort in JPL's NEO

Coordination Office for the precise computation of asteroid orbits for close-approach predictions and impact probabilities. IAWN had heavy responsibilities should a large asteroid pose a serious threat: assisting governments to analyze impact consequences and to plan mitigation responses. Zhang-Wei, Kayla, and their colleagues labored with no particular urgency. Based on calculations for discovered objects in orbit around the Sun thus far, JPL estimated that it would be over a hundred years or so before a large one could threaten the Earth. But science had its own allure.

Kayla knew the observatory well, having visited there many times: first as part of a high school field trip, then as part of her math and physics classes at CSU Dominguez Hills, now as part of her Caltech astronomy and astrophysics classes. She'd again be staying for a few days at the Palomar Monastery, the lodging facility so-named as only male astronomers had stayed there in the early days of Palomar operations.

Kayla smiled as she pulled away from the curb. It was good to be smart. She got on the Interstate highway and brought the old car up to speed, a bit over the posted limit. She reached over and popped a can of Gatorade. It would be an hour or so. She had time to think and reflect, especially after last night's gunshot alarm clock. Kayla had been in high school when she had boarded a big chartered bus for a field trip to Palomar, her first. This was part of a Caltech program to let underprivileged teens see the world beyond Watts. The gunshot that had awakened her last night brought back a flood of memories, not all of them good.

DeShawn
[12 Years 256 Days before Impact]

Kayla's morning drive on the interstate highway toward Palomar was again monotonous. Over the drone of the engine and tires of the old car, her thoughts drifted to DeShawn Brown. How could she forget him?

An only child, DeShawn had lived in the apartment right next door to Kayla, also an only child, in the same building of the Jordan Downs Projects on Grape Street. Her parents, a tall handsome father and a short beautiful mother, had always seemed to have a little more money than his. They had bought Kayla an old Erector Set and a set of Lego tiny, interlocking plastic bricks. Kayla and DeShawn spent hours together on the floor in one apartment or the other, safely inside behind barred windows, building all sorts of imaginative things. With a very quick mind, her little construction projects always outshone DeShawn's.

When they were in the third grade together, she had built a small tower with nut-and-screw-fastened metal pieces set on a two-layered pedestal made of the little plastic bricks. The upper layer could be rotated on the lower one around a common pivot point. She added a little salad oil to help smooth and ease its movement. The little tower looked like an oil derrick with an extended arm of her design that could be rotated. On its end she clamped a plastic letter opener from her father's desk drawer. It had a plastic magnifying lens on one end. Fastened onto her mechanism, it could be tilted.

On a bright sunlit day, she and DeShawn brought what she called her "tower of solar power" out onto the sidewalk. As the Sun moved in the sky, she made adjustments so that the bright dot of intense light stayed focused on the concrete, its track an arc. She tried to explain how it all worked in relation to the Sun, due to the Earth's rotation and axial inclination. DeShawn just placed dried grass at the apex of focused light, fascinated when it smoked and burst into tiny flames. He moved the rig near a crack in the sidewalk; ants were scurrying to and from their home beneath. He executed some hapless ones at the focal point of his death ray. Kayla didn't like that, so she moved her tower away from the ant entrance. DeShawn complained. A childhood argument followed. Then they were distracted, DeShawn much more than Kayla.

Throbbing bass sounds from big rear speakers underscored heavy rap lyrics coming from a big four-door Lincoln Town Car, riding a just a few inches above the street on wide tires mounted on chrome wheels. It had been painted deep purple. The interior held four young Black men, each wearing a purple, back-facing baseball cap. Even though the car had air conditioning, all the windows were rolled down in the hot, dry Southern California air, with elbows hanging out. The driver slouched down in his leather seat. His right hand hung down limply from his wrist over the top of the steering wheel to guide the big machine. His head moved slightly back and forth on a supple neck, precisely in time with the deep beat of the music. As the car slowly passed, a back seat passenger had a smug, proud expression on his face. He looked at Kayla and DeShawn and extended a contorted hand: three fingers out, forefinger curled back touching the thumb. He was trying to communicate something, but Kayla and DeShawn had yet to learn the sign language of the Grape Street Crips. Kayla recoiled. DeShawn was mesmerized, fascinated as if that car held powerful men in a chariot from a dark powerful place. They were.

As they grew up, Kayla and DeShawn often walked together to the nearby grade school and middle school. But different social groups had different gravities. In high school, they walked with others with different social connections. Like most girls in their formative years, Kayla mentally outpaced the boys, including DeShawn, but she did so by an even much wider margin. Whether in arithmetic, algebra, or science, she often found herself helping DeShawn get his homework done, laboring to get him to actually understand what he was doing. As they grew they remained friends, but DeShawn resented her mental superiority.

In high school, their separation continued to widen. Kayla was often asked to come to the head of science and math classes to explain what was being taught. Almost as an obligation, Kayla continued to help DeShawn in the privacy of their apartments. Their circles of friends changed. DeShawn started hanging out with boys with low-slung pants, baseball caps worn backwards, strutting down the hallways with "don't mess with me" attitudes sculpted on their faces.

When the annual California Science and Engineering Fair was announced, Kayla's teachers, parents, and friends expected her to enter again, this time as a senior. The announcement happened to coincide with a travelling book fair held in a Watts neighborhood community center.

People came to look over old books, but mostly to sell the ones they had; they needed the money. Kayla strolled amongst book-laden tables. She picked up a hard-bound tattered jewel and opened it. The pages reached out and pulled her in: *Theoria Motus*, by a name she immediately recognized from her math classes ... Gauss. She asked the vendor to please hold it for her. Back at the apartment, she pleaded with her mother for enough money to buy the old reprint. And she got it. Kayla poured through and devoured *Theoria Motus* in the midnight quiet of her bedroom. She not only could handle the equations, but actually understood Gauss's iterative method used to predict the solar orbit of the large asteroid Ceres some two centuries earlier, using just a few measured observations that had been made by an Italian astronomer of the day.

A pair of posters with equations and solar orbital geometries, supplemented with printed explanations, at first seemed an obvious entry for the science fair. But this wouldn't do for Kayla. She wondered, What if the orbit of a large asteroid was predicted to cross the Earth's orbit? What if the calculated timing of both bodies brought them to the same place at the same time? Should the accuracy of the orbit prediction be sufficient to warn and take action?

Her parents couldn't afford to buy her a computer, but Kayla had access to some in the study hall at her high school. She used the same observations, at first just three, and then all 19 of them as used by Gauss, a genius scientist and mathematician. But she added small errors to the measured right ascensions and declinations, and to the times of these measurements, individually and collectively. The number of combinations became enormous, so she did just enough to show the sensitivity of the predicted orbit to observational errors. Rather than using an electronic calculator, she used a spreadsheet application. Her poster boards showed the celestial geometry of Ceres, Gauss's equations, a description of his methodology, and the spread of location predictions as two-dimensional probability distributions. Copies of her more-detailed report were at the table to be taken by the science fair's judges. Her display and report could stand alone on their own; they had to. She won First Place.

With her win, top math and science grades, Scholastic Aptitude Test results, and Advanced Placement tests, she netted a scholarship to California State University at Dominguez Hills. The distance from Watts to the campus was relatively close, seven miles, or infinitely far depending on one's measure. It was too far to walk, certainly hazardous after sunset. But there was public transportation that mollified most concerns.

Students and faculty at Dominguez Hills were diverse; admission and employment were determined by the power of their minds, not their ethnicity nor the hue of their skin. Kayla added to that diversity. She had been offered a scholarship not because of her color, but because of the power of her mind.

***

Drifting into the center lane without realizing it, well over the speed limit, a rude horn snapped her out of her day-dream. And just in time. The Temecula Parkway exit was coming up fast. More road lay ahead as she ascended from arid land to the pine trees on the rolling hills around Palomar Mountain, then to the parking lot of the observatory itself. She strode with authority into the control room; they all knew her. She flipped open her laptop computer and confirmed that QW7's ephemeris had been correctly loaded. Kayla went outside with a can of Gatorade, sat on a folding lawn chair, and watched the sunset. The sky dimmed though a series of beautiful striated hues on the horizon that changed to solid blue-black above. Back inside, the massive telescope moved almost effortlessly on a thin film of high-pressure oil and was pointed at where QW7 was predicted to be. Then it was confirmed and tracked. Time-variant right ascension and declination data flowed into the computer's memory. Kayla watched a computer monitor; there it was, her space sister, QW7 skating alone on the absolute black velvet of deep space. With a variant of mathematical inversion techniques pioneered by Gauss, the track of QW7 would be calculated. Kayla reached into her briefcase and pulled out the old book originally written by Gauss, set it on the desk in front of the monitor, and gave it a reassuring pat before putting her hand back on the computer mouse.

Zhang-Wei and Kayla worked diligently together, hammering out solutions on the anvil of a supercomputer. Their tools were sophisticated: orbital theory, complex mathematics, asteroid and space-probe track data, and, above all, their minds. The catalyst and stimulus for their work was Apophis, a rather large asteroid that had passed close to the Earth years earlier. With orbit modeling at the time, Apophis was predicted to pass very close to the Earth in 2029, with a probability that it could collide. The forecast probability of impacting the surface was small, 2.7 percent, but it was not zero. It was a long prediction, many years out. Later, with more observations, including more-accurate position data from the huge radio antenna in the Mojave Desert and orbit model improvements, anxieties had been calmed. Apophis was still predicted to pass close in 2029, but modelers expressed confidence that it would miss. So there was no need to spend time and effort to deflect Apophis, even if there were the means to do so. National and international budgetary bottom lines wouldn't be affected. What-to-do hand wringing disappeared.

Centuries earlier, a noble Englishman, Sir Isaac Newton, and a German, Johannes Kepler, had provided the requisite theory and equations for the motion of space bodies that obeyed the universal law of gravitation. For two bodies, the Sun and a planet, or comet, or asteroid, predicting their solar paths was possible well before the advent of electronic computers. But the universal law of gravitation had consequences. As an asteroid orbited the massive Sun, there were gravitational tugs on it by the Sun's other orbiting bodies: its planets, their moons, and very many other asteroids, some large enough to be considered minor planets. There were very many N-bodies. To add to the complexity, every orbiting body gravitationally affected every other orbiting body, slightly tugging and nudging, adding to the uncertainty of their orbits. The number of pair-wise combinations was huge, all acting at nearly the same time with speed-of-light delays considered. Depending on the required prediction accuracy, some bodies were estimated to be inconsequential and omitted from the calculations in order to save computer time. However, if a large killer asteroid were to be predicted to come uncomfortably close to Earth, accuracy would be *the* thing, as far in advance as possible. Unlike the 2-body problem, solving an N-body problem wasn't possible analytically by using well-understood equations that enabled calculating an exact solution. Predicting orbits laden with N-bodies required various applications of numerical integration and approximation and supercomputer-enabled probability estimation. One method used for this estimation was called Monte Carlo, named after an area in the Principality of Monaco known for its ubiquitous gambling activities.

The track of an asteroid, based on observations, was not without error. The more observations the better, preferably taken over a time-arc of years. There was a critical point. It separated history from the future. It was the end of the observed trajectory. At that location in space, an asteroid's position and associated three-dimensional velocity vector would be the initial point for the predictive model.

Shrinking the probability fuzz around these parameters was the objective.

There would always be uncertainty at any forecast time. Zhang-Wei and Kayla, like others had done, were resorting to a brute-force method to estimate uncertainties: repeatedly sampling the probability space surrounding the position and velocity of the starting point, Monte Carlo style, then gathering the predicted end points to define the uncertainty space.

Zhang-Wei, Kayla, and a few of their close cohorts at Caltech and JPL were now approaching the problem in a slightly different and ingenious way. Kayla had been grappling with the ever-present N-body problem.

Over coffee after Zhang-Wei's class one day, Kayla had brilliantly suggested using stochastic-dynamic theory, carrying along the probability-fuzz ellipsoids at each step of the forward integration process. While not theoretically pleasing from a pure physics standpoint, stochastic methods enabled by supercomputer processing could lessen the errors of the predictive starting point. At any predictive time, probability distributions would be there, obviating the need for the less-accurate and burdensome Monte Carlo method.

They then borrowed an application from a completely different discipline. Kayla's mother cleaned the home of two retired professors. Their research delved into the physical and chemical sciences, specifically focused on metallurgy. To reach a desired end-state of a metal's ductility and hardness, a tedious iterative process could be applied: annealing.

Zhang-Wei and Kayla subjected orbital mechanics and the N-body problem to Adaptive Simulated Annealing, ASA, a probabilistic technique for approximating the overall optimum of a given function. For an asteroid's orbit, the complex function was the position and velocities of all the solar orbiting bodies and their gravitational interactions.

But this improved accuracy had a heavy price: computational load, the time it would take a supercomputer to anneal to a solution, or more accurately, a set of time-variant solutions. For the observed trajectory, the number of iterative simulated annealing steps was a selectable parameter. For forecasted trajectories, the duration of the forward time step, the shorter the better. The annealing parameters at each step had to be chosen. All would soak up floating-point operations at increased precision. Depending on parameter selection, convergence to orbit solutions years out could take days or weeks.

Kayla applied their latest ASA model against the recent trajectory of QW7 as she had observed at Palomar. At various imposed lead times, she changed the point that separated the observed past from the predicted future. Zhang-Wei and Kayla hovered over a computer monitor at JPL as data scrolled by and error graphs displayed. They stood and gave each other a celebratory "high-five" slap. But there was more work to be done in the approval process before it would become the standard model at JPL.

In the excitement, Kayla gave no thought to DeShawn. He was in prison now, using his mind just to survive.

American Ka'bah
[12 Years 180 Days before Impact]

In pre-dawn darkness, the heavy articulated garage door rolled slowly down and closed. A small dashboard-mounted light changed from green to red. The heavy metal-backed door was now firmly locked by stout cross-latches and electronically alarmed. Reassured, Adam backed out from his driveway onto the tree-lined street. As he drove off, Adam glanced with pride at his big brick home in a northern suburb of the nation's capital. The early morning traffic on the Beltway was thin. He pushed his black Mercedes S-Class sedan up to a comfortable cruising speed as classical music filled the interior. He was on his daily pilgrimage to Fort Meade, to the National Security Agency, NSA, his ka'bah. Adam passed easily through main gate security. The armed guard recognized him and the sticker on his car, waving him through. Adam swung the big Mercedes into his select parking space. With memorized codes, fingerprint readers, retina scanners, and through a manned check point, he limped along through the layers of security to the inner sanctum of the leaders of the Agency.

Adam eased himself down into his leather chair. He winced slightly from the expected pain. Like an electric shock, it radiated out from his right hip. But that passed as he massaged it with the heel of his hand as a sedating wood aroma enveloped him. Adam rolled the chair up to his massive desk made of unfinished cedar, hand-hewn from trees grown in Lebanon, trees he had selected himself before they were felled. The natural oils in the wood cast a calming scent around him. Adam often needed such calming, from more than his reconstructed hip joint.

He logged onto the secure server to review highly-classified message traffic that had arrived since the last time he'd been at his desk. And that was late yesterday, Sunday evening. Adam entered a code through the small, glass, touch-sensitive keypad embedded flat in the desk while he placed the fourth fingertip of his other hand on the reader that recognized his unique fingerprint pattern of ridges, arches, loops, and whorls. The heavy right drawer unlocked. It rolled out with ease on smooth bearings. A small, thick-sided safe filled the drawer. Adam opened the now-unlocked lid on the top of the safe and withdrew a single paper document, the only item within. Something had happened in the last 24 hours. It was labeled with special markings known only to a very few. As he stressfully read and absorbed its highly-secret contents, his hip began to ache. He had gotten used to reading and massaging at the same time. This document was an internal memorandum, the contents now transferred indelibly into his keen mind: reports, tasks, names, global places. Electronic communications were convenient, but some secrets required old-school methods. Adam spun his chair around and fed the memo into the shredder, as was absolutely required. It hummed and turned the inked paper into minuscule pulp.

Adam glanced up at the wall behind his desk. On it hung a pair of low-altitude commercial aerial photographs, behind glare-reducing glass in cedar frames made from the same trees as his desk. The photos and their meanings were on the complete opposite ends of the security spectrum. Anybody anywhere could buy them. But there was a bit of pride embedded in the one that showed the large, cubical Islamic shrine, the Ka'bah of Mecca, wrapped in a large black cloth with bands of Quranic verses brocaded in gold. In the photograph, the Ka'bah was surrounded by concentric circles of the faithful, some of the nearly two million pilgrims gathered there during their annual pilgrimage: the Hajj.

The other photograph was of a large rectangular solid, the NSA building, which was clad in outwardly-black, one-way glass. From the air, at first glance, this iconic Fort Meade structure looked similar to the one in Mecca. Instead of a cluster of pilgrims, it was surrounded by a sprawling array of parked cars of the believers in a different faith: the security of a nation. Very few people knew that he was in both undated photographs when they were taken. Certainly no surprise for the NSA photograph; he worked inside this very building. However, Adam had also been among the believers that surrounded the Ka'bah. His beliefs back then were not Islamic, but rigidly conformed to the dictates of Christianity, as they did now.

***

Scottish blood flowed through Adam MacKellar. He had been a top student at Georgetown University, majoring in Arabic Studies with emphasis on the Arabic Language, specifically the predominant dialect spoken in the Kingdom of Saudi Arabia. A tall, gangly Virginia boy, he hoped to eventually land a job with the State Department. He had been in a post-graduate program leading to a Master's degree. But his plans were interrupted by four commandeered aircraft that were flown into the Trade Towers in New York City, the Pentagon, and a field in Pennsylvania. He hadn't received his advanced degree when he was visited by two non-smiling men clad in dark suits. They wore sunglasses despite being in an office provided by the University. The Central Intelligence Agency, CIA, offered him immediate employment to ply his skills. His professor highly recommended him as a gifted student. Adam hesitated. Their offer was tinged with coercion and implied personal threats. Adam learned from that.

Adam's well-practiced Arabic linguistic skills were so good that native Arabic speakers thought he was from Saudi Arabia, until they looked at him. Pale skin, blue eyes, and red hair spoke to his Scottish heritage. Initially, his skills were best used inside the CIA, translating intercepted voice and message traffic, which he did very well.

But the CIA soon had different, more urgent plans for him. Brown contact lenses took care of his blue eyes. A special chemical designed in the CIA research basement, semi-permanently turned his skin to light olive-brown. Red hair wasn't unheard of in the Kingdom, but black hair was predominant. That was more easily changed and maintained. His facial bone structure was neutral; not Caucasian, not Arabic. And his nose was long and straight, with a slightly bulbous tip, another plus. Somewhere along the procreative line, some Arabic DNA may have been introduced into his Scottish lineage ... possibly from a raven-haired beauty at an old pub in Edinburgh.

With a deep bank account, and identification and travel documents wonderfully-forged in the basement, Adam wound up in the Hajj of February, 2002. There he met, or rather targeted, some men from Riyadh who shared his apparently radical faith. With carefully-crafted conversations in the coffee shops of the capital city, he was drawn into more private venues where Allah and the principles of al-Qaeda were more openly discussed. Through very obscure drop points, information made its way from the U.S. Embassy in Riyadh to the CIA in Langley, Virginia. Targets were selected. Accidents just somehow happened. People clandestinely vanished. Some were publicly evaporated by laser-guided Hellfire missiles from unseen drones circling high above, controlled by satellite link from somewhere in Nevada.

Suspicions had arisen for one particular Hellfire assassination. One in the small group was an al-Qaeda operative. He planned to drive to Yemen through the desert. His plans were shattered into a million pieces on a dusty road. Back in Riyadh, deductive reasoning kicked in: who knew what and when? Adam's undercover Arabic façade was removed, followed by a midnight chase of a taxicab with him inside. A flash of cash had convinced the driver. Adam barely made his way to the safety of the Embassy, but not before a bullet shattered his right hip. Secretly squirreled out of the country, Adam healed with the aid of inserted titanium pins. He arrived back at Langley headquarters with a distinctive limp and new directions. He'd made a name for himself and a future in a dark world.

***

"The general will see you now." Adam limped in and sat down across the big desk from the NSA Director in a corner office larger than his. The steely-eyed fighter pilot that flew that desk wore four stars, command pilot wings, and a chest full of ribbons.

"Well, Adam, how'd your meeting go at Caltech?"

"Sir. That Lajos Vadja is one piece of work, but a genius piece of work. I think I got his attention."

"How far along is he with quantum computing?"

"No way of knowing that. This is extremely complicated. Einstein stuff. But if there's a breakthrough, it'll most likely happen there."

"We must have it first. How's the interception?"

"Very good, actually. We've monitored and recorded all of his phone calls and emails. We've even hacked into the security camera video stream from the laboratory to his home. He hadn't thought of that vulnerability. We've got video recordings of activity in the lab."

"Adam, I don't need to remind you that we've not gone through the courts for a warrant. Our necks are hangin' way out there."

Adam leaned over slightly, reached down and rubbed his awakened hip. "I know. I know. But all that would have taken far too much time and we'd have lost valuable intelligence."

"What's the latest?"

"We've been monitoring Liu Yang's communications with mainland China, which shot up just after my visit. I think I inadvertently smoked him out when he saw me leaving the secure lab. You've seen my lapel mini-cam photo of him. He certainly didn't know me, but my stare and body language must have given me away. Don't need a warrant for those foreign interceptions. Just damn amazing! He made airline reservations to Shanghai that night, first class, mind you. I watched that son of a bitch take many photos of computer screens in the lab and spend a bit of time at the keyboard. He's made off with what Lajos wanted to keep very close-hold. That embarrassing breach is known at Caltech in very limited circles. We've got a heads up from our buds at the FBI. Apparently Liu erased or corrupted critical technical files. That's bad news for us; good news for the CCP."

"Have you seen our latest interception and decryption of Chinese internal communications? It just came in from downstairs."

"No."

"Well, something's happening. I've forwarded it to the Langley folks. They're tracking this, like they do many things."

"What's going on?"

"There's been an outbreak of some lethal virus in Hubei Province, far south of Beijing. Pneumonia-like death rates have been soaring. We've intercepted encrypted traffic between Beijing and a virology lab in the province's capital city, Wuhan."

"Sir, probably just coincidental, but that's where we've tracked Liu Yang. On the other hand, supercomputers have been used in virus and genome research around the world, and right here in our own country. Quantum computing could be a very big deal for research being done in that lab."

Their meeting over, Adam went back to his office, pulled out a bottle of Scotch, and poured himself a glass. At his level in the Agency, as Deputy Director, certain perks came with the job. He took a long sip and reflected that cryptology, the making and breaking of codes, lay at the very heart of the NSA. The Agency had literally been at the forefront of computer development since its inception decades earlier as the Armed Forces Security Agency. The most advanced computers first went to the NSA, followed by the service with the second-biggest need for high-speed computing: weather. NSA dealt with human intelligence; weather people dealt with natural intelligence, the observed and forecast state of the atmosphere. Well-read, Adam knew that weather had proved critical in wars long before computers came on the scene. Chinese General Sun Tzu, who wrote *The Art of War*, famously guided military strategy: "Know the enemy, know yourself; your victory will never be endangered. Know the ground, know the weather; your victory will then be total."

Liu Yang's theft and Sun Tzu's fundamental strategy now bothered Adam greatly: would the Chinese make the quantum computing breakthrough first?

Compass, Square, and Cross
[9 Years 355 Days before Impact]

Adam rechecked his calendar. Raphael would be landing at Dulles International Airport that afternoon. As with earlier visits, Adam would pick him up. This very close friend and confidant worked in France's General Directorate for External Security, the French equivalent of the CIA. They both had a close British friend in MI6, but at the last minute Ian was unable to make the trip. Raphael was certainly known and trusted by the CIA and the NSA, but they didn't know about this visit.

From the Beltway, Adam drove out on the crowded toll road to Dulles as Raphael made his way through passport control and the luggage carrousel to the agreed outside meeting point. Adam pulled up, jumped out, and welcomed him. "*Mon ami*, Raphi. *Mon ami.*"

In French-accented English, Raphael replied, "Good to see you, Adam." They shook hands, each with a finger folded back. This ancient form of public cryptography, a secret signal that they both belonged to the same clandestine organization, wasn't needed. They knew each other very well, but continued this practice as a form of close camaraderie and common clandestine purpose. With Raphael's luggage in the trunk, there was causal small talk in the big Mercedes on the way to Adam's house. But nothing serious, as a matter of habit … just in case. That could wait.

Inside his secure garage, Adam lifted out one piece of luggage. Raphael took it and went knowingly to his room, the same one as on previous visits. The bed was still unmade and comfortably crumpled, just as he'd left it. Except for Adam, the big house was vacant and had been so since his bitter divorce.

It was better that she was gone from his life. She'd incessantly wanted to know more about what he did for the government, and about the wine cellar. It had been a big bone of contention, too much for a fragile, hurried marriage to a beautiful girl from Wichita.

Following his return and recovery from his mission in Saudi Arabia, Adam had moved inexorably up in the government ranks and pay scale to where they could afford the big suburban home. He'd hoped that would make her happy. With no children, it had ample room spread over two stories, and a nice backyard for her roses. But it didn't have a basement. The realtor had said something about the high water table and feared leaks through concrete walls.

His boss at the agency had seen the well-recognized occupational strain and suggested that Adam needed a hobby to relieve the stress of clandestine security work. Adam liked a good glass of wine at a good restaurant or bar in the nation's capital, and there were many of both. Bottles of expensive wine started showing up in a kitchen cupboard, on closet shelves, then in a wine cooler, followed by a closet with a floor-to-ceiling wine rack, converted with refrigeration to keep wine at just the right temperature. Adam was really into his new hobby; his wife, not so much. He wanted a classic wine cellar where before the advent of refrigeration, cool subterranean temperatures were maintained by thick concrete walls and the surrounding cool soil. He hadn't cleared this idea with the mistress of the house when the backhoe showed up in their backyard. A deep rectangular pit was dug next to the rear of the garage. Piles of dirt were hauled away. Then the carpenters came. They built plywood forms, surrounded by rubber sheets, for poured concrete that spewed out from a rotating tank on a truck. Her favorite rose garden was trampled; there was a lot of mud and mess tracked into her pristine home by Adam. The cellar floor, walls, and ceiling were quite thick, with their thick rubber-sheet edges sealed with tar to prevent water intrusion. Adam finally showed her the plans and kidded that it could also be used as a bomb shelter, the capital surely being on somebody's nuclear target list. She didn't laugh. Access to the cellar would only be through the back of the garage, down a steep set of stairs, through a heavy door at the bottom landing. Soon, Adams's two foreign associates, Ian and Raphael, became more-frequent visitors, always adjourning to the cellar, locking the door to keep her out.

A decision was made in the cellar by the threesome. Adam embarked on a self-help project. Hiring a special contractor could have aroused suspicions, and the contractor would know. Soon, unmarked boxes of special materials arrived: rolls of flat, narrow copper strips and wide, fine-meshed copper screening, all ordered from a distant company in Utah near the copper mines. Like wallpaper, Adam bonded the screening over all of the interior surfaces of the cellar: floor, walls, and ceiling, ensuring the edges touched and overlapped each other. This included the two fresh air vents in the ceiling, in and out; air passed through them, but electromagnetic energy was blocked. Strips of copper were fastened to the four edges of the door and to the interior of the entire door frame, so that uniform copper-to-copper contact was maintained all the way around when the door was closed. Thinking ahead, he penetrated the electronic shielding. A high-bandwidth fiber-optic cable went from a computer modem through a well-sealed hole in one wall to the vast Internet beyond. If needed, the cable would merely be disconnected to fend off computer forensic tracking. To keep keyboard and computer emanations from leaking out down a copper wire needed to carry power into his cellar, Adam went the extra mile and managed to install an isolation transformer and power-line filter. The transformed room was as electronically secure as some of the spaces where Adam worked.

All had been going well, in Adam's mind, until Raphael's visits became more frequent. French, handsome, mysterious, he'd caught the eye of Adam's wife. The feeling may have been mutual. Despite the stereotypical French view of love and life, nothing had happened. But bitter suspicion and arguments ensued. Her hometown in Kansas now had more appeal for her. That pushed the marriage off the cliff. The trust between the members of Adam's group was much more important than his mere marriage, which he came to view as a distraction from his real mission in life. Raphael and Ian, too, were not encumbered by marriage.

Raphael freshened up and came out holding a rather pricey bottle of Rémy Martin XO brandy he'd hand-carried from Paris. They went into the garage through a secure door from the house, then down the dimly lit narrow stairs. The vault-like door was pulled opened after Adam correctly spun the dial of the lock back and forth a few times. He taught Raphael the combination. Inside the cellar, the light switch was thrown and the door firmly pulled shut. Their meeting room was now a Faraday cage, trapping electromagnetic signals from getting out, including those from the powerful computer at the end of the table and the monitor and keyboard attached to it. He'd relocated most of his wine bottles back to the refrigerated closet in the house above, but a small wine cooler under the end of the table held the good stuff.

Raphael set the bottle of Rémy Martin by two cut crystal glasses that caught the light with rainbow glints. Adam pulled out a bottle of Domaine Serene Monogram Pinot Noir, born in a western valley of Oregon. Both bottles were opened and their contents transferred carefully to the awaiting glasses; brandy for Adam, wine for Raphael. Then the binding toast: "To Solomon's Temple. To Knights Templar." Only then could this meeting of considerable substance begin, reviewing the state of the world ... and opportunities.

Nothing was hung on the copper-coated walls lest the mesh be compromised by a nail or screw. But there were objects on slanted stands on narrow tables, including framed reprints. One was of a painting of George Washington holding a trowel and a scroll, wearing an apron of Freemasonry with the compass and square embroidered on it. The other was of Benjamin Franklin, also a Freemason and co-signer of the Constitution. Between them was a large, solid bas-relief of the Masonic symbol, sculpted of brass: the compass and square with "G" within their grasp. On the other side of the room was a rather large frame on a floor stand. It held a coarsely-woven white cloth tunic with an embroidered red cross, as if it had been worn by a

Crusader in the Holy Land. The Crusaders had attempted to change the order of that part of the world. Failing that, their motivation had continued through the centuries, becoming necessarily secretive.

Adam, Raphael, and Ian secretly formed their own Knights Templar cell. It was not affiliated with any Masonic body. In addition to the fundamental beliefs of the Scottish Rite, the threesome's philosophy contained the idea that a single action might well upset the delicate world balance of power and change the course of human history. Having access to the deepest secrets held by their governments could enable an appropriate action that could lead to a new world order ... one of their choosing.

The two retrieved elite Montblanc pens from their pockets and set them on the table next to the crystal glasses, with formality. Raphael's was gold-plated, Adam's was the silver StarWalker model. Both were engraved.

Absolutely no cameras nor electronic devices could cross the thresholds of their respective inner sanctums, in either direction, without detailed inspection and scrutiny. There were security firewalls and sensitive detection devices in each of their organizations that could detect a small thumb drive carried in a pocket or briefcase, in a shoe or under a foot, but not so much for a flash memory chip in the cap of a metal Montblanc pen, especially if it were engraved as a gift to them from the organizations they served. Even so, their pens had been subjected to careful by-hand examinations more than a few times, until trust was established with those at the checkpoints. Then, tiny chips were stored in their pen caps, chips that could accurately store a lot of information, highly-classified information. X-ray scanners at check points couldn't penetrate their Montblanc pen caps.

Adam fired up the computer. The big LED screen at the end of the table came to life. "Well, Raphi, what have you got?"

Raphael removed the cap from his pen and tapped the open end gently on the table; his memory chip fell out. He inserted it into an adapter. Adam inserted that into the USB port of the computer. Adam did the same with his chip. Descriptive text and images were displayed.

Raphael began, "Adam, we learned about the suppressed protests in Hong Kong. It lays out the plans of the CCP."

"Yes, Raphi. We've also decrypted the communications on this matter sent by those Communist atheist bastards. Here's something new that we collected through our space-borne Eavesdrop system. The CCP's militarization of the Spratly Islands in the South China Sea has plateaued. Expect to see big oil rigs sprouting up on those shallow, scraggly atolls."

"Very interesting, Adam. Now look at this! Remember when a former officer of Russia's military foreign intelligence service was thought to have been injected with a rare nerve agent? Allegedly, he'd been suspected of becoming a British agent and was killed under direct orders from the highest level. From signals intelligence and from corroborating information from one of our French operatives in Moscow, that direct order has been confirmed. Old Cold War habits die hard. It's too bad Ian couldn't make it. Maybe he could've confirmed the allegation about the Russian becoming a British agent."

They went through item after very sensitive item. It was obvious that they were virulently anti-Communist. The two of them were only slightly less tolerant of those that followed different religious beliefs than those that had driven the Crusades and the Knights Templar. Raphael and Adam took short mental breathers to sip French brandy and Oregon wine.

After the brief interlude, Adam spoke first. "Raphi, I'm afraid I've got some bad news, and some worse news. That effort to develop quantum computing at Caltech has suffered a serious setback. A Chinese post-doc in their lab ran off with their latest findings, but not before vandalizing the files in the lab, a huge setback. I'd thought they were in the lead. Now I'll have to visit others that are working to be the first in quantum computing."

Raphael lamented, "That's too bad. And dangerous. We've been tracking the efforts at the Paris Centre for Quantum Computing. No breakthroughs yet."

"Yes, very bad. Last week I went to see the director of the Caltech effort to demand that he remove a Chinese national from the lab, the one we've been following. It wasn't soon enough." Adam brought up a high-quality image of Liu Yang, the one taken with his lapel camera while in the Quantum Computing laboratory.

Raphael asked, "May I copy that image? We have an operative in China. What's the worse news?"

"China could be the first to develop reliable quantum computing! If so, this'll require that our encryption methodologies be changed and operations adjusted to respond to the timeline of quantum computing decryptions of their encryptions. We could be playing speed chess with one eye closed and one hand tied behind our back."

"Adam, that would be a very different world."

Adam and Raphael downed the last of their drinks. Raphael went to the core of their meeting. "Any good news? Do you see any opportunities? I do not."

"No, Raphi, but there is something out in the open, in the *Washington Post*. A Spanish astronomer at the big observatory in La Palma discovered a large object that's passing through our solar system. Well, actually, he's Basque, but you know about the sensitivities in Spain."

"Will it come close to us?"

"No. But many telescopes will be trained on it. It's named Elcano."

"Are there any opportunities during Elcano's passage?" Raphael asked hopefully.

"No … no, I can't see any. It's just a distraction, but not enough of a distraction."

Keck II
[9 Years 325 Days before Impact]

Kayla rolled over from a soft muffled sleep, looked up at the ceiling, then out the bedroom window at the nearby foothills of the San Gabriel Mountains. A few seconds passed. Then she was wide awake, alert. She hadn't slept well. Wearing little, she slipped out from under the covers. In the brisk shower, her mind quickly spun back up to speed and raced through a torrent of facts, figures, and data: primarily Elcano's predicted trajectory relative to the Earth and its orbit as a function of time. QW7, her adopted asteroid, was also in the back of her mind. Calculation and re-calculation at JPL had shown that Elcano would cross the Earth's orbit twice, almost in the plane of the ecliptic, but miss by a non-threatening distance. But maybe there was a different collision possibility. Had she dreamed about it? She wasn't sure, but she had to check it out.

The discovery of Elcano at Gran Telescopio Canarias had caused quite a stir among the professional and amateur star-gazing community. Elcano had *not* been bumped out of the Asteroid Belt but had come from beyond the solar system. Many telescopes around the world were now trained on it, capturing more data and images for this rare passage.

It was a short drive from the apartment above Zhang-Wei's garage. With purpose, Kayla strode past the familiar displays of JPL's successful space missions, then past the large dimly-lit mission control room with its plethora of computer monitors, large high-resolution electronic wall displays, and fatigue-fighting blue light. People were busy at rows of consoles monitoring the space probe Juno as it orbited Jupiter. She found the familiar side room and entered with an electronic security card, sat down at one of the computer terminals, and logged on. It would become her window into an enormous trove of astronomical data, complex algorithms, and enormous computational power.

A bearded post-graduate student with a long ponytail and an earring sat at the next terminal. He smiled and winked at her. They had classes together. With her neatly trimmed afro and beautiful face atop a tall slender body with long legs, Kayla had a gravity of her own. She ignored him. Others in the room, things around her, and the room's quiet sounds evaporated as she concentrated. Using JPL's Small-Body Database, Kayla retrieved predicted orbital data for 467317 (2000 QW7) and Elcano. Soon, she had a representation against a black background of the Sun, the Earth's orbit, QW7 on its closed elliptical path, and Elcano on its open hyperbolic trajectory. At its farthest distance from the Sun, at orbit aphelion, her QW7 had been beyond the orbit of Mars.

With a mouse click, she set the image into motion. As colored dots, QW7 and Elcano slid along their colored trajectories, neither coming dangerously close to the orbiting Earth. Displayed date and time increased while the distance between QW7 and Elcano decreased. She slowed the imagery, then stopped it when the QW7-Elcano distance was at a minimum, a very short calculated distance. She quickly realized that in just five days, the two displayed dots were calculated to come almost together.

This validated the vision she'd had in the shower ... or was it in her dream? The two bodies would most likely miss, but there was a small probability that they could collide, aided by mutual gravitational attraction. From her science fair days in Watts, she was now more than aware of the gradient fuzz of probability density surrounding each predicted location. The minimum distance between the most likely locations of QW7 and Elcano was calculated to be less than one one-thousandth of the average Earth-Moon distance. Kayla slapped the table and shouted, "Dammit, they could!"

The pony-tailed young man flinched. Kayla apologized for her outburst. She felt that she could be a real-time witness to something very important, maybe as dramatic as the impacts of the Shoemaker-Levy 9 fragments on Jupiter; maybe more so! She couldn't wait to tell Zhang-Wei.

Kayla drove over to Caltech and walked into Zhang-Wei's office without knocking. The look on her face told him that she had something really important to say. She explained her findings. Zhang-Wei logged on to the JPL system from the terminal on his desk. He confirmed her QW7-Elcano findings. He cautioned, "Great work! But I wouldn't make a big deal out of this, not publicly, not yet."

"Why?"

"They'll likely miss, considering the respective uncertainties. A recorded impact would be spectacular. A miss in space is one thing, but a wrong impact prediction quite another. Reputations and legacies must be considered, including those of Caltech and JPL. Remember, you have a promising career ahead of you."

She pulled up a chair and sat right across his desk from him. "I understand. But I've busted my ass for you and your research. I want the opportunity to be the first to observe and confirm a very rare collision in space, even more rare than Shoemaker-Levy."

"Where? Palomar?"

"No! I want a telescope with high resolving power, one of the two Keck telescopes on Mauna Kea; I know you have some influence over their scheduling."

"When?"

"Look at the data! The time of closest point-of-approach of QW7 to Elcano is five days from now!"

"Five days! What's the timing? From Mauna Kea, will you have nighttime observing opportunity?"

"Yes, definitely! Who do you think I am? I've run the calculations for the possible collision point as seen from the position of Mauna Kea. I've even checked the weather forecast. I'll have a good view in clear skies not long after nautical twilight against a moonless sky. Perfect!"

"You do know that the observing run schedule for both Keck

telescopes is locked into place, well beyond two weeks."

"Yes, yes, I know all that. Unlock it! This is more important than looking at some distant galaxy, or whatever."

"I think I can make this happen. I've got a few research markers that haven't been paid. There'll be an unhappy astronomer or two, and your name will not be a secret, nor will mine."

"Please! Make it happen."

He sat back and let out a long sigh. "Kayla. You know with Russian forces in the Ukraine, if you observe a collision, it may be relegated to the back pages of the newspapers."

"Yes, that's possible. But our periodicals will cover it, and the astrophysical community will know."

"Relax. Relax. Make the airline reservations and schedule time at the remote facility. I'll drop you off at the airport."

"Remote facility? Hell, I want to go to the top, to see this famous state-of-the art telescope, walk around and check things out, just like I've done at Palomar."

"OK, OK. Make sure you have reservations at the Mid-level Facility. Somebody may have to be bumped from their reservations there as well."

Three days later in her Mid-level Facility room, Kayla slid off to sleep wrapped in remembered thoughts that turned into a dream, a nightmare. She saw herself studying at a table in her small bedroom, her work illuminated only by a flexible-neck lamp. She was working on trigonometric identities and solving simultaneous equations, her homework from a class at CSU, Dominguez Hills. Her focused thought was interrupted by deep bass sounds that penetrated the walls and rattled the window. She had heard such sounds before when she and DeShawn were operating her "tower of solar power" on the sidewalk. Often it was from the same Lincoln Town car. But other cars from other gangs had driven slowly down the same street, to do business. Tonight, the car was a big Cadillac, not purple, but red. It slowed and stopped right in front of her building. She turned off the table lamp, stood, and pulled aside the shade to safely peer out from the darkened room through the iron security bars. The throbbing music stopped. She couldn't make out who was sitting in the big car, just shadowy figures. To her surprise, DeShawn walked out of the apartment complex and over to the car. He leaned in though the car's open passenger-side window. In less than a minute, DeShawn turned and ran back into the Projects carrying something. The car didn't move. To her amazement, and fear, she heard the front door of her apartment slam shut, followed by her father walking slowly up to the car. Two men got out. She heard a verbal confrontation ending with gunshots that sliced through the night air. The men quickly got back into the car and sped off, tires burning. Her father slumped down into a dark clump that remained motionless on the sidewalk, like a pile of dirty laundry.

After a long day of work, Kayla's mother was sound asleep and wasn't awakened by the gunshots. Kayla ran out and knelt down in a widening pool of blood from her dying father as he gasped for breath from the gaping bullet holes in his chest. He reached up and grabbed her wrist and looked into her eyes. With his other hand, he pulled his 3rd Armored Cavalry Regiment brass challenge coin from his pocket, proudly received during the Gulf War in Iraq. That coin, a Bronze Star Medal, and post-traumatic stress were all that remained after his honorable discharge. He had let Kayla play with the coin as a child, but normally kept it in his pocket for good luck when applying for jobs back in his Los Angeles hometown. That luck rarely came, except when he had married a strong, employed woman and fathered Kayla. With haunted wide eyes he rasped out, "Kayla … I love you," as he pressed the coin into her palm. Then the light in his eyes went out. He should have thought more tactically before confronting the Bloods' encroachment into their neighborhood.

Kayla awoke and sat straight up, at the same place in the dream. She'd had this dream many times before, since its real-life script had played out on Grape Street. Her cell phone alarm went off as if it had been tied to the ending of her dream. She glanced over at the nightstand for reassurance; her father's challenge coin was still on the old book where she'd set it.

Kayla lifted the black-out shade and looked out the small windows toward the southern horizon. The Sun had long since disappeared below the shoulder of the mountain to the west. The blue-pink shaded pastels of the sky and the digits on her cell phone told her it was time to go. She used the bathroom and splashed cold water on her face. Kayla was ravenous and devoured an energy bar. She folded up her laptop, stuffed it alongside the detailed notebook in her briefcase, fished out a small backpack and filled it with energy bars and cans of Gatorade. *Theoria Motus* was placed alongside the Gatorade cans, and she dropped the challenge coin into her pocket. She pulled the door shut and almost ran headlong into a handsome, middle-aged guy with a pony tail and stubble beard. He looked a lot like the graduate student back at Caltech that always flirted with her. "Oh, excuse me!"

"Please. Not to worry. I'm the observing assistant for Keck II tonight."

She extended her free hand and said, "Hi. I'm Kayla Williams, grad student from Caltech. That's where I'm headed." More people came out of their rooms and made their way past them in the narrow hallway.

He continued, "It's an evening ritual around here when astronomers, observers, and support staff take to the peak and spread out among the observatories."

"Well, I guess I'm one of them. Should be sort of like operations at Palomar, just higher."

"Not quite … not quite. I'm Josh. I'll be supporting your observing run, operating the telescope. We've been expecting you. I'll help you check out the near-infrared imager. Your people in California caused quite a fuss with their last-minute rescheduling. They must have some connections."

"He does, I mean, they do. This is part of my PhD research. My advisor helped make this happen."

"He must be one powerful dude. You can follow me up the road. It's just gravel in places. There's no way to get lost. I won't be driving fast. There aren't any guard rails in places, and the mountain sides are steep. There are tight switchbacks. There've been accidents. Just stay behind me, and use a lower gear."

"How's the weather been?"

"It snowed last night. The observing run was completely wiped out by clouds. We had some unhappy astronomers. Your intervention created a few more. But the forecast for the next few days calls for clear skies, cold and windy. The road's clear."

Kayla pulled her four-wheel drive SUV out onto the road and started the eight-mile trip, behind Josh. She'd have some time on the way up to think more about her observing run at the top. She reached over and patted her backpack. Her ticket out of Watts, *Theoria Motus,* was inside; she hadn't forgotten it back in the room. Kayla reached into her pocket and rubbed the brass coin between thumb and forefinger, hoping that physics, luck, and Keck II would cooperate.

Kayla fully realized that Elcano, coming from outside our solar system, was only the third interstellar object to be confirmed since humans began observing the heavens with telescopes. Before Elcano, Oumuamua was discovered by an astronomer at the University of Hawai'i in 2017, using imagery from a very special pair of telescopes at the 10,000-foot peak of Haleakalā on the island of Maui. The primary mission of the Panoramic Survey Telescope and Rapid Response System there, Pan-STARRS, was to detect Near-Earth Objects that threaten impact. Kayla had studied Oumuamua. She knew very well that almost two years later, a Russian amateur astronomer and telescope maker had discovered a comet on a never-to-return trajectory. It was unlike the famous Halley's Comet, which was in a highly-elliptical orbit with a return period on the order of the average human life span. Rather than ascribe a philosophical, mythological, or spiritual name, the discoverer's name became the comet's name, as he had requested: Borisov. Both Oumuamua and Borisov dove through the plane of the ecliptic at very steep angles, before being flung around by the gravity of the Sun and sent on their way at a high inclination into deep space beyond the outer planets. Unknown to Kayla, Elcano was about the same size as the large, spherical asteroid Ceres, its orbit first calculated by the author of the book in her backpack: Johann Carl Friedrich Gauss.

As she drove up in the fading light, Kayla noticed a small pile of volcanic rocks toward the end of a footpath. She could barely make out a garland of purple-white flowers set around it; a Hawai'ian lei like the one she'd seen earlier. Some of the protestors she'd seen by the Onizuka Center had hiked up to this spot, as had been done by the ancients. These descendants had performed a sacred ritual, calling on Wākea and Pele. The desk clerk's words at the Mid-level Facility crossed her mind: *kapu*. For Kayla, it was too late to turn back.

The steep gravel road turned into one with pavement and guard rails. Kayla looked around as the Sun slipped below the western horizon. The red-orange light gave the place an unreal, ethereal quality, reflecting off the huge white domes of the pair of Keck telescopes. Their large eyelids were closed, in protective mode. These metal shields would roll open for their telescopes to gaze upon the universe with mechanical precision down to a billionth of a meter.

Kayla followed Josh around the final curve leading to the Keck facility. To her northwest, about 500 feet lower and about a half-mile away, was the site of delayed construction for the TMT. The time of First Light was now indefinite for the enormous telescope. A site on La Palma had been promoted and considered, but rejected. The Hawai'ian protesters had preferred La Palma and, of course, any other location.

Kayla pulled into the parking lot and backed in as Josh had done, matching the other vehicles. It took more people than Josh to run and maintain the massive, precisely-tuned and aligned optical machines. There were traces of snow where the parking lot met the building. Kayla jumped out, grabbed her backpack and briefcase, leaned into the stiff freezing wind, and followed Josh into the long low building that supported the pair of telescopes. Kayla blurted out, "Jesus Christ … it's damn cold!"

"I'm not sure if Jesus had anything to do with it, but that's the price you pay to be closer to God's universe. Set your things down here. I'll give you a quick tour and introduce you to the support astronomer, Susan, a grad student from the University of Hawai'i.

She flew over from O'ahu. She got here early to help check things out, to get things warmed up and ready."

Kayla set her briefcase on the table. The laptop inside contained the ephemerides for Elcano and QW7. Kayla anticipated their collision.

Epiphany
[9 Years 324 Days before Impact]

Kayla had worked often at Palomar as part of her doctoral studies. But Keck II's engineering, work spaces, and the telescope itself were much different. Quite a few years had passed since the Hale telescope was completed on Palomar Mountain.

Josh and Kayla wouldn't be alone. The night attendant welcomed them. He'd troubleshoot problems as needed and make sure everything was done correctly and safely. He pointed to a rack of portable personal oxygen systems. Kayla had seen elderly smokers, suffering from emphysema, with plastic tubes in their nostrils, lugging around green bottles near sea level. Being young, healthy, and self-assured, she declined.

As had been requested from Caltech, the near-infrared imager had been installed. Adaptive optics would help shed atmospheric scintillation and provide the imager with precisely-focused light.

The control room had that familiar look to scientists everywhere: computer monitors with keyboards and mouse pads sat on tables. Kayla insisted on downloading the forecast ephemerides for Elcano from her laptop, despite the fact they'd been transmitted to Keck II by Internet link; she wanted to be sure. Josh raised his eyebrows in exasperation and looked at the ceiling.

The sun had set and the time of astronomical twilight had passed. There were no clouds, and the Moon wouldn't rise for another five hours. The maze of stars in the darkening sky emerged. Kayla glanced at the digital clock on her unfolded laptop and the date/time display on one of the monitors for the big telescope. They matched, second by digitally-ticking second. As the Earth turned, Elcano would rise above the horizon in 37 minutes and 54.2375 seconds, if the ephemerides were correct. They were based on data from many telescopes to date, as processed at JPL.

Susan, the graduate student from the University of Hawai'i, stood and politely introduced herself. Kayla felt a little lightheaded and decided an energy bar and a can of Gatorade would push that aside. She offered the same to Josh and Susan and asked Susan where she was from.

Susan described the Presidio Heights district of San Francisco and mentioned that she hadn't needed a scholarship; her parents had paid for everything outright for her to attend the University of California, Berkeley. That's where she'd met Josh in astronomy classes. She said that she'd always wanted to live in Hawai'i, then held up her right clenched fist, little finger and thumb extended: the *shaka* sign for hang loose. Josh did likewise and bumped his similarly-formed fist against hers. That told Kayla a lot.

Kayla's unfolding description of her life on Grape Street in the Watts section of Los Angeles was certainly in stark contrast. Josh and Susan sat almost hypnotized while Kayla described in vivid detail how the Bloods had executed her father. She went on to describe her first visit to Palomar that led to her winning the state's science fair. She took out her copy of *Theoria Motus* and described its motivational involvement. Kayla set it on the table, then set her father's brass challenge coin upon it. Josh and Susan realized that they were listening to somebody with hard-earned substance, who didn't mind using ghetto language to fit circumstances.

The big eyelid, the protective dome cover, was slowly opened. Light from the infinite universe fell upon the polished hexagonal segments, as if together they formed a giant retina. Gathered and focused light was guided into the actual retina: the near-infrared imager. Since its formation, the Earth continued to spin on its tilted axis. Like a very fine Swiss watch, the Keck II mirror smoothly, almost imperceptibly, moved to stare in the direction of the predicted right ascension and declination, computed for the local time and location of Keck II. A near-infrared image appeared on one of the monitors. More typed commands and a mouse click; a bright yellow laser beam pointed spaceward along the path toward the predicted location of Elcano. Adaptive optics kicked in and the image sharpened considerably. Infrared spectral data and their changing graphs appeared on other monitors. Everything was being recorded.

Elcano had a large signature, owing to its size being on the order of Ceres, something that would be estimated later. The infrared image wasn't precisely at the predicted location, but close enough for confirmation and further refined alignment. Instead of using the predicted ephemeris to point the big machine, it would now track the center of the image, yielding track data that would produce the actual ephemeris.

Kayla asked Josh and quickly confirmed that Keck II was tracking and recording the actual sky position of Elcano, part of the reason for her visit. It would be visible for just over three hours before disappearing below the horizon. All data during the passing arc of observation would be transmitted to JPL for them to update and refine the Elcano ephemeris, also shared worldwide. Observing arcs for the next two days had been scheduled. More would be demanded if the weather didn't cooperate.

Kayla saw it, but Susan was the first to mention the smaller infrared spot very near Elcano. Together they appeared to be like a double asteroid, one much smaller than other, or at least less bright in the near infrared. Kayla knew the other was asteroid QW7, but said nothing.

Due to their relative speed to each other, passing in opposite directions, the observed angular spread and apparent distance between them shrank in the minutes ahead. Toward the end of Kayla's observing run, Elcano and QW7 appeared to come together. She sat spellbound, not taking her eyes off of the image monitor. If a collision had occurred, the enormous amount of heat generated would make a very dramatic show in the near infrared … but there was nothing. The heat image of Elcano did not change at all. The recorded infrared temperature jumped slightly as QW7 slipped past the apparent limb of Elcano. QW7 had passed on the far side and its image had been occulted by Elcano. Possibly it had struck the unseen side. If Elcano were rotating, which was likely, the heat signature of the impact crater could come into view later, the following night. Elcano was slipping below the horizon. Like all astronomers, Kayla knew she was witnessing history, after the fact, due to the speed of infrared light from Elcano and QW7 and the distance from them to Keck II.

Just then an elderly man with a white beard, an unlit pipe in his mouth, horned-rimmed glasses, and a ski jacket entered the control room. Earlier that day he'd checked into a beach hotel in Hilo. He carried one of the observatory's personal oxygen systems. A clear plastic tube led to a small pair of tubes in his nose. Kayla wondered if they were needed because of his age, or maybe due to a life of pipe-smoking to look the part of a scholarly professor, or maybe just because he didn't stop to acclimate at the Mid-Level Facility. She didn't ask.

Susan immediately stood up. He was indeed a professor, Susan's advisor from the University of Hawai'i. She introduced him to Kayla. His part of the conversation was curt, since his part of an observing run had been eclipsed by the one for Kayla. But his point of interest would be visible for another 15 minutes, and he wanted to use his remaining limited time. The object of his and Susan's interest was a star in its death throes, a supernova far, far beyond the galaxy. He had requested a different imaging device, but there wasn't enough time to change out the near-infrared imager that had been installed for Kayla. The installed one would have to do for him as well. The big telescope was smoothly swung into a new direction and elevation, the laser beam re-activated.

The professor was obviously irritated, but Kayla felt that a rather large rock floating around near the Earth's orbit just might be a little more important. QW7 was here and now, not light-years away, not millions of years ago. In deference to scientific social graces learned from Zhang-Wei, Kayla uncharacteristically bit her lip and just held her tongue; he'd also reminded her that she did have a career, so don't step on it, that Watts was in her rearview mirror.

She thanked Josh and Susan, folded up her laptop, grabbed her things, said goodbye to the professor, and headed to the door. She stumbled, almost falling. The room seemed to swirl as she felt a twinge of nausea. The air *was* thin. It was time to head back down to the Mid-Level Facility from Keck II. With a slightly-bilious brain, she still had the common sense to drive down the steep road in the dark very slowly, putting the automatic transmission into second gear to keep from overusing and overheating the brakes. She'd be back tomorrow evening, and the next, for more rescheduled blocks of time on Keck II, further pissing off the professor. The secrets of the supernova would have to wait.

Back in her room, Kayla felt tired, heavy-eyelid tired. But she had to email Zhang-Wei. "Good data on Elcano at Keck II. Sent to JPL. Appeared to have occulted QW7. It may have impacted Elcano on far side. Should know after more observing runs. University of Hawai'i professor upset, but no problem. You probably know him, beard, glasses, pipe-smoker, forgot his name. Thin air got to me. Getting much-needed sleep now."

Her inbox showed an unread email from the same address she'd just used; her mind cleared enough to click it open. "Was told about the data sent from Keck II. Tiger is happy."

Zhang-Wei and his team at JPL updated Elcano's ephemeris and sent them to Keck II. The next evening Kayla watched as the big faceted mirror was trained on the horizon, moving slowly as the Earth turned. Then Elcano appeared, as newly and accurately predicted. With adaptive optics, the higher-resolution image revealed QW7 on the other side as compared to imagery from the night before. It had *not* impacted Elcano, as Kayla had expected, even hoped. But she knew that the probability of an interstellar body colliding with an asteroid was almost infinitely small. But for nearly-infinite periods of time, likelihoods increased as testified by lunar craters and pock-marked asteroids. Regardless, she let out a disappointing sigh. Kayla now knew that QW7 would not make the astronomical headlines and bring her name along with it. Or would it?

She directed, "Josh, track the smaller image."

"I can't. That's not on the approved observing run."

Kayla didn't like the tone of his voice, sounding like he was getting back at her for having to jump though his ass at the last minute to change and coordinate her observing runs. "Bullshit! Just fuckin' do it!"

"What did you say?"

"Do it! How'd you like to do your post-doc work selling Mai-Tais on the beach?"

Josh grimaced as his fingers danced across the keyboard. Imperceptibly, Keck II's 880 pounds of hexagonal mirrors were now trained on QW7. The angular spread between Elcano and QW7 increased as the night continued. More composed, Kayla now requested, "Josh, display right ascension and declination for the second object."

Josh and the Keck II system complied; position data on the well-known asteroid were now being displayed and recorded. On the fly, on her laptop computer, Kayla brought up the previously-predicted sky positions of QW7 relative to the location of Keck II, its ephemeris. She scrolled through the long table to arrive at the current time. She glanced back and forth rapidly between her laptop and the changing data on one of the monitors. The positions were obviously different. Elcano's gravity had significantly changed the trajectory of Kayla's sky sister!

There was certainly enough computer power at Keck II to run QW7's predicted positions and compare them to the evolving observed positions of her just-deflected asteroid, to compute the angular distance between them as a function of time. But the hardware and software infrastructure environments used by the JPL Solar System Dynamics group and Keck II were different. Installing the JPL application and testing the interfaces would have been time consuming. Checking data the old fashioned way by visual inspection would do, at least initially, to identify that there was indeed a trajectory change worth worrying about.

Kayla continued comparing the observed positions of QW7 with the predicted ones on her laptop. They diverged. She thought that perhaps Elcano's gravitational attraction had decelerated QW7 into a captive orbit, or that the much smaller asteroid had enough relative speed and momentum to break free and had been slung out into a new direction. Unknown to Kayla and others at Keck II, QW7 had skimmed past Elcano within 1,000 meters of its surface. With no atmosphere to drag it down into an impact, QW7 continued on its deflected trajectory, having skated past Elcano.

As Elcano and QW7 disappeared below the horizon, a still-irritated professor walked in. Kayla engaged him in an objective, pointed conversation. There was tension in the rarefied air. Susan and Josh watched, just in case they had to intervene. Kayla explained that something very important may have happened. She tried to draw his attention away from the inter-galactic light-years distance of the supernova down to the scale of astronomical units in the solar system. She described that the smaller image was of well-known QW7, emphatic that its orbit had changed and that its determination could be very important. Kayla dramatically concluded, "JPL has already classified QW7 as being potentially hazardous. In its new orbit, this potential must be quantified with the possibility that it may pose a real hazard to somewhere on Earth."

She grabbed her things for the trip back down to the Mid-level Facility, turned, and added with a tinge of sarcasm, "It may not be large enough to cause the extinction of dinosaurs, but certainly enough to kill many people, to wipe out a large city! I'm going to ask for more observing run interventions for more measurements until we can get a handle on its threat. Sorry."

An unhappy bearded face, and his students, watched her leave the control room.

Down where the air was a little thicker, at the Mid-Level Facility, Kayla felt better and sent an email with the latest information and her urgent request. QW7's new orbit could make even bigger news than if it had impacted Elcano. She followed this up with a phone call directly to the Director of JPL, who was also the Vice President of Caltech, even though she was probably in bed. She had been, and was now a bit groggy. Kayla was very excited and convincing. Emergency wheels rolled, and the JPL Director's elevated position swung into action. More observing run schedule changes hit the fan at Keck II, direct orders from the highest administrative level. Days were added, as many as needed, for Keck II to be under Kayla's control when QW7 would be in view, even more days if there were weather cloud-outs.

Without opening the email from the JPL Director in her inbox, she immediately emailed Zhang-Wei: "QW7 did not impact Elcano. Repeat, did not. Must stay longer to track changed orbit. JPL Director has the ball. Get your calculating shoes on. Head over to get your group into action. Has to be done right! Please feed Tiger and give him his renal meds. Don't forget to clean his litter box!"

Reality
[9 Years 308 Days before Impact]

The flight from Hilo to Los Angeles droned on. Kayla was eager and excited to get back and learn of JPL's calculations for QW7's altered orbit. Her laptop computer was up and running on battery power, set on the fold-down tray. She reviewed the data. As powerful as it was, her computer's memory and processor could no way handle a modestly accurate orbital calculation. Just as well. A spoiled brat of a boy in the seat in front of her thought bouncing back and forth was a good way to pass the time. Finally, Kayla just gave up, leaned her head against the window, and gazed down on the blue Pacific. It was dotted with cumulus clouds, brilliant white in the morning sunlight. She wondered if her mother could see them, from beyond her ashes.

Kayla had come a long way since *Theoria Motus* and winning the state science fair. She and DeShawn had taken starkly divergent career paths, she the road to becoming a recognized astrophysicist, he wrapped more tightly into the illicit drug economy of Watts, and its consequences.

***

Kayla could have been evasive when the narcs paid her a visit. But the callous gangland death of her father loosened her tongue. Kayla just told them what she'd seen and heard on the street. Crack cocaine and other mind-bending, life-ending drugs netted a tidy income for street dealers, some more than she'd ever hope to earn as a professor. Kayla was a Caltech grad student. Money was tight. She commuted from the Projects. Her widowed mother was tough and determined, a tiger mother as black as a panther. She worked long hours cleaning the household filth of others to put food on the table, to afford a used car for Kayla, and the gas it required.

Kayla's information unwittingly netted DeShawn a few years in a California penitentiary. The Crips soon found a replacement for his drug distribution system. They looked for the rat and thought they'd found her, ready to pull away from the curb on her way to attend classes.

Kayla looked over to her right and saw one of DeShawn's gang friends that she remembered. He'd invited her to become a member, to help with their business, to be initiated, and to be passed around. Her blunt refusal and her acceptance at Caltech had galled him, and the gang. To them, she'd become White. Kayla recognized the flashed hand sign for the Grape Street Crips while the assassin's other hand held the pointed pistol. She heard the sharp *crack!* The bullet came through the right corner of her windshield and tore across her left cheek. He ran off after the hit. Blood flowed out between the fingers of her left hand which she held tightly against the straight shallow wound. A slightly different aim and her lights would have gone out. She drove to the hospital with one hand, then showed up for classes the next day, stitches hidden under a small bandage. Professor Vadja wondered; Professor Huang asked.

Life changed after that near-fatal gunshot through the windshield. Death threats started appearing in their mailbox and slid under their apartment door. One of her mother's clients, a man and wife, retired Caltech professors, learned of this and invited Kayla and her mother to stay at their small home near the institute, at least until a safer place to live could be found. Kayla and her mother squeezed into the small second bedroom. Kayla slept on an air mattress on the floor and parked on the street. The splintered hole at the corner of her car's windshield told a story to those walking by.

Concerned questioning by Zhang-Wei resulted in his offer for Kayla to stay in his empty guest quarters. She accepted. He'd purchased the Pasadena home from a couple whose mother had died. They no longer had a reason to stay in Pasadena. They'd built a cozy apartment for her above the garage, complete with a tiny kitchen, stove, refrigerator, and small bathroom with a narrow shower. The beautiful view of the San Gabriel Mountains through the gabled window made up for the cramped accommodations. The meager furnishings were still there, part of the deal when he'd purchased the house. He thought that his mother back in Taiwan could be convinced to spend her golden years close to him. Until then, Kayla could live there.

Kayla's mother became a live-in housekeeper and caregiver for the retired aging professors. With their recommendations, soon she was cleaning the homes of others in the neighborhood and could easily walk to her work. She called the housing authorities and gave up the apartment in the Projects on Grape Street. Kayla stopped by for short visits to check on her.

Finally, it couldn't be avoided. Kayla invited her mother to meet Zhang-Wei at his home and to see her small garage apartment. It was awkward, but Zhang-Wei was accepted. Little did either of them know that Kayla would be living above the garage with another, a stray tomcat adopted by Kayla; Tiger was found feral and wandering around.

An unseen risk silently crept in. Food was comforting and an inexpensive form of entertainment that also helped relieve stress. It also added more than a few pounds to Kayla's mother, accompanied by diagnosed diabetes and high blood pressure. Nothing too serious until the coronavirus pandemic swept away the professors and Kayla's mother. She'd languished away on a ventilator in the ICU of a local hospital, and Kayla was prohibited from being by her side when the end came. Kayla was only able to look into the cardboard box at the crematorium to say goodbye, before it was slid into the furnace. She left with her mother's ashes in a porcelain urn. It now rested on a shelf above her bed.

***

The bumps of the landing-gear tires brought Kayla back to reality. Lost in thought, she hadn't even remembered the descent.

At the pick up curb, a silver BMW sedan pulled up. She tossed her stuff in the back seat and jumped in the front.

"Welcome back. You've made life interesting back here," said Zhang-Wei. He drove into the dense Los Angeles traffic on wide freeways, back to their refuge at the foot of the San Gabriel Mountains and to Tiger, her beloved gray tabby. Zhang-Wei had told her that finding the cat was more than accidental, and that the cat would bring good luck. It was meant to be.

Kayla asked, "Well, did you have a chance to process the QW7 data from Keck II?"

"Yes."

"And … ?"

Zhang-Wei's voice lowered and slowed. "It does not look good. We must be very careful how the information is released, but it must be released soon."

"What?"

"It looks like Elcano gravity-decelerated QW7 into a new orbit."

Irritated, Kayla responded, "Hell! I know that."

Zhang-Wei again became the teacher. "Kayla, just listen. The standard model has it crossing the Earth's orbit in two places, in an Apollo orbit with its aphelion still extending beyond the orbit of Mars, but not by much. Initial calculations with the current approved model give it an orbital period of 1.71 years and an inclination of 11.97 degrees with respect to the ecliptic. Before the encounter, its period was 2.72 years with an inclination of 4.15 degrees; quite a change."

"Do you realize how big QW7 is?"

In an exasperated tone, Zhang-Wei replied, "Yes, Kayla … I do … as certainly do you. In just under 10 years, QW7 and the Earth are predicted to come very close. With our limited observing arc, the model has it coming by at about twice geostationary satellite altitude with a 1.2 percent chance of surface impact. But the number of initial observations is lean. Weeks or months of position data are needed for a sufficiently accurate orbit calculation."

"My god!"

"Oh yes … your god … and my god," Zhang-Wei replied.

Kayla then stepped into the geopolitical realm. "This should be reported to the Minor Planet Center and posted on the JPL Sentry website, and the site run by our Italian friends in Pisa. Get more telescopes on it, more observations!"

"Kayla. Hang on. Do you think world governments and their leaders should find out about this from a computer screen, from panicked scientists knocking on government doors in the middle of the night?"

"Oh."

"It gets worse. I ran an abbreviated version of our stochastic-dynamic application with your adaptive simulated annealing approach, using JPL's recently updated Development Ephemeris. The N-body problem is still very much a problem, far too many gravity-interacting masses orbiting the Sun. I increased the number of the larger bodies, to increase the accuracy of the prediction, including those in near-Earth orbits and potentially hazardous. It took days for the JPL computer to anneal to a trajectory solution for the closest point of approach. I had to make some approximations or else it would still be running. I looked up the results just before I left to come and pick you up. The probability of impact using my, I mean our, methodology is 2.8 percent. As you very well know, the standard model only includes the dynamic perturbations caused by the planets, the Moon, and a few of the larger N-bodies. Our model has it passing within geostationary satellite altitude! I've asked for an emergency meeting with the President of Caltech, the Director of JPL, who you woke up, and NASA's Planetary Defense Officer. He's flying in. I've added a few members of my JPL team, and that certainly includes you. You may be grilled on what happened at Keck II."

"What about the probability-density ellipsoids in 4D time-space?"

"The stochastics are a little loose. The massively parallel processor is running our N-body annealing, using more bodies and more dynamics and physics. We're including radiation pressure, relativistic components, and even the Yarkovsky effect. It'll take two more days to get the result, just before the meeting."

Kayla added the obvious. "If we knew the mass of QW7, that would tighten things up considerably. That could be determined if we knew the mass of Elcano, knowing how it had perturbed the orbit of QW7."

"Yes, Kayla ... if only."

"Zhang. You know of the agreement with the International Astronomical Union."

"I do. But since the preparation lead will be around nine years, and not centuries, this information must be released carefully, as accurately as possible. We don't want a false alarm with the unnecessary panic that happened with the premature release of the XF11 prediction."

"How about Vadja's quantum-computing black hole, to speed things up?"

"Not yet. That would bring together two uncertainties: the accuracy of our new approach, and the reliability of quantum computing itself. The trustees are aware of other problems behind the black door at IQIM, or at least as aware as Lajos has permitted. I overheard that there's another problem with Lajos, a big problem, and that he may be removed from his position."

"Problem? Removed?! Well, he can be, shall we say, eccentric. It must be something serious."

Zhang-Wei remained silent, thinking, then, "Kayla, what do they say about me?"

"Oh, you're highly thought of, but your abacus demonstration does throw them off."

That harmless statement went to the core of his being. The comfortable ambience of the interior of his BMW tensed. He remained silent as he sped past other drivers, weaving in and out, honking at freeway idiots. Silently, they were processing the shared information. He slowed to take the off-ramp.

Zhang-Wei spoke first. "This is quite troubling."

"Has Lajos offended the trustees again, demanding more money, more equipment?"

"No … there's been a breach in security. One of his post-doc staff, one of his former students, absconded with key quantum-computing information, possibly breakthrough information."

"What the hell … ?"

"And rumor has it that all the reports and data files have been erased or corrupted."

"Well, son of a bitch!"

"He hasn't responded to my emails, text messages, phone calls … nothing. I drove to his big house. He didn't come to the door."

"Really? Maybe he just decided to move into a less auspicious house, one more suitable for a Caltech professor than a billionaire corporate executive."

"No, I don't think so. I went to personally see him at IQIM. I had trouble getting past that damn black door. The staff there hadn't seen him for a week. They were very agitated, as if somebody had disturbed the hive and the queen bee had gone elsewhere. It appears that a very expensive ruby-silicon wafer from a darkened room is missing."

"Good grief! Lajos is moody at the best of times. Maybe he's having a nervous breakdown. Or, he's been compromised."

"You're not alone in thinking that. Caltech has quietly brought in investigators, I think. Even though Lajos's work is privately funded through the institute, it has national security implications."

Zhang-Wei pulled into the driveway. Kayla pulled her things out of the backseat and made her point: "QW7 may have national security implications as well."

He pulled something from the door pocket and handed it to her. "I think you should know about this."

"What is it?"

"It's not urgent. But you should read it, later."

Kayla slipped the folded sheet of paper into her computer case, then lugged her things up the side steps of the garage to the small landing, unlocked and opened her door. Tiger heard and ran over, weaving happily around her legs, eager to be petted. Kayla bent over, scooped him up, and held him against her cheek. His comforting, rhythmic rumbling purr was heard, felt … and needed.

At the kitchen table, she retrieved the paper handed to her and sat down. She unfolded it and immediately saw the IAU logo and title followed by: Elazar San Martín Etxarte, Spain, 1940–2022. Below was the full life and professional history of the Basque astronomer. It ended with "Discovered interstellar body, Elcano, at Gran Telescopio Canarias." She leaned back, thinking, as if she were trying to communicate with Elazar, to thank him. She realized that if not for him, the passing interstellar body may not have been discovered, if at all, until well after its encounter with QW7, delaying the discovery of QW7's altered orbit, astronomers possibly thinking that it was a newly-discovered asteroid. That could have taken years, leaving no time to deflect QW7 from a possible Earth impact.

***

The Director of the Minor Planet Center and NASA's Planetary Defense Officer entered the room. They had flown in late just the night before. Others from JPL, Zhang-Wei's team, had arrived earlier. Then Lajos Vadja entered, full of his dark gloom, and took a seat. Kayla leaned over and quietly asked Zhang-Wei, "Where have they been hiding him?"

He whispered back, "I don't know. But with his genius mind, he's a welcome addition to this critical gathering. He's not bashful when things don't line up."

A security guard was posted outside to make sure nobody could put their ear to the locked door. The big screen had been lowered, the JPL Director standing alongside. Zhang-Wei sat next to Kayla. The President of Caltech sat on the other side of the table, next to the NASA people.

The Director spoke. "Welcome, ladies and gentlemen. There has been a very interesting potentially-dangerous development. Kayla Williams, studying astrophysics, went to the Keck II observatory in Hawai'i to gather more data on a passing interstellar object. It was first observed at the big telescope in the Canary Islands. At the request of the discoverer, it was named Elcano. You may have read about it. Kayla, please tell us what you observed."

Kayla walked up and stood at the podium, confidently. She tried to appear calm, but kept touching the scar on her cheek. Kayla explained that she had expected to witness asteroid QW7 possibly impacting Elcano, but had only witnessed their passing, QW7 being occulted by the much larger Elcano. Her voice tensed as she described that after the two bodies had very closely passed each other, QW7 had been deflected, or rather, decelerated by gravitational assist into a new orbit, and that she had urgently sent position data to JPL to determine its new ephemeris. She lowered the lights and clicked through the Keck II near-infrared images of Elcano and QW7 as they approached each other, apparently merging, then spreading apart. Kayla thanked the JPL Director for her support that essentially turned Keck II operations over to her control on Mauna Kea's peak. She concluded: "QW7 is in a new orbit, a more dangerous one."

Kayla brought up the JPL graphic simulation of the QW7-Elcano encounter. The standard display of orbits and position dots was overlain on the Elcano dot on its hyperbolic trajectory from beyond the solar system. As the two bodies approached in nearly diametrically opposite directions, she expanded and slowed the display to where they were represented by larger circles approximating their relative sizes. The extremely rare near-capture and release was beautiful to watch, with QW7 skimming close to Elcano. To Kayla, they were a space pair skating on black. She zoomed out and stopped the display with QW7 on its altered orbit. She step-advanced the display until its time matched that of the clock on the wall. "Ladies and gentlemen, this is where QW7 is, approximately, as we speak."

Kayla sat back down, and Zhang-Wei took to the podium. But before he started, he held up his abacus and did a quick multiplication, using the same two numbers he'd always used since Taiwan. Some eyes widened. Not everyone knew of his distinctive lecture trait. He set the abacus down on its edge, to be seen, then began, "Using our best validated model, with the initial data from Keck II, the asteroid has dropped from an Armor orbit into a lower-energy, shorter-period Apollo orbit, crossing the Earth's orbit in two places."

A hand shot up from the Planetary Defense Officer. Zhang-Wei acknowledged him. "Yes, Sir?"

"Will QW7 pose a serious threat?"

Zhang-Wei smiled, almost as if this were a planted question, asked on cue. "Yes," was his simple reply.

He started and sped up the motion on the display. Days and digital years ticked by as the Earth completed each orbit of the Sun, with QW7 missing the Earth by wide margins as it also sped around the Sun. He slowed the display when QW7 and the Earth were on obviously converging paths, then stopped it when the two dots merged. "Our current Standard Dynamical Model has it coming between the Earth and the Moon in less than ten years, mid-June, 2032."

Lajos knew the model results, but asked anyway, "How close will it come?"

"As shown in the lower left, nominally about 72,000 kilometers, twice geostationary satellite altitude, but with a 1.2 percent chance of impacting the surface."

"That's close! Have you considered all the inaccuracies?"

Zhang-Wei winced inwardly at the implied assault on his capabilities, but maintained his composure. "Professor Vadja, considering our current computational accuracy, it could be much closer, with a greater probability of impact. As you well know, we've been working on a new more-accurate model that merges numerical integration with stochastic annealing. It takes more time, even on a state-of-the-art supercomputer, but we're confident that it is more accurate and reliable. Our latest run gives it a 2.8 percent chance of impact on June 15, 2032. Whichever model is to be believed, the time to respond is now. The new model brings great urgency with very little time to act."

Lajos went for the jugular. "How much faith do you have in that new prediction?"

"Enough to warn those on Earth to react to a 2.8 percent chance of collision, or greater. QW7 had already been a Potentially Hazardous Asteroid in an Armor orbit. Now it's in an Apollo."

The Defense Officer went to the heart of the matter. "Is it possible to predict where it will strike the Earth? Whom should we warn?"

"That's not possible … yet. The latest prediction of the annealing model has the most likely location mid-latitude, Central Russia.

The JPL Director added, "Whom do we warn and how; that's what needs to be decided. We don't need a public repeat of the poorly-worded information that hit the newspapers for asteroid XF11 back in '98. The astronomical community gave the public mental whiplash with various announcements of impact risk. It reflected badly on our ability to accurately predict the orbits of hazardous asteroids."

The Defense Officer stood, a lined-face, seasoned man. "Let's meet with Homeland Security officials. Let them decide. This should become an agenda item at the United Nations, but that's not our call."

Zhang-Wei interrupted with, "We should wait until the new model has a full run with additional observations. We'll have the answers in about two weeks."

"Two weeks?!"

"Ladies and gentlemen, considering the N-body problem and observational uncertainties, nine plus years is a very long time to integrate. The computational load to achieve sufficient accuracy is enormous, even for our best computers. Our current methods have QW7 missing the Earth at a greater distance. Other international space agencies will probably show similar results. Our developmental model will deliver more-precise results, but at greater computational cost."

A suggestion was offered, inadvertently exposing a raw nerve. "Let a quantum computer at IQIM have a go at it."

The Caltech President responded, "A post-doc left with the latest findings, besides corrupting important files before he left. We're reconstituting the laboratory at IQIM."

Lajos's sullen face and deep frown went deeper. He did not anticipate this public embarrassment.

A JPL astrophysicist innocently raised his hand. "Maybe the Feds can find him ... and the missing information."

"That may be difficult. He's a Chinese national, and he's now back in China."

The gathering squirmed in their seats: technical piracy, now a rogue QW7. With the Chinese connection revealed, people in the room glanced at Zhang-Wei. Even Kayla did ... unintentional, reflexive racism.

The lights were brought back up. The Defense Officer stood at the head of the long conference table. "Ladies and gentlemen, I need not remind you that this must be held in absolute secrecy until we're ready to make our case at the national level. Absolutely. No. Leaks! Do you all understand?"

Kayla raised her hand.

The Defense Officer pointed at her. "Yes?"

"What about defensive measures? The DART impact on Dimorphos will happen next month."

"Miss Williams, data for its orbit change around Didymos won't be known until the end of the year. We'll then know if a kinetic impact could be effective. There are a lot of concepts and theories on how best to deflect a dangerous asteroid, but none have been built or tested."

Kayla muttered, "Well, that better change ... and in a hurry."

Awakened
[9 Years 301 Days before Impact]

The Caltech-JPL team boarded the Metro Silver Line at Dulles. Their flight from Los Angeles had been turbulent. They were glad to be on the ground. The green foliage of the hardwood tress lifted their spirits, despite the message they carried. Nobody spoke as the train dove deep beneath the Potomac River, then resurfaced and finally stopped at L'Enfant Plaza near their hotel. They checked in, tried to relax, then met privately to go over their presentation one more time with Zhang-Wei and Kayla. Lajos was also part of the team, even after the quantum computing fiasco in his lab.

The next day a van picked them up for the ride north to the Department of Homeland Security. The meeting had been arranged with a secure phone call. There were no messages. Such digital information was vulnerable to interception. They were met at the main entrance and escorted through layered security to a meeting room deep within the building. Twice, security staff using scanners required explanation of the wood-framed set of beads on dowels carried in Zhang-Wei's briefcase. His abacus got a very thorough inspection. Lajos thought that this was his kind of place. Finally, after the last check-point, Zhang-Wei whispered to Kayla as they walked, "A little different than JPL security."

A massive oak conference table filled the room. Around it sat the Secretary of Homeland Security, the Secretary of State, the Secretary of Defense, and their immediate staffs. The President's National Security Advisor, the Ambassador to the United Nations, and the Administrator of NASA were also in the room, as well as the President of Caltech and the JPL Director ... and Adam MacKellar.

Kayla could feel administrative and bureaucratic power so thick she could almost cut it with a knife. Introductions were made all around. Adam's and Lajos's eyes briefly met, then averted. Lajos quickly pondered why this red-haired man was again crossing the trajectory of his life.

Formalities over, the Administrator of NASA began the meeting. He was a political appointee that had been approved by the Senate, earlier a Congressman. He took to the podium in front of a large lowered screen. He'd been thoroughly briefed by his top staff about the recent meeting at Caltech. "Ladies and gentlemen, we have a real asteroid threat. QW7, a large asteroid, was discovered in 2000 with a telescope atop Haleakala through our successful Near-Earth Asteroid Tracking program. This asteroid had posed no threat for the foreseeable future. However, it's been deflected by a passing interstellar object into a new orbit. It'll now come very close to the Earth in just under 10 years, with a very real possibility of impact."

The National Security Advisor raised her hand. "Is it large enough to do serious damage?"

"Yes, very much so. It's larger than the Empire State Building."

"Too large to burn up in the atmosphere?"

"For sure. The entry shock wave will be devastating enough. That, and its ground impact, will destroy a large area as if a hydrogen bomb had gone off."

Open free-form dialogue spontaneously ensued from around the table. "Where will it strike?"

"At this point, there's too much uncertainty in orbital prediction. But the latest model shows that it could land in the northern hemisphere."

"That's pretty broad. North America? Europe? Russia? China?"

"North America to China in the mid latitudes, but we strongly caution to not focus on that, publicly at least. It'll most likely miss. There are too many uncertainties at this point. It could even arrive at a grazing angle and skip off the top of the atmosphere."

"What do you suggest?"

"Before we get into that, a little more background and detail is necessary. I'd like to introduce Kayla Williams, a doctoral candidate at Caltech. She was at the Keck II telescope on the top of Mauna Kea in Hawai'i to get data on a passing interstellar object, Elcano. If not for Kayla, we would've lost valuable time, critical time."

Kayla looked a little uncomfortable at the podium. She took a deep breath and absentmindedly briefly touched her face scar. Then she carefully described what had occurred. On the screen were displayed a series of near-infrared images from Keck II, as she'd shown back at the Caltech meeting. They appeared as pixelated yellow-orange blots against a black background, one much larger than the other. As she toggled through the images, the smaller one appeared to be absorbed into the other. "The larger one is Elcano. The smaller one is asteroid QW7. They are coming at each other in almost opposite directions. These were recorded by an infrared imager at Keck II. They are *not* colliding. QW7 passed closely behind Elcano."

The next set of images showed QW7 reappearing on the other side. Kayla explained, "It was decelerated, slung around, and released into a new orbit. I extended my nights at Keck II to get more observing arcs of position to send to the Jet Propulsion Laboratory. Oh, by the way, Elcano is on its way out and has crossed the orbit of Mars."

Kayla was in the moment. In an unplanned think-it-say-it mode, she continued ad lib, "Back in 2011, asteroid YU55, as big as QW7, passed by the Earth closer than the distance to the Moon. JPL accurately predicted this miss-distance. The world's population was informed, but a warning wasn't needed. But with JPL's latest prediction, a warning about QW7 is needed. *Now!*"

Without waiting for his planned introduction, Zhang-Wei quickly went to the podium, thanked her, and took control. He knew she was passionate about this. He was unsure just what would come out of her mouth next in a room full of powerful people. He hesitated, went back to where he'd been sitting, and returned quickly to the podium with his abacus. He went through a calculation in seconds. The moved beads echoed in the room. He set it down on its edge as if it were a trophy, which it was. He forgot to introduce himself. Puzzled glances were exchanged around the table. A staffer whispered, "What the hell is that all about? Is he a U.S. citizen?"

Zhang-Wei heard this, glared in that direction, then introduced himself and launched into his presentation. His descriptions and graphic presentations were spell-binding. He explained that the computationally-intensive algorithm had included the interactive gravitational effects of the planets and large asteroids, relativistic effects, and much more. Behind him on the big screen, the orbital ballet went from just before the Elcano and QW7 interaction, to the current position of QW7, to the time of the predicted possible Earth impact. He stopped the image as QW7 neared the Earth, then displayed them in increments of days, then hours, then minutes. He included graphic representations of predicted probability distributions. At each step, he zoomed in to show the layers of error probability, displayed as two-dimensional encompassing zones around QW7, white fading to gray, then to black, representing zero probability. The same incremental zones were shown around the Earth and around the Moon. There were a few puzzled faces. He answered the unasked question: "Even though we know the positions of the Earth around the Sun fairly well, and of the Moon around the Earth, there are still some uncertainties the farther out we go in time, including exactly where the surface of the Earth will be as it rotates on its axis."

Where the non-black areas of probability overlapped, the colors changed to shades of red, showing the levels of joint probability, meaning that there was some likelihood of occupying the same red-shaded space at the same time: a collision. As Zhang-Wei stepped the display forward to June 15, 2032, the larger circle, the Earth, and the smaller circle, QW7, came together surrounded by bright red. It looked like an explosion, with the maximum joint probability shown at the center as 3.5%, larger than the earlier model run back at JPL.

From somewhere in the room came, "June 15th, 2032 ... 3.5 percent ... hmmm. Looks like a 96.5 percent chance it could miss."

Zhang-Wei's reply was more rhetoric than accusation. "Yes, but would you like to take that chance?"

The Secretary of State noticeably flinched, not used to being put on the spot in public. He didn't answer, but whispered something into the ear of a staff member; an orbit of power in the political universe had been disturbed. The President of Caltech quickly stood up and defused the tension. "Thank you, Professor Huang." Zhang-Wei sat back down.

The Administrator of NASA went to the podium and grabbed both sides of its top. The abacus was still sitting there. "We have some suggestions as a starting point. First, we recommend that the President send a secure alert message, a communiqué to the leaders of all nations. He may wish to speak to some of them personally, but that's his decision."

"What's the bottom line of the communiqué?"

"We've prepared a draft. It's in the folder in front of each of you. Very importantly, in the message, in personal communications, and in following meetings, a predicted impact area on the Earth will not be given, repeat, *not* be given. It is far too early to cause unnecessary panic and area evacuations. The fact that a large asteroid might impact the Earth somewhere, in as little as nine years with the potential to cause significant loss of life, will cause enough panic. Even if it strikes the ocean, the resulting tidal wave would result in the deaths of millions of coastal residents."

"What steps should be followed?"

"There's been a lot of thinking and planning over many years within and beyond our shores about asteroid threats. Under the UN, international organizations have been formed and have matured. We're part of the International Asteroid Warning Network and the UN-mandated Space Mission Planning Advisory Group. The NASA-funded Minor Planet Center plays an important role, as do many other international organizations. In summary, they, or rather *we*, collectively focus on the following basic steps: search, detect, track, characterize, predict, warn, plan, coordinate, mitigate."

"Where are we now?"

"We're in the warning phase, broadly speaking, with a relatively short lead time. Please include us in the communiqué distribution. Upon receipt, to live up to our responsibilities, we'll immediately send out a notice and all of our data on QW7 to the international astronomical community."

From a Homeland Security staff member, "We didn't do so well with the meteor that exploded over Chelyabinsk in Russia, now did we? No warning at all!"

"Yes, but back in 2008, we correctly predicted the time of an asteroid air burst over the desert of Northern Khartoum."

The inquisitor had apparently done his homework and replied, "That gave us a whole 21 hours."

"But it was a small asteroid. The one over Chelyabinsk was only about 20 meters across. It slipped through our observing sieve, but the mesh has gotten tighter. From earlier observations and studies, QW7 has been estimated to be from around 300 meters to 700 meters across; like I said, larger than the Empire State Building. We'll be entering the warning phase with some urgency, with planning and coordination on its heels. We are talking about years, not decades. There will be a lot to do in a short period of time, designing the means to deflect or destroy QW7, constructing and testing a system, and building the heavy-lift launch vehicles to get it to the asteroid in sufficient time. Getting international consensus on mitigation may be more difficult than actually deflecting QW7 from its current orbit."

The Secretary of Homeland Security walked to the center of the room. "Thank you very much for your time and energy on this threat to our national security, and the world's. You'll be escorted out to your waiting transportation. We're going into executive session in preparation for tomorrow's Cabinet-level meeting with the President in the White House."

The President of Caltech made a spontaneous request. "We feel quite strongly that Caltech and NASA's Jet Propulsion Laboratory should become the center of any international effort. With NASA support, we've designed and landed sensor packages on Mars, including a number of rovers controlled by radio link. Hell, more to the point, we've orbited probes around asteroids, sent back their pock-marked images."

"But other nations have done pretty well in space, haven't they?"

"Yes, for sure, some in partnership with us. Yet, there are echoes of the 1960s Space Race and the Cold War that still haunt us. Also, there's the national pride of European nations, Russia, India, Japan, and China, especially China."

From somewhere in the room, "What about the problems in Ukraine?"

The Secretary of Homeland Security replied, "We'll take that into consideration when we speak to the President. International politics may have to be considered. Russia is a prominent spacefaring nation. For a time, we had to ride their rockets to get to the International Space Station."

The Administrator of NASA interjected, "Defensive measures will almost certainly involve an unmanned system. NASA's Jet Propulsion Laboratory must control the mission after the post-launch handoff."

"You assume that if one is developed in time, that U.S. launch vehicles will be used. The Russians and Chinese have demonstrated some very heavy lift capability. The weight of the device, or devices, may be a constraint, especially if they're kinetic impactors."

"That's to be determined. Caltech offers to host any and all international meetings to be held to address the threat. They have the facilities, plus we can showcase JPL for attendees not yet convinced. Funding assistance for conferences and expanded JPL operations would be appreciated."

The Cellar
[9 Years 299 Days before Impact]

Evening summer air drifted around them with flashes of lightning as they boarded the van for the ride back to their hotel near L'Enfant Plaza. Lajos was the last in line. Adam walked closely by, bumping into him as if by accident, quickly slipping a folded note into his hand. The van wound through the nation's capital. Lajos opened the note: "8 pm Willard bar."

Back in the hotel room of the Caltech President, the team did a hot wash-up of the critical Homeland Security meeting and discussed the next steps that awaited them back in California.

The nation's capital had excellent restaurants. Reservations were made. Lajos stood to leave. "Sorry, but I want to have dinner with an old friend, a former student of mine. I'll not be joining you."

The cab pulled up outside the Willard InterContinental Hotel. Lajos stepped out, then into the plush historic lobby. People seeking government favors had intentionally wandered into that very same lobby. President Ulysses S. Grant had often gone there for a brandy and a good cigar, so as not to offend his wife with these manly vices, she back in the White House nearby. The frequency of such liaisons increased. A moniker had been born: lobbyist.

The hotel concierge directed him to the small elegant room, a meeting place for the city's political and social elite since the hotel was established in 1847. Lajos entered the bar and homed in on the head with red hair, as if it were a beacon. He took a comfortable high seat next to Adam who was pretending to read a folded copy of the *Washington Post*. Without looking at him, Adam asked, "Do you like brandy?"

Lajos also looked straight ahead and replied, "Yes. But it must be good, not like the cheap Pálinka I remember in Budapest."

Adam set the paper down and raised two fingers; he'd been here before. "Sasha … Rémy Martin, neat."

In Russian-accented English, "Yes, Mister MacKellar." As Sasha poured the golden liquid, "The weather is warm outside, not like I remember in Siberia. I was nursed on vodka to stay warm."

Lajos frowned. Memories returned of Russian atrocities in Budapest. Two snifters were set before them.

"Lajos, let's talk of life. Do you believe that people and events have changed the order of the world, *can* change the order of the world?"

Lajos looked pensive, pondering that question. He had to admit to himself that he wanted to be one of them, and that quantum computing would be the event. "Yes. Yes, I do."

With an extended welcoming hand came the answer to an unasked question, "Adam … Adam MacKellar."

Lajos tentatively grasped Adam's hand. "I hope it will be nice to have met you, again."

"Nice has nothing to do with it. It looks like Sasha's people are trying to change the order of things in their neighborhood." Sasha was polishing a wine glass, pretending not to hear. A hush fell over the room. Adam broke it quietly with more historical anecdotes. "You do know that Abraham Lincoln changed the order of the world, or at least this part of it. He stayed at this very hotel before his inauguration. If the South had successfully seceded, the outcome of the First World War may have been different."

Lajos felt like challenging Adam on some obscure aspect of Theodore von Kármán, but resisted. Theodore had changed the order of the world, with rocketry developed at the foot of the San Gabriel Mountains.

Adam reached further back. "Zheng He, a Chinese Admiral in the Ming Dynasty, could have changed the order of the world. Zheng commanded a fleet of hundreds of huge merchant sailing ships, each much larger than those of Columbus, decades earlier. He and his ships had sailed as far as the east coast of Africa, returning with goods and wealth long before Columbus was born. But the Ming Dynasty, for a variety of reasons ... palace intrigue, threats from land invasion, and ancient politics among them ... had the ships burned or ordered they be left to rot at their docks. What if Zheng He had sailed ships east and had bumped into what is now America, long before Christopher's discovery from the other side? Would we be sitting here now, speaking Chinese instead of English?"

Lajos reflected for a moment then answered. "Probably. The order of the world would have been changed, in a big way."

Adam knew history better than Lajos knew physics, and Lajos knew a lot. He skillfully directed their conversation down through people and events that had indeed changed the order of the world, or could have if certain people had not died, or an event had taken place, part of the mind-flexing "what if?" hypothetical analyses of history. As they sipped their brandy, Adam briefly touched on a number of turning points: the Crusades, the Bubonic Plague, Karl Marx, Vladimir Lenin, the Spanish Flu pandemic, and Mao Zedong to the Manhattan Project and the killing of student protesters at Kent State University. Adam dwelled on the Crusades, emphasizing that Salah ad-Din had changed the order of the world in the Mideast. Adam hypothesized" "If Salah ad-Din's soldiers had been defeated by the Christian crusaders, would terrorists have flown planes into our buildings?"

Lajos discussed the Kent State disaster with greater interest, telling Adam about a family member who was shot by the Russians during another student revolt: the 1956 Hungarian Revolution. Hearing that, Sasha looked away and raised his eyebrows, but Adam tracked him and said, "Sasha, it looks like some of your countrymen are trying to change the order in Ukraine, and maybe the Russian Federation in the process."

Sasha gestured with raised hands, palms out as if to show that they held nothing. "That is none of my doing."

Adam turned toward Lajos. "I am certain that quantum computing will change the order of the world. But that order will be different depending on who is first. Many are trying, but we had thought it would come out of your laboratory at Caltech."

"Yes … would have, could have, except for that bastard Liu Yang!"

A few heads looked over from the other side of the circular bar. Adam extended his hand, palm down and motioned for Lajos to lower his voice. He leaned close, looked Lajos in the eye and whispered, "We are intercepting Liu's communications and are tracking him. We have resources in-country."

Lajos's eyes widened, his mind whirred. He asked himself, Who *is* this man?

"Lajos. I see something that may change the order of the world: QW7. We should discuss this in another place. Why don't you stay over? I'll pick you up at your hotel at 8:00 pm tomorrow night, sharp."

Lajos took a nice evening stroll through the National Mall back to his hotel near L'Enfant Plaza. He felt it would do him good, to clear his head. Only a few sprinkles landed on him from a dying thunderstorm. It reminded him of walks when a student back in Budapest.

Back in his his hotel room he changed his flight reservations, then called the Caltech president to tell him that he'd not be returning tomorrow but on the following day. He learned that the Caltech president would also be staying over.

***

Turbulence uncomfortably jostled the aircraft. A warning tone was heard, and passengers were warned to remain in their seats. Again, thunderstorms had to be avoided. The Caltech people were in their private thoughts about QW7, the future, and their role in it. The President of Caltech and Lajos weren't onboard.

A severe jolt struck; seat belts kept passengers from lifting off and hitting their heads on the top of the cabin. Passengers by windows watched the wings flex, as designed. Zhang-Wei patted

Kayla's hand. "If you pray, give special thanks to the engineers that designed and the workers that constructed the wing-spar of this aircraft."

To passengers' relief, the flight smoothed out. The long flight ended with big rubber tires chirping on the runway at LAX. The Caltech-JPL team spread out to their cars or waiting cabs. Zhang-Wei and Kayla went to long-term parking and his BMW. It was late. Tomorrow would be another day, a very busy day.

The next day came early. Zhang-Wei was in his JPL office, waiting. Kayla was in another room at a computer terminal preparing the QW7 information and data package for transmission. A JPL administrator knocked on Zhang-Wei's door, opened it, and announced, "High-priority message!"

Zhang-Wei went to the special room and scrolled through the displayed text of the official Presidential communiqué. World leaders now knew about QW7's altered orbit. He went quickly to where Kayla waited and gave her a smile and a firm thumbs-up. Data, including right ascensions and declinations, infrared images, and spectral analyses streamed out under IAWN agreement. She listed Josh and Susan at Keck II as part of the observing team, as a kind of peace offering for the language she'd unleashed there. World astronomers would soon know the details of QW7's new orbit. Observing runs at many observatories would change, even the schedule of the Hubble and Webb space telescopes. Ground-based radio telescopes were enlisted in the QW7 observing effort; their accurate position data would also be needed.

***

The President of Caltech had stayed behind to meet with the head of the FBI. He wanted to get to the bottom of Liu Yang's high-tech heist and data vandalism, but quietly. Public revelation wouldn't be good for the institution's reputation and could put future federal funding for important research at risk. The FBI chief leaned back in his chair, touching the tips of the fingers of both hands lightly together as he framed his short statement, "I've received pressure to tap the brakes on this investigation. It's being handled slowly, a number of administrative levels below my oversight, out of sight."

"Is there nothing you can do?"

"No need. Liu's back in China. There are other agencies more adept at handling this. Please, don't make an issue of it. Let it die."

"Well, we've reassigned the principle investigator."

"That's enough."

***

The big black Mercedes pulled up to the curb at 8:00 pm, sharp. Lajos was waiting. Adam was at the wheel. Lajos opened the door himself, climbed in, and pulled it shut, the solid sound a testament to German engineering. He was surprised to hear the first strains of Strauss's Blue Danube Waltz. Adam had timed it perfectly, touching the play icon as he drove up. Nothing was said as the majestic genius of the symphony swelled around them from multiple speakers. Lajos leaned his head back and closed his eyes. He was taken back to his time at the university in Budapest where he and fellow students discussed physics and listened to the grand music of an earlier era composed in that part of the world.

Adam pushed an overhead button and drove down the long driveway to his impressive home. A light on his dashboard turned green. He arrived at the garage just as the door completed its opening, again timed perfectly. As it automatically closed behind them and latched with a thunk, the indicator light turned red. Lajos got out and Adam motioned for him to follow. "Would you like to see my wine cellar?"

"Yes, of course. I like quality wines, especially French reds."

Adam spun the digits of the dial on the door at the bottom of the stairs. With the rotation of its lever handle, he pulled the heavy door open. Lajos couldn't help but notice the physical trappings of a Faraday cage as he stepped across the threshold. He wished that he had installed the same information protections back at IQIM. On the table was a nice Château Greysac Médoc. How had Adam known?

Its cork had been removed, the wine left to breathe to perfection during Adam's round trip to L'Enfant Plaza. He now filled two crystal wine goblets as Lajos sat down. Nothing was said. Lajos quickly scanned the room, fixating on the brass compass and square on the side table and the red cross on the other side of the room.

Adam lifted his glass and proposed a toast, "Here's to you, Lajos, and your future." They each took their mandatory sip to keep from committing the toasting sin of setting a glass down before doing so. "We know that you have been relieved of your responsibilities at IQIM."

"How did you know!?"

"It is my job to know, not yours to know how."

Lajos confessed, "I learned of the deflected asteroid threat, and I'm working my way back into the Jet Propulsion Laboratory where I know my engineering and data-processing skills may be of value."

"We were hoping that to be so, but it was confirmed when I saw you walk through the door of the meeting room at Homeland Security."

Ever suspicious, Lajos asked, "What do you want of me? I'll have no real authority."

"We know that, but you'll have something very valuable."

"What's that?"

"Access."

Lajos speculated, "Many people have access into JPL. The requirements are not that stringent."

"That will change, my dear Lajos ... that will change." Almost boasting, Adam continued, "We'll know of the needed changes even before the President of Caltech and the head of NASA will know, and they'll be making them."

"What changes?"

"Security, Lajos, security. There will be some international objections. But what is the most capable place on the planet to control space probes and to change the orbit of QW7? Why, JPL, of course. But with so much at stake, security and access control will multiply one-hundred-fold."

"What has this to do with what we were discussing at the

Willard?"

"Lajos. What will be the objective at JPL?"

Lajos was certainly smart enough to know. "To determine and predict trajectory, to alter that trajectory, maybe with a massive nuclear bomb. But I have other ideas."

Adam now applied "what if?" not to history, but to the future. "We believe that QW7 could change the order of the world. You know ... smite the common enemy. More equitable social compacts and a different world leadership could come out of the dust if subtle actions were to be taken at just the right time."

The dark side of Lajos came out. "Yes, Adam, that is possible, but I have little faith that fundamental human nature can be changed. The human race has lived with its curse since the beginning."

Adam was firm. "Of course you realize that the world's order has already been changed, first the coronavirus pandemic unleashed by China, then that policeman in Minneapolis who knelt on the neck of a Black man. How we police ourselves and share the common wealth has changed. And now, Ukraine."

"Yes, it has been a turbulent, stressful period. I lost two close friends, faculty members, to the virus, one a professor emeritus that lived next door. Then, as if that weren't enough, protesters streamed through my neighborhood, some threatening to take our homes, if not our lives. That was nothing like the Hungarian Revolution. It was more like what Lenin would have wanted."

Adam probed. "I notice that the student that discovered the QW7 deflection at Keck II is a young Black woman with a scar that speaks of her past. Was she brought onboard at Caltech to satisfy diversity objectives?"

Lajos reflexively shouted, "No! She was a student of mine and very capable, the top of my difficult classes. She came from a tough Los Angeles neighborhood."

"Do you think she'll be involved in QW7 operations at JPL?"

"Certainly. She's helping Zhang-Wei develop a more-accurate asteroid orbit prediction methodology that will be critical."

"Yes. We know of this, and that she's living over his garage."

Nyame
[9 Years 292 Days before Impact]

The presidential communiqué on QW7 had been released to foreign leaders. Data followed, spreading worldwide into the minds and computers of astronomers and astrophysicists ... and journalists. JPL's Center for Near-Earth Object Studies updated their Internet-accessible Close Approach Data Table. Based on JPL's Solar System Dynamics standard model, the Minimum Orbit Intersection Distance of QW7 was forecast to be 34,562 kilometers from the surface, less than 10 percent of the distance to the Moon. This model was based primarily on the gravitational Kepler orbits of the Earth and QW7, but with the integrated adjustment of the perturbations from just a few of the N-bodies. The closest point of approach to the Earth would most likely occur 2032-Jun-15 21:46 Coordinated Universal Time. This approximately agreed with the QW7 predictions of other international agencies. Professionals, interested amateurs, and just the curious had open access to information that could result in a massive life-ending event ... somewhere. In line with established international protocols, the first press release was issued, but not from JPL.

IAWN PRESS RELEASE: ASTEROID DISCOVERED IN DEFLECTED ORBIT WITH RISK OF EARTH IMPACT - College Park, Maryland, USA, August 22, 2022. Asteroid 2000 QW7 was decelerated into a new orbit by the gravity of a passing large interstellar body. The near collision was observed July 23, 2022, with the Keck II telescope at the peak of Mauna Kea, Hawai'i. Since its deflection, QW7 has been tracked nightly by astronomers around the world. Impact monitoring systems at NASA's Center for Near-Earth Object Studies at the Jet Propulsion Laboratory and ESA's Near-Earth Object Coordination Centre determined from subsequent observations that the chance of impact is near 1.0 percent. That is, chances are nearly 99 out of 100 that the asteroid will safely pass by the Earth, approximately June 15, 2032. Additional observations will enable a more-accurate calculation of the orbit with the possible elimination of risk. The asteroid is calculated to approach within 35,000 kilometers of the Earth's surface. Based on long-studied apparent brightness of QW7, the size of this asteroid is approximately 300 meters to 700 meters. IAWN disseminates this information in accordance with United Nations General Assembly resolution. IAWN is an international network of organizations that detect, track, and characterize potentially hazardous asteroids. IAWN will publish updates of impact probability as this asteroid is tracked.

Orbit accuracy would improve as more telescope observing-arc data were received, especially when supplemented with measurements from ground radio telescopes when QW7 was close enough to reflect back pulsed signals of sufficient strength. With the position and time uncertainties of both QW7, and the Earth itself, the minimum distance was essentially a predicted impact, albeit one with a small probability. QW7's size had been estimated from observed infrared and visible-light brightness, part of Kayla's earlier research. That size certainly got people's attention. An exploratory space probe would be needed to visit the asteroid to nail down QW7's physical parameters.

Zhang-Wei and Kayla's ASA model addressed the N-body problem. Their model would provide a more alarming prediction: a small yet higher probability of impact. But the ASA model was still in development and verification. It inconveniently soaked up a fair bit of supercomputer time.

For the world, a common enemy would now do wonders for

international cooperation, especially when the enemy was thought to arrive in somebody's Earthly neighborhood in nine years, maybe your own neighborhood. The attention of public officials and government leaders was certainly warranted.

An emergency meeting of the UN Security Council was called. It would be held in the designated chamber of the UN Conference building in New York City.

Earlier, the Security Council had met in that same chamber on another stressful matter: the Russian invasion of a neighbor. The Russian Federation was a permanent member of the Security Council. The Russian representative felt the heat of world opinion amid back room rumblings about their removal from the Council. For the representative, and the President of Russia, QW7 was a welcome distraction, deflecting global attention from their grisly regional conflict.

Of course, the press had again been invited to the open Security Council meeting. Newspapers and televised commentary helped fan the flames of world awareness, well beyond those with telescopes, their data, and orbit models. Decisions and actions would be needed with an urgency fueled by the stark 9 years and 294 days of remaining time.

***

Kayla rolled her head side to side with dreamy flashbacks of the gunshot that nearly took her life back in Watts. Her mother was gone now, felled by a coronavirus lung infection. Kayla's father had also been taken from her, by force. The pain of their loss still remained. She sleepily reached over to the night stand and patted her old book: *Theoria Motus*. She touched her dad's challenge coin resting on its cover. The Sun appeared over the San Gabriel Mountains, warming her face. Aging Tiger stretched, yawned, and placed his paw on her cheek. Kayla glanced at the bookshelf that held a white porcelain cat, a gift to Zhang-Wei from his mother. It had been made in Taiwan, despite its Japanese heritage. It had been often argued that this feline statuesque talisman had its roots in ancient China. Its right paw was raised, inviting good fortune. It rested next to a porcelain urn with the ashes of Kayla's mother, whose fortune had run out. Zhang-Wei had thought Tiger cat, and Kayla, needed a companion and had given her the porcelain cat. A raised left paw would have invited customers; but there would be plenty of those in the coming months, wanting to know the most likely when and where of QW7's impact. Zhang-Wei had explained that according to Chinese mythology, real cats can see things that people cannot. That attribute would be needed at JPL in the coming years, months, and days. Old Tiger was the living embodiment of his porcelain companion. If only either could speak.

Zhang-Wei was still asleep in his adjacent house, exhausted by their all-night session at JPL, putting the final touches on their new asteroid orbit prediction method. It awaited formal blessing by the JPL Director. If ever there were a time when accurate asteroid orbit prediction was needed, now was it. Zhang-Wei had met privately with her and got right to the point. "Ma'am, respectfully … do you want the answer fast, or do you want it accurate?" The Director wanted both; but as with any complex, multi-component system, there would be trade-offs.

Kayla started her morning ritual by walking down the wooden steps and borrowing the morning newspapers from Zhang-Wei's front porch. Two papers awaited her. There hadn't been a formal vetted warning on QW7. Until then, the fuzzy press release would have to do. By hurried back-channel agreement with the IAU, that would be done at the end of the upcoming urgent Defence Conference to be held on the Caltech campus. With a fresh cup of coffee in her hand, she leafed through the *Los Angeles Times*. There was an article buried on the interior pages, something about an asteroid that would come close to the Earth in 2032, about as close as a big asteroid had done in 2011, closer than the distance to the Moon. The reporter had not attended the UN emergency meeting and overlooked the Associated Press feed. A deadline had driven the article's limited content.

The New York Times was much different. Tiger jumped up on the table. She gave him a good petting as she absorbed the article. She certainly knew all the details, and then some. Kayla wanted to see how those details were conveyed to the public, some of whom, somewhere, were potentially at grave risk. The paper's main building was not far from the UN. A story about the same asteroid, expanded in some detail, appeared on the front page. Their senior journalist had attended the UN meeting on the asteroid threat. The headline grabbed Kayla's attention: "Large asteroid could strike the Earth in 2032." The first sentence began with, "Calculations at NASA's Jet Propulsion Laboratory ..." The article went on to describe how this already-discovered asteroid had been deflected into a new and dangerous orbit and referred to it as 467317 (2000 QW7). For readers' convenience in the remainder of the article, the Minor Planet Center's catalogue number and the year of the discovery had been stripped away, leaving QW7 as its name. The seasoned science reporter was unable to find a name for QW7.

He'd done a feature article on the threat of asteroid 99942 (2004 MN4) when it was reported that it would pass very close to the Earth in 2029. That asteroid had been given a rather un-cheery name: Apophis, the Greek name of the mythological evil serpent that dwells in eternal darkness, who nightly attempts to swallow the Egyptian sun-god Ra. It seemed to fit with its unofficial name as dubbed by attention-seeking journalists: Doomsday Asteroid. At first there was considerable concern; but later radio telescope data enabled a more accurate prediction. It was forecast to miss the Earth, 13 April 2029, to pass within about 4.6 Earth radii from the surface ... close enough to awaken governments of the need to develop an asteroid deflection system. QW7 would add to that motivation.

The reporter had seen fit to not describe the necessary but arcane method that determined the alpha-numeric designation QW7: the half-month of discovery, the order of discovery in that half-month, and the number of cycles through the alphabet to arrive at that letter. The full designation was complex to the layperson, but there were thousands of potentially hazardous asteroids to catalogue. QW7 was just one of them, now in a dangerously-modified orbit.

Kayla had not discovered QW7, but she had discovered its altered orbit; a re-birth, a celestial re-incarnation. Kayla was an independent person with grit. Without checking with Zhang-Wei or anybody else, she proposed a name to the Minor Planet Center: Nyame, the all-knowing, all-powerful supreme Deity of the Akan people of Ghana.

Kayla's ancestors hadn't come through New York's Ellis Island in that great wave of European immigration. When she asked about such things, her father explained that her great-grandparents on both sides of the family hadn't immigrated, but they'd fled the Jim Crow South. Without written records, ancestry further back was lost in the fog of time. The only thing they were most certain of was that Kayla was a descendant of slaves, like many others in her poor Watts neighborhood.

While she was unsure of its statistical veracity, she succumbed to sending in a saliva sample for a DNA ancestry check. The resulting pie chart had a big wedge for Ghana, one of the sources of slaves captured and stuffed into wooden sailing ships, hauled to the New World, and forced to work in the fields of their European masters. Back in Ghana, people still clung to their ancient spiritual beliefs. The big statistical wedge drove her to wander through different stacks at the Caltech library and do Internet searches. She learned more about her roots, and about Nyame.

Her eyes widened when she read that the Akan people's supreme creator of the universe was also referred to as the Sky Deity. On Mauna Kea she encountered Wākea, the Sky Father of a different culture. Was it coincidence, or was it meant to be? She knew the answer. She submitted Nyame as QW7's name and awaited their decision.

News of a possibly dangerous asteroid spread beyond the reaches of *The New York Times* and *Los Angeles Times* to shamans in Ghana and protestors in Hawai'i atop Mauna Kea. As the Sun set, chants accompanied the ancient hula as dancers lifted their hands to Wākea, the Sky Father. But their words had changed since Kayla had first encountered them at the Mid-Level Facility. Now they called upon Wākea to direct QW7 to strike the site of the TMT and also sweep away the existing telescopes. Since QW7's altered orbit had been observed with Keck II, the protestors felt their request was justified.

In Ghana's rugged, lush, forested highland, a village with conical, thatched roofs was alive with beating drums and gyrating dancers in colorful garb around a central fire. Villagers clapped and chanted to the rhythm as a shaman looked skyward to the starlit heavens. He reached out to their Sky Deity, Nyame, to push the asteroid away. He was in unknown opposition to the spiritual request on the other side of the Earth.

Meanwhile, esteemed members of the IAU Working Group for Small Bodies Nomenclature poured over the requested name for 467317 (2000 QW7). There was some debate since the requestor, Kayla Williams, had not discovered QW7. That honor fell to the automated Near-Earth Asteroid Tracking system on Haleakala on the island of Maui. The principal investigator at the time for NEAT was JPL's famous Eleanor Helin, now deceased. For some reason neither she nor her two co-investigators had requested a name for QW7. But Kayla had discovered its new orbit and made a compelling case for her requested name. The IAU decided. Kayla was notified by the Minor Planet Center that QW7 would be named Nyame. The announcement of the asteroid-naming included the phonetics for it as spoken in Ghana: *nee-yah-meh*, with *nee* the stressed syllable. It would become a household word, a name practiced by astronomers, reporters, and TV news anchors.

Conferring
[9 Years 271 Days before Impact]

Shortly following the UN emergency Security Council meeting in New York City, the first day of the Asteroid Defense Conference at Caltech arrived with more than enough public awareness. Zhang-Wei and Kayla parked as close as they could to the big round building, the Beckman Institute's huge auditorium capable of seating over 1,100 people. With other invited astronomers, scientists, and government people from around the world, they walked alongside the long pond with its gentle streams of arched water to get to the main entrance. The water-feature was peaceful, but there were others crowded on the adjacent grass lawns. They had a not-so-gentle interest in QW7.

The general public usually had some interest in reports of asteroids that would pass near the Earth. The prediction of another pass usually garnered 'ho-hum' responses, unless they were astronomers. But the fact that an emergency meeting of the UN Security Council had been held, concerning the threat of an asteroid collision, awakened news people and those that read what had been written. Some reporters and their editors tended to embellish things, riding on the back of the yellow journalism of the past. It sold papers, drove radio and TV news program ratings, triggered Internet mouse clicks on computer screens, and finger taps on cell phones.

By sheer coincidence, just after the UN meeting there was a massive volcanic eruption in Indonesia that wiped out entire villages. It was accompanied by a large killing earthquake and a tsunami that swallowed up coastal villages around the Bay of Bengal. The Earth was indeed a restless place. Now, as if divinely driven, the deep black realm of space was following suit.

The horrific news from Indonesia and India, newspaper articles and TV news programs about QW7 and the press release about the scheduled conference at Caltech became a spiritual trip wire. Agitated people gathered around the Beckman Institute and held large hand-lettered signs: "Repent … The End is Near … Come to Jesus." A fervent young man with a Southern accent held a Bible high above his head. He shouted a warning sermon, something about the Fourth Horseman of the Apocalypse, riding on QW7, bringing well-deserved death to the sinful Earth. On the wide, low wall surrounding the tranquil pond, an apparent Buddhist monk wearing an orange robe sat in the lotus position, eyes closed in meditation, arms held forward, palms of his hands up. Zhang-Wei remembered seeing such things in Taiwan and wondered if the monk was trying to communicate with QW7, maybe trying to deflect it with the power of his meditating mind. He looked around at the Christian apocalyptic side of things, thinking one would offset the other, leaving the fate of QW7 and the Earth in the hands of the learned gathering inside.

TV trucks, with their long extended antennae, drove down the concrete walkways and parked on the lawns. Reporters and their assistants with shoulder-mounted video cameras clustered around the base of the steps leading up into the entrance. As Zhang-Wei and Kayla made their way through the throng, a microphone was thrust at them as cameras flashed. He pushed them aside and made it through the door into the welcoming arms of security staff, complete with inspection of handbags and an archway that detected metal. The guards were armed. There had been threats.

The auditorium was packed. More news reporters with their videographers stood along the back wall. Planning and administration of the conference had been enormous and precise. With most students at home for the summer, visiting attendees were housed in empty dorm rooms. They'd be close to the big auditorium and the Beckman Institute's spaces that were to be used as meeting rooms; time was of the absolute essence. This was a working decision conference with assigned task groups. Attendees didn't just get past security and wander into the auditorium and hopefully find a place to sit. Each and every seat was assigned. A seating map with seat numbers and name list was given to participants as they made their way past security. Included was a security badge with serial number and facial photograph. Worldwide, more people wanted to attend than for whom there was room. Deciding who could attend, or not, was nearly as complicated as calculating the trajectory of QW7.

Zhang-Wei and Kayla found their adjacent seats, next to Lajos. In the astronomy and astrophysics community, there were close partnerships and collaborations. People from Pisa sat nearby. In the auditorium there were many acknowledging head nods with serious faces and small hand waves. Zhang-Wei raised his eyebrows and took note when the founder and executive director of the B612 Foundation, a former NASA astronaut, walked in. The wide-ranging community was gathered to address a common threat: QW7.

But there were other ramifications: international trade and treaty negotiations, the conflict in Ukraine and other regions, and interlaced economics that could override or distort the best plan that the world's top astrophysicists and engineers could recommend. A multi-faceted recommendation to the UN was the focus of the conference, and that would be the framework for the decisions that lay in the immediate years ahead.

There was some mumbling when a man in a blue uniform entered and took his seat. He caught the attention of reporters when he ascended the stairs into the auditorium. There were four stars on each shoulder of the Chief of Space Operations for the new United States Space Force. Like aviation itself, there had been a need to focus and protect United States and allied interests in space. There was certainly an increased interest in space, the same space that enveloped the Earth and QW7, and the near-space through which rockets would be launched to defend the Earth. He knew that blasting an asteroid to bits with a massive nuclear bomb could be on the table. Rockets with nuclear bombs would have his keen interest. Over 50 years earlier, under the auspices of the UN, nuclear powers of the day signed the Outer Space Treaty: the United States, the United Kingdom, and the Soviet Union. Other countries signed on in the following years, but not all followed up with their government's ratification. Among the binding principles was the prohibition of placing weapons of mass destruction on any celestial body, or otherwise stationing them in outer space. QW7 was indeed a celestial body. The General arranged to be in the conference group devoted to deflecting the asteroid. There, he could keep an eye on things that could be indirectly threatening, like a large hydrogen bomb on the tip of a rocket. Military intelligence agencies had been alerted. Adam MacKellar at the NSA had taken note. The Russian contingent sat in a group. They were known and immediately recognized, and uncomfortably felt the stares of others. The President of Russia had rattled his nuclear weapons saber. Use of overwhelming force seemed to be in the Russian psyche. Lajos was confident that a massive nuclear bomb would be recommended by the Russians.

The President of Caltech stepped to the podium. The auditorium was filled with a low chatter. Rather than asking for quiet over the loudspeakers, the lights were dimmed and brightened a few times, to get everyone's attention. It became quiet. He welcomed them to the California Institute of Technology and the Jet Propulsion Laboratory, even though that was a few miles away. He then introduced the Secretary-General of the UN, the keynote speaker. If ever there were a time for nations to be united in a common purpose, now was that time.

The Secretary-General had gray hair and a lined face that spoke to his wisdom in world peace, politics, and his early engineering life. He'd been the prime minister of his country and was now in his second term as Secretary-General. Well-respected and trusted, he had been recommended by the 15-member Security Council, then appointed by the General Assembly representing nearly 200 member states. He spent a few minutes describing the structure of the UN Security Council, its five permanent members and the current ten non-permanent members. For some of the attendees, top scientists, this was mind-numbing bureaucracy. He smoothly transitioned to their task, recounting the steps that had been taken to identify QW7 as a threat: detecting, tracking, and predicting its new orbit. It had already been characterized physically, due in part to Kayla's research. The emphasis was certain: continued tracking by multiple observatories, space-based platforms, and ground-based antennae for accurate predictions and warnings, then deciding on just how to mitigate the threat: how to deflect QW7.

He turned the podium over to the Administrator of NASA who dropped the other expected heavy shoe. "Ladies and gentlemen. As you well know, we do not have a proven asteroid deflection system. The expense, and the formerly-distant threat thought to be many decades off, has lulled all of us into a measured, affordable pace of test and development. We do not now have the luxury of time. We must decide quickly, predicated on the accuracy of our predictions, on how to mitigate this threat, or even if we need to. Only a few optimum launch opportunity windows for heavy-lift rockets lay before us in order to rendezvous with QW7 as soon as possible. But the time to design, build, and test a deflection system will erode away our remaining time. National and international resources must be cooperatively focused. There are a number of theoretical concepts; one will be tested in 10 days with the DART mission. This conference will stay in session until the basic design of a deflection system is agreed upon, as well as a plan for its development, testing, and deployment." The Administrator of NASA merely reaffirmed what everybody in the auditorium already knew, professionally and instinctively.

He thanked the community in advance for their hard, dedicated work, then made a request for recognition. "Ladies and gentlemen, please give a hand to Miss Kayla Williams. At Keck II this last July, she was the first to observe that QW7 had been deflected into a new orbit, giving us extremely valuable lead time." Kayla stood, completely surprised, while attendees clapped. Kayla acknowledged the adulation and sat back down. Zhang-Wei patted her hand. The Vice President of Caltech had remembered that early-morning phone call from Kayla and had suggested this moment of recognition. The NASA chief continued, "Miss Williams is a PhD candidate, and I have it on good authority she will likely receive her degree. I also have it on good authority that the International Astronomical Union has approved her proposed name for QW7 in its new orbit: Nyame." Kayla was pleased that his pronunciation was phonetically correct, as spoken in Ghana.

Lajos just sat stoically. There would be no recognition for him. He scanned the seating assignment list. Lajos cast his stern gaze across the auditorium. There, in the far corner, was Adam MacKellar. Of course, there were more in attendance than astronomers and astrophysicists. Political and national power would be as important as the power of the rockets to launch the soon-to-be-determined deflection system. But what power did Adam have? Why had he been invited, or even been allowed to attend?

The NASA Administrator continued. "It's been reported in the news that the UN Security Council voted that the Jet Propulsion Laboratory will be the command and control center for orbit prediction, deflection operations, warnings, and press releases." What he didn't say was that the vote was 13 to 2, with the Russian Federation and China voting no ... not a particularly good way to launch an international effort. "We've begun adding security in and around JPL and will be installing secure high-bandwidth communications to the European Space Operations Center, the Russian Mission Control Center for Roscosmos, and the Beijing Aerospace Flight Control Center, as has been agreed. Representatives from those agencies will have seats in the Mission Control Center at JPL." He didn't reveal that another data communications channel would be installed at the National Security Agency in Maryland. Adam also had power. The NASA Administrator concluded the opening plenary session with, "Please adjourn to your respective working groups. We look forward to your recommendations as soon as possible ... I want daily reports of your progress!"

Prediction
[9 Years 264 Days before Impact]

The news blackout was strict. Reporters were prohibited from sitting in on working group deliberations at the Defense Conference. Guards were posted by the doors to the meeting rooms. Positive identification was required to enter. Participants were warned not to leak any of the deliberations. Rumors and misinterpretations were silenced. Reading how the sausage of collaborative science, under stress, was being made would not be good for a nervous public. Warnings and asteroid defense plans would be released in due time, after the end of the conference. There was no working group public transparency, to the ire of some scientists.

Starved for information, newspaper reporters, editors, and TV news anchors picked up on the publicly announced naming of asteroid 467317 (2000 QW7) and that a beautiful Black woman, a Caltech astrophysicist, had proposed it. Articles with her photograph, showing the scar on her cheek, soon appeared; they explained the history of the Akan people of Ghana and their Deity, Nyame, who knows and sees everything. Reporters showed up on Grape Street. The dead, cold lump of space debris came to life. Spiritually personified, it became a real, living, and deadly enemy.

Some Nyame newspaper articles found their way into the California State Prison cell of DeShawn Brown and into the hands of the Crips in South Los Angeles. Kayla's assigned failed assassin even felt some remorse. Despite having been deemed a drug snitch, her stock rose in all corners of the Los Angeles Black community.

African culture and the roots of slavery were again being openly discussed across the nation, if not the globe.

This wasn't a calming influence for those standing outside of the Beckman Institute. People with different signs started showing up, signs held high with the name Nyame on them. Verbal conflicts arose between people with different spiritual beliefs; the young man with bible-waving oratory was one of them. The history of slavery was folded in, resonating with social justice movements and the protests of a few years earlier. The threat of Nyame was not bringing people together, which was the goal of the Defense Conference.

Zhang-Wei, Kayla, and Lajos would be making the case for the expanded N-body full-physics model using adaptive simulated annealing. Despite the quantum computing disaster at IQIM, Lajos was brought back into the fold at JPL. His brain was needed, despite his personality. But he'd be working for Zhang-Wei, not the other way around, part of the JPL mental triumvirate in the Solar System Dynamics group. Of course, there were others in the international community that worked on this complex problem. They came well-prepared with their models' QW7 orbit predictions. The trajectories were similar, but the forecast relative positions of the Earth and QW7 over 9 years out differed significantly, with impact probabilities ranging from a low of 2.5 percent to the high of 8.3 percent from the latest ASA run. But there was price to pay for increased accuracy. The computation took 2 weeks on NASA's supercomputer that could process at 150 petaFLOPS: 150 quadrillion floating-point operations per second.

The Russian Federation's presentation started with a just a hint of confrontation, with a reminder that the polynomials of Pafnuty Lvovich Chebyshev were at the soul of JPL's development ephemeris of the known planetary bodies. The stern Russian attempted some humor suggesting that, in the limit, the desired accuracy of the solution of the position of Nyame could take 9 years to compute, just as it was arriving. He added, as if speaking to students in a classroom, that Nyame itself perfectly integrated all the forces involved.

That netted a Hungarian glare from Lajos. A quantum computer could have easily handled even the most complex of formulations in seconds rather than weeks, but Liu Yang had changed all that. Lajos gave an especially hardened look to the astrophysicists from Beijing. He darkly thought that maybe they were harboring Liu.

Complex equations, algorithm flow charts, tables, graphs, computational loads, and accuracies were the red meat of the session. There were no real surprises as these scientific advances were promulgated in peer-reviewed journals and had been the foci of a number of conferences. The session was polishing old rocks, but a new stone was thrown in the pond by Zhang-Wei.

Theory was one thing, verification quite another. He was at the podium. One of his verifications was almost serendipitous, using the pre-deflection orbit of QW7. He performed his abacus calculation, then spoke. "Colleagues. Back in September of 2019, QW7 made a close pass, coming within 0.036 astronomical units of the Earth. My graduate student, Kayla Williams, went to Palomar to get observed data over a five-day arc. This accurate track has been one of the baselines for our verification. To tighten it up, we added the location and track data from the Arecibo Radio Telescope in Puerto Rico, before the disastrous collapse of its instrument platform into the big dish."

From somewhere in the room, "QW7 or Nyame. Which is it?"

As for most of the conference attendees, the naming was a surprise to Zhang-Wei. He gave a brief glance to Kayla then replied. "Yes, yes. We can refer to it either way. When Kayla did her work at Palomar, it was QW7."

A hand shot up. "Hale does not have the pointing accuracy of today's telescopes."

"Yes, we know. But back in 2019, it had something more valuable: QW7 up close. Would you want Keck II at 3.6 astronomical units or Palomar at 0.036?" Zhang-Wei went on to carefully explain that he used observing arc data from the very first observation of QW7 in August, 2000 through observations up to 2010, 9 years prior to September, 2019, to initialize the latest version of the ASA model. He compared the predicted track to the track as determined by the Palomar observations and the Arecibo measurements. The error statistics were impressive and applicable to the current threat, even though it was now in a different orbit, a Nyame orbit thanks to Elcano.

"My dear friends. You know of Juno. It took over 5 years to reach Jupiter. Your space agencies have had similar probes into the solar system. We've collaborated on some of them. With our Deep Space Network antennae, an atomic clock, and Doppler-shifted radio signals, we located Juno with meter accuracy and velocities with equivalent precision on its way to Jupiter, somewhat better than using right-ascension and declination and mathematical inversion to determine trajectory. My close partner, Professor Vadja, will explain our process."

Like a dark angry cloud, Lajos took to the podium. His face scanned around the room like an antenna looking for an enemy ship. Socially deficient, he started. "Listen carefully. The N-body problem belongs to all of us, but also for Juno as it responded with a track that had to be corrected with its thrusters. After a track correction, the new positions were fed into our model. Its predictions were compared to future positions at various lead times up to the next track adjustment. The chart behind me shows the verification for each of the between-thruster corrections."

A timid hand was raised. "Lajos, we don't have the Juno data."
"Of course, Wilfried. You hadn't asked for it."

It took 6 days, long hours, and heated words before the Prediction Group agreed to a recommendation. There was much discussion and argument. Normal collegiality was stressed to arrive at a balance between the accuracy of the final trajectory of Nyame as it either struck the Earth, or barely missed it, versus the time needed to compute a new orbit, when additional observations became available before and after a deflection had been applied. Two weeks of time were required on NASA's most powerful supercomputer. But the group's model recommendation had a political bent. NASA's JPL ASA model would be the benchmark for all actions and decisions, including warnings. With some realistic political deference, the track predictions of the European, Russian, and Chinese space agencies could be released to the public, but with appropriate cautions and caveats. It was envisioned that press releases would show the JPL-predicted track relative to the Earth with associated location probabilities; but other tracks could be shown to give the general public an appreciation of the uncertainties involved. This would be similar to hurricane predictions, where colored tracks like entangled strands of spaghetti were shown on a map where they crossed a coastline, complete with watch/warning probability zones. The public, primarily those living in coastal regions, were very used to such warnings. At any given forecast time, there would be a NASA-modeled prediction of Nyame's most-likely location. Around that point would be ellipsoids of decreasing probability, like concentric egg shells. This was true even for the Earth, considering the slight errors in the predicted location of the center of the Earth and where the surface of the Earth would be as it rotated.

Lajos correctly and strongly interjected that if radios and their antennae were to be landed upon Nyame, position and track information could be much more accurately determined, and much more quickly, using the Deep Space Network. Valuable time, life-saving time, could be saved as Nyame approached, guiding both warnings and deflection operations. He brought that concept into the Deflection Group.

Lajos wrapped up his presentation with a graphic that showed elongated probability ellipses centered on a dot where Nyame could strike with a 3.0 percent probability. The next two ellipses were for probabilities of 2.0 percent, 1.0 percent, and down to the boundary of 0.0 percent. Integrating over the areas of ground-intersected probabilities, the overall chance was 8.3 percent. Lajos carefully explained: "That location and the probability ellipses are the intersection of the probability shells of the Earth and Nyame. Obviously, there's a 91.7 percent chance, according to the latest run of the ASA model, that Nyame will miss."

An astrophysicist from the European Space Agency raised his hand. "It looks like the most likely point of impact is Vilnius in Lithuania, with some probability that it could land on Moscow, Berlin, or even London."

Zhang-Wei stood and interjected, "Yes, but more telescope observations in the months ahead will narrow that down, change the probability distributions, and likely change the center point. This is just a real example of what can be gleaned from the ASA model. It took two supercomputer CPU weeks to arrive at what you see."

In his deep voice, Lajos cautioned, almost threatened, "This graphic must not leave this room. If a space probe is landed on the asteroid, the prediction will be significantly tightened using NASA's Deep Space Network to locate Nyame within a few meters, with corresponding accuracy for velocity. If we do that, we should make big rocket thrusters part of the package. But I'll bring that suggestion into the Deflection Group. The model output you see will be transferred to the Warning Group. They'll drape it with an appropriate narrative for the public. There's already sufficient anxiety."

Before Lajos clicked to remove the big graphic from the screen, someone in the back of the room, with scientific transparency on his mind, quickly raised his small cell phone and silently touched the white dot on the display.

Deflection
[9 Years 264 Days before Impact]

The Deflection Group was animated, energized much more than the Prediction Group. It was one thing to accurately predict whether Nyame would miss the Earth; if it didn't, where and when it would strike quite another. If there were some probability of impacting the surface, the prediction became immensely important. Prediction Group members were encouraged and allowed to cross-flow and attend Deflection Group sessions; Lajos was there. The where, when, and how of deflection, and its result, greatly depended on the accurate modeling of Nyame's orbit before and after a deflection, so there was a natural and necessary fundamental tie with the Prediction Group.

Those in the Deflection Group were proud not to be passive observers to a potential catastrophe. In their collective hands was the determination of how to deflect Nyame to miss the Earth, or to miss by a wider margin. The feasibilities, pros and cons, of all the possible deflection options were presented. As with the other working groups, the Deflection Group was firmly challenged to be comprehensive. Intense debates followed as they wrestled with their charter and choices. Needing time for more study and analyses wouldn't be an acceptable answer. The clock was ticking.

The possibilities quickly narrowed. The estimated size and mass of Nyame and 9.72 years were effective filters. Concepts that required long lead times, either for their development or their application, were rejected outright: gravity tractor, laser ablation, light sail, ion beam, focused solar energy, and reflective coating. That left kinetic impactors, nuclear detonations, and rocket thrusters.

With the upcoming NASA DART mission, kinetic impactors initially held some sway. But colliding significant masses directly opposite the center of gravity of a tumbling Nyame, to effect required velocity changes, could be quite difficult. If more than one were to be used, targeting the later ones to intersect Nyame on its new deflected trajectory could be almost impossible.

Nuclear detonations had some appeal, especially to the Russians. They touted their Tsar Bomba, code named Ivan, the most powerful nuclear weapon ever created and tested, and that they could develop an even more-powerful one. But there were prediction difficulties. One was whether the detonation would fracture and spilt Nyame into pieces, each hazardous, converting Nyame into multiple impact threats; the other was tracking the fragments for individual predictions. Yet another was accurately modeling the vector impulse of evaporated, ejected material of to-be-determined asteroid composition: rubble, solid, or some combination of both.

What was needed, as skillfully stressed by Lajos, was an incremental, controlled system: that would be nuclear rocket thrusters landed upon Nyame. Commanded firings from JPL would impart a velocity change, a new direction and speed for Nyame. The deflected orbit could be observed, measured, and additional deflections commanded in step-wise fashion, until arriving at a trajectory that would miss the Earth, or pass by it with a very low percentage of impacting the surface.

Regardless of the final decision of the working group, it would still require precious time to design, build, and launch a deflector system and rendezvous it with Nyame.

As with the Prediction Group, the Deflection Group had real-time access to databases and super-computing resources. On a large screen was an interactive graphic display. The new Apollo orbit of Nyame was shown along with its 2 intersections with the Earth's orbit, and the intersection point where Nyame and the Earth were predicted to be at the same time, at the point of minimum separation. That point was also shown in a different frame of reference, a mathematical plane through the center of the Earth and perpendicular to the asteroid's trajectory. The working group used this sophisticated application not to actually plan a deflection mission but to evaluate the options. Mass of payload, date of launch, and the time to intercept Nyame were key variables, but the most critical was the asteroid's mass.

For selected dates, three orthogonal components of asteroid velocity change, Delta-V, were chosen: along the velocity vector of the asteroid, cross-track, and normal to its orbital plane. For the estimated mass of Nyame, the application quantitatively revealed what all in the room knew instinctively. The earlier the date, the smaller the net Delta-V required for the same change in end-point position. If only they could go back a few decades, a smaller number of less-massive kinetic impactors could have done the job. But Nyame's new orbit hadn't existed decades ago. Everyone knew they were trapped in a tightening vice of remaining time. They felt the pressure of 9.72 years. From that, they would have to subtract the time it would take to prepare and launch kinetic impactors, plus the time it would take for them to get there to strike Nyame.

The speaker at the podium offered what everybody already knew. "We'll soon have the results of the Double Asteroid Redirection Test mission. The probe strikes Dimorphos today, the moonlet of Didymos in the binary pair. Its orbit around Didymos will be analyzed. We won't have the results for a month or so. The orbital velocity change may be small, millimeters per second. You saw the results when we applied that magnitude of change in the Deflection Application."

From the back of the room, Lajos raised his hand and spoke bluntly. "DART is a pretty little test on a body much smaller than Nyame. Considering their relative velocities and their relative masses, tons would have to be thrust into Nyame at very high velocities to make any difference in the remaining years to possible impact."

The graphics on the screen revealed additional sobering information. Based on known heavy-lift launch vehicles, the maximum mass was calculated that could be put into a transfer orbit, then boosted into a trajectory to arrive at Nyame with the correct relative velocity and approach angle. The application showed that many more than a few rocket-launched kinetic impactors would be needed.

But there were other ways to change Nyame's velocity vector. The Russian astrophysicists suggested that one, or more, nuclear detonations near the asteroid could do it. No need for precisely-calculated approach angles and relative velocities. Equivalent megatons of radiated power could rendezvous near Nyame and be positioned with the same velocity vector at the correct relative three-dimensional bearing, orbiting in space-flight formation.

Again, Lajos spoke bluntly from the back of the room. "We're wasting our time with kinetic impactors and nuclear detonations! There are many things we do not know sufficiently: the mass of Nyame, its shape, its density, its center of mass, or where it will be in its estimated 72-hour rotation, and even what its axis of rotation is. We don't know if it's a pile of rubble, made of solid iron-nickel, or a combination of both. There are too many risks with nuclear detonations. We might make matters worse."

"Professor Vadja. We can launch a space probe to rendezvous and determine those things, maybe even landing on Nyame. With communications antennae and the Deep Space Network, we'll also nail down position and velocity. Nuclear bombs will be launched separately to arrive at the same time, then positioned and detonated based on the data from the probe."

Lajos sharpened his teeth and cut back, "My goodness, von Kármán must be rolling over in his grave! That may be feasible, but too many risks. Nyame could be fractured into a dangerous pattern of space buckshot, threatening more than one place. Plus, the optimum launch window for an investigative probe with minimum time-of-flight to rendezvous has passed. Our focus must be on the next launch window, and have everything ready to go by then."

"Well, professor, if not nuclear detonations or kinetic impactors, what do you propose?"

Lajos was now in his stride. He walked to the front of the room and took command of the podium so people wouldn't have to turn and crane their necks to see him. Most knew him, or knew of him. Lajos laid out his concept of launching payloads from different sites, all to arrive at Nyame at nearly the same time. "Colleagues, one of the payloads, the first to arrive, will be like the successful rendezvous with asteroid Ryugu by Japan's Hayabusa2. It successfully landed small rovers with sensors on the surface. In addition to high-resolution imagery, we now have Ryugu's rotation period, axis of rotation, its size and shape, bulk density, and measurements of its weak gravitational field. Ryugu is like a pile of rubble, not suitable for a nuclear detonation deflection; Nyame could be the same."

From the back of the room, Alexei spoke with a deep Russian-accented voice, "And just what do you plan to do with the other payloads? Are they to be nuclear bombs?"

Lajos knew the person behind that voice from previous encounters. "My dear Sasha. There will be trajectory-altering, powerful rocket engines landed on the asteroid, pointed outwards. They'll be just like the hydrazine thrusters used on long-distance space probes, only a hell of a lot bigger. As we've talked about, the radio transmissions used to communicate with those rockets will also be used with our Deep Space Network to precisely and quickly determine position and velocity."

Lajos continued as if giving one of his infamous classroom lectures. People in the room had been subjected to his verbiage at earlier technical conferences. He described that each payload will have a star tracker, a sensitive inertial sensor, communications antennae, and nuclear cells to power everything. Sharp corkscrews in the legs will twist into the surface to anchor themselves. Adjustments on the legs will align rocket thrust directly opposite the center of mass. As Nyame rotates, and possibly wobbles, Lajos explained that rockets would be commanded by secure uplink to fire for specific durations in a modeled sequence to produce a desired net Delta-V. Following the collective rocket nudges, Nyame would be accurately tracked for a few weeks. The ASA model would be applied to predict the closest point-of-approach to the Earth and the probability of ground impact. The process will be repeated as Nyame nears, until it's on a safe trajectory or the rocket fuel runs out. Lajos accompanied his lecture with system engineering and program management charts with interrelated project tasks: estimated durations, completion times, and estimated costs. He'd come prepared.

Alexei spoke rather brusquely. "And just what type of rockets do you plan to use? A binary chemical rocket will weigh very much, and ones light enough to be launched and transferred into a trajectory to Nyame will have limited thrust."

Lajos rose to the challenge. "Have you forgotten nuclear thermal rockets, the use of a uranium fission nuclear reactor to hyper-heat liquid hydrogen into a high velocity jet? Both Russia and the United States worked on this monopropellant technology during the Cold War. There'd been successful ground tests aimed at shortening the time for a manned mission to Mars. Our countries lost interest, and funds were diverted to rocketry to carry nuclear weapons for mutual annihilation. Compared to heavier chemical rockets, its specific impulse is much greater, more than double."

Alexei replied, "Of course, Lajos, that is very well known. Your government has set aside hundreds of millions of dollars to design and test such rockets. But you've been stymied by converting weapons-grade uranium into low-enriched uranium. We've not been so constricted. We'll get our people to Mars first."

"Sasha, your tests haven't gone so well. Lives were lost in the Nyonoksa accident you tried to cover up. It would've been better to set your sights on Mars and not long-range, low-level, high-velocity cruise missiles. We both have the technology. Such rocket engines can be designed, tested, and manufactured as quickly as the asteroid landers that will cradle them. I think our Chinese brethren have been doing similar research and development. It would be a team effort that unites us."

Alexei interrupted. "You saw in my presentation that a large nuclear detonation near Nyame can deflect it. We can park it close on the correct aspect angle. The temperature of the irradiated surface will eject material and thrust the asteroid into an opposite direction. We have enough material in storage from the good old days of the Cold War to make very powerful nuclear devices, and we have the heavy-lift rockets to get them there. We'll be able to launch devices sooner than any of these other schemes."

Those in the room squirmed. Launching a large nuclear bomb into space could make some nations a bit nervous, plus it was against UN policy on the peaceful uses of outer space. The head of the U.S. Space Force quietly took note. But this was an emergency. Alexei emphasized that they had an Angara-100 heavy-lift rocket on the pad at the Baikonur Cosmodrome in Kazakhstan, and they could swap out the space probe with a nuclear device in short order.

Lajos fired back. "What if it takes more than one detonation?"

"We can launch more."

"Alexei, Alexei. You can't park them in formation. The first detonation will disable the others and possibly fracture Nyame into smaller, yet lethal, fragments. Subsequent deflections will be much more complex. Which ones will you choose? How will you know?"

The silence in the room answered the questions. Lajos continued and fleshed out his concept. The covey of landed rockets would not only be able to communicate with mission controllers at JPL, they would communicate with each other through an asteroid local-area network. Parameters for the execution model would be securely uplinked prior to the execution sequence and transmitted back for confirmation. Then, the countdown would be allowed to continue. If the command message were not confirmed, a command would be uplinked to stop the countdown. The countdown would be governed by the atomic clocks of the asteroid local area network. The time to uplink the execution model, receive confirmation, and, if necessary, stop the countdown ... all governed by the speed of light and the relative distance ... would not be a limitation.

Professor Li Chen broke in. "Lajos. Why do you not fire all the rockets in the correct sequence until all fuel is exhausted, giving the asteroid one large velocity change?"

"Li, my good friend, that's possible. But what if we're wrong? Then all operations will be focused on where to evacuate. We'll only apply enough thrust to barely miss the Earth, leaving liquid hydrogen for subsequent trajectory corrections if needed. It's possible that we could over-correct and actually increase impact probability, with no options remaining."

"Professor Vadja. The mass of QW7, I mean Nyame, is somewhat larger than that of a space probe."

"Yes, Doctor Chen, we certainly know that. But, like jiu-jitsu, a small amount of force precisely applied can move a larger opponent into a new direction."

"Lajos, how will you make such a calculation?"

Lajos replied, "We'll select an aim point just sufficient to miss, about geostationary satellite altitude. We'll run the ASA model in reverse from this spherical tangent point, so that the reverse trajectory splines with the actual trajectory at the point when the rocket-firing sequence begins."

Professor Chen calmly stood up from the front row and turned to face all in attendance at the working group. "We would be playing brinksmanship, I think that is the American term, with people's lives. How close can you fire a gun at a person's head and still miss?"

That set the tone for discussions that went on into the next days. It was good that reporters weren't in the room. Heated language was exchanged; complex equations and charts were flung on the screen. Rather than discussing abstract theories and raw basic research, they had to make a decision on what deflection system should be pursued. Different countries shouldn't be tinkering with the same asteroid. Votes were taken until a super-majority was achieved. There were hard-nosed holdouts for kinetic impactors and nuclear detonations. Lajos's plan of controlled, nuclear thermal rocket thrusters on Nyame became the recommended deflection system.

Alexei's close friend quietly showed him the cell phone display with the image of the latest prediction of where an un-deflected Nyame could impact. His hometown, Moscow, was not at the center, but within an uncomfortable probability ellipse.

***

Back home, in an underground meeting room in the Kremlin, they would come up with their own secretive plan: the largest hydrogen bomb ever conceived, atop a huge Russian rocket ... all cloaked as a probe to Jupiter.

Warning
[9 Years 253 Days before Impact]

The Defense Conference wrapped up after ten laborious, bleary-eyed, long days, ending with a proposed international agreement. Formal signatures by national leaders would follow for their commitment of resources and to prepare their nations. Zhang-Wei and Kayla's ASA model would be used to predict Nyame's orbit, closest point-of-approach, before and after rocket deflection firings. Other nations' models were not officially sanctioned. Warnings, press releases, and press briefings would be based on the output of the ASA model.

The Earth already had a common threat: global warming. The Intergovernmental Panel on Climate Change, the IPCC, had been formed some years earlier as a body of the UN. Following suit, by Defense Conference dictate, the Intergovernmental Mission Control Center was formed, the IMCC. JPL gained another moniker and mission. While global warming loomed, Nyame threatened on a different time scale.

For asteroid deflection, international cooperation was focused on nuclear thermal rocket thrusters, with their instrument and communications packages, to be launched and landed on Nyame. Heavy-lift launch vehicles, modified for deflector payloads, would be used. There was much to be done, equivalent to the Manhattan Project or the first Moon landing, with very little room for slips in the tight schedule. The Administrator of NASA announced it all, in detail, from the podium of the big auditorium of the Beckman Institute at the close of the conference. News media were lined up along the back wall. To help ensure consistency, they received a carefully-crafted press release just as it was electronically transmitted from Mission Control at JPL to the Associated Press and to other national and international agencies.

There was a template to guide the Defense Conference Prediction Group that drafted the release. JPL's Center for Near-Earth Object Studies held biennium Planetary Defense Conference Exercises, complete with orbit predictions for a hypothetical asteroid. The exercise in 2017 had been uncanny. Its scenario: an asteroid in an Apollo orbit, about the size of Nyame, and a predicted impact in nine years. It came with a set of briefing slides intended for the public that included hypothetical planned missions to assess the characteristics of the hypothetical asteroid, and the launch of hypothetical kinetic impactors.

The first IMCC press release for Nyame was essentially a warning for Lithuania, based on the latest ASA model run. While alarming, the press release was intended to be calming, lest panic ensue. A lot could change in the years ahead, especially if a deflection were attempted. Subjective assessments of low, medium, and high varied considerably from astronomers and astrophysicists, to the governments of nations, to the average person on the street.

IMCC PRESS RELEASE, OCTOBER 02, 2022. ASTEROID POSES LOW THREAT OF EARTH IMPACT. An asteroid could pass close to the Earth in approximately 9 years 253 days. There is a small chance that it could impact our planet near Vilnius, Lithuania. The asteroid, officially designated 467317 (2000 QW7), named Nyame, was observed on July 25, 2022, to have been decelerated into a new orbit by the gravity of a passing interstellar body. Nyame has been tracked extensively since then by observatories around the world and telescopes in space. The likelihood of impact is low, according to the Intergovernmental Mission Control Center (IMCC) at NASA's Jet Propulsion Laboratory in Pasadena, California. Nyame should not be cause for public concern at this time, as there is a high probability that it will safely pass by our planet. As the asteroid is extensively observed in the months ahead, its orbit will become better defined. In all likelihood the possibility that it could impact the Earth may be eliminated. Based on observed brightness, Nyame's representative size ranges from approximately 300 meters to 700 meters, but it is too distant at this time for astronomers to make a more accurate estimate. The accompanying diagrams show the orbits of Nyame and the Earth, along with their positions when Nyame's orbit change was discovered and the position when Nyame is expected to pass close to the Earth. The third diagram is an expanded view of the intersection point of the two orbits when, with the current uncertainty, the asteroid is predicted to cross the Earth's orbit June 15, 2032. The Moon's orbit is shown for scale. Through international agreement and cooperation, an asteroid deflection system will be developed and launched in the near future, to change Nyame's orbit to make it completely miss the Earth. Any warnings will be issued by the IMCC.

The press release was intentionally watered down to prevent premature panic. A reporter from the *Los Angeles Times* felt that he had to re-burnish his reputation after his thin, early reporting following the emergency UN meeting. Somehow, he'd been furnished the clandestine cell phone image taken in a Prediction Group session. He included that hair-raising graphic in his extensive front-page article. Revealing that the graphic had been provided by an anonymous source did little to comfort an anxious public. If this impact forecast had been withheld, what else was being kept behind closed doors?

It wasn't long before reporters started showing up on the streets of Vilnius, complete with man-in-the-street ad hoc interviews: "How does it feel to be in the crosshairs of Nyame?" Similar questions were heard in other capital cities: Moscow, Paris, London. Those living in the Southern Hemisphere breathed a sigh of relief.

***

The tour group flowed into the impressive JPL Mission Control. Some had been here before, some hadn't; Adam MacKellar hadn't. Lajos was in the throng, giving advice, answering questions, even when not asked. The newly-formed IMCC, also known as the Space Flight Operations Center, was the communications hub for the Deep Space Network. Huge parabolic antennae were in 3 separate locations: Barstow, California; Madrid, Spain; Canberra, Australia. Each antenna location was separated by about 120 degrees in longitude, enabling continuous communications to spacecraft nearly anywhere in deep space as the Earth rotated, handing off one to the next. Adam was keenly interested and asked many questions as he peered over the shoulders of controllers at their consoles, busy communicating with space probes and with the Perseverance rover on the surface of Mars. Images of the surface of the red planet on computer screens added to the obvious technical heft at JPL. And there were other responsibilities, one being Apophis, predicted to pass close to Earth some 7 years hence.

Zhang-Wei and Kayla walked into the shared Operations Center and over to a pair of consoles and spoke to the operators sitting there. Lajos touched Adam's arm and pointed them out. "Yes, yes, Lajos. I know who they are; Professor Zhang-Wei Huang and his graduate student, Kayla Williams. I know more about them than you do."

"Of course. But do you know their Solar System Dynamics group is working on the orbit of another asteroid?"

"Which one?

"Apophis."

"I thought you had a good handle on that one, that it would pass very close, but with zero chance of impact."

"Yes, that's true. But now they've applied their ASA model, to tighten things up. The previous dynamics model had it coming within 4.6 Earth Radii of the surface, April 13, 2029, with zero percent probability. The latest prediction has it missing by 4.5 Earth Radii; still at zero percent."

"Good thing, Lajos. There's no program to deflect it, and little time left to get the hell out of the way if it were predicted to strike."

"Adam, if that were predicted to happen, those damn Russians would propose their brute force nuclear bomb method, with barely enough time to build, launch, and get it to Apophis."

The tour drifted off into other areas. Representatives of the other four member nations of the UN Security Council were shown their designated private offices and their computer monitors in Mission Control. With the unresolved differences in the Ukraine, the Russians received suspicious glances.

Offices were planned to contain systems for password-protected access for high-bandwidth communications with the space agencies of their home countries. United States-imposed sanctions had to be overcome for the link to Roscosmos in Moscow. Initially, orbit calculations, warnings, and press releases would be evaluated and coordinated. Tensions would heighten when a deflection system was in place and uplinked command messages needed IMCC approval. In addition to continuous armed patrols around the building, people would need to pass through a guarded entry point and get past a retina scanner and fingerprint reader. Some deep-thinking, free-spirit astrophysicists and engineers balked at this level of planned security, but the very fate of somewhere on Earth was at stake. Not everyone on Earth was equally motivated. Layered security and operational control-system architecture had been borrowed from the Cold War control of nuclear weapons, which was still in place: one or two demented people couldn't bring about a nuclear exchange. Nyame was not made of fissile material ... but could be turned into a weapon nonetheless.

As the tour wound down, Adam made his way over to Lajos as they headed for the main doors. He tugged on Lajos's arm, holding him back. Soon, the two of them were alone in the foyer. The few that noticed them were not alarmed; Lajos was a frequent visitor. In a low voice, Adam made a request. "Lajos. I'm sure there are other areas we weren't shown. Can you be my tour guide?"

Lajos didn't answer verbally, but merely furrowed his thick brows and gave a quick affirmative nod. Lajos showed Adam the emergency generator system that instantaneously powered JPL, should commercial power be interrupted. It was expensive, smoothly providing power within one-half cycle of the 60 cycle power that fed the building. Computer systems didn't feel any interruption, as well as JPL's communications system. They passed more rooms, some for the storage of necessary things, shelves and shelves of them. Adam noticed an unmarked door with a cypher lock. Lajos attempted to just walk past, as if the room were of little consequence. Adam again restrained Lajos by the arm, "What's in there?"

"Oh, that's the data communications hub, full of wires and servers, a rat's nest," Lajos nervously replied.

Adam glanced around the hallway, looking for security cameras. He had been well-trained in the ways of the CIA and NSA. Adam felt that there could, or should, be some recorded surveillance, but didn't note any. "I'd like to see what's in there."

Lajos knew the cypher and opened the door. Adam was greeted by a beautiful, confusing labyrinth of colored wires that interconnected rows and stacks of servers with their rapidly-blinking colored lights, like an abstract work of electronic modern art. In an instant, Adam wielded his cell phone, panning the room, touching the white circle on the phone's display.

Now it was Lajos's turn to put a restraining hand on Adam. "What the hell are you doing?"

"Don't ask. You remember my first visit, don't you? It wasn't in time to prevent you from fuckin' things up! Liu Yang stole your research."

Lajos coldly realized that he was in a tightening vice, feeling the pressure of their meetings, especially the one in Adam's cellar.

***

Kayla scrolled through thousands of lines of code for a subroutine of one of the modules of the ASA model. One obscure convergence algorithm was taking too many cycles, and too much time, in her view. The Defense Conference had been exhausting, but provided necessary focus. She was back at it. Zhang-Wei was also, sitting at the next terminal. JPL was a veritable beehive of activity. Kayla leaned back in her chair, eyes closed, thinking. Her keen mind could hold disparate thoughts at the same time. She shifted from one thought to another and opened an Internet website for visiting the California State Prison for men in Lancaster. Zhang-Wei glanced over, "What's that?"

"Something personal."

***

Tiger awakened her with a persistent paw on the scar of her cheek, meowing. Her breakfast ritual was hurried. Kayla pulled the door closed and walked down the steps. She pivoted toward her dented old car just as Zhang-Wei walked out. "Hey, there's somebody I want to see. I'll be back this afternoon," she said. He hesitated, then waved and drove off toward JPL in his BMW.

Kayla clipped her seat belt and glanced at the hole in the windshield. She headed north and peeled off the Interstate at Antelope Valley. Her trip would be longer through a dry, brown, barren landscape. Lancaster was on the other side of the mountains that she could see from her bed in the garage apartment. This was her first visit to a penitentiary. It wasn't at all like her trips to Palomar Mountain far to the south. Soon she was in the high desert named after the Mojave Tribal Nation.

The surrounding high chain-link fence was topped by razor wire that spoke of those inside being dangerous to society, being rehabilitated if not punished. If it was hard for them to get out, it was difficult for Kayla to get in. She scheduled the meeting online and felt she had to sign her life away, weathering intrusive website questions. At the main entry, she again had to submit to interrogation and inspection. Everything she had was put in a locker, but she was frisked all the same before walking through the metal detector. All sorts of things could be and had been smuggled into the prison. The guards were taking no chances. They escorted Kayla into a bare room with two old chairs at a table with paint-chipped legs. The ambience of this place was low on California's budget priority list. The stark space had high windows to the outside world. Guards looked in. She took a seat, then waited … and waited.

Finally, DeShawn was escorted in. As with all the other prisoners, he wore a two-tone blue outfit: comfortable loose-fitting pants, blue shirt and a darker blue jacket. Each shirt or jacket announced their status in yellow letters: CDCR PRISONER. Just in case they happened to wander off campus, the people of Lancaster, or all of California for that matter, would see that they belonged to the California Department of Corrections and Rehabilitation. DeShawn slouched into his chair and looked at her with a hostile attitude.

"Kayla. Why you wan' t' see me?"

She just stared at him, thinking to herself, Why *did* she want to see him? Kayla didn't really know, especially since one of his gang buddies tried to kill her. But something in the back of her brilliant brain, maybe a twinge of guilt, told her it was the right thing to do, to clear the air. After all, they'd grown up together on Grape Street and were friends until high school.

Kayla hadn't planned what to say; she should have. "DeShawn, I was just thinking about you and wondered how you're doing."

"How you think!? Thanks to you, I be locked up. Ma momma hasn' come t' see me, no letters, nothin'. Hey, it wasn' ma idea t' shoot you"

Kayla bristled, "I didn't rat on you. I just told the narcs what I'd seen out my window. I didn't mention your name. You were just in the wrong place at the wrong time when they made that sweep." Then, without intent, some of the language of her youth came out. "Not my fault you dealin' hard stuff when the narcs in the ghetto bird seen you!"

DeShawn nodded slowly, realizing she was right, then shot back, "I be readin' 'bout you in the papers. Made a name fo' yourself, probably by fuckin' the professahs. You got one nice ass, top nice long legs. Woulda made a dam' good hoodrat, fuckin' the guys. Mickey the Cobra wanted a piece a your fine ass. Before the dam' narcs, I was a playa' in the hood. Had ma choice."

Kayla jerked back at that sharp broadside, then returned fire, cutting to the quick, "Speaking of mothers, mine died from covid."

That set DeShawn back. He'd known Kayla's mother as a hard-working, caring person and changed his language. At the table, he wasn't among his gang buddies; no need to impress them with bonding language from the street. "Oh, I'm very sorry. She was nice."

"OK, Deshawn. When you get out, you've got to stay away from grinding drugs in the hood. How much longer do you have?"

"Twelve fuckin' months! What the hell am I spose' t' do? What kinda' job can I get with my ma record? Washin' cars? Cleanin' toilets? Sweepin' streets?"

For Kayla, answering those questions was almost as hard as understanding astrophysics. In her gut, she knew that he'd be drawn back into the black hole of the Grape Street Crips. She held out an olive branch. "I can stop by to see your mother, maybe give her a little help. Can I tell her that you're going straight?"

"You stay 'way from ma momma!"

Their eyes locked in a long silence, exchanging words without sound. As if by some exterior command, they both stood at the same time. They both knew the visit was over. She extended her hand. DeShawn recoiled, "What the hell is that? You gon' White?" He flashed her the hand sign for the Watts Grape Street Crips. A few Crips were in the same prison; they stuck together ... they had to.

Kayla turned and left the table ... and DeShawn. She had attempted to replace the first girder on building a bridge back to her Watts neighborhood. She had a premonition as strong as the one that foretold of the close encounter of QW7 with Elcano, that just maybe that bridge should be strengthened. But why?

Testing
[8 Years 5 Days before Impact]

As the months passed, two forces came together following the Defense Conference: motivation and money. Nyame, in its altered orbit, provided the motivation, governments the money. Teams of the world's top engineers and program managers responded across international political boundaries. This synergy was very powerful. In less than two years, the results were on calibrated test stands in a broad scrubby desert of a shallow basin near Yucca Mountain.

Decades earlier, a different synergy had been in full swing at the Nevada Test Site: nuclear bomb testing stimulated by the Cold War with the Soviets. Radioactive contamination and fallout from above-ground testing had been an afterthought. A different government nuclear program later moved into the neighborhood: Nuclear Engine for Rocket Vehicle Application, NERVA. Tests were conducted at a special site with a crusty Western name: Jackass Flats. NERVA eventually wound down, leaving radioactive waste management in its wake. But the concept had been proved: heat for accelerating thrust-producing hydrogen through a narrow nozzle could be provided by the nuclear fission of uranium. Russian scientists had also come to this realization about the same time. They also used stored liquid hydrogen, then super-heated it by pumping it through the linear cores of a small but very hot nuclear reactor. Pound-for-pound, this yielded much more thrust than from the binary reaction of heavier chemicals, liquid or solid, to heat things up.

Nyame brought things full circle at Jackass Flats. Buildings, roads, and test stands again sprouted from the barren desert grit. Scientists, engineers, and fissile material returned. Signs warned: Use of Lethal Force Authorized. Fences and armed patrols kept idle curiosity out. The risks of handling radioactive material had to be taken, small when compared to Nyame's threat. Seating had been erected like those seen at outdoor sporting events. It was at a supposedly-safe distance from the separated pair of test stands. Each had a full-scale nuclear thermal rocket, an NTR, designed for remotely-controlled operation on the surface of Nyame.

The contingent from JPL had arrived, having been escorted from the main gate under the intense mid-day sun. The temperature of the dry air was climbing quickly from its chilly overnight low. Kayla and Lajos were among the visitors. They came by comfortable air-conditioned buses from Pasadena. The time to fly from Los Angeles to Las Vegas was much shorter, but when added to the time to get to and from the air terminals, through security, and the wait times at the airports, it was about as fast to go by bus through Death Valley, with no transportation mode changes along the way. Kayla thought of DeShawn when they passed through Lancaster, thinking he should have been released by now.

The viewing stand was crowded. Hats of various styles were worn or made available for those unfamiliar with the desert sun; some were billed caps, others were broad-brimmed. Bottled water was handed out with the advice to stay hydrated. Different languages could be heard: German, Russian, and Chinese, besides the prevalent English. Big cameras on tripods were set up on the ground in front of the stair-stepped seats. Loudspeakers kept everybody informed of the countdown and what they were about to see. A black sedan with tinted windows and government plates pulled up; Adam MacKellar and two others, in their distinctive dark suits and aviator sun glasses, stepped out and up into the crowd. This critical NTR demonstration was preceded by months of testing of various components at different scales. There had been some failures; one with two deaths, an American and a Russian, but that had been kept from the media. A successful public demonstration would now assure the world that the essential part of the asteroid deflection system was on schedule.

This demonstration had something more, much more. The rocket firing controls at the two test stands were connected by a local area network, similar to the one envisioned for the surface of Nyame. A command message would be transmitted from JPL to a geostationary communications satellite, then relayed down to antennae at the test stands ... a small-scale simulation of the planned deep-space communications. The message would initiate a local automatic count-down to start a series of firings for each NTR, first one, then the other, then both, followed by different patterns of planned durations from seconds to minutes. Two things had to come precisely together for each NTR firing: neutron-absorbing rods mechanically moved; valves opened and liquid hydrogen pumps activated.

People in the stands could follow along using the handout that listed the sequence of firings. Repetitive, controlled, timed, reliable rocket firings were absolutely critical to nudge a tumbling Nyame into a desired direction.

Zhang-Wei was in JPL Mission Control. At their assigned seats were the designated representatives of the UN Security Council nations when the command message was sent. They all witnessed the confirming return message within the expected time window, which would be much longer, but known, when communicating with the landers arrayed on Nyame. When the acknowledgment message was received, with the same control parameters, the countdown was allowed to proceed. Otherwise a stop message would've been transmitted. This was announced to those in the stands, and everyone's eyes flicked between their watches and the test stands. Then, NTR1 fired, precisely on schedule.

A tall, yellow-orange vertical exhaust plume was seen against the low mountains in the background. Some expected to hear the deep vibrating rumble made by the explosive force of a chemical rocket. But what was heard was a higher-pitch sound, like a blowtorch on steroids. NTR1 shut down, on schedule, 10 seconds passed; NTR2 fired, then shut down after 30 seconds. Thirty more seconds passed. Then both NTR1 and NTR2 fired at exactly the same time. The on-again off-again sequence, different timings, and durations continued for the next hour. The last firing was completed. Of course, there had been a secret dress rehearsal a week before, and everything had worked just fine. Those in the viewing stand stood motionless in the now hot desert wind. Then they erupted into applause and cheers. Even Lajos had a rare, uncharacteristic smile, as did Adam. Kayla gave a high five to a journalist from India standing next to her. The firings had been at maximum design thrust. Measured specific impulse was reported to waiting engineers.

High Bay 1 in JPL's Spacecraft Assembly Facility was also the scene of considerable activity. A full-scale prototype lander cradling an NTR mock-up, including radio antennae, computers, hydrazine thrusters, star tracker, inertial sensors, and cameras was being built. Engineers and technicians in white cleanroom attire were busy as bees. The press peered through the high windows of the viewing gallery; a few were escorted into Mission Control, all perfectly timed with the demonstration at Jackass Flats.

The four-legged lander in High Bay 1 was the prototype for the following planned nine landers, each mated with its NTR. Each would be tested extensively, then sealed in nose cone payload modules designed to sit atop the heavy-lift rockets at their launch sites in the United States, the Russian Federation, China and India, as agreed. Special airlift would distribute the modules, saving precious time. Ground crews would accompany them, assisting mating operations at each launch site, including the loading of liquid hydrogen into the NTR tanks.

A month earlier, Nyame had passed relatively close to the Earth, close enough to net accurate distance and velocity measurements from radio telescopes. It had been decided not to rebuild the big one at Arecibo. But there were others, including the antennae of the Deep Space Network that had been used as radio telescopes. Ranging and Doppler-shift velocity measurements were added to position and time data from optical and infrared telescopes. Zhang-Wei oversaw the integration of these data to initialize the ASA model which was run on the JPL supercomputer at maximum precision, maximum N-bodies, and minimum time step. The launch window for that minimum time to rendezvous with Nyame, at this relatively close distance, had long passed. Space probes, let alone a deflection system, were not available at the time. Now, if the development schedule held, NTR quadrapods would be atop their heavy-lift rockets when the next optimum launch window arrived. That window was bearing down.

The output of the ASA model was discussed at length in the back reaches of JPL. Adding to the complexity were the gravitational tug of the Earth and atmospheric drag, both altering the final probabilistic trajectories to surface impact. The center of the impact probability ellipses had shifted, close to and just north of Vyazma in Russia, about 200 kilometers west of Moscow. The impact probability at the center had increased to 4.1 percent, with an overall 9.1 percent probability of a strike somewhere within the outer elliptical edge of zero likelihood. The time of center-point impact had shifted 2.6 minutes earlier. The ellipses still stretched, narrow and elongated, from Moscow to London: the risk corridor. Compared to Moscow and Saint Petersburg, and the land around these major cities, the area around Vyazma was sparsely populated; fewer people to scare. There was tense debate within JPL whether to release these specific impact data, along with the ellipses on a map. It was decided to wait for the critical NTR demonstration to give increased confidence that Nyame would very likely be nudged into an Earth-missing orbit. Consequently, Nyame's un-deflected orbit and impact prediction would become irrelevant, they hoped. Combined with program management assessments of the availability of heavy-lift rockets with NTR landers, the decision was made to release the prediction, map, ellipses, and all.

Kayla and Lajos were on the way back to Pasadena when the warning and press release went out and spread over the citizens of Vyazma and Russia.

The next days were hectic for JPL, and eventually for Zhang-Wei. Warnings and press releases since the Defense Conference, about every 4 months, hadn't changed much since Vilnius had been in the crosshairs. The slight increase in the probabilities, and the very fact that there was a change as Nyame was closer in time, had caused public concern. If not the probabilities themselves, the trend had become alarming. This was exacerbated by the tendency of the news media to write in alarming tones, to be competitive. Articles about approaching Nyame appeared on the front page on some newspapers. TV news anchors led with the story. Ratings were still important. Limited press conferences had been given with earlier releases, but questions as to the when and where of possible impact were altered as to the why of the change in prediction.

Zhang-Wei was called upon by NASA and Caltech. Lajos was avoided. He was known to be direct and rather blunt and wouldn't necessarily be calming. A press conference was held at the Beckman Auditorium. With carefully prepared slides, some with orbital graphics and underlying equations, Zhang-Wei briefed the latest on Nyame and fielded questions. Doomsday prophets and religious zealots again crowded around the auditorium as reporters and their camera crews pushed their way through. For some reporters, the outside scene was just too tempting. Photographs and video clips of activities on the green grass of Caltech accompanied news narratives.

Professor Huang took to the stage with nothing but his abacus in hand. He started his dialogue after demonstrating his prowess with the ancient calculator, completing the winning calculation again in a mere 2 seconds. Videos of that habit were merged with those of happenings outside, which didn't provide a confidence-building impression. But Zhang-Wei's briefing was impressive. He explained what all the graphs and equations actually meant. Bringing immense complexities down to the level of the layman proved difficult. Websites and Facebook pages soon filled with as much information as people were able and willing to digest. "We'll just have to trust them" was the attitude of the average person on the street.

***

The predicted center point, having moved into Russian territory closer to Moscow, caused concern in the Kremlin. The Plesetsk Cosmodrome would receive intense, very secretive attention to modify the Jupiter probe to something much different. With characteristic dark suspicions, they internally asked the honest question, "What if the NTR deflection system fails?" They could be exposed to the laws of orbital physics. A huge nuclear space detonation could convince Nyame to head elsewhere.

***

The Beckman Auditorium soon saw more activity, but on a more optimistic note. It was the backdrop for the Caltech June commencement ceremonies. With Southern California weather, the annual conferring of degrees was done outside. A sea of students in black robes and their guests sat on white folding chairs that filled the long, wide green lawn. It was standing-room-only attendance. Many stood in front of buildings that framed the long grass plaza. The Caltech Orchestra added pomp and circumstance to accompany the procession of distinguished faculty, each with wide stripes on the sleeves of their robes, including Professor Zhang-Wei Huang and Professor Lajos Vadja. Everyone stood to honor their entrance down the grass center aisle through those seated.

In their colorful academic regalia, speakers took to the elevated podium: Chairman of Caltech's Board of Trustees, the President of Caltech, and a world-famous alumnus, an astrophysicist. With their academic discipline colors draped over their black robes, names were called one-by-one to receive Bachelor's Degree diplomas. Then, for the Master's Degree recipients, hoods in their college's colors were placed over their shoulders. This was followed by those that had attained the lofty Doctor of Philosophy degree. They received a hood of blue velvet, lined in orange with a white chevron stripe. Kayla Williams was among them. For her, it had all started in the sun ... the mounted, moveable magnifying glass on a Grape Street sidewalk, with DeShawn frying ants. She thought of him as she walked up, stood proudly, and had the hood placed over her shoulders.

There was more recognition, almost as important as when the NASA Administrator had cited her at the start of the Defense

Conference in the building right behind them. A surprised Kayla was called back to the podium to receive the doctoral prize awarded to a student whose PhD thesis reflected extraordinary standards of innovative research. Her treatise on Adaptive Simulated Annealing had fit the bill, aided by Professor Huang's strong recommendation. She had been recognized for discovering QW7's deflected orbit. Now she was recognized for the orbital model to predict its position, as Nyame, eight years into the future.

Those in the seated throng rose and applauded. There were others standing along the sides. One wore sunglasses, a black blazer over a collared purple shirt, black slacks. Next to him stood a husky man, bulging muscles revealed by a tight-fitting purple t-shirt of the Grape Street Crips. Above all, they wore attitude for all to see. Tattoos on faces, necks, and arms spoke to membership. Their initiation requirements had been different: no classroom grades, no technical papers, and no theses. It had demanded more: committing an armed robbery, being beaten by gang members in a so-called bull pen, or doing a drive-by shooting. One of them had done a walk-by shooting for membership. That had left the scar on Kayla's cheek.

Kayla walked back to the podium to receive her award. She almost tripped on the steps. Kayla was distracted. In the corner of her eye, she saw DeShawn's contorted-fingers, the identifying hand sign of the Grape Street Crips. She thought, My god! What's he doing here?

A slender woman in a flowing tie-dyed dress, Birkenstocks, rainbow-dyed hair, and a nose ring stood next to DeShawn. She'd seen the hand sign but had no idea what it meant. She did notice that both Kayla and DeShawn were Black. She spoke without thinking, "Isn't it wonderful to see such diversity. Are you related to her?"

The pair looked at this woke hipster as if she had come from Mars. Deshawn slowly answered, "She's our sista."

"Oh. That's nice."

Hacking
[6 Years 185 Days before Impact]

The cellar meeting had been good. Adam's knights discussed Lajos Vadja at length and his necessary involvement for them to control nuclear thermal rockets on the errant asteroid. Ian and Raphael hadn't met Lajos, but already didn't care much for what they'd heard about his blunt arrogant attitude, attributes that were barely tolerated, even if wrapped in genius. What they did admire was his access at JPL ... and the leverage Adam held over him.

The trio had discussed other global opportunities: quantum computing, the vulnerability of the Panama Canal, secret use of the Uyghurs in Western China. They now had a singular focus to change the order of the world: Nyame. Well placed, it could bring a nation's economy and might to its knees, but which nation?

Ian and Raphael were winging their way on overnight red-eye flights back to England and France. Adam had dropped them off at Dulles. He was headed back, not to his Washington, D.C., home but to Virginia State Route 123. He knew that divided four-lane road very well. In the fading twilight, his headlights illuminated the big green highway sign that again welcomed him to the George Bush Center for Intelligence. The left-turn arrow changed to green; he swung into the wooded road. Dead-serious signs warned the casual and the curious. Unless you worked there, or had official business, don't even think of driving farther. A Federal statute was listed. Daylight and night-vision cameras recorded everyone and everything along that short road.

Less than a mile later, Adam stopped and flashed his credentials at the main gate, then waited while they were checked by a no-nonsense, machine gun-toting, crew-cut guard in a black cable knit sweater. That level of security was comforting. After parking, he again was checked at the main entry to the imposing building. Inside, Adam stopped for a brief moment in front of the white marble wall with rows of black stars, in honor of those agents who had given their lives serving their country. He had known three of them, before he'd moved his career over to NSA. One star could have been for him if a bullet in Riyadh had struck a little higher than his hip. In-country intelligence collection was a dangerous business.

He made his way through internal layers of security: keypad codes, fingerprint readers, cameras everywhere. Not surprisingly, Adam was headed to a dark corner of the Office of Technical Service. He arrived at the research and development laboratories in the basement, a familiar collection of rooms off the long hallway. Adam had affectionately called them his basement wizards. Complex, one-of-a-kind, mostly-electronic, high-tech devices had come out of those labs. Sometimes they were the ingenious integration of stuff purchased at Radio Shack; other times, the components were made there from the ground up, even the fabrication of computer chips themselves. Such things were needed to intercept and eavesdrop on the communications of potential enemies, sometimes friends, remotely or close-up. Behind locked doors, they were designed, assembled, and tested by the best in the dark business.

The electronic keypad and fingerprint scanner outside a particular door recognized him. The flashing red light above the door turned green, the lock released. Adam entered, and the heavy steel door clicked comfortably into place behind him. His Montblanc pen had also made it past security.

Adam was expected. A friendly, familiar voice welcomed him, "So, my long-lost friend, what can we do for you?" Henry had waited for Adam past normal work hours, but intelligence didn't run on a normal time schedule; there was nothing normal about it. You labored by the demand, not the clock.

"Hank, I need a piece of your magic." Adam fished out some

high-resolution photographs from the inner pocket of his leather jacket and spread them on the table. To the untrained eye, the images showed rows and racks of servers, bundles of colored wires, and tiny colored lights. These photographs had been taken at JPL with the help of Lajos.

"Where the hell is this?" Henry's question was rhetorical; he knew it couldn't be answered.

"Can't say, Hank. You know the drill." A flash memory chip fell out from the cap of his pen. "The images are also on this. It's yours."

"Thanks, I think." Henry picked up a big magnifying glass and examined the prints under an intense light. "Looks like top-end servers." Adam knew when Henry got to the special mega-pixel images on the chip that he'd be able to identify the make and model numbers of the servers and other components, and the ports for the interconnecting colored wires. Henry understood this sort of thing very well; it was his job. He'd be able to visually untangle JPL's electronic Gordian Knot of communications.

Adam recognized that look on Henry's face and got right to the point. "We need to automatically intercept outgoing digital messages and automatically modify them, outbound and return, out-haul and in-haul, without messing up Ack Nack confirmation. It all has to be as if we'd not been anywhere near. No digital fingerprints."

"Do you know the message format?"

"Yes. It's on the chip." Adam's people had been able to intercept the satellite-linked communications during the nuclear thermal rocket demonstration at Jackass Flats, but that information would absolutely not be given to Henry. It was within the cellar's compartmented security controlled by Adam.

"Ya know, Adam, even with our fastest chips, there'll be a slight delay, a few nanoseconds in both directions. It'll be undetectable, unless someone's looking for it. What parts of the message do you want to change? There's a lot of housekeeping crap, checksum, parity bit checks, and all that."

"We're interested in specific bins used for time and duration. They'll have their times. We'll have ours."

"Sounds like Stuxnet stuff; Iranian centrifuges driven to self-destruction."

"No. We're not trying to insert a worm. Changed initiations and durations are required. Basically, our target will send a message to remotely control a nuclear reactor, for it to activate at some future time, and stay activated for some period of time. The message received by the nuclear control system will be sent back. If the outbound and inbound messages match, they'll let things proceed. If not, they'll send a control message to stop the operation."

"This isn't for a Russian nuclear power plant, is it? Another Chernobyl?"

"Like I said, Hank, can't say. But it's not a Chernobyl event, if you're having second thoughts."

"I assume you'll want to communicate with whatever we come up with. We'll set up a dark website with a user-friendly interface to enter your time and duration data. It'll live on our special server, a black hole, even compared to the dark web. You'll communicate with our server. It will communicate with my device."

"Great. Our operative cell will have a very anonymous IP address." Henry pictured some walled-off basement room in a dark corner of the globe. He didn't realize that Adam's cell was in a cellar just two miles away.

"Hank, can you slip this project in your budget somewhere, between priority cracks?"

"Don't worry about that. A message from your boss filtered down and landed on my desk, said to do whatever you needed. We'll get right on it; get back to you in a couple weeks, maybe a little longer. Adam, my friend, can't rush genius, ya know."

"I know, I know. You sound like an echo from the old days."

"Hey. I have a new secret weapon. I call her my little dragon lady, ethnic Chinese, parents came from Taiwan, but she doesn't mind the label. She specializes in making electronic little beasties with digital data stingers. She was an MIT prodigy. She designed our special server."

"Oh, by the way …we'll also need to know where and how to insert your thing in that room."

Henry replied, "You don't want much, do you? There's been

some promise in making conformal flexible computer chips on flexible circuit boards." Henry placed his finger on one of the photographs. "Hell, nothing promised here, but maybe the device will look just like this long flexible yellow wire."

Adam shook Henry's hand with a very firm grip, as he had in the early days of their friendship in the agency. He made his way back out through the security phalanx, including the grim-faced guard. He turned left onto Route 123. Adam couldn't the get the vision of Henry's dragon lady out of his whirring mind, evaluating and integrating the possibilities. She could come in handy in the Liu Yang case. Next stop: home and cellar.

***

Adam sat in his comfortable NSA leather desk chair, swiveled part-way around to where he could see the Ka'bah in Mecca where he'd been immersed in the sea of believers. He drummed his fingers impatiently on his cedar desk, waiting for the hot-line beep. He'd arranged the meeting at NSA, not NASA. In the bureaucratic jungle of Washington, D.C., at this high level of bureaucracy, who was the visitor and who was the visited said a lot about relative power. The Administrator of NASA had come to discuss the request of the NSA Director, who pushed a special button and summoned his deputy. Very shortly, Adam walked in and was introduced to the new head of NASA, the result of a newly elected President from the other political party. They shook hands.

Adam spoke first, "The high-bandwidth trunk line with JPL is up and running."

"I know that. I've been briefed. Pardon me, but why do you need access to the position data for Nyame and the other orbiting bodies? JPL has everything well in hand."

Neither Adam nor his boss liked that question, or the attitude behind it. "We just need access at the same level as do the other four nations. They need the data to run their models for the agreed cross-check on JPL warnings and press releases. We just want to stay on top of things, so we don't have to bother you and the folks at JPL."

The NASA Administrator nervously adjusted his tie. "I don't agree … but we'll comply. We do work for the same government, after all."

Adam inserted another request, "One more thing. We need to run ASA in RTM, I believe it's called, reverse tangent mode, to determine the deflection times for the nuclear rockets when finally planted on Nyame. Our techies will give your techies our operating system."

"This will be done, as well as version-controlled modifications. ASA in both modes is a very heavy burden. Do you have the run-time?"

"What do you think? Hell, yes! We've partitioned the use of our massively parallel system for its occasional use for Nyame. It's just a matter of priorities. Just consider us as an operational backup to JPL."

***

The flight from LAX was smooth. First Class was very comfortable. The champagne was excellent. Lajos felt he deserved it all. Adam picked him up at Dulles as if Lajos were a foreign dignitary. Nothing was said on the ride in the Mercedes, but the classical music was a grand distraction. He was to give a private lecture on astrophysics and orbital mechanics ... in the cellar. There was no hotel for Lajos this time; an upstairs bedroom would do, as strongly suggested.

Adam escorted Lajos down the stairs and into the cellar. Ian and Raphael were sitting at the table. They didn't stand, which irritated Lajos. The table held crystal glasses and bottles: French brandy, Oregon wine, and English stout ale. Lajos was given his choice; he selected the brandy. Names weren't exchanged, but heads nodded as they spoke. Lajos took their measure; they silently returned the favor. The Frenchman was elegant, handsome, and elite. The Brit was short, with a round, ruddy face and slightly red nose, suggesting a love affair with stout.

Lajos inserted his thumb drive into the desk-top computer.

The slides for his lecture appeared on the big screen. He spoke slowly, dismissively, as if his audience were mentally beneath him. They weren't. While deep theory and complex mathematics were beyond their grasp, they certainly could comprehend the N-body problem, the Adaptive Simulated Annealing method, accuracies and uncertainties, and the long time it took a massive computer to spit out the prediction. For Adam's knights, rising to the top of an intelligence agency required more than average intellect. Lajos got to the part about running the ASA model in Reverse Tangent Mode from a selected miss point near the Earth.

Adam asked, "Lajos, do we need to know how it works, the theory?"

"Yes, most definitely, you do."

They didn't, but Adam relented. It wasn't worth arguing when bull-headed Lajos was in his element. And he had a captive audience; they needed Lajos. Adam gave him this sweet carrot to balance the threat of the big stick he held over him. A captive audience, they all had the same motive. Lajos explained the means supported by mind-numbing mathematical theories and conjectures. "Gentlemen, you've been secretive. I just assume you'd like to direct the asteroid yourself to suit your purpose. I have my suggestions, but I'll defer to your judgement."

Raphael shot back, "That is wise, Lajos, that's very wise. We have the means to deflect careers … and lives."

Threatened, Lajos glared but continued. "Mass won't be known with sufficient accuracy until the accelerometers on the quadrapods tell us the net result of a series of rocket firings. And that must be further confirmed by the resulting new trajectory which will take up to two months of observations. With a limited amount of liquid hydrogen, we mustn't waste it on trial and error."

Adam got down to the essence. "What's the solution?"

"The ASA model, but applied in a very special way, thanks to me and Paul Erdős."

"Who?"

Lajos verbally beat his chest, he couldn't help it. "He was one of the most brilliant mathematicians to have come out of Budapest

University, the same school I attended years later, the same school that produced Theodore von Kármán; we're all Jewish and Hungarian. Erdős was probably the best in the world."

"How does he fit into the solution?"

"The ASA model gives us the most accurate position and time of the closest point of approach. But we must know what Delta-V to apply, and when, to put the asteroid on a desired path. At a specific future point in its orbit, we can simulate various velocity changes and run the ASA model for each; a computational monstrosity. But I had a better idea, and worked with Professor Huang and Doctor Williams to apply the ASA between two points."

Ian blurted out, "On the Earth."

Visibly frustrated, Lajos rolled his eyes. No ... in space! One is the closest point of approach desired; the other is a future point on the asteroid orbit, when the first of a sequenced set of rocket firings takes place. The ASA model can be run from either point, forward or in reverse, N-bodies and all, but the ends of those trajectories won't match the points selected. This was a most difficult problem. That's when I turned to the theories of Paul Erdős: discrete mathematics, approximation, set and probability theories. Would you like me to cover his theories and conjectures?"

Ian answered for the group, "Bloody hell, no, for Christ's sake! Get to the point."

"As you wish. In a very complex way, at each micro time step from each end, estimated trajectories in two-body fashion are shared and compared, then relaxed according to an Erdős conjecture and the total N-bodies. Then the next time step, the process repeated until the adjusted trajectories meet at the half-way point, mid-trajectory. It's a beautiful thing."

Adam encouraged him, "And ...?"

"And ... one selects the desired closest point of approach and runs the ASA in Reverse Tangent Mode, so-called because the new trajectory is tangent to the old one at the point of first rocket firing."

Lajos gave a pop quiz, "And why do you think that's important?"

As if he'd been sandbagging all along, Adam replied, "Because you can compute the net change in velocity needed to achieve the new trajectory, and program the rocket firing sequence accordingly."

Lajos picked up a glass and took a sip of brandy. "Very good, Mister MacKellar. A gold star for you."

Adam realized the immense power in all of this. If his knights selected an end-point as their preferred impact point on the surface of the Earth, the Delta-V required would be determined, and the programmed timings would also be determined, delivered courtesy of a yellow wire that was in a drawer of the table.

Lajos injected a bit of reality. "But there is a penalty: ASA in RTM takes 50 percent longer than a straight ASA run by itself."

Raphael had had some mathematics instruction at *Sorbonne Université* in Paris, before he realized he was better suited to study global politics and international relations. He raised his hand, as if he were a student.

Lajos called on him. "Yes?"

"As Nyame approaches its closest point to the Earth, the distance along its orbit and remaining time will shrink. ASA in regular and RTM will likewise shrink, will they not?"

"Yes, you're quite right."

They would have a few more years to think about all that; by then, all the NTR landers would be hopefully anchored to the gritty gray surface of Nyame, assuming they could be built and launched in time. After more cellar deliberations, the secretive triad would select an on-Earth point to change the world's destiny. There was a more-immediate requirement. They thanked Lajos for the presentation and stroked his considerable ego, all three clapping.

From the table drawer, Adam pulled out a photograph and a coil of yellow wire with a server connector on each end. "Lajos, please replace the yellow wire marked in this photo with this one, part of routine maintenance. I'm sure you'll know how to do this."

"What's this for?"

Adam smiled and reverted to business as usual, his tone somewhere between matter of fact and overt threat. "Please, don't ask, if your career and health mean anything to you."

The drawer was still open. Something evil, compact, and black lay in there. He'd had it since his CIA assignment to Saudi Arabia.

Adam pulled it out and set it on the table, for emphasis ... a loaded Glock. "And, by the way, please send us the command message format used at JPL to control the Perseverance rover on Mars."

Lajos remained cool, "How do you want me to get that to you?"

Adam scribbled an email address; long gibberish on both sides of the @ symbol and handed it to Lajos. "Commit that to memory."

For Lajos, that was easy. He finished his brandy.

Quadrapods and Nose Cones
[5 years 185 Days before Impact]

Reporters clambered onto comfortable air-conditioned buses that took them through Lancaster, across arid land, then to the west gate of Edwards Air Force Base. It was the birthplace of advanced aviation research; the sound barrier had first been broken over that desert. Like a herd of school children on a field trip, they were guided to the engineering test site: low man-made hills in the Mojave Desert. The wind was nearly calm as had been forecast and required. A prototype hung at the end of a long cable from a tall crane. The asteroid lander looked like a lunar lander on steroids. A big cylinder over the main body housed weight equivalent to the planned nuclear reactor. It was topped by an upward-pointing rocket exhaust cone. Four large cylindrical pressure vessels with hemispheric ends were fastened between the heavy-duty, fold-down legs, just above the wide circular foot pads.

Lunar landers of the Apollo program had four legs, so the number of legs on the asteroid lander was no surprise to the visitors. However, the public had been spared the simulations, tests, and debates among NASA engineers; three, four, or five legs? Or more? Nyame's gravity was weak. On-asteroid static weight supported by the legs would be very much less. But the purpose of this asteroid probe-with-lander was much different. A powerful rocket would put enormous load on the legs, pushing against the surface of Nyame. It had been decided, four was optimum, considering static center-of-balance, and the restrictions of rocket payload launch weight and nose cone dimensions.

A week earlier, press interviews had been given at JPL. Reporters looked into the Spacecraft Assembly Facility, High Bay 1, where this prototype had been constructed. One of the engineers had said simply that it was a platform for a nuclear thermal rocket to be placed on the surface of Nyame. He was quickly corrected by a fellow engineer who said that it was a quadrapod. The more-appropriate name was reported in the news; the generic name for a four-footed thing had stuck.

The full-scale quadrapod was lowered slowly to the measured sloped surface, covered by a mixture of gravel and rocks in a designed spectrum of sizes. There were other man-made mounds for testing. Data and imagery from landings on near-Earth asteroids Eros, Itokawa, Ryugu, and Bennu, and the DART impact against Dimorphos, had been used as a guide. Engineers attempted to replicate their regoliths, the rocky surface materials covering bedrock, or possibly just more rubble. Whether Nyame was a complete pile of rubble or had a solid core, its surface was likely similar to those asteroids. Even the very weak gravity of a drifting asteroid was a sufficient vacuum cleaner of space debris, if given a very long time.

The descent rate on the unwinding cable was about the same as planned for the actual asteroid landings, just a few centimeters per second. In a very weak gravitational field, bouncing off the surface would not be good. Swiveled hydrazine thrusters on the landers would guide them gently to the surface, then swing up to hold them there until helical screws fastened them down. Onboard autonomous feature tracking, as had been used for the Bennu landing, would enable large boulders to be avoided. Load cells had been inserted in the legs and in the suspension line to measure weight in an attempt to replicate the gravity of Nyame. Its extended feet, four circular pads, came to a gentle rest. The quadrapod inclined, matching the slope of the surface. Two tests were conducted for this and the many other crane-assisted simulated landings on various regolith types with various slopes.

The lead NASA engineer for the quadrapods spoke directly into the camera. "Nuclear thermal rockets will be landed on the surface of Nyame, being simulated here. Nearly all of the weight is taken by the crane cable, to simulate the weak gravity of the asteroid and the lander's effective weight."

A reporter interrupted, "Sir. Is Nyame's surface like what we see here?"

His reply had a tinge of irritation, "We don't know for sure. We haven't been there yet. But we do have images and data from landings on other asteroids." The engineer went on to describe more detail than the public needed to know. After the quadrapod made its suspended landing, long helices, sharp-pointed corkscrews on each leg, wound their way through the holes of the foot pads into the rocky grit. These were intended to anchor the quadrapod to the surface as much as possible. When compressed by a rocket firing, the regolith's slight elasticity could reflex and kick the quadrapod off the surface when the firing cut off. The depths of the simulated asteroid regolith varied from 1 meter to 3 meters. If impenetrable rock were encountered, the corkscrew automatically stopped, lest it lift its round flat foot off of the surface. It was an example of superb NASA engineering.

In the desert heat, threaded rods in each leg turned. The prototype quadrapod tipped slowly until the unseen center line of the vertical rocket cone pointed to the Earth's center of gravity. "Ladies and gentlemen. What you see now is the lander automatically adjusting the length of each leg so the NTR's thrust line is directly opposite the center of mass of the Earth. The same will be done on the surface of the asteroid."

The same reporter, who hadn't done his homework, interrupted, "Why does it need to do that?"

"It's complicated, but if not done, the rocket's thrust would serve to add rotation to Nyame, in addition to making an inaccurate nudge to change Nyame's orbit."

"Is Nyame rotating?"

"Yes, slowly tumbling. But not enough to fling off gathered rubble. It could also be wobbling, but we won't know the details until we get there. It'll all complicate the NTR firing sequence. Based on the periodicity of its observed brightness, it tumbles end-over-end about once every three days. That's slow compared to our reference asteroids, roughly the same size with roughly the same gravity. The composition and depth of the surface layer of Nyame could be different."

The announcer looked around at the now-silent reporters. "Now, if there are no more questions, let's get back on board."

A short distance away was a big NASA building. It was undergoing modifications to convert its large spaces into filtered-air cleanrooms suitable for assembling spacecraft. From a central inner office, they peered through a sealed window into one of the rooms. "Ladies and gentlemen, complete quadrapod landers will be assembled in there and the other assembly rooms of this facility."

Workers in white cleanroom suits were taking measurements. Held vertically in large, caster-wheeled, roll-around steel frames were two halves of a nose cone fairing that would hold a complete lander during launch. Some were testing the ceiling-mounted gantry crane, lifting and moving test items around.

A keen reporter asked, "Why don't you use the two high bays at the Jet Propulsion Laboratory? We've watched the prototype being built in one of them."

"Good question. Once the final design is verified and locked down, nine landers will be built and sealed in their rocket nose cones. The two high bays would be a fabrication bottleneck, and transportation logistics must be considered. Plus, fissile material in the nuclear reactors of the rockets is an unacceptable, unnecessary risk. Nuclear thermal rockets will be assembled and tested at Jackass Flats, then transported here, trucked overland." News of the deaths at Jackass Flats during NTR testing hadn't gone over well at JPL.

Reporters tapped furiously on their cell phones or spoke into them. Video cameras caught it all. An older woman scribbled notes on a paper pad, the old fashioned way. She asked, "How will the assembled landers be transported to the rocket launch sites?"

"Another good question. Heavy-lift aircraft with large volume capacity will be flown in, using Edward's runways. Sealed nose cones, with bottoms designed for mating with specific rockets, will be carefully loaded and flown out. Ships would be slower than aircraft, and the logistics at the receiving ports would be a problem."

"What aircraft will be used and where are the rocket launch sites?"

"We'll have more on that later. One of the launch sites is at Vandenberg Air Force Base. One of the completed nose cones will be transported there by truck. That won't take too long. All the others will be transported by aircraft."

***

His boss stood next to him, somewhat anxious. Adam watched the two big computer monitors in his office. The ASA model reached the end of its massive crunch of vast numerical arrays starting with the latest observed position data for Nyame. Accumulated errors were slightly less due to the reduced time to potential impact. Nyame was a few months closer in that variable; the time required for numerical integration and simulated annealing had shortened.

Finally, output data tables and graphics layered-up on the screens. He selected the display of probability ellipses on the Earth's surface. The point of most-likely ground impact shifted slightly toward Moscow, with a slight increase in probability and slight change in time of impact. The areas of the ellipses were slightly smaller. Unknown to his boss, all that remained of Adam's day was to pick up Ian and Raphael and bring them to the cellar, after watching the evening news special.

But there were internal concerns at NSA. "Adam, this had better be worth it. You've taken a fair bit of computer resources offline for over two weeks. Intercepts, decryptions, and analyses have all suffered."

"Sir, this trumps other priorities. We're in the same hemisphere. A little error in timing and that damn asteroid could land in our backyard."

"You don't trust the operations at JPL?"

"I do. But as President Reagan said, trust but verify. NASA is supposedly in charge, but the whole operation is lashed up with two countries that don't have our best interests at heart. They are members of the IMCC."

"So, we need to spy on them?"

"We're not spying, just verifying. We'll see what warnings and press releases come out. Here, we'll have unfiltered ground truth."

"Break, break, Adam. How goes the Liu Yang investigation?"

"We've intercepted some communications dealing with computers and computing. Our brethren in McLean have been working it. MI6 has done better. One of their operatives in Hong Kong has made her way into the interior. They have eyes on."

***

Brandy, wine, and dark stout sat on the coffee table in the front room of Adam's house, no need to head to the cellar yet. Trying to be a good host, he set out a bowl of peanuts and a plate of crackers with brie and cheddar. They comfortably sat on a couch and lounge chairs in front of the huge LED screen. It wasn't the evening news. Warnings triggered special TV programs and front-page newspaper articles dedicated to Nyame. For some people, it was like watching the next episode of a drama series, only this one was real with a life and death plot. They knew the main character, Nyame, and the supporting cast. Social media served to lather people up with facts and intentional falsehoods. Predicting the end of somebody's world became a drumbeat; websites were set up for that purpose. Bible sales and church attendance had risen; so had suicides.

People in Russia watched their televised programs with somewhat greater interest. Since their classroom days, they knew of the Tunguska event in Siberia over a century earlier. A mere decade earlier, the Chelyabinsk meteor was still fresh in their minds. With typical Russian negativity, they wondered if Nyame was their fate ... as if brutal tsars and the October Revolution hadn't been enough.

The anchor of this program sat across from a panel of experts to field questions. Lajos sat there stoically with furrowed brows. Kayla and Zhang-Wei had avoided this one. On the big screen was the computerized orbit diagram of JPL's online Small-Body Database Browser. It showed the current position of the Earth and Nyame, its orbit as determined by the last ASA model run. The anchor started with a rather blunt statement, "Good evening. Nyame is getting closer," as if the Earth and Nyame were on long, straight-line intersecting paths. In their relative orbits, that distance would grow and shrink predictably. He sped up the motion, then stopped it when the two respective dots came together. The graphics were changed to a close-up 3D depiction showing the track of Nyame relative to a moving and rotating Earth, as a gray dot on a red dotted line, missing by a close distance. "This is the most-likely track of the asteroid, but there are unavoidable uncertainties."

That set off panel discussions as they described 3D probability ellipsoids, as best they could for their national and international audience. Discussions led to Nyame's physical characteristics. The real image of an asteroid was shown looking like a big, gray slightly-bent potato. It was shown in apparent rotation, images pieced together from a series of stills taken from a Japanese space probe. The Caltech astrophysicist on the panel reminded viewers, "That is not Nyame, I repeat, *not* Nyame, but asteroid Itokawa, about the same size as Nyame. Itokawa is a pile of space rubble, maybe two piles held loosely together. That's why the odd shape."

"Professor Johnson, do we know the physical properties of Nyame?"

"No. We do know it rotates slowly with low centrifugal force. It could be another rubble pile. Or it could be solid iron-nickel, like some of the meteorites that have struck our planet."

Professor Vadja broke in, "If solid iron-nickel, it would be the worst for people somewhere, because more of its mass will survive the atmosphere."

Ian took a long drink of the Guinness stout he held. "Solid iron-nickel. That should scare the hell out of everybody, don't ya think?"

With an eloquent French flip of his hand, Raphael commented, "Yes, Lajos is a real charmer. He needs some makeup, and somebody should trim his eyebrows."

As if on cue, the program shifted to one of hope, a description of the plan to deflect Nyame. Panelists answered questions about nuclear thermal rockets. The video changed to the test quadrapod landings in the Mojave Desert and the large cleanrooms at Edwards Air Force Base. Animated graphics showed an artist's rendition of one landing on an asteroid's surface, then its NTR being fired. The program ended with images of two behemoths of the air: the C-5M Super Galaxy and An-124-100M Ruslan. "These aircraft will ferry the quadrapod landers, sealed in their nose cones, to the rocket launch sites."

Raphael stood. "Let's hope that all works. Let's get down to business, *mes amies*.

They made their way down the narrow stairs and sealed themselves in the cellar. Adam fired up the computer and opened the clandestine email from Lajos. "This is the format of the command messages being sent to Perseverance on Mars. I visited my old friend in the CIA. His assistant came up with a different interface. My story for this was convincing, hidden by the veil of secrecy that still separates us."

"Adam, what's the plan?"

"From this room, we'll alter the message for the camera on Perseverance and have it move in a direction opposite than that commanded. That should get somebody's attention, and prove that the yellow wire works. Lajos will watch, and let us know."

Perseverance and Plesetsk
[5 Years 7 Days before Impact]

She picked up Tiger. Her old cat was in the twilight of his years. Kayla hugged him tight with long petting strokes, then set him down in her very own Pasadena home. Working for NASA at JPL had changed her financial orbit, nudged along by a bank mortgage. She also drove a new car, a small but efficient all-electric vehicle. Kayla turned the corner, and gave her horn two quick taps as Zhang-Wei was coming out from his house. Both were on the way to JPL. The ASA model would dump its results that afternoon. They'd be part of the internal multi-national coordination for the warning and press release that evening, another tick-tock of Nyame's inexorable countdown clock.

There was a bit of commotion that morning from a different corner of JPL: the Mars Perseverance Rover team. They hovered over monitors reviewing the latest camera images from the Jezero Crater. They commanded Perseverance to roll to the edge of what appeared to be a river channel billions of years old, when the surface of the planet had held enough water to sculpt it. Big rocks had carefully been avoided on the overland trek. Stopped at the edge of the channel, they uplinked the command message for the camera to pan to the right. The returned images revealed that the pan had been to the left, at first unnoticed. Then, from one of the monitor positions came, "What the hell! What the fuck happened?"

It wasn't a disaster. The imagery was spectacular and revealing. But raw sensitivities remained for any mistakes. In a side meeting room, the team went over the messaged communications with Perseverance via the Deep Space Network. Lajos sat next to a gray-haired engineer who had been around when a NASA probe had plunged destructively into the Martian atmosphere. The crusty old engineer was blunt, "Somebody or something fucked up! Attention to goddamn detail is our job. We don't want a repeat, like confusing English and Metric units as we did with the *en route* data of the Climate Orbiter."

Lajos was uncharacteristically quiet. The room of frustrated engineers couldn't determine the cause after tedious fault isolation attempts. A bright-faced junior engineer, an MIT post-grad, offered a possible reason, or scapegoat: the Sun. He uploaded graphics and data from the Space Weather Prediction Center in Colorado. "Sir, we are near solar maximum, Cycle 25. Last week there was a major solar event, a huge flare coupled with a coronal mass ejection. High-velocity charged particles caused a magnetic storm that affected Earth-orbiting communication and navigation satellites. Particles from the solar belch swept out in their spiral path and over the Martian surface and Perseverance. It looks like the particles arrived at Mars about the same time that our command message arrived."

The old engineer replied, "So, young man, you think our message got garbled on arrival? Then why the hell did the return confirmation message match what we sent?"

With forced respect, "No, Sir. The problem occurred *after* the confirmation message was sent back, after the command data we'd sent had been ingested in Perseverance's computers. A charged particle or charge buildup in the electronics likely caused a bit to flip, generating a false signal, turning the camera in the other direction."

"Well, young man, we thought of that. The computer chips and circuit boards are metallically shielded, within weight limits. The computer system is triple-module redundant, continually cross-checking in case a high-energy particle or accumulated charge errantly changes a one to a zero."

"Sir … maybe all that was not enough considering the strength of this coronal mass ejection, the particle concentrations, and their velocities. The folks in Boulder say this was a record setting event."

The old engineer turned to the brooding face next to him. "Lajos, what do you think?"

Lajos spoke with calm confidence, his deep voice resonating. "The Sun; that's what did it. Our engineers are similarly hardening the electronics on the quadrapods. There could have been electronic damage on Perseverance. I strongly recommend you send another command message and confirm the mechanical result. But you can do what you want." He stood and turned. "I'm going to lunch."

The meeting ended abruptly. Another message was sent to Perseverance. Controllers at consoles waited on tenterhooks, relieved when the imagery confirmed the commanded and expected rotation of the camera.

Well before that test, Lajos had eaten lunch at home, lox and bagel, sitting at his computer. He sent a very short message into a dark crevice of the Internet ... Yes.

That one word brought a smile to Adam's face in his cellar. A necessary part of changing the order of the world had been verified. It had worked! But it wasn't all by mere chance. Prediction was in the name and charter of those solar people in Boulder. Adam had done some planning and timed his message to the yellow wire, taking advantage of the frequent camera-command messages expected over the duration of the charged-particle sweep across the face of Mars.

He sent a dark email to Ian and Raphael. They celebrated.

***

Controllers in the Edwards tower watched the huge aircraft descend on final approach. The An-124-100M Ruslan was certainly impressive. The crew looked down on a sea of tan; the famous dry lake bed. C-5M Super Galaxy aircraft were already on the ramp; they were impressive as well. Two more Ruslans would soon be landing. There would be more aircraft than needed, as backups, should one or more of them be grounded because of mechanical problems. The logistics schedule was tight.

All the aircraft had one capability in common: airlifting things that were both heavy and large. Quadrapod NTRs in their rocket nose cone fairings fit that category. Rockets on launch pads awaited them. C-5Ms could have handled all eight quadrapods, as had been heatedly argued. The Ruslans could load nose cones larger than had been designed. However, the C-5Ms could be air refueled; no en route stops to slow things down. But geopolitics won over common sense concerning Nyame's threat. The Russians wanted a very public piece of the action, especially since they were in Nyame's un-deflected crosshairs. Rockets were on the launch pads at the Baikonur and Vostochny Cosmodromes. The Russian pilots and their Ruslans would publicly help save Mother Russia. Some wondered whether it was worth saving.

Leading up to the gathering of this air cargo armada had been armed truck convoys from Jackass Flats. The parking lot around the assembly rooms of the modified NASA building had been crowded for months. Assembly and system checks occurred around the clock. Visitors' quarters on base were full up. Some people had been ordered out, making room for the aircrews. Rows of travel trailers were parked right outside the fabrication building, saving commute time for the most essential engineers and technicians.

The rocket-launch window was approaching. The remaining time pinched; they all felt the pressure. The time from launch to landings on Nyame was critical. The launch window had been determined by the complex mathematics of the transfer orbits connecting the relative positions of the Earth and Nyame. If missed, the next launch window would be much later, greatly increasing the NTR energy required to sufficiently deflect Nyame. Almost two years earlier would have been greatly preferred, but the quadrapods with their NTRs could not be completed in time, let alone the rockets to boost them into their transfer orbits. If the rockets launched during the upcoming window, the time from launch to rendezvous with Nyame would be 331 days. After arrival of the quadrapods, precious time would be needed for probative measurements for the landings themselves, and remote system checks before the first NTR would be fired.

After long hours in the air, relaxation and camaraderie were needed; all pilots flew together in their different world. The Russians found it, a short walk from their assigned quarters. As fate would have it, a few C-5M pilots were already relaxing, bending their elbows on tables in the bar. Russians and Americans wore their distinctive flight suits with ranks, names, national patches. They also wore their pride. The Russian crews spoke English far better than the Americans spoke Russian. Shots of vodka and whiskey were exchanged.

The speed of thought broke through the language barrier, landing on the Cold War. For some, their parents had flown Boeing and Tupolev bombers with sufficient nuclear capability to assure mutual annihilation. This irony wasn't lost on them. Soon there were bear hugs, as if they were long-lost family members at a reunion. For those that flew, they *were* family, a bond that extended across political borders. They discussed their planned payloads; they'd be carrying nuclear reactors, not nuclear weapons.

A California state flag hung on the wall. The image of a brown grizzly bear walking on a mound of green grass, next to a red star, got the Russians' attention. Their own burly icon predated California's by centuries. Shots of vodka were raised to the bear on the flag, and to the red star.

There just happened to be a fighter pilot in the room, now a test pilot, sitting at another table. He listened to the Russian accents. Testosterone fueled his impulse. He shoved himself away from his table, chair legs screeching, fell intentionally backward onto the floor, then held his arms and legs straight up and yelled, "Dead Bug!"

Many dove to the floor and assumed the same position, but not all. Unfamiliar with this quaint custom, the Russians were too slow on the uptake. The last one still standing had to buy a round of drinks for everyone there. Bourbon was demanded amid the laughter.

Not to be outdone, a Russian pilot moved chairs away from a large round table, returned from the bar and set empty shot glasses and open bottles of vodka on the table and announced, "*Medved priblizhayetsya* ... bear is coming!"

An American pilot asked, "Say what?"

Instruction was given, in broken English. "Place money on table, dollar bill, Americans; we, 100 ruble note."

The American sensed a drinking contest with a monetary prize. "OK. Then what?"

The answer was given, "Hide from Russian bear, under table. Must wait, no legs out to bite, bear will leave." All participants tossed their financial contributions on the table and crawled into the cramped space underneath for protection against the phantom Russian bear. The instigator joined them, pushing in and shoving around for space, she intentionally next to the handsome test pilot. For her, this drinking game had another objective. When confirmed by all that the last leg had been tucked under, another Russian pilot announced, "*Medved ushel* ... bear gone. Stand up. Drink to leaving."

Everyone crawled back out, stood up, poured and tossed back straight shots of vodka. Again, someone yelled, "*Medved priblizhayetsya*" followed by "*Medved ushel*" when it was safe. There were more cycles of this, uncounted, hiding from the bear and drinking to the bear's departure, money placed on the table each time. Even the American pilots got the hang of it in passable pronunciation, "*Medved priblizhayetsya ... Medved ushel.*" Finally, there was only one pilot that managed to not only crawl out from under the table, but to actually be able to stand up and toss back a shot, all alone, the final requirement for victory. The pile of money became hers. The test pilot managed to struggle out and stand up at the same time, but gravity and a spinning room pulled him back down to reality, shot down by a female Russian transport pilot, no less. A tall muscular woman, she had been raised in the logging camps of Eastern Siberia, very used to vodka to warm and ward off the bitter winters. She had literally drunk the men under the table.

Fortunately, it would take a few days to load out the aircraft, leaving enough time to meet the minimum bottle-to-throttle requirements. This was pretty much a global standard. Human bodies burned off alcohol at about the same rate, regardless of culture or bravado, but with some metabolic gender difference.

The quadrapod airlift pilots recovered in their quarters. The test pilot had met his match under the round table at the bar. Exhausted, he lay in bed unable to move, wrapped in the arms of the strong Russian woman from Siberia.

***

In the bowels of the Kremlin, an aged warrior had argued successfully that if their huge nuclear bomb were not detonated, not used to deflect the asteroid, it could be kept in the same trajectory. Both would arrive at the Earth at about the same time. The trajectory of the reentry vehicle could be adjusted before reaching the top of the atmosphere. If the asteroid were to impact, a nuclear weapon could be detonated in the chaos, taking out an old enemy, or a new one. It had been designed to automatically do so, at a specific altitude following a reentry deceleration trigger. Such an opportunity was too good to pass up, to change the order of the world to fit the Russian vision dating back to Lenin.

Farther north, an air traffic controller keyed his microphone. He reported altimeter setting, low visibility, and calm surface wind. A big Ruslan descended on long final approach over the vast, green northern boreal forest. The pilot averted his eyes from the rising sun and glanced left. An Angara A5 heavy-lift rocket was being serviced from the big blue gantry. The rocket stood majestically though the white blanket of shallow ground fog under the brilliant blue morning sky. With the sun at low angle, the scene was stunning. Another, in the control tower, had been a military pilot, seasoned in the ways of drinking vodka with his pilot comrades. He lifted binoculars to his eyes, watched the approaching aircraft and announced, *"Medved priblizhayetsya."*

This bear was quite real and swung onto the parking ramp at Plestsy Aeroport. Trucks and heavily armed security waited: no nonsense, Russian style, old world. The big turbofan engines wound down. Silence returned to the remote airfield. Components were carefully transferred to the convoy of trucks parked under the wings, then were driven through the green conifers the few kilometers to Cosmodrome Plesetsk. The most powerful hydrogen bomb ever constructed anywhere on Earth was carefully installed on a special space probe in the cone-tipped cylinder. It was larger than Tsar Bomba, the largest ever exploded. The Angara A5 nose cone fairing sat atop a liquid-fuel rocket surrounded by four liquid-fuel boosters.

An unseen reconnaissance satellite passed overhead.

***

Of course, he had been read in to the intelligence compartment. Adam reviewed the Top Secret information, the integration and analysis of information from various sources. Keen analysts at the National Reconnaissance Office had poured through the overhead images of the Ruslan at Plestsy Aeroport and the clustered activity around the rocket at Cosmodrome Plesetsk. The CIA had a carefully-developed card up their clandestine sleeve. He was a well-paid asset in Mirny, a small town built exclusively to house those that supported the cosmodrome. When not doing his official job, he also trucked in things to keep the workers happy: vodka and frozen fish from Arkhangelsk 200 kilometers to the north. Now he delivered other things to other people: ground photographs taken with a telephoto lens and hand-written reports recorded on old-fashioned microfiche. All had been transferred the old-fashioned way, a dead drop in Arkhangelsk. This still netted the death penalty if discovered, a nasty habit held over from the Cold War. Adam's people had intercepted and decrypted message traffic between Moscow and Plesetsk. This intelligence was a team effort. Adam asked and NASA confirmed that the optimum launch window for a probe to Jupiter had already come and gone.

What now sat on the big rocket in Northern Russia was not a research space probe to Jupiter, the Russian cover story. Adam picked up the secure phone to the U.S. Space Command. A hydrogen bomb, even one launched into a transfer orbit away from the Earth, was a clear violation of the old Outer Space Treaty. This would cause more concern in Huntsville than at the UN. When presented with this information in the White House Situation Room, the President decided *not* to call out and embarrass the Russians on this matter. Means and methods, including the Mirny asset, could have been put at risk. Plus, delicate trade negotiations and stiff sanctions were also on the table.

If JPL knew what Adam now knew, Lajos and the IMCC asteroid deflection people at JPL would not be thrilled with Russia's apparent planned disruption of Nyame's orbit using brute nuclear force. But something rather important slipped through the intelligence net. If known, the President would have made a much different decision. The hydrogen bomb itself, atop the Angara A5 at Plesetsk, was shrouded within an ablative re-entry nose cone, not at all needed for the airless void surrounding Nyame.

***

Kayla invited Zhang-Wei over to her place, a kind of house warming, too long delayed. But that was understandable considering the pace of activity at JPL. The doorbell rang; she opened the front door. Old Tiger limped over slowly and rubbed against her ankle. Zhang-Wei held out a pineapple, a fresh one grown in California. "For you, Professor Williams, for your good health in this home."

She accepted and cradled it with one arm, as if it were a child. "Please come in, Professor Huang." They both broke into laughter at this silly charade of formality. Before she pulled the door shut, she caught a glimpse of a big Cadillac sedan passing slowly by. She couldn't see through the dark-tinted glass, but she knew immediately. DeShawn and the Grape Street Crips knew that Kayla had moved, and to where. He was just confirming, hoping that Kayla would notice this different kind of drive-by.

"Kayla, back in Taiwan, you would be expected to roll the pineapple, with just your hands, through all the rooms for your good health and good fortune."

She just grinned at him, "I'll do that later." She set the pineapple on the table, in the middle of the spread of food and drink. More guests were to arrive soon.

"I have some important news. My mother is coming to visit."

"That's great. I look forward to meeting her, the one who raised such a brilliant mathematician, abacus and all."

"Well, actually, she's coming to stay."

"Really?"

"Yes. When those in Taipei signed the Reunification Agreement, she'd had enough."

Kayla reasoned, "But that is to take place over 50 years, gradually. Generations will pass to heal the wounds. After all, they are of the same blood."

"Kayla, you don't understand. Our forebears suffered greatly under the heel of Mao Zedong. Putting Taiwan under the Communists is too much for her. Look at what happened with Hong Kong."

"Are you going to find a place for her, your house, or a house here in Pasadena?"

"In Taiwan, generations live in the same house, the eldest the most revered. I think, or hope, she may like the apartment above the garage, where you'd lived. She'd be very close to me and have privacy."

"That would be nice. It's comfortable. You may have to decorate it to suit her tastes."

"Oh, I've thought of that. I've been shopping. One more thing; she wants grandchildren."

Kayla knew that Zhang-Wei worked very long hours and had a very thin social life. She stared at him. "Why are you telling me this?" The room filled with a different tension.

Fortunately, the doorbell rang. Lajos and two JPL astrophysicists were on the other side. As she let them in, Lajos explained, "I almost didn't make it. My flight was delayed, almost cancelled."

"Lajos, welcome. Say, you've been back and forth to Washington a lot these days. Are you doing work with the big folks at NASA?"

"Yes. There's a lot to do; briefings and questions. I don't want to bother you with the details."

Kayla flicked a quick glance at Zhang-Wei. They'd assumed that NASA Headquarters had been on his itineraries.

Lajos continued, "Did you watch the big aircraft takeoff this morning with my asteroid landers?"

Kayla opened a can of beer and handed it to him. "Lajos, the quadrapods are not yours. They're the result of international engineering."

"Yes, Kayla, but I successfully drove the nuclear thermal rocket deflection concept at the Defense Conference. The landers are my children."

All in the room had to agree. With a glass of wine in hand, one of the guests walked over to the big screen TV and turned it on. No surprise, just about every channel had a summary of recent events at Edwards, starting with the careful loading of the quadrapods in their nose cones, rolled on their sides into the cavernous cargo bays of the huge aircraft. Done with great care, the nose cones barely fit in the C-5Ms. This was followed by video clips of aircraft taking off as viewed from the departure end of the runway. As each passed overhead, the camera was turned to follow its climbing departure. The deep whine of the turbofan engines filled the room. When video of the last aircraft departure ended, the excited announcer informed the vast audience, "Ladies and gentlemen, these nuclear thermal rockets are headed to Nyame."

Lajos almost exploded, "My God!! Some idiots out there will think the aircraft will fly the quadrapods to Nyame."

Kayla touched his hand, "No, most will not."

Launch
[4 Years 337 Days before Impact]

Trajectories around the Sun were fundamental in the complex equations. JPL's Solar System Dynamics group had been hard at work. They had been in close coordination with rocket and quadrapod engineers; delivered mass and the time to do so was the focus. International representatives looked over the broad mathematical shoulders of Zhang-Wei and his very experienced team, including Kayla and Lajos. Their results were checked, cross-checked, and rechecked

From many months of intense observation since the discovery of QW7's altered trajectory, the plane of Nyame's orbit, with a period of 1.7238 years, was inclined 11.9682 degrees from the Earth's ecliptic. Other driving factors were in the mathematical mix: heavy-lift rockets and their staged thrust to insert NTR quadrapods into near-Earth parking orbits, without their nose cones, there to await commanded impulse-thrust acceleration into transfer orbits to Nyame. Minimum fuel Hohmann transfer was not used. Minimum time was the objective, constrained by quadrapod mass and the mass of its liquid hydrogen that could be carried from liftoff to rendezvous. Enough fuel had to remain to decelerate each, in order to nestle them near the slowly-tumbling asteroid in spaceflight formation, like space-borne bees clustering near the hive.

The optimum time window was narrow to launch the quadrapods into their initial orbits. All had to be in their parking transfer orbits before the window arrived. The other side of the timeline had been compressed by the time that had already been used to design, build, transport, and affix NTR quadrapod nose cones to the heavy-lift launch vehicles. The remaining ground launch window was too short to use one site for the nine payloads. International cooperation was mandatory.

Quadrapods and nuclear thermal rockets were only on the drawing boards when the previous window had come and gone. If the approaching launch window was missed, the next was almost two years later. That would leave much less time to deflect Nyame and require more NTR thrust than could be landed on it. Deflection operations would only change the most-likely point of impact and its probability, not eliminate them.

Humid heavy air drifted across the east coast of India from the Bay of Bengal. Even though the sun had set, the crowded outdoor viewing stand was enveloped in sweltering heat. The launch window was open, and there were no tropical storms to threaten operations. Those attending expected dramatic nighttime launches from two different launch pads, separated by a few minutes. But these were especially important; the nose cones on India's big Unified Launch Vehicles carried NTR quadrapods destined for Nyame.

NASA engineers and JPL astrophysicists could easily have stayed in California and watched the televised launches. Most did. But interests were heightened by pressure from NASA. Lajos had volunteered and had led a small JPL group.

International news had covered the arrival of C-5Ms from California at the Tirupati International Airport. The big nose cones were slowly and carefully offloaded and trucked the 90 kilometers to the assembly buildings at the Satish Dhawan Space Centre on an elongated barrier island. The logistics of the overall plan came together, here and at the other five launch sites.

The viewing stand was not open to the general public. By-invitation-only credentials had to be shown by reporters, camera crews, and special guests. Ian and Lajos met in the throng with a handshake, forth fingers folded back. Some strings had been pulled in Washington, D.C. for Ian. Lajos had been drawn into Adam's group.

The flights from London and Los Angeles were long and tiring, despite business class accommodations. Both men arrived days earlier to shake off jet lag. The hotel restaurant served authentic curry dishes. Descendant from the days of the British Raj, Indian restaurants were common in England and in Ian's village outside of London. He knew what he liked, what to order and what not. Arrogant Lajos, feigning culinary expertise, didn't take his advice. He asked for something authentic, traditional. After his mouth cooled down, he spent more time in the bathroom than in bed. The night of the launches, the two reconvened in the corner of the viewing stand.

"Lajos. How ya feeling, mate?"

"Better, no thanks to you."

"I warned ya. Phaal Curry is a bit warmer than paprika-spiced Hungarian goulash."

"Ian, I could have gone to any of the other launch sites, but I wanted to come to India."

"Why?"

Lajos answered with a hint of disdain. "I've been to India before, attending astrophysics conferences. These people produce some of the world's best mathematicians. Chess was born in the north. Top theoreticians have come from this land, and still do. Some of their theoretical thoughts are buried in the model that predicts Nyame's path."

Their idle chat was interrupted by the countdown being announced over loudspeakers. They watched huge rocket engines erupt and collectively light up the landscape like a rising sun. Acoustic waves beat against their chests as the big, heavy-lift vehicle rose into the night. A short time later, the performance was repeated from a different launch pad at Satish Dhawan.

A similar scene unfolded half a world away, on the East Coast of Florida. Like Satish Dhawan, the Kennedy Space Center was located on a coastal barrier island. As predicted, there were no approaching tropical storms out in the Atlantic to delay the planned launches. C-5Ms had landed on the long runway that had been used for Space

Shuttle returns. The ground transport of the quadrapod cones over the short distance to the huge Vehicle Assembly Building were watched by an exuberant press. "Made in America" was thrown in for good measure, repeated by the President at a televised press conference.

Adam MacKellar, like many others, wanted to come to watch, to be part of something that would help him change the order of the world. Raphael had flown in from Paris to join him. Adam greeted him with the special handshake. "*Mon ami*, Raphi. *Mon ami*."

They watched the liftoff of the Space Launch System rocket, and waited for the second. Both nose cones had been affixed to their rockets in the same building, then rolled-out to their respective pads.

All was going well when the countdown for the second launch was stopped. A deviant reading from a liquid hydrogen high-pressure turbo-pump rudely landed on the computer of an engineer in the Launch Control Center. As with other managers of the main systems, she had the power to stop the launch. All function-monitoring stations, including weather, had to report "in the green" status, or the countdown to core engine ignition would be stopped. Minutes passed; the wait seemed interminable at the viewing stand, and across the nation. Pressure mounted. But facts were facts, and data were data. The ghost of the Challenger disaster four decades earlier still hovered in the big room. Phone calls were made at the highest levels, risks assessed, and reassessed. The decision was made. Delayed, but still within the launch window, the SLS rocket lifted off and headed out across the Atlantic Ocean, through the overcast clouds, out of sight. Over the unseen horizon, before the solid rocket boosters peeled off, the abort command was given. Everything crash-landed in mid-ocean. A sub-orbital launch would have put Europe at risk. Adam and Raphael looked at each other and slowly shook their heads. Now there were 8 quadrapods, if things had gone well at the other launch sites.

Launching radioactive fissile material carried known risks, for all the launches. These were risks well worth taking, but Nyame also carried risks. There were plans for all the launch sites should a quadrapod nose cone fail to reach low-Earth orbit. Recovery and disaster teams were positioned downrange, on the oceans and on land, just in case. The splash point for the aborted launch from the Kennedy Space Center was accurately determined. A deep-submergence dive vehicle was on its way aboard a fast U.S. Navy surface ship. A leaking reactor on the ocean floor was to be avoided, according to environmental protection plans.

Zhang-Wei felt uncomfortable on Chinese soil. The launch site was on Hainan Island, nearly as large as Taiwan. His mother was strongly opposed to his trip when she learned that the big rocket on the launch pad at Wenchang was named Long March 7. The actual long march led by Mao Zedong had left scars in the family that had never healed.

Fluency in Mandarin and his Chinese persona had been seen throughout China and the world. He was interviewed when he arrived at Haikou Meilan International Airport, as was Kayla. Their positions at JPL and their lead involvement in the prediction and deflection of Nyame had been nationally interesting, driven by ethnic pride.

The arrival of C-5Ms at Haikou Meilan had caused quite a stir. The quadrapod nose cones were offloaded and trucked some distance to Wenchang. The Chinese Communist Party had lobbied hard for their Xi'an Y-20 heavy-lift aircraft to deliver the quadrapods. But the slightly smaller dimensions of the Y-20 cargo bay made for a too-tight fit. Engineers were very unwilling to redesign the size of the quadrapod and its surrounding nose cone.

Wenchang had two launch pads and two vehicle assembly buildings to support them. This was to be a double nighttime launch, again separated by a few minutes. On the strictly-controlled viewing platform, Zhang-Wei acted like a tour guide for Kayla, translating the rapid dialogue. They could have easily gone to Florida or nearby Vandenberg Air Force Base, where the quadrapod nose cone had been trucked from Edwards. But she had more than an oblique interest in China, as did he. It hadn't been that many years since the coronavirus pandemic had spread across the world and killed her mother. She didn't know, but suspected that the origin of the virus was the result of an experiment gone wrong in a Chinese virology laboratory.

They heard the countdown in Mandarin. Kayla now wished she had decided differently. She was the only Black person on the platform, or in the hotel, and garnered as much attention for that reason as the successful rocket launches.

On the flight back to Los Angeles, they discussed that the firing of the NTRs would be based on the ASA model in its Reverse Tangent Mode, and it would provide the data for computing the controlled firings of the NTRs on the quadrapods they had witnessed being lifted into space.

Cosmodrome Vostochny in far eastern Russia, not far north of the Mongolia border, had a Yenisei rocket on the pad. The delivery of the nose cone had caused more of a sensation than the launch itself. After landing at the Ulyanovsk Vostochny Airport, the aircrew disembarked from the big Ruslan and waved for the cameras. The aircraft commander, a tall Russian woman, clenched her fist and turned her wave into celebratory fist pumps. Soon, she was interviewed.

Cosmodrome Baikonur, where the other Yenisei rocket would be launched, was being leased from Kazakhstan. While part of the former Soviet Union, things had changed. Now, the cosmodrome was on the land of an independent nation, free to negotiate the expensive rent to use the place. While images of the launch from Baikonur would be seen on television, the operations at Vostochny were covered to a greater extent, justification for the expense of further developing the site, lessening dependence on the site of the launch of the world's first satellite, Sputnik I, from Baikonur.

Before the 8 payloads were inserted into their transfer orbits to Nyame, people around the globe were treated to a montage of these Earth-saving launches in virtually every aspect of the news, accompanied by excited commentary. This took the edge off the latest warning and press release from JPL. The most likely impact point had moved closer to Moscow, the probability of impact had increased to 9.3 percent. The people of Moscow would have to live with that, besides the following warnings for almost a year. It would take this time to achieve rendezvous of all 8 quadrapods, landing them on Nyame, and activating their NTR thrusters, before a revised trajectory could be confirmed.

A rocket launched from Plesetsk earned just a footnote in a few newspapers and short articles in scientific journals on what was to be learned in orbit around Jupiter, years later.

Others knew differently.

***

Zhang-Wei and Kayla wove their way from the parking lot through the familiar buildings of the JPL complex, virtually a small city. They had walked this route many times and came up to JPL's Space Flight Operations Facility as the sun peered over the San Gabriel Mountains. The air was dry and cool; morning shadows were long.

Security was very noticeably tighter. In addition to an armed guard at the main door, pairs of armed guards were seen patrolling the perimeter. Even though the interior security guard at the access control desk knew them very well, they were subjected to identification checks including fingerprint readings and iris scans before a newly-constructed interior door was buzzed open. This was now strictly applied to everybody, including observers and engineers from the countries involved in tracking, predicting, and issuing warnings for Nyame.

The critical deflection system was being added to the mix. Tighter security was warranted. The motives of those who were outside of the QW7 Defense Conference had been worrisome enough. Some, not many, but enough, had other views of the deserved fate of the world. Known only to a very few, death and bomb threats had been received. Fearing that the authors of these threats had more than a passing knowledge of spaceflight operations, armed patrols were seen circling the communications antennae at nearby Barstow, the

Goldstone site, and those near Madrid and Canberra.

Eight quadrapods launched from six sites had entered their transfer orbits to rendezvous with Nyame. For the U.S. launches, even the failed one, NASA's Mission Control Center in Houston had had control. Now, as also done at the other launch mission centers, ground control had been transferred to JPL for the covey of space-borne quadrapods. India, China, and Russia also had sites for deep space communications. But regarding longitudinal coverage, each had fewer sites with resulting blind periods. Even if they had 360-degree coverage, centralized coordinated control at JPL had been determined at the Defense Conference.

Kayla came into the Mission Control room. It was crowded. People stood behind those seated at the many consoles, the guarded Deep Space Network at their fingertips. Lajos waved her over. "Kayla, this is the start of something extremely important."

She rolled her eyes, "Yes, Lajos. I know, I know."

"Come over here. This young woman is communicating with one of the two quadrapods launched from India. I was there, you know."

"I'm sure it was impressive, as well as the two launches Zhang-Wei and I witnessed at Wenchang."

Lajos shrugged that off and continued, "The three 34-meter antennae at Goldstone are slewed in the direction of the outbound group of quadrapods. We're reserving the use of the big 70 meter antennae for communications farther out. It's now being used for Perseverance communications." He excitedly pointed to the monitor, "There! See? That's the signal."

Slightly annoyed, the controller turned and said, "I'll be sending up test messages, confirming that I have control of the onboard hydrazine thrusters, netting position, and velocity data to define and further refine its transfer orbit track."

Lajos just had to add, "Yes, yes. The antennae out in the Mojave Desert will track them until eclipsed by the horizon in four hours. The three 34-meter antennae at the Canberra site will pick them up."

Representatives from Russia and China hovered near consoles behind the seated controllers. They seemed to have a kinship with the quadrapods launched from their country, even though they had been designed and built in America. Nyame was bringing people together in a different way.

Lajos strolled back and forth behind the seated controllers, nodding when satisfied with what he saw. Zhang-Wei was in his office, with Kayla, checking on the status of the ASA model run.

The yellow wire in the communications room remained dormant. After the Perseverance test, its intended time had not yet come.

***

Zhang-Wei sped down the California freeway with Liang, his mother, by his side in the front seat. There had been a misunderstanding at passport control at LAX. She was still seething. The lines were long, and the young immigration officer was tired and minimally trained. To have confused Liang Huang as coming from the Peoples Republic of China, and not the Republic of China, Taiwan, was over the top for her. There were different views of national sovereignty. Security guards had to come over to see what the yelling was all about. Fortunately things calmed down, her passport was stamped, and she was let through into the waiting arms of her son. The verbal reunion by the luggage carousel was in fluent Mandrin, even though Liang could speak passable English.

Zhang-Wei proudly showed his mother around his house and the property outside. Liang was impressed with the view of the mountains. She commented that the air felt good, being less humid than the moist, subtropical atmosphere that covered Taiwan. But this was now to be her home. He gently held Liang's arm and escorted her up the steps into the waiting apartment above the garage. Despite being a man, he had done a very good job decorating and furnishing the space. To top it off, on a book shelf there was a porcelain cat with one paw raised, the right paw inviting good fortune. It had been Liang's gift to him, and his gift to Kayla.

Kayla had taken both her mother's urn and the porcelain cat to her new home. But she returned the cat figurine when she learned that Zhang-Wei's mother was coming to live with him. It was the right thing to do. Plus, she had rolled the pineapple throughout her home for good luck, and Tiger was still alive. She walked the few blocks from her place, then up the wooden steps. "Hello, hello … anybody home?"

"Kayla, please come on in." Liang turned to see and noticeably did a double-take. Zhang-Wei continued, "I'd like you to meet my mother, Liang Huang. Mother, this is Kayla Williams, absolutely my best student. We work closely together at the laboratory nearby because of the asteroid Kayla discovered and named."

Kayla had done her homework and made a deep bow of respect, her hands at her side. Liang bowed in return, but not as low.

"Happy meeting you, Kayla. My son wrote about you." Not that it was necessary, but he hadn't written about her African heritage. Liang had to suppress fleeting tribal feelings; she stared and realized that Kayla was quite beautiful, despite the scar on her cheek.

Zhang-Wei pulled out chairs from under the small kitchen table and went to prepare coffee for Kayla and tea for his mother. Conversation was slightly forced with Liang innocently asking some probative questions about Kayla's past, including where she was from. For Liang, Los Angeles had more meaning than Watts. Zhang-Wei went down to retrieve his mother's luggage. Sensing it was a good time to go, Kayla stood. "It was a pleasure meeting you. You raised a wonderful son, a brilliant professor."

"Thank you. Much hard work … very much." Then Zhang-Wei lugged in two very large suitcases.

As she went out the door and down the steps, Kayla said, "I'll see you tomorrow." The walk back in the shade of the trees was pleasant. She didn't notice the car with dark-tinted windows slowly following her.

Rendezvous
[3 Years 342 Days before Impact]

No envelope, no stamp; the crumpled invitation had been stuffed in her mailbox. It wasn't for a Caltech faculty social event or a neighborhood backyard barbecue. She spread it out and stared at the scrawl: "Momma's. Midnight. Grape Street."

After Lancaster, even though DeShawn had suggested otherwise, she'd made a daytime visit to his mother in the Watts Projects on Grape Street. It hadn't gone well. She should've expected the reception. The carefully opened door had revealed long-held suspicion and hatred. With the chain still latched, bitter words flowed out through the narrow separation, "You fuckin' bitch! You ruin' ma son's life, ma only chil'. You grew up togetha'. Don' come back" The door was slammed in her face.

Despite his mother's feelings, DeShawn had gone to Kayla's graduation. Maybe he was building a bridge back from the other side. The informal invitation was not signed, but she knew who it was from. And why meet at his mother's place? Driving down Grape Street in the middle of the night could be anything but safe.

Her all-electric vehicle had been plugged-in at the back of her garage since she returned from JPL that afternoon. She got in and checked the gauges. Its batteries were fully charged. The indicated maximum range would get her to Grape Street and back with stored electricity to spare … if she didn't get shot like she had been years ago. Kayla backed out of her driveway and drove off into a starlit, moonless California night. She rubbed the scar on her cheek along the way, to accompany her thoughts.

Grape Street was still familiar, but new buildings had sprouted near where she'd lived. According to the *Los Angeles Times*, the Projects were being revitalized.

Parked cars were jam-packed on both sides of the street. Her headlights led the way; a few streetlights tried to push away some of the darkness. Kayla could make out the old, ubiquitous features: metal and chain-link fences, and steel bars on doors and windows, even on second story windows. That much hadn't changed since she'd left the neighborhood for good with a fresh gunshot wound. Small groups of furtive people stood in the shadows, looked around, looked at her. Some talked in muffled tones, exchanging things, doing business. Kayla hoped there would be a parking space at the building where she and DeShawn had grown up together. Kayla wanted to walk quickly from her car to the entry door of her old building. To her surprise and relief, there was an empty space for a car right out in front. She swung in and parked.

Memories flooded back. She saw the spot on the same cracked concrete where DeShawn had tracked down and killed hapless ants with the solar death ray from her mounted magnifying glass. A little farther down the sidewalk was where she'd said goodbye to her father as he bled out from a gaping gunshot wound. She was now parked in the same place where a bullet had come through the windshield of her beat-up old car and sliced her cheek. It shocked her to see two men standing exactly where the earlier gunman had stood and shot her. One of them walked over towards her, flashed the hand sign of the Grape Street Crips, leaned down, tapped her window, and motioned for her to roll it down. This was serious Crips muscle, the reason the empty parking space was there. Kayla had been expected; a transfer point was needed.

She was very hesitant to roll down the window, but did so when she saw the .45-caliber pistol gripped at the end of the arm that hung down at his side. "How you, sista? I be there when you got your degree. You 'member me?" He reached in, unlocked the door, opened it, and told her to come out.

"Where's DeShawn?"

"Not here." He grabbed Kayla's forearm and led her to another car with a driver inside. He opened the back door, pushed her in, put a cloth sack over her head, and pushed her down flat. "Jus' chill out; we be takin' you t' see DeShawn."

The route weaved around through an intentional maze to a back alley. The driver pulled into a driveway and stopped. Kayla heard the snarling of a pit bull and the clanking of a gate being unlocked, pulled open, and then shut after the car lurched forward. The escort then flung open the back door and pulled her out and down a narrow passageway, past a small house to a squat, cinder-block building with no windows that had once been a garage. Kayla then heard taps: twice, a hesitation, then three times. Somebody on the other side recognized the entry code that changed nightly and opened the heavy door. Kayla was ushered in, almost stumbling on the threshold. The sack was removed.

She squinted. The overhead fluorescent lights were bright. Not even her thoughts could hide from the glare. There, at the head of a long table, sat a proud DeShawn Brown, slouched back into a big chair. Kayla looked at the others sitting around the table, an ethnic rainbow: Hispanic, Asian, Black, White. Their eyes stared at her with the intensity narrowed by lives hard-lived. Glasses, guns, and whisky bottles were on the table; white powder, a straw, and a razor blade rested on a small, square sheet of glass at the other end. Next to these escapes from life was a large laptop computer, its screen folded open, an encryption app displayed.

"Kayla. How you doin'? Set your fine ass down."

She slid out a chair, sat down, and scooted herself up to the table.

He continued, "So … lets get down t' business." Since his release from Lancaster, DeShawn had indeed focused on business. Gang-turf warfare had consumed his time. Shootouts had killed many of his Grape Street buds. He'd done his prison time with some of them. DeShawn had managed to call a truce with other gangs in Watts, to discuss things of mutual benefit. He'd been very convincing, a skill he'd acquired in Lancaster, organizing the prisoners who had Watts connections. There was enough drug pie to go around. Fighting was wasting people and time. He led the formation of a small consortium with its own street constitution and electoral system. DeShawn had made it to the apex, his path lubricated with a little blood along the way. Business at the executive level was now conducted in the garage blockhouse. Hand-carried orders and encrypted emails came from there, distributed to disciplined soldiers that sold hard drugs with big profit margins. That business extended across the border with Mexico. One of those at the table lived in Tijuana, a wholesale supplier. DeShawn's organization was much like the reconstituted Mafia that had gone quietly underground; no more very-public assassinations on the street that made the papers. Competitors that strayed into DeShawn's new world were taken care of quietly, out of sight, their bodies never found. As had been the case around old Las Vegas, the Mojave Desert served that purpose. DeShawn had genius equivalent to Kayla's; organizational genius for far different operations.

Kayla fidgeted, tapping her fingers on the table, rubbing her cheek. "Just what business do you have in mind?"

"We be doin' some checkin'. Ma people be dam' good at that. The budget for the Jet Propulsion Lab is big. We like a cut, maybe for protectin' the place, as a start, replacin' the guards we seen."

"I can't do that, even if I wanted to."

"Oh, hell! You be fuckin' famous, discoverin' and namin' that fuckin' asteroid."

Knowing she couldn't, Kayla replied, "There could be other things. I'll just keep my eyes open for you. I'm busy as hell right now."

"OK, OK. Hey, when we gonna see what Nyame look like? I like to see ma enemies, look 'em in the eye 'fore I take 'em out."

"Soon. In about a month."

"I be lookin'. Hey, why you gon' White?"

"What the hell are you talking about? I'm as Black as you."

He leaned back and laughed. "It ain' the skin, but the attitude, the culture. You left ours. But I guess you still our Grape Street sista."

Kayla felt a twinge, a knot in her stomach. Dead silence filled the room. Unfinished business over, Kayla stood, was hooded, and led out into the night and into the backseat. The car accelerated and again weaved through back streets. She had no idea where she'd been, as DeShawn required. The car finally was brought to an abrupt stop. The cloth sack was removed, a card was handed to her. All it had on it was a phone number. "We be contactin' you. If you wan' t' reach us, call this."

Kayla was let out and heard, "See you, sista," as the back door was slammed shut. Her electric vehicle was still there, having been guarded all the while. She got in. It was small but accelerated briskly. Alone, Kayla found her way out of Watts faster than she'd driven in. Tomorrow would be a busy day at JPL.

***

Deceleration commands had been uplinked. Distance shrank. Velocity vectors matched that of the errant asteroid. The quadrapods had arrived. Each bristled with the best technologies that human beings could produce, each with a nuclear thermal rocket built at Jackass Flats. Cameras on the spacefaring quadrapods had picked up Nyame over a million kilometers away. Precise orientation data, refined with onboard star trackers, had enabled controllers at JPL to adjust trajectories with vectored bursts from hydrazine thrusters. This wasn't the first time a space probe had a planned rendezvous with an asteroid. The brilliant professionals at JPL were well-practiced.

One quadrapod was brought near Nyame. An image soon filled its digital camera's field of view. A high-gain antenna was rotated to point precisely back toward the Earth. Narrowly-focused radio waves carried streams of data. The modulated signals were gathered up by the big 70-meter dish near Madrid. The imagery bits were sent through the labyrinth of intervening communications links to arrive at JPL, there for a computer to spread them into a visual array.

A hush fell over Mission Control. Nyame's ugly, high-resolution face appeared, beautiful to some. They had seen close-up images of other asteroids. But this visual revelation was much different, considering what was at stake. Kayla, Zhang-Wei, and Lajos stood next to each other in the back of the crowded room, eyes fixated on the big monitors on the wall. Like other airless asteroids and celestial bodies, like the Moon, Nyame had space acne. Craters of various depths and diameters pockmarked its ancient gray surface. Rocks, big and small, were strewn about on gravel and grit. Quadrapod landings would have to be done carefully.

Zhang-Wei put his hand on her shoulder. "What do you think, Kayla?"

"As expected, but way different than the pixelated IR image I saw at Keck II."

Lajos was less eloquent, and feigned fear. "It's a big evil bastard." He wondered if God was thinking of this, or of the plans of others.

The shadowy potato-shaped image, like a football with blunt ends, was reviewed at the IMCC. The approved press release with Nyame's image flashed around the world. Newspapers, television programs, the Internet, and social media had had their described nemesis since the Defense Conference. Now, it had a face.

Tedious probing and surveillance began. Nyame's gravity was too weak to hold a quadrapod close with any appreciable orbital velocity. Two of them were maneuvered with their hydrazine thrusters around the slowly tumbling asteroid. Lasers determined distance. High-resolution cameras built a database of the entire regolith surface from tiny pebbles to larger boulders the size of a quadrapod. Spectrometer data revealed the physical properties of the surface. Gridded images from all angles enabled determination of shape and dimensions and calculation of volume.

Since its discovery on Kayla's birthday, ground-based visual, infrared, and radiometric measurements had accumulated. She had intensely studied these data as part of her research. With surface reflectivity and emissivity assumptions, estimates of characteristic size ranged from about 300 meters to 700 meters. Its shape could not be determined from afar, but the rhythmic periodic change in reflected brightness suggested something other than spherical: a tumbling, elongated shape.

Now its size and shape were known: an approximate ellipsoid

373 meters long, 206 meters across its circular cross-section, its diameter. It was a dangerously large asteroid.

Nyame's spin state was accurately determined. Its axis of rotation cut through the midsection of the ellipsoidal shape, nearly perpendicular to the long axis. Nyame was tumbling slowly end-over-end, lengthwise, with a rotation rate of 4.901 degrees per hour; a period of 73.454 hours. This was close to that determined from ground-based observations of the variation of reflected light intensity. Its non-principal axis of rotation was almost zero, but even this slight wobble had to be considered when determining when and for how long the landed nuclear thermal rockets would be fired.

As with the Earth's 23.5-degree inclination with respect to the ecliptic, Nyame's axis of rotation was inclined 13.6457 degrees to its orbital plane, which itself was inclined to the Plane of Ecliptic by 11.9682 degrees. Based on these data, Lajos and his crew set out to determine the optimum locations to bed down the quadrapods to impart yet-to-be determined velocity changes.

Onboard the quadrapods were pairs of radar sensors, with different wavelengths, that sounded the depths of the regolith; about 5 meters to 10 meters was the result. There had been insufficient centrifugal force to fling off the space detritus that had accumulated over millions of years. The imagery had first suggested that a pile of rubble was threatening the Earth. However, Nyame turned out to be a hybrid. The surface belied what lay beneath. The relatively shallow layer covered a solid, iron-nickel core that could survive a burn through the Earth's shallow atmosphere. Nyame indeed was a dangerous asteroid; a *very* dangerous asteroid.

Mass was estimated by inertial sensors onboard the probing quadrapods. Composed mostly of iron-nickel, the mass of Nyame was more than had been first estimated from a distant Earth. That number pulled alarmed engineers and astrophysicists to a back conference room.

The number of quadrapods, the designed thrust of the nuclear thermal rockets on each, and the amount of liquid hydrogen they carried had been driven by many factors. The mass of Nyame was the most critical. It now became questionable whether there was enough total thrust to impart enough net change in velocity, Delta-V, to nudge Nyame away from an impact. The few in the room, including Lajos and Dimitri, strongly felt that this possible problem should be kept very secret. They had crossed swords at the Defense Conference, and continued to do so in JPL. Dimitri, part of the mandated international team, hinted aloud that Lajos's concept was coming apart. With a deep hoarse whisper, Lajos leaned over close, "One big bomb would have come with more unknowns, and more risk, and you know it. *Zatknis.*"

Dimitri flinched at Lajos's Russian approximation of "Shut the fuck up!"

Zhang-Wei and Kayla waited for the golden data. Observing arcs from many telescopes, supplemented with radio astronomy, had yielded reasonably accurate position and velocity data to initialize ASA model runs. That had resulted in predicted impacts very near Moscow with heart-stopping, panic-inducing probabilities. From Deep Space Network antennae, radio signals were transmitted, received by the quadrapods, and transmitted back; the frequency shifted slightly due to relative velocity. Doppler shift for radio waves worked in deep space, as well as for atmospheric sound waves from the passing of a high-speed train. With atomic clock accuracy, line-of-sight position was determined down to a few meters and velocity down to fractions of centimeters per second. Averaged over all eight quadrapods in close formation with Nyame, position and velocity data were calculated, recalculated, confirmed, and passed to Zhang-Wei's group.

The Yarkovsky effect was already part of the ASA model; Kayla had done the software modification. The velocity-changing effect on a rotating body was small, on the order of the distant forces of some of the N-bodies used in the complex integration. Shape, rotation, thermal, and reflectivity properties of the surface regolith had been approximated. Now, they were much better known from up-close measurements. Nyame wasn't a nice spherical shape with the axis of rotation perpendicular to the ecliptic. The effect of the lag between the absorption of light from the sun and the re-emission of infrared radiation as micro-thrust was small, but very complex. Kayla had handled it; Zhang-Wei agreed. ASA prediction accuracy had been improved. Kayla confirmed overall data entry.

DeShawn's offer cluttered a corner of her mind. She concentrated hard and unleashed the ASA model. It would be the last prediction before the first deflection operation.

****

The imaged map of Nyame's surface determined possible landing locations for all eight quadrapods. Sufficiently flat areas without large rocks were sought. The sloped sides of meteor craters were to be avoided. Sensitivity analyses for Nyame, and for threatening asteroids in general, showed that changing the along-track velocity vector netted the greatest change in the distance of the closest point of approach to the Earth. For a tumbling Nyame, optimum landing site selection, with the tangential velocity change constraint, was a complex problem. But Lajos and his team were up to the task. Nyame's period of rotation and orientation of its axis relative to its orbital plane were added to the mix. For these landing zones, with the same dynamic properties, its total mass and its center, a firing algorithm was crafted: when and for how long to fire each nuclear thermal rocket to achieve a net velocity change.

Landings were done one at time, carefully, replicating what had been done on a man-made regolith in the Mojave Desert. Natural Feature Tracking, using the high-resolution imagery, was used to avoid large rocks, something that had been developed for the touch-and-go landing on asteroid Bennu. Four large pads gently touched the surface. The quadrapod was held there by thrusters automatically swiveled outward, as sharp helical screws wound their way into the strata of rubble. Sensing the orientation of the gravitational field, the length of each leg was automatically adjusted until the relation of the rocket's thrust vector to the center of mass was just right. Over the course of days, the next quadrapod was moved into position and landed, then the next, and the next.

The last one, also the first to probe and measure, was maneuvered around Nyame, sending back images of the other quadrapods on the surface; aerial reconnaissance in the vacuum of space. The scenes were dramatic. On sunlit sides, quadrapods stood on legs with shadows cast across the gray surface. One lander had settled uncomfortably, for the controllers, near a rock about a third its size. Finally, this last quadrapod was brought to the surface and anchored.

The final arrangement was a pair of quadrapods at each end, four around the middle girth of Nyame. The radio-linked local area network was brought up and tested. The quadrapods could now communicate with each other and JPL as their high-gain antennae were programmed to slowly move in response to Nyame's slow rotation. Line-of-sight was periodically occulted for some, but the local area network ensured all quadrapods received intended data. Returned data confirmed that it could handle uplinked firing parameters, timing and duration, and communicate them back. All was in place. The ASA model, in Reverse Tangent Mode, would provide the target Delta-V.

More than a lot had happened since Elazar Etxarte had been driven by his student to Gran Telescopio Canarias on La Palma, and since Kayla Williams had driven herself up to the peak of Mauna Kea to Keck II. The focus of the international effort was ready … ready to deflect Nyame. That coordinated press release would soon hit the streets ... and the human psyche.

Dimitri said he needed a break. He strolled through dappled sunshine on the JPL campus, smoking a strong cigarette; smoking wasn't allowed inside. While standing next to a tree, as if trying to hide, he touched the send icon and sent an encrypted text that landed on a computer in the Kremlin. It arrived a day after an encrypted message from Roscosmos Mission Control Moscow: "*Medved priblizhayetsya.*" The bear held a nuclear bomb and had also rendezvoused with Nyame, but farther out. Undetected, it was in a parallel orbit, drifting there, just in case.

In the shade of another tree, Lajos sat on a park bench as a pair of armed guards walked by. He waved and waited until they passed, then held a cell phone close to his mouth.

The firing model had been sent to NASA headquarters. Even

though all the needed brain-power was at JPL, and then some; bureaucracy was strong. Secure communications had been used. Regardless, a powerful agency had intercepted it.

Adam looked up at the photo on the wall of the Ka'bah in Mecca, then down at the message. He smirked as he read other interceptions: a decrypted and translated message from Pasadena to Moscow, and another one within Russia, something about a bear coming.

***

The TV news anchor was handsome, well-known, and trusted. He wore horn-rimmed glasses to convey intelligence he didn't have. But, superficial or not, ratings were important, especially during this time of a real asteroid threat. They wouldn't let this crisis go to waste. Off camera, he had read a copy of *The New York Times*. Nyame's first image was in a feature story with a disquieting headline: "Killer Asteroid!"

In addition to increasing network viewership ratings, he thought his job was to calm the public with an on-air interview with the Administrator of NASA and NASA's Planetary Defense Officer. But there was some last minute shuffling. The President of Caltech had been added. The brain trust at JPL that did the heavy lifting would have to sit this one out. They didn't mind, except for Lajos.

In the studio, all four sat at a table in front of two big displays. One showed all of Nyame close up, the other showed a landed quadrapod with a second one in the distance, both on one end of Nyame. The guests were introduced, but that was hardly needed considering the news media coverage of Nyame, NASA, and JPL in the preceding months.

"Welcome, gentlemen. We've arrived at the moment of truth, haven't we?"

The Administrator of NASA replied, with a forced air of calm confidence, "Yes, we have. With multinational cooperation, we launched and landed eight quadrapods, each with a thermal nuclear rocket to deflect the asteroid." That comment merged smoothly with the previously-seen montage of rocket liftoffs, starting with Cape Kennedy and India's Satish Dhawan Space Centre. All launches were shown in rapid sequence, except the failed one. The Planetary Defense Officer gave a running commentary. His words, and the sight and sound of the fire and fury of big rockets, were comforting to the general public. If humans can build such things, then surely they can take care of this deadly asteroid.

The news anchor interjected, "You said that all eight have landed now, right?"

"Yes. That took a few days. It challenged the people at our Jet Propulsion Laboratory in Mission Control, but they accomplished this astounding feat flawlessly."

The President of Caltech interrupted, "It's an international team effort. The Intergovernmental Mission Control Center is at JPL, but many of those there have come through our institute."

With that, the Administrator of NASA adjusted his tie, a nervous habit when stressed. He directed the conversation to the images of a quadrapod on its gray, rocky landing area. "This is one of eight, this one at the end of the asteroid, which is essentially shaped like a big football with rounded ends, as you can see in the first image." He had wanted to have the NASA logo emblazoned on the fuel tanks of each lander, but this was an international effort; he'd been overruled by the President of the United States. "That inverted cone is the business end of a powerful nuclear thermal rocket. This one, and the others, will be fired in a tightly-controlled sequence considering Nyame's slow rotation, all commanded from JPL. When done, the asteroid will receive a precise, planned push, a nudge, in a specific direction to change its velocity and its orbit to miss the Earth."

"Will there be more than one nudge?"

"Quite probably. We'll have enough liquid hydrogen for more nudges. We must evaluate the trajectory change and use that to initialize a very complex model to predict where it'll be in the vicinity of our planet, sometime on June 15, 2032. With the quadrapods on the surface, we'll know that trajectory change very accurately, lessening the uncertainty of the prediction."

The Caltech president touched his ear, an arranged signal. The displays now showed the faces of Zhang-Wei and Kayla Williams, her face intentionally turned to hide her scar. "These two people are the products of Caltech who are leading the effort, with others of course, to model and predict the orbit of Nyame. Miss Williams, a Caltech post-doc, is the one who discovered the change in the asteroid's orbit and was given the honor of naming it."

On cue, the anchor stated, "They could've been here, but I understand that they're busy back at JPL."

"Yes. The latest model run just finished a few hours ago. We have the prediction if we were to do nothing." A map was brought up showing elongated ellipses with close spacing, their center now between Minsk and Moscow. "Using the quadrapods for more-accurate position and velocity data, this prediction of the risk corridor is more accurate. The increase in overall probability from 9.3 percent to 15.3 percent is a bit alarming. But we now have the means to change its trajectory and its likelihood of impact."

"When will the first nudge take place?"

The NASA administrator again adjusted his tie. "Soon."

For the residents of Minsk and Moscow and those in between, especially Russian leaders, soon seemed a very long time. Plans could be made for evacuation of the cities and their surrounding areas; relocating millions of people somewhere would be a daunting task. The first out would not be people, but the priceless holdings of the Hermitage Museum. Ruslans would deliver them to Arkhangelsk, where, under military guard underground, they would wait out the arrival of Nyame. The data on Nyame had been shared globally, including with Russian astrophysicists. They advised those in the Kremlin that they now were able to determine the distance and relative aspect to the asteroid to enable them to move in and detonate their massive hydrogen bomb. Russia's best vodka was passed around the room, easing the tension.

Nudge
[3 Years 208 Days before Impact]

Delta-V was on everyone's mind at JPL. Even the news media spoke of it, but in more general terms: nudged velocity change. The first collective rocket-nudges of Nyame approached, with urgency. The dark cloud of astrophysical truth hovered over them: the shorter the time remaining to possible impact, the greater the nudge required to achieve a change that would result in a predicted zero probability of impact. Nyame's originally underestimated mass exacerbated the problem. Liquid hydrogen remaining in total, and on each quadrapod, were critical limiting factors. Fuel load measurements were transmitted back to JPL. Amounts were carefully accounted and husbanded.

The latest trajectory was calculated through the digital labor of a supercomputer framed by the ASA model. Nyame's predicted path intersected JPL's defined B-Plane. This flat mathematical surface sliced through the center of the Earth, perpendicular to the asteroid's passing trajectory. The intersection point on the B-Plane was the forecast closest point of approach, more formally the MOID: Minimum Orbit Intersection Distance. The most likely miss distance prediction was 0.9521 Earth radii from the surface. With that prediction came the haze of location uncertainty. Even with enormous computational power, the N-body problem was a dastardly thing at this required scale. The Earth, too, had its location and rotation uncertainties. In combination, probability ellipses intersected the Earth's surface. They were very narrow and very long, essentially defining a linear risk corridor. Their mutual center was still between Minsk and Moscow.

A desired intersection point was reset to 2.5 Earth radii on the B-Plane, along the same radial from the Earth's center. A larger, more comfortable distance could've been selected, but the Delta-V would've required the total rocket thrust available.

Zhang-Wei, Kayla, and others oversaw running ASA from the 2.5 Earth radii intersection point in Reverse Tangent Mode, so that the other end of the computed reverse track splined smoothly with Nyame's predicted orbit in 21 days. From the firing algorithm, the first rocket thrust would start exactly at that time and location. When the last rocket was fired, the required net velocity change would be imparted, nudging Nyame into an altered orbit. The required velocity vector change was passed to those responsible for firing the rockets. Firing times and durations were determined, checked, and rechecked by Lajos and the other international players, trusting and verifying. The confirmed values were inserted into the command message transmitted to the quadrapods on Nyame. They were received and shared, for redundancy, through the on-asteroid local area communications network, because some high-gain antennae would be occulted when the transmission arrived. Some hours later, a second redundant transmission was made. In all, timing and duration values unique to each quadrapod were loaded into their onboard computer memories to control their nuclear and liquid hydrogen control systems. The values that had been ingested by each numerically-identified quadrapod were transmitted back. To their collective relief, all was confirmed at JPL: what they received matched what had been sent. The return message also confirmed that the countdowns on each quadrapod, governed by their atomic clocks, had started. By unanimous vote of the IMCC principals, including Zhang-Wei, Kayla, and Lajos, the on-asteroid countdowns were allowed to continue. Considering the velocity of the signals in each direction, a time buffer had been inserted in the countdown. If everything was not just right, a message to stop the countdown would be sent in time, stopping everything.

The yellow wire had eavesdropped passively on the two-way

passage of digits, then reported them to a converted wine cellar in a Washington, D.C. suburb.

＊＊＊

There had again been some grumbling in the NSA trenches. Access to computer resources was constrained, restrained, and delayed. Some intelligence analyses, interceptions, and decryptions had to wait.

Adam also waited, he in the cellar by the computer terminal for a message from Lajos. It arrived and was instantly decrypted. It simply read: 2.5 radii, 55.66024, 32.49015, the last two numbers being the latitude and longitude of the point between Minsk and Moscow with the greatest probability of impact; 2.5 radii was the distance from the center of the Earth through that surface location, on that radial.

Back in his office, Adam fed those numbers into the ASA model on the NSA supercomputer. Some days later, firing times and durations were spit out and compared to values captured by yellow wire. They matched.

The dramatic result would be seen on the monitors at JPL, and on the evening news.

＊＊＊

Nyame's first nudges began and continued over the course of 73 hours. Cameras on the quadrapods were message-commanded to rotate and align to look up at rocket exhaust cones for visual confirmation. Additional cameras on the pair of quadrapods at each end of Nyame were oriented to view each other. Aboard each quadrapod, when their programmed countdown reached zero, control rods moved, nuclear fission occurred, and reactor core temperatures spiked. At the same instant, valves were opened and liquid hydrogen was pumped through the closely-packed cluster of linear tubes in a very hot reactor core. Heated instantly to thousands of degrees, the hydrogen changed state, expanded violently, accelerated, and thrust out through the nozzles of an outward-pointing cone. Sir Isaac Newton's action-reaction still worked. Accelerometers recorded the result. The reported data synchronized perfectly with the imagery. Hot bright yellow plumes of hydrogen were dramatically seen against the cold black of deep space; artistic beauty on ancient gray rock. The scenes were also somewhat eerie. The bright exhaust illuminated the areas around the quadrapods' feet, giving the regolith a strange yellow-gray hue.

Due to Nyame's slow rotation, it took over three days to complete the firing sequence. Images of the rocket-firing ballet on Nyame's ends were received and distributed with a descriptive press release. Those in control at the IMCC would have to wait over two months to confirm the altered trajectory and see where the ASA model predicted the closest point of approach and the associated Earth-impact probability ellipses. Hopefully, the residents of western Russia, and those in a basement room in the Kremlin, would breathe a little easier.

Rocket firing times were released beforehand to the operators of space-borne and ground-based telescopes; some were in the backyards of amateurs. Yellow light could be seen in the night sky when magnified by the big telescopes. Mars, too, was in the scene. It appeared near Nyame, by virtue of the viewing geometry, even though separated by millions of kilometers. Relative to Mars, Nyame was tiny. But hot nuclear thermal rocket plumes turned it into a visual and infrared man-made pulsar. The periodicity of these light-pulses, separated by hours, was determined by Nyame's rotational position and whether firing rockets were occulted by being on the opposite side. Recorded telescope images soon were seen on news programs and Internet sites, coupled with the impressive on-asteroid imagery. Some scenes were sped up to show the variation over three days of nighttime viewing.

***

Adam drummed his fingers on old Lebanese cedar, waiting for the summons. His red phone beeped. He expected this. Adam had the nudging numbers. Computer resources were back online to support the national security mission, but not for long. Weeks of post-nudge track data would be shared by JPL. The ASA model there, and at NSA, would predict a new track and the risk of impact. Adam had spent considerable time bringing the new NSA Director up to speed on why their computer resources were being spent on asteroid track prediction, in addition to what NASA was doing at JPL.

Adam poked his head in the Director's office door, a no-nonsense four-star Army General with extensive combat tours in Iraq and Afghanistan. "Yes, Sir."

"Come in, Adam. It looks like the eggheads in Pasadena are going to save Russia. With what those assholes did to Ukraine, they deserve a big rock to land on their heads." He clicked the remote control. A big screen on the wall came to life. Last evening's recorded news was replayed, the part with a series of scenes of nuclear rocket firings on the ends of Nyame. That imagery was more than impressive, almost as impressive as if humans had landed on Mars.

Adam rubbed his hip firmly. "Pretty dramatic, don't you think, Sir?"

"Yes, very much so. But more importantly, it was reassuring to millions in Russia. Now, reassure me."

"All is going as expected. The timing and duration values that were sent to the quadrapods on the asteroid matched our computations. Our main-frame ran the model in reverse, in so-called Reverse Tangent Mode. It took some time."

"Yes, I know, I know. Are you sure of the results?"

"Boss, they share that data with observatories so they can be sure to capture the show. Hell, they even posted them on the Internet." Adam didn't divulge that he had other means, a yellow wire, to know the data. But there were other concerns.

"Christ! I need more reassurance than that."

"We have no choice, Sir, other than to wait for the post-nudge track data and run the predictive trajectory model again."

"You know, Adam, I have to brief the President and the National Security Council on the latest impact prediction, well before they see it in the Washington Post or on the evening news ... even before they hear it from the Administrator of NASA."

Adam stood to leave. "Is that all, Sir?"

"Yes. But keep me informed."

Adam finished with the best reassurance he could provide: "You'll learn the prediction when I do. We have a good estimate of run time."

Adam stopped dead in his tracks when he heard the next apparently unrelated question. "I hate to pick at an old scab, but whatever became of Liu Yang?"

"The CIA lost track of him in Wuhan, when the pandemic broke out. He may have died, or those communist bastards squirreled him off somewhere for his quantum computer secrets."

Alone in his cellar with his thoughts, Adam sipped some very good brandy. His hip throbbed as he composed the message. It called for a very important meeting. Ian, Raphael, and Adam would discuss, in the cellar, the extremely-powerful lethal capability that now lay at their feet; they could direct Nyame to change the order of the world. The decision would be in their collective hands, to be debated and argued. Written only in their minds, each would bring their preferred targets. They'd discussed them before, but now it was decision time. Adam clicked the send icon. The clandestine invitation was on its way, made a little more formal, in deference to Raphael, ending with, *"Répondez s'il vous plait."*

Raphael and Ian did ... the dark way.

With one hand, Adam guided his big, new black Mercedes all-terrain SUV. With the knuckles on his other hand, he deeply kneaded his hip. He had traded in his aging sedan for a model that looked like a military staff vehicle handed down from the Third Reich. He had paid a specialty shop handsomely to install a top-end stereo system and speakers throughout. Wagner's Ride of the Valkyries engulfed his thoughts, but not softly. The quality was equivalent to a performance of the National Symphony Orchestra at the Kennedy Center.

He pulled in at the pick up area at Dulles. Ian and Rafael waited together by the curb; they'd arrived on the same flight having met in Paris to discuss the meeting. Adam jumped out, folded back a finger of his right hand, gripped their hands, and welcomed his accomplices. "*Mon ami*, Raphi. *Mon ami*. And you too, Ian, ya bloody bastard."

Adam swung back onto the toll road and turned the volume down. Ian spoke first. "Christ! This is a big ugly rig!"

"Yes, Ian, it is big and ugly. I thought it more appropriate for what lies ahead. We have more destructive power in our hands now than any country or army ever."

Raphael nodded, "*Oui, oui, mon ami*. The music is perfect for us. Turn it back up."

They were not female Norse Valkyries. Adam's knights rode together in comfort, not on mythical horseback. They would decide who'd live or die.

Eventually, the heavy door was pulled closed, sealing the Faraday cage of the cellar. Glasses were charged with Louis XIII Black Pearl brandy that Raphael had brought. Deserved by the moment, it was the very best. Adam made the obligatory toast. They raised their crystal glasses toward the red-cross of Saint George on the white cloth, the cross of the ancient Knights Templar. "To Solomon's Temple. To the Knights Templar."

Three Montblanc pens were set on the table, but their contents would not be needed. Adam kicked off the meeting. "Ian, what did you think of the rocket show?"

"Fucking fantastic!"

Raphael immediately chimed in, "Fabulous! *Magnifique*! Our plan is coming together."

Adam got right to the point. "Ian, what is your recommendation?"

Ian gave a surprisingly thoughtful answer. "Obviously, Beijing should be the target. I had first thought Moscow, but Russian world influence is waning, especially after their fuck-up in Ukraine and in the Baltic. China's influence is waxing. The CCP is there, and that part of China is densely populated, also with critical industries."

"Raphi, what say you?"

"This was very hard. I sat overnight on a bank of the Seine, near my apartment, thinking of the consequences, the morality of killing millions, almost all of them innocent."

Adam slammed his fist on the table and retorted, "Goddamn it, Raphi! Don't go all wimpy on us. We've come a long fuckin' way to get to this point of changing the future. Do you think the Crusaders worried about such things when facing the forces of Salah ad-Din?"

"*Merde*, Adam! Have you conveniently forgotten? We've kept the spirit of the Knights Templar alive on French soil. I agree with Ian; Beijing."

"Well, gentlemen, I vote with you both. Beijing it is. We *will* change the order of the world, with just retribution for what those monsters did unleashing the coronavirus. On the radial from the center of the Earth through the latitude and longitude of Tiananmen Square, I will set zero Earth radii, and run the ASA model in reverse to get the required rocket firing parameters. Those will be inserted into our yellow wire before a planned uplink for a nudge."

Ian asked, "When's the next nudge uplink from JPL?"

"After the trajectory from the last nudge has been observed and ingested, and the ASA model has finished. We'll just have to wait and see the predicted point of most-likely impact and the associated probabilities. Even if zero percent, they'll almost certainly want to give Nyame another nudge, and another, until the hydrogen runs out, just to be on the safe side of things.

Now it was Raphael's turn, "What's the plan? Shall we meet back here?"

"Of course. We and our yellow wire will be part of history. It could wind up in a museum, more important than Turing's computer, the Enigma machine, or the Enola Gay."

***

They hovered over the results, worried. Post-nudge trajectory observations had been used to initialize the ASA model. Now the model had done its thing as designed by Zhang-Wei and Kayla. There was a non-zero probability of an Earth impact, but with a different location of the ellipses centroid. It had moved from Russia to the Pas-de-Calais on the northwest coast of France. On a more positive note, the impact probability had decreased from 15.3 to 5.8 percent. Due to its size and solid iron-nickel core, if it struck the surface, land or water, the preceding downward spreading shock wave would cause additional wider catastrophic damage. Nyame could wipe out millions of people covering swaths of land in France and England, much of Paris and London, and produce tsunamis down the English Channel and up into the North Sea to further spread disaster, inundating coastal areas, especially the Netherlands.

The IMCC warning was far different than the press release following the Defense Conference. Flashing across the globe, probability ellipses were depicted on a map of Europe. Regions beyond the outer ellipse had 0.0 percent likelihood of impact.

IMCC NOVEMBER 24, 2028 WARNING: POSSIBLE ASTEROID EARTH IMPACT IN 1129 DAYS. The international intergovernmental team at the NASA Jet Propulsion Laboratory commanded nuclear thermal rocket thrusters on asteroid 2000 QW7 (Nyame) and deflected its orbit. With extensive post-deflection observations, Nyame is predicted to impact near the Pas-de-Calais with a 5.8 percent probability on June 15, 2032, 13:23:24 Universal Coordinated Time. Other impact locations farther from this location and other times are possible, with less certainty. Nyame will most likely completely miss the Earth. However, due to the asteroid's size and impact risk, evacuation planning is warranted at this time. Cities and municipalities within 600 kilometers of Pas-de-Calais and the coastal areas of the English Channel and the North Sea should review evacuation plans. The next rocket deflection operation may eliminate the risk of ground impact. When known and validated, the new forecast track and impact probabilities will be released

In advance of the warning, the President and the National Security Council received a briefing from the NSA Director, as informed by

Adam from their run of the ASA model on the NSA supercomputer.

This was immediately followed by a three-way hot-line call initiated by the United States President to the President of the French Republic and the Prime Minister of the United Kingdom. Their response was predictable. "We must make the next nudge as soon as possible!" The President attempted to ease their concern, saying, "The next deflection operation will be soon, as soon as the next observations and our fastest computer will allow."

Ian and Raphael took serious note, and each independently emailed Adam using the dark channel. "We must act now!" Adam snickered, thinking that their motivation may have been two-fold: to move the impact point close to Beijing, and to move the crosshairs away from their countries.

Error!
[3 Years 66 Days to Impact]

They could feel the panic and pressure from the English and French members of the IMCC and from across the Atlantic. Zhang-Wei and Kayla needed a break. They could have spoken privately anywhere, at either of their residences in Pasadena or in a JPL private office. But they chose a student café on the Caltech campus. Zhang-Wei remembered very well the conversation he'd had over coffee with his best student, Kayla, after his class one day. Kayla did also. They now walked into the same, open airy space within the corner of high glass-exterior walls and went to the same end of the same long communal table. It had been fashioned from a 400-year-old oak tree that had lived on what became the Caltech campus. Zhang-Wei had always felt something special was soaked into the dense fibers of that wood: hundreds of years of accumulated wisdom from Indigenous peoples, Spanish missionaries, Chinese laborers, and the westward expansion of Europeans. He drew his fingers lightly across the surface of the old oak.

Student heads turned. Thanks to Nyame, Zhang-Wei and Kayla were famous well beyond local academic circles. A graduate student boldly came over to talk to them. Zhang-Wei politely raised his hand, a gentle stopping gesture. "Please, Robert, we have something to discuss."

Kayla went to the counter and returned with two cups of mind-stimulating black coffee.

In the intervening years, he and Kayla had published an

astrophysics text. Of course, the iterative equations of the ASA model occupied many of the pages of the thick book. A bright, fresh young face of an undergraduate excitedly appeared in their midst. She set the hard-bound volume before them. "Please, could you sign this?" They did.

Zhang-Wei and Kayla were left nearly alone to discuss Nyame. They tried not to notice the young eyes that watched them with awe. They had more notoriety than the movie stars in nearby Hollywood. Beyond their reputations, each was distinctive in their own right; she with a beautiful yet scarred face; he with a piercing stare and an ancient bead calculator. Almost absentmindedly, he pulled out his abacus, did the calculation, and set it down between them. Students pointed and whispered; they knew about that abacus.

"Kayla, do you remember discussing the annealing algorithm you suggested at this very table?"

"Yes, Zhang, I certainly do."

"That was fortunate. It's become a key part of the ASA model, greatly increasing accuracy even though it needs more computer run time. Life and death decisions are now based on it."

"Yeah, I know. The model's running in reverse mode as we drink this coffee. The required Delta-V should enable the next nudge to deflect Nyame to a near miss, away from the Pas-de-Calais, with near-zero probability of impact."

"I certainly hope so. There's not much time left, and there's only so much liquid hydrogen remaining for thrusting operations. You were in the meeting. There's enough for maybe two more nudges, depending on required velocity changes."

"Zhang, I hate to speak ill of anyone, but have you noticed Lajos lately?"

"Yes. He does seem a bit distracted, aloof even. We're all under a lot of pressure, local and international. I even received a call from the President."

"Really!"

"Yes. He wanted to know my opinion of the accuracy of our predictions for Nyame. I'm sure he's briefed often by the top people at NASA. I told him that I, or rather we, had absolute confidence in the model. He appreciated that, but I could tell he was uncomfortable with my probability description. He wanted a yes-or-no answer."

"Good grief! So does the rest of the world. Maybe Lajos is embroiled in what information the President receives. He seems to be flying back to Washington more frequently. Lajos says he has to coordinate something or other with NASA, but won't say much about it."

Zhang-Wei withheld his instinctive gut-felt feelings. "Yes, most likely … most likely. But Lajos is Lajos."

"Say, how's your mother doing?"

"Just fine. She likes her cozy space above the garage. Sometimes she reminds me about grandchildren.

"I don't mean to pry, but I understand that you visited your old neighborhood."

Kayla reflexively touched her scar. "Yes, I did. When you grow up with someone right next door, when our parents were friends, it's hard to just write him off. He's a human being, too."

"I understand, but please be careful. He lives in a far different world. We don't want to lose you; I don't want to lose you."

Kayla glanced at the clock on the wall. "You won't. Now let's get back to see what velocity change is needed for a 3.1 Earth radii miss. As you argued, a miss distance less than that would still have a non-zero probability of Earth impact. The reverse tangent run should be done in an hour."

"Kayla, what do you think of the ASA prediction of Apophis?"

"It's more accurate. It is what it is. The probability of impact is near zero. The world has enough to worry about with Nyame on the horizon."

Zhang-Wei donned that serious stare of his. "Anyway, there's absolutely no time left to launch a nuclear bomb to intercept it on its final run-in. A nuclear weapon could've been feasible, but a fragmented Apophis could result in many ground impact points ... asteroid buckshot."

***

Adam was on the entry records. He knew it, but didn't care. An array of security cameras and retina and fingerprint scanners documented his arrival, three hours before the President would receive the briefing from Adam's boss.

From his NSA office, Adam had directed execution of the ASA model in reverse, but not from the miss distance set by the IMCC. The principals at JPL were still in heated trade-off discussions and calculations of Delta-V nudge versus remaining liquid hydrogen. Dimitri and Lajos were in a white-hot argument. As part of Adam's plan, Lajos argued for show, to delay. Adam had selected central Beijing at zero Earth radii from the surface. Adam's B-Plane was not through the Pas-de-Calais, but through Beijing. Precise and demanding, Lajos had included an atmospheric drag adjustment. Due to its mass and relative velocity, the momentum of Nyame was enormous. But the atmosphere would slightly slow it down, changing where it would impact, also changing the area covered by the entry shockwave. Adam got a jump on the model's execution at JPL. Lajos had helped slow things down with his heated dialogue. It would be some days before both computers provided their solutions, enough time for Ian and Raphael to return for the execution of the plan, from the cellar of a home in a nice quiet neighborhood with tree-lined streets.

"Well, Adam, are the folks in Pasadena going to give Nyame another kick in the ass?"

"Yes, Sir. They've selected a miss of 3.1 Earth radii from the surface. It's the shortest distance that's likely to have a have a zero percent probability of impact. They could've increased that distance, but they're careful not to use up the liquid hydrogen remaining."

The hardened combat veteran sitting across from him thumped his knuckles loudly on the desk. "Shit! I commanded forces in the Hindu Kush, had to react to the uncertainty of the Taliban. Everything about that damn asteroid reeks of uncertainty: forecasting it, tracking it, nudging it. JPL's playing a little bit of brinksmanship, aren't they?"

"Yes, Sir, they are. But they have no choice. I've got the rocket firing times for the next nudge, before them. I got a head start with an earlier execution of the reverse model on our computer."

"Good show! That's what I like to see. Initiative in the trenches. Let me know if the numbers match."

"Yes, Sir."

Back in his office, Adam downloaded the different dangerous numbers into his flash memory chip and inserted it into the cap of his Montblanc pen. Even at his elevated position, security at the Agency was very tight when entering or leaving. His metal pen again made it past the security check points and their detection devices, back to his cellar at home.

That evening, Adam again drove out on the toll road to gather his forces, as if it were for the 12th-century Battle of Háttin in the Holy Land. The Knights Templar and Crusaders had suffered defeat at the hands of Salah ad-Din, which had changed the order of the Mideast for centuries, up to the current day. Adam had a shattered hip joint from Riyadh to show for it. His enemy was now farther east. Adam and his knights had more than swords, arrows, maces, and spears. They had a much larger weapon: Nyame.

The pick up curb at Dulles was crowded. Ian and Raphael were in the milling throng, dragging luggage on their small wheels. Again, they flew over on the same aircraft. They made their way to the big Mercedes, easily seen over the heads of the sea of people. Quiet did not await them in the big SUV. The power of Beethoven's Fifth Symphony filled the interior.

Ian broke the spell, asking, "Well, Adam, do ya have the numbers?"

"I certainly do, Ian. Soon our little yellow wire will have them and the rocket controls on the asteroid will have them, with none the wiser."

Raphael laughed, "Until they observe the resulting track and update the prediction."

"Raphi, Raphi. Have you little faith? We couldn't have planned this better if we'd tried. Sometimes things just fall into place. God is with us."

Raphael bristled, "I have faith in Jesus our Lord, stronger than yours. What the hell do you mean? How is God helping us execute millions of human beings?"

The last notes of the fortissimo of Beethoven's Fifth Symphony trailed off to the powerful sound of kettle drums. It fit the moment. Adam turned off the stereo system. Road noise on the toll road was nicely muffled. "Lajos brought this to my attention. But even I could figure it out using JPL's orbit viewer. When the rocket-firing transmission is made, Nyame will be nearing the other side of the Sun, beyond the orbit of Mars, cut off from our view."

"What the bloody hell does that do for us?"

"Ian, Ian. You do remember the trial run of the yellow wire, don't you?"

"Yeah, sure do. That yellow plastic connector did its thing."

"Damn right! And the Sun belched, big time, a coronal mass ejection. The high velocity particles arrived at Mars and at the Perseverance rover when the command message to rotate the camera had arrived."

"Yeah, that coronal mass ejection was observed and its consequences analyzed. It got the blame, giving our camera test good cover. But how will the Sun help us now?"

"I'll tell you in the cellar."

Again, the heavy door was pulled shut. Louis XIII Black Pearl brandy, from the same bottle, was used to toast the cross of the Knights Templar.

Raphael said, "I think I know."

Ian was full of himself. "Do ya now, my dear French friend? Have ya forgotten Trafalgar?" Adam donned a wry smile. He'd heard such friendly banter between them before, digging up old European bones.

Raphael continued, "Those at JPL will eventually know that the orbit they'd intended did not occur, with a much different most-likely point of impact. Who or what will they blame?"

Ian blanched. "That could result in a deep security scrub of the entire place. Our skinny yellow friend could be discovered. There may be enough rocket fuel remaining for them to correct what we're about to do. We'll be cut out ... and that'll be that."

Raphael retorted, "Ian, *mon ami*. God's created uncertainty will cloud their minds. Solar probes around the Sun have provided views from the other side, but there's no operational monitoring system. A large solar flare or coronal mass ejection could've occurred, or maybe not. High-velocity particles may have swept out over Nyame, or maybe not. They'll not know for sure. Our learned friends at JPL will be going crazy. They'll not suspect our intrusion, but they'll need a reason for the trajectory error. Their reputations and much more will be at stake."

Adam applauded, "Very good, Raphi! Very good. You see, God *is* on our side."

Raphael responded, "Enough with your philosophy! Let's get to it, before I change my mind. Remaining time is precious. The values must be in that yellow wire before the communication uplink to Nyame is executed."

Adam took the time to add, "You know, my friends, Carl Sagan had warned about what we're about to do."

Raphael nodded, "Very certainly. They're trying to perturb Nyame's track, to make its orbit benign . We'll now transform its orbit to impact the Earth where *we* choose."

Adam fired up the computer at the end of the table. With a few clicks, an awakening message was sent to the yellow wire at JPL, triggering a return confirmation. The black link was established.

Three expensive pens lay before them. Adam picked up his, removed the cap, and tapped it on the table. He inserted the lethal memory chip and its adapter into the computer. A table of values popped up, quadrapod identification numbers 1 through 8, their rocket firing times and their burn durations. Another quick click; they were ingested into a formatted message to the yellow wire. "Gentlemen, this is the moment we've worked for, have waited for, have lived for."

Raphael was silent, pensive.

Ian blurted out, "Let 'er rip!"

Adam wanted to savor the moment. He picked up his glass that still held premium French brandy and proposed a toast for the ages:

"To the future ... to a new world order."

Raphael and Ian raised their glasses, touched Adam's glass, and responded, "To a new world order!"

All three tipped their glasses up and downed the brandy, every last drop.

Adam didn't use a simple mouse click on the send icon. Rather, still holding his glass up high, he struck the Enter key with a downward hard thrust of his stiff, firm forefinger: "To the future!"

***

Nyame approached solar aphelion beyond the orbit of Mars, over 427 million kilometers from the Earth on the direct opposite side of the Sun, in so-called superior conjunction. Orbital velocity was slowing to a minimum. After numerical modification by the innocuous-looking yellow wire, Adam's Beijing numbers left the big 70-meter dish at the Canberra site just before noon, aimed a few degrees from the direction to the Sun. Traveling at the speed of light, the changed numbers reached the antennae of six quadrapods 23.67 minutes later. Two quadrapods were occulted, on the opposite side from the arriving signals, but the local area network took care of them. Adam's numbers found their way into control programs for nuclear reactors and the control valves for releasing liquid hydrogen. The same unobstructed antennae that faced the Earth redundantly transmitted the confirmation message of the stored values back to Canberra, then relayed them back to JPL. The yellow wire converted them to the values that had been originally intended. The countdowns had started on Nyame. The first rocket, on its middle girth, would be fired in 40.276 hours, just as Nyame disappeared behind the Sun. The numbers were confirmed at the IMCC. The countdown was allowed to proceed. Then, the wait.

It would be some time before the relative positions of Earth, Sun and Nyame enabled nighttime observation. The Hubble and Webb telescopes in space could be brought to bear on the problem, but they were limited by how close to the direction of the Sun they could look without damaging sensitive optics. The firing sequence was hidden by the Sun.

Finally, Nyame could be telescopically seen in the night sky, but still too far away for radar astronomy to track. Legions of ground telescopes were expectantly turned towards it. The altered trajectory was defined and refined. The points did not match those calculated by the ASA model. Concerned astrophysicists, domestic and foreign, at the IMCC spent stressed hours at their computer terminals analyzing and sharing these data, discussing their concerns. The observed track was slightly different than that determined by the ASA reverse trajectory; but how different?

Zhang-Wei and Kayla oversaw the initialization of the ASA model with the observed new trajectory and released the computer to predict Nyame's closest point of approach. Then, another wait as time-stepped annealing grappled with the N-body problem.

***

The gate guard waved the big Mercedes SUV through. At this early hour, everything was quiet except Adam's anticipation. He calmly made his way through the layers of security into his office and looked at his computer monitor. He was a little late; the answers were already on the screen: latitude, longitude, date, time, and probability. A smile of long-withheld satisfaction came over his face. Adam leaned back in his big chair to savor the moment, then made the call without speaking. He heard the reflexive, "Transportation."

Adam replied, "Clover."

"Yes, Sir." The phone went dead. Adam made the second necessary phone call.

An answer came out of a sound sleep, "Yes?"

"Clover."

With that code word, the head of the NSA sprang into action. He was used to early-morning missions in Afghanistan that needed his releasing commands. He gave his long-suffering wife, the spouse of a career military man, a peck on her cheek.

"Again?" she asked rhetorically.

"Yes, again." Hurriedly, he splashed cold water on his face, spat out breath-cleansing mouth wash, dressed, grabbed his leather valise, and headed out the door. A black sedan with tinted windows, a siren, and red and blue lights on top was in his driveway. The stern-looking driver held the rear door open. "Good morning, Sir."

"Good morning yourself. Now, step on it!"

The roads were empty, but the flashing lights and siren were turned on as the speedometer bumped 100.

Adam heard the steps coming down the hall and opened the door just as his boss arrived. "This better be good, Adam."

"Sir. I'm not sure if it's good, or better; it's the latest prediction for Nyame."

"What's the rush? I've always made it over to brief the President well before the warnings came out of JPL."

"Sir, this is much different, with national security implications. Look at this."

"Holy shit!! That's close to Beijing! And with 34.7 percent!"

"Sir, you need to call an emergency meeting at the White House; the President and the National Security Council in the Situation Room. You can use my phone."

The call was made. A different code word was used that set emergency recall wheels into motion. "Adam, come with me. There's sure to be more questions on this prediction."

The National Security Council was seated when the NSA two-man contingent arrived. With a thumb drive transfer, a map of China was displayed on the big monitors with a center point and surrounding probability ellipses, 34.7% standing out in red. All stood as the President and Vice President entered. When all took their seats, the sleepy-eyed President asked, "OK, folks, what have we got?"

The NSA Director cut to the quick, "Mister President, there's a 34.7 percent chance the asteroid will strike near Beijing, almost fifty-fifty. See? There's the most-likely point of impact."

"I thought they'd fired those rockets to change the course of the asteroid to miss."

Adam interrupted, "Excuse me, Mister President, but that's what they thought also."

"What the hell happened?"

"We don't know, but the deflection operation occurred on the far side of the Sun. An unseen solar flare with high-energy particles could've messed things up."

"Who knows about this?"

Adam replied quickly, "Us and the people at the IMCC at JPL. They're probably taking some time as to what their warning and press release should say."

"Aren't there Chinese representatives at the IMCC?"

"Yes, Sir."

The Chairman of the Joint Chiefs of Staff broke in. "We've got two carrier battle groups exercising in the Straits of Taiwan. Two Chinese aircraft carriers have been playing chicken with us. Their fighters have buzzed our carriers; supersonic. The Chinese will be suspicious of why the asteroid is now pointed at them."

The President blanched. "What do you suggest."

"DEFCON 3 in the Straits; DEFCON 4 for our remaining forces."

"Isn't that an overreaction? Won't that military readiness posture increase tensions?"

"Possibly, but since concluding the Reunification Agreement, the mainland has been pushing hard to speed up the transition to their long-held, One-China policy. The asteroid prediction, even though three years out, may cause them to overreact."

The President polled the Security Council. After a long, thoughtful, stressful pause, he commanded, "Do it!"

***

There was a choke point, by design: the computer terminal in Zhang-Wei's JPL office. He, and often others, Kayla and Lajos among them, examined ASA model output parameters and the prediction before releasing it internally. Such information could be critical, and this common-sense check had been inserted into the process. The repercussions from the Pas-de-Calais warning were still being felt in Europe, and in the office of the U.S. President. This time there were others waiting for the Minimum Orbit Intersection Distance, the location of the most likely point of impact and its likelihood.

The Administrator of NASA and his armed escort crowded close as the prediction rolled up on the screen. As with earlier predictions, the office door had been locked tight, another guard stood outside. Jaws dropped. Nyame would pass 0.292 Earth radii of the surface with a 34.7% probability of impact for the displayed latitude and longitude. With one mouse click, a map with probability ellipses was brought up. The centroid was near the city of Taiyuán in Shānxī province, about 300 kilometers southwest of Beijing! The Administrator raised his hand, spoke into his cell phone and commanded, "Lock down!"

Very quickly, all the entrances to JPL were locked. No-nonsense guards with automatic weapons stood by them, inside and out. An internal operative went into the communications room. Adam's little yellow wire wasn't noticed. All electronic means of communication with the outside world were shut down, even to the Deep Space Network. Inside the room, fingers danced across a keypad to release a small cover revealing a red switch. It was thrown to the marked "JAM" position. Unknown, except to a very select few, cell phone jammers had been inserted in various corners of JPL. Now, they were activated. Physically and electronically, everybody inside of JPL was sealed off from the outside world, even those managing other space probe missions. Over loudspeakers was heard, "Asteroid defense ... mission control conference room ... conference room ... *NOW!*"

Many were already there. The room soon filled. The probability impact map was on the big display, as were the associated metrics. Silence filled the room as the information was absorbed. Almost instantly, the Chinese representatives on the IMCC pulled out their cell phones, frantically tapping on icons and numbers. Li Chen was in the group; he'd been a participant at the Defense Conference. They spoke in rapid hushed Mandarin about their phones not working.

The Administrator of NASA stepped to the center of the room, directly under the map displays and flicked on his hand-held microphone. "Ladies and gentlemen. This is the latest prediction following the latest deflection of Nyame. Obviously, it is of some concern. The building has been secured and all communications have been disabled. Nobody will be allowed to communicate or leave until the warning has been approved and released."

An old, gray-haired grumpy engineer shouted from the back of the room, "Obviously there's an error! Something or somebody fucked up, either the deflection operation or the prediction model; maybe both!"

Kayla flinched. Zhang-Wei glared and spoke. "The ASA model has always been the approved benchmark. Other models at other space centers have been in general agreement. Something went awry with the deflection."

Now it was Lajos's turn. He did a good job of expressing feigned ire. "Hardly! We do not make mistakes; *I* do not make mistakes. We've accounted for everything, even Jupiter. There are other things out there to change the velocity of the asteroid. Other than the Sun, Jupiter is the largest mass in the solar system, one of the more-significant N-bodies. It was almost in alignment with the asteroid on the other side of the Sun when the deflection operation began. The tug of Jupiter, even Ceres, was accounted for in the firing algorithm."

Dimitri interjected. "Well, my old friend, just what the hell did cause the problem?"

"The Sun."

From the other side of the room, "You mean a solar flare, charged particles, like those that messed up the camera commands for Perseverance?"

"Precisely."

"Well … there's been no warning or observation of such an event."

"Of course. Nyame was on the other side of the Sun, beyond observation by the space weather forecasting people. We don't need confirmation. What else could it have been?"

Kayla thought to herself, What else, indeed?

Discussions raged for an hour. Finally, the Administrator of NASA added necessary calm leadership. "We can't sit on this. It is what it is. It is what we have. It must be released … carefully, admitting to a deflection or prediction problem. Other space centers also have the post-nudge track data and will soon, if they haven't already, apply their own orbit models."

Within two hours, the warning was drafted and the vote taken. Kayla watched Lajos with his normal air of arrogant self-confidence. But something was different … his smile. Kayla had never seen such an expression, as if he knew something others did not. This bothered her. Off in a quiet corner, she brought this to Zhang-Wei's attention but couldn't explain an objective cause for her concern. Zhang-Wei had to admit that his gut-feelings were similar. They were scientists, not psychologists, but still ... ? Kayla went to her desk and touched her father's challenge coin atop *Theoria Motus.*

The blackout and lock down were lifted, the doors were opened, the warning was released.

IMCC APRIL 10, 2029 WARNING: POSSIBLE ASTEROID EARTH IMPACT IN 1163 DAYS. The international intergovernmental team at the NASA Jet Propulsion Laboratory commanded nuclear thermal rocket thrusts on asteroid 2000 QW7 (Nyame) and again deflected its orbit. With extensive post-deflection observations, Nyame is now predicted to impact near the city of Taiyuán, Shānxī Province, China, with a 34.7 percent probability on June 15, 2032, 11:14:32 Universal Coordinated Time. Other impact locations farther from this location and time are possible with less certainty. Nyame will still most likely miss the Earth. Due to the asteroid's size and the predicted probability of impact, mitigation and evacuation planning should be done at this time for cities and municipalities within 600 kilometers of Taiyuán. Due to solar activity, high-energy particles likely interfered with rocket firing controls.

Suspicions
[3 Years 60 Days to Impact]

Except for curious astronomers, Apophis was an unwelcome distraction. Observations of its approaching trajectory had been used to initialize JPL's ASA model to update and refine the reassuring short-range prediction. About the size of Nyame, it was forecast to pass within geostationary satellite altitude on the 13th of April, 2029, a Friday, no less. Despite the near-zero percent likelihood of surface impact, the public-relations timing couldn't have been worse. The warning of Nyame's possible impact, dangerously near Beijing, had hit the streets just three days earlier. Mystics, soothsayers, and people with Friday-the-13th suspicions clamored that Apophis was a dress rehearsal for a real impact in just over three years; to them, the two asteroids were personified and in collusion. In irrational minds, the etymology of Apophis and Nyame added to their illogical rhetoric.

In his cellar, wrapped in quiet solitude, Adam was unusually content. He relaxed, sipped good Oregon wine, and read through a paper copy of Sunday's *Washington Post*. The small fibers of compressed pulp felt good in his hands and his hip didn't hurt. Thanks to his ingenious deflection hack, Nyame had been nudged into a trajectory for an Earth impact with a much higher probability. News of this had nudged Apophis off the front page. He leafed through and came upon the article about Apophis and read it with ironic satisfaction. It brought back memories of Mecca, the Hajj, and the hip-piercing bullet in Riyadh. He shifted from paper to electronics and retrieved the Islamic calendar online.

Preparation for the Pilgrimage to Mecca had been underway, with the Hajj to start in a few days. On a clear desert night, pilgrims had watched Apophis transit the sky. Observatories in the Kingdom had been trained on Apophis. Each had been filled with different pilgrims with a different faith: astronomers. Imams had known of the approach of Apophis and had sermonized about its meaning at their mosques during the Asr, at late afternoon prayers that day. A New Moon had been unseen in the daytime sky and had set with the Sun, followed by the darkest of nights. With unaided eyes, thousands had been able to see the bright point of light moving amid the stars; sheiks, imams, and mullahs were in the throngs. Far from city lights, desert Bedouins took special note and had also prophesied. Powerful telescopes had netted accurate position data as Apophis passed.

Always seeking to increase readership, the *Washington Post* article quoted a radical imam: "Apophis heralds the coming disaster of Nyame." At his mosque, the imam happily explained that this was suitable for the infidels that had mistreated Islamic believers in northwestern China.

Adam smirked, thinking that godless communism should have been added to the justification. Then he readied himself for his red-eye flight to Los Angeles.

***

The top dogs were there: the Administrator of NASA, the Planetary Defense Officer, the JPL Director, the President of Caltech. Certainly, the international members of the IMCC all came, as helpful watchdogs. The conference room filled. Like all the other attendees, Zhang-Wei, Kayla, and Lajos had to pass through a metal detector and shed all electronic devices or anything that could record an image or communicate. Adam MacKellar was there. He had asked his boss to help him finagle a NASA invitation to the emergency meeting.

The doors were pulled closed. Armed guards were posted

outside. It was a small-scale replay of the Defense Conference, but at an undisclosed location. Protestors and doomsday activists were chanting outside of the main entry to the JPL campus and around Caltech's empty Beckman Institute auditorium.

The NASA Administrator took to the podium in front of a large display: a map of China with overlaid ellipses and their centroid. "Ladies and gentlemen. We've written this off as data corruption due to a solar flare, which may or may not have occurred. I *repeat* … may or may *not* have occurred."

In the next hours, model descriptions and verification data replaced the map. Discussions were direct and heated.

Lajos had again come prepared. "The rocket firing algorithm is correct, to put Nyame on a trajectory as determined by the Adaptive Simulated Annealing model. Dimitri, Li Chen, their people, and others have all reviewed and validated the firing model. There are *no* errors; there *were* no errors."

Zhang-Wei stood his ground. His abacus had made it through security and now rested on the podium. With its old beads, he quickly did the calculation, his abacus a talisman. He summarized the heart of the matter: "We are absolutely confident in the ASA predictions and this model's use to determine the required deflection."

The Planetary Defense Officer shot back, "We're looking for kilometer accuracy."

"Yes, but three years is short in trajectory-prediction time." Zhang-Wei put things in perspective, as a validation. "Apophis was discovered almost 25 years ago. With what we had at the time, there had been a 2.7 percent probability of impact in 2029. With subsequent radar and optical observations, the prediction was refined and Apophis was taken off the risk table. We recently refined its trajectory with our ASA model, which brought it just a bit closer to the surface. As you all know, the Apophis close flyby occurred five days ago, and that close track was captured by a number of Mideast telescopes. Including gravitational effects, the ASA model was near-perfect in its prediction."

From the back of the room, "When should we do the next nudge? The longer we wait, the more deflecting-energy required. We've seen the post-nudge down-linked data. A lot of liquid hydrogen was used up."

A frustrated Planetary Defense Officer replied, "After we figure out what the hell went wrong! And not before."

Lajos intruded. "The problems were undoubtedly caused by the Sun. What else could it have been?"

Silence followed the almost rhetorical question. Then, from somewhere in the room came an old, raspy voice. "Carl Sagan … you remember him, don't you? He, and Steven Ostro of this very laboratory, warned of the possibility of intentionally transforming a benign asteroid trajectory into an Earth-impacting one."

A collective gasp spread over the room. For a few, this bolstered their guarded suspicions. Adam and Lajos glanced at each other, but remained stoically calm. Like an actor on the New York stage with a Shakespearian part, Lajos stood, "Such a suggestion is ludicrous! How in the hell could that have been done? The IMCC and JPL are in control of everything, with strict verification of communications with the quadrapods on Nyame."

The Administrator of NASA took to the podium. "Such nonsense must not leave this room. Do you all understand?! It will only serve to foment panic. Our press releases and issued warnings are the benchmark."

Zhang-Wei stood. "Sir. Pleiades II has been our supercomputer for the ASA model. It has extensive self-checking for computational errors. While highly unlikely, an arithmetical error could have occurred."

"What do you suggest, Professor Huang?"

"Access to the El Capitan II supercomputer at the Lawrence Livermore National Laboratory, or whatever they call that place these days."

The Administrator of NASA looked at the IMCC international representatives and chose his words carefully. He knew that Nyame oversight modeling was being done at the NSA, and that the El Capitan supercomputer at Lawrence Livermore simulated nuclear detonations. "That's reserved for national defense."

Adam and Lajos again made secretive eye contact.

Zhang-Wei continued, "Sir. Respectfully, we're concerned about international defense. We should run the ASA model on both computers at the same time and compare results to remove the possibility of an arithmetical error."

"I'll see what I can do. We should've been doing this from the beginning."

Zhang-Wei emphasized, "We'll need to do that. But considering their operating system, confirming that our model is correctly installed on it, will take time; then we can run the ASA in Reverse Tangent Mode on both computers."

The NASA Administrator agreed, as did a majority of the IMCC members; not unanimously, but a majority.

Adam internally breathed a sigh of relief, as did Lajos. The time to install everything on El Capitan would give them the necessary head start on the NSA computer to come up with the numbers to further deflect Nyame to strike closer to Beijing.

Zhang-Wei let his mind suspiciously wander. There were other, large space communications antennae that belonged to the countries represented on the IMCC: China, France, the Russian Federation, and the United Kingdom. He automatically dismissed any notion that France or the United Kingdom had surreptitiously communicated with the landers on Nyame to change the rocket firing sequence. But any communications intruder would have to have not only motivation, but the modeling and communications details only available within the very secure JPL. While very unlikely, he couldn't dismiss the possibility that for the predictions for Nyame, the probability of outside interference was not zero. The Russian Federation still had the 70-meter antenna at Yevpatoriya, and the Federation still had tight control of Crimea despite sanctions. China's 64-meter antenna in Jiamusi could do the communications. Zhang-Wei stopped himself. Accusations without substantiated proof would fracture the teamwork at JPL, let alone the world's trust in IMCC warnings.

Kayla listened, observed, and vividly recalled her premonition that Elcano and QW7 could collide, and that the Pleiades constellation research by Professor Etxarte had served to identify Elcano. She didn't mentally detour into the remote likelihood of other nations secretly communicating with Nyame landers to cause an Earth-impacting orbit. As those in the meeting spoke of the Pleiades II and El Capitan II supercomputers, Kayla had another premonition, equally as strong as the possible collision of Elcano and QW7. As the meeting drew to a close, she again noticed the demeanor and unusual smirk of Lajos. She didn't know much about Adam MacKellar, but had recognized him from the Defense Conference. Kayla had noted the glances between Adam and Lajos; her unease deepened.

***

Kayla acted on raw instinct, sometimes necessary for survival in Watts. She now sat on the other side of a desk in an office she had never visited before: JPL Security.

When Kayla and DeShawn had focused her magnifying glass on a Grape Street sidewalk, they had no way of knowing that someone had managed to insert a very small computer, a Raspberry Pi device, into JPL's Information Technology network. Those hackers had stolen sensitive government data for NASA's Mars missions. Over a decade later, another hack enabled the theft of over 500 megabytes of data for a major mission system. All of this finally resulted in a not-so-friendly visit by NASA's Office of the Inspector General. In the aftermath, cyber security at the famous laboratory had necessarily been increased. Following the Defense Conference and the formation of the IMCC, JPL security had been increased much more. This included security cameras in the ceilings of all the hallways, at all entrances and exits, and in the Mission Control Center itself. Rather than bulky, unsightly cameras suspended on brackets or within obvious domes of red glass, they were recessed above the ceilings with only tiny, unnoticeable lenses in small recesses.

Kayla began her uncomfortable probe, "Is there a camera covering the entrance to the Comms Room?"

"Yes, but not inside the room itself. The door has a cipher lock."

"Do you retain all the video imagery, or is it overwritten?"

The Security chief squirmed in his chair at the pointed questions. "Ninety days are stored on our real-time servers for immediate access and review. All imagery is archived on another server before being overwritten."

"Would it be possible to review all imagery from that camera starting from the year 2023?"

"Sure. You can use that room over there, where I do video reviews. I'll set up a special file from the archive for you. Are you looking for specific individuals?"

Now it was time for Kayla to squirm. "Yes, but I'd like to keep that confidential."

"Well, we have the latest facial recognition software. If you can upload frontal, full-face reference photographs, you'll save a lot of time."

"Does your interface have a USB port?

"Of course; more than one."

"When can I use the room, in private?"

"This afternoon, after lunch. I'll let you in. But I'll have to log your entry."

Kayla stood to leave. "No problem. I'll be back. Thanks."

Back in her office, Kayla inserted a thumb drive into her computer. In a few seconds, she was on the Internet, then at the Caltech website and the Professional Faculty listings. There he was, almost jumping off the monitor: "Lajos Vadja, Professor of Computer Science and Mathematics; Jet Propulsion Laboratory Senior Research Scientist." His broad Magyar face glared out at her: strong check bones, bushy eyebrows, furrowed eyes. Not too many faces like that, she thought; should be easy for the facial recognition algorithm.

Kayla brought high-protein energy bars and a bottle of fruit juice from the cafeteria. The Security chief let her in the locked room and gave her a quick tutorial on the interface. She absorbed it quickly. Kayla was left alone behind the closed door. She uploaded Lajos's digital face and retrieved archived video by calendar year. The camera viewed a long, brightly-lit bicolored hallway: horizontal white and lime green. The door to the Communications Room was on the left, a long row of doors to private offices on the right; framed space-themed photographs of NASA missions hung between them.

She clicked the search icon. In an instant, there was Lajos walking toward the camera, a constantly-adjusting red rectangle framed around his face as he moved, but he'd not stopped at the door to the Communications Room. The imagery then jumped forward in time to when Lajos's face was again detected. Kayla kept the pointing-finger cursor over the stop icon as imagery clips leapt forward, with people going in both directions when Lajos's face appeared. Then, there he was, stopping to finger the cypher lock of the door on the left. But there was more in the image, another man: Adam MacKellar. He appeared nervous as he glanced around the hallway. A few seconds of his full face had been recorded. She downloaded his image to her thumb drive, then continued searching more years of the archive. There were three times when Lajos had entered the room, not noticeably carrying anything. But a small computer could be easily carried and hidden.

While working on her PhD under Zhang-Wei, she'd been given access to JPL to further her research. She'd been greeted with a welcoming tour and a personal briefing on internal security. Kayla was told about the Raspberry Pi hack and its consequences, and that she was never, ever to bring such devices into JPL or ever wander around the IT niches of the laboratory. With that etched firmly into her memory, she now suspected that Lajos, or maybe Adam MacKellar, had had the opportunity to install such a device ... and maybe had done so.

Her next stop: Zhang-Wei. Together, they met in the Security Operations Center with the head of cyber security. He ordered a complete scrub by his people of the Communications Room.

Quietly, thoroughly, without fanfare, that room was inspected as never before. The NASA Administrator wasn't informed, considering his admonition about the possibility of a clandestine hack into the communications links with Nyame. Every cubic centimeter of the room and the racks of equipment were searched. Since the earlier breaches, the Communications Room had been tidied up. The inspectors had to work around and through the plethora of neatly-bundled cables of different colors, some of them yellow. Each server and power supply had security seals with dates when they'd been affixed; none had been broken. Everything on the IT design list was accounted for; there were no unaccounted components in the rows of servers.

Within one bundle was a yellow cable fabricated by careful hands in the basement of the CIA Headquarters building. It intentionally looked exactly like all the other yellow cables. It wasn't noticed.

Lenin
[3 Years 37 Days to Impact]

All that had been needed were seven. But at the urgent behest of China, 14 members of the UN Security Council had voted to hold an emergency meeting. The United States had abstained from the vote, the topic uncomfortable. The issue was not about a threat to national sovereignty or territorial integrity, but about the latest prediction of a well-known dangerous asteroid apparently bearing down on China, and much too close to China's capital.

The UN meeting room was cavernous; 15 national representatives sat around a semi-circular table. There was tiered seating on one side for interested attendees and a huge digital display monitor above them on the other. The international press was there for the televised meeting. The representative from China would speak first. Before she did, the monitor displayed what had been seen at the JPL emergency meeting: a map with elongated concentric ellipses.

The Chinese member of the IMCC at that close-hold meeting near JPL, Li Chen, had heard the NASA Administrator's admonition about the possibility of Nyame's deflection system falling into the wrong hands. But, as soon as he could, Li sent an encrypted message to the Central Committee of the Chinese Communist Party.

Rather than in her native Mandarin, the representative of China spoke in almost perfect English with a slight accent. Her face appeared on the monitor, TV screens, computer monitors, and cell phones around the world. "My country is at grave risk because of United States incompetence. Responsibility must now be turned over to Guójiā Hángtiān Jú, our National Space Administration." Under her control, the image on the big screen reverted to the mapped ellipses and the displayed 34.7%. She theatrically droned on for the international audience, and for the Chairman of the CCP, concluding that the deflection could have been intentional, but not describing how. Implied was better than described, since informed description was beyond her technical grasp.

The United States Ambassador to the UN spoke next. His face reddened; a vein on the side of his bald head seemed to be bulging out. "These accusations are outrageous! We are all part of a team to prevent disaster, or at least until now. China had selected their top astrophysicists for membership on the team at the IMCC. Asteroid track data and model applications have been very transparent, well beyond the Jet Propulsion Laboratory. Now is not the time to change horses in the middle of a dangerous stream. There are only three years left. Time must not be wasted."

The representative from Russia spoke next, in Russian. For viewers, the volume of his voice was suppressed; the translator's voice was heard. "At the UN-mandated Defense Conference, we had strongly suggested that a nuclear detonation be used to provide the necessary deflection energy. Now, the bed has been made and nobody wants to sleep in it." He continued in an authoritarian voice, concluding with, "There may be time to launch a nuclear bomb to do the job. Russia stands ready." The representative had not been informed of the large hydrogen bomb that now orbited in distant formation with Nyame.

***

The Front Range of the Rocky Mountains was grand and idyllic, more than a mile above sea level. Solar physicists at the Space Weather Prediction Center continuously gathered data and imagery of the Sun by observatories around the world and satellites in orbit. Analyses and predictions were their products, stressful important work. Stress increased considerably for the Director. Across his desk sat the Administrator of NASA and a senor FBI agent. A second armed FBI agent stood outside the locked office door.

The NASA Administrator tried to be congenial. "Thank you for taking the time to meet with us," as if the Director had any choice.

The Director curtly replied "I told you. We've gone over the observed activity and our forecasts of the Sun for the period of time when the asteroid's rockets were being fired, when it was behind the Sun. There were no coronal mass ejections or large solar flares observed on the face of the Sun that we can see. If there had been such activity, high-energy charged particles could have swept out in their spiral paths and affected the computers in the quadrapods on Nyame. But, I'll tell you again, the Sun was quiescent. We're long past solar maximum and unsure of the activity on the unseen side of the Sun, even considering its 27-day period of rotation. That's our analysis. Just what do you want?"

"A public release about increased solar flare activity during that period, your reanalysis."

"Reanalysis?!"

"Yes, I know. But solar flares and coronal mass ejections can and do happen at any time, even during solar minium, right?"

"Certainly. But none did during that time, or just before on the edge of the Sun, and then carried around to the hidden side on its rotating surface."

The FBI agent cut in, "You are aware of the fact that budgets are not always firm, that investigations are uncomfortable, and that neighborhoods are not always safe. I'm sure you'll know what to do."

The not-so-friendly visitors left. The Director had studied at the Universidad Complutense de Madrid for his PhD, and had even taken a class from Professor Etxarte. He felt somehow connected to what was going on with Nyame, but not connected enough to lie. Now he was being asked, or forced, to put a spin on scientific facts. He sat and seethed at his desk for a few minutes, then called up the files of the Prediction Center's solar products for the period in question. It pained him, but he went through the formal reanalysis and amendment process and released a modified electronic document.

***

The President of the United States would have spoken at the UN if it had been a meeting of the General Assembly, as had been done many times since the formation of the UN. Instead, he chose a televised speech from the Oval Office of the White House, carried to virtually all corners of the Earth. The President had briefly considered speaking from the podium in the Press Briefing Room, but there he might've had to field questions or just not take any. He was strongly advised against that venue. His objective was two-fold: reassure nervous populations that the IMCC had things well in hand, and defend the reputation of the United States space program and the Jet Propulsion Laboratory. Talking points from NASA lay before him on his desk, his prepared speech on the ever-present teleprompter. He adjusted his tie slightly, took a deep breath, and focused on projecting calm, confident, knowledgeable leadership. A digital clock on the camera pedestal showed decrementing numbers. A person standing next to the camera operator pointed at the President; he was on the air.

"Good evening. An asteroid poses some risk to the global community. We have worked closely with our international partners over the last six years and have implanted the means to deflect it into a safe orbit to completely miss the Earth. The intergovernmental team at NASA's Jet Propulsion Laboratory has the supercomputer power to predict its path and to determine deflection parameters. An unexpected solar flare corrupted data that had been transmitted to the rockets on the asteroid. That error will be corrected as soon as possible. I ask everyone to remain calm and listen to the advice of your governments. Thank you, and God bless America." The less said, the better.

The President was off the air, and relieved. He was immediately followed by televised panels to interpret and tell viewers what the President had just said. Ratings and viewership were at an all-time high, surpassing elections ... for the countries that had them. Russia and China put their own spins on his words.

***

Kayla hesitated, weighing the risks, then made the call. After a brief interrogation, the voice on the other end said that she'd be picked up in an hour. "You be ready, sista."

She sat in her front room, peering out at the street, expecting a long, low purple limousine with dark-tinted windows. But DeShawn had lowered the public profile of the Grape Street Crips; why draw unwanted attention? A nondescript, gray four-door Chevy sedan pulled up on the street. The windows weren't tinted. A tall Black man got out wearing nicely-creased tan slacks and a blue polo shirt; no purple hat on backwards, no tattoos, and no tight-fitting purple t-shirt. He walked casually to the front door and rang the doorbell. Kayla opened it, expecting to give a lost driver needed directions to somewhere. "Can I help you?"

"Don' need no help. DeShawn be waitin'."

"Wait a minute." Kayla went back in to get her briefcase. It was unusually heavy. He let her into the backseat. There, an associate of the revitalized Grape Street Crips was ready with a cloth sack. "Chill, baby. You gotta wear this. Lay down flat." He pushed Kayla down, out of sight. She tightly gripped the briefcase handle as it rested on the floor.

The car accelerated smoothly. Kayla could sense turns and speed changes, and could tell they'd entered a freeway by the road noise and that of other cars and trucks. A deceleration was followed by more twists and turns, starts and stops, then coming to a final one. She heard the big garage door roll up as the car rolled in. Then the door rolled down with a metallic echo. They led her out and between rows of trucks in a moving and storage company, DeShawn's up-front business. In a windowless back room, she was pushed down on to a hard chair; the sack was pulled off and her eyes adjusted to the bright light. She focused on the slouching figure across the table: DeShawn.

"How you doin' Kayla? Look like you got problems, big problems. We be watchin' the President. You be needin' our help?"

"Yes, but not like you think." She set her briefcase on the table and snapped open the latches. Crips guards immediately pulled out their pistols and pointed them at her head. "Take it easy, guys."

DeShawn grimaced and glared at the assigned driver who should've inspected the briefcase before Kayla was pushed onto the back seat.

She carefully opened the briefcase, revealing two large glossy photographs that sat on top of bundles of money. Many similar transactions had taken place across this table. She slid the photos to DeShawn, then tipped up the briefcase. Bundles of $20 bills spilled out, $50,000 worth. She'd lowered her bank account substantially, but she could afford it.

A broad smile spread over DeShawn's face. "Sista. Now we be gettin' somewhere. What you want? Take out these White dudes?"

Kayla slid a thumb drive across the table. "No. Their digital images are on this."

DeShawn noted that her reply was not immediate, that she had to roll that question around in her mind. "What you want, then?"

"Track down where the red-haired one lives. I've found out that he works for the National Security Agency, so he probably lives somewhere in the Washington, D.C. area. His name is Adam MacKellar."

"What 'bout the otha' one?"

"He's Lajos Vadja, a professor at Caltech that does research at the Jet Propulsion Laboratory. I don't know where he lives, exactly. He often flies back to Washington to coordinate with NASA, but he may be meeting with this Adam MacKellar."

"What should we do if we find 'em? Take 'em out?"

"No. Just report back to me."

"We can do that." DeShawn fingered the cash on the table. "This be a down payment."

"I figured as much. Send someone out to my place to report in person; call first."

"Got it, Kayla. Anythin' else?"

"No."

DeShawn still refused to speak using standard English grammar. He certainly could if he'd wanted to; he'd done well taking an English course offered back in prison. But he had good leadership and management skills. He intentionally spoke in the language of his gang; trust was critical. "My boys take you back now. We be in touch."

As soon as she was escorted out of the room, the bag over her head, DeShawn flipped up his laptop computer monitor, inserted the thumb drive, and started composing a message that would be encrypted and sent to his franchise in the Trinidad neighborhood of the nation's capital. A few years earlier, he'd flown out there and managed to broker a peace deal between the local Crips and Bloods. This turned into a low-profile syndicate, administratively linked with Crips, Bloods, and other gangs in major cities. The boys in the Trinidad hood would carry out Kayla's ask.

***

The President of Russia strode through the long narrow hallways to the underground meeting room in the Kremlin. Two armed guards accompanied him; one could never be too careful. The room had previously been a private chamber of a Russian emperor. This President had watched the emergency meeting of the UN Security Council. He was proud of the speech by the ambassador he'd appointed, but didn't think much of the later televised speech from the White House. Mutual trust and respect remained thin.

Not many people knew of the massive hydrogen bomb that had been launched from Plesetsk, that it was not a space probe to Jupiter. The few that waited in the room did, including and especially, the Director General of Roscosmos, the agency of the Russian Federation responsible for space operations. All stood as their President entered. His escorts were instructed to wait outside the thick door. Then all sat down at the long table to get down to the serious business at hand.

While taller, he looked uncannily like Vladimir Lenin of Russia's October Revolution. Shrewd and balding, he'd intentionally grown a mustache and a narrow goatee before his last election. He'd spoken of times in an older Russia.

The President spoke first. "Comrades, what is the status of the bomb we have named in honor of Lenin?"

Out of respect and a tinge of fear, the Director General used the Russian archaic term of address. "Sudař. Before I get to that, we just received an encrypted message from Dimitri. He's part of the intergovernmental team at America's Jet Propulsion Laboratory."

"I know, I know. What does our Dima say?"

"Sudař, he confirms that there is uncertainty in the deflection of the asteroid. And a lack of confidence in the process."

"What about the predicted impact?"

"Sudař, the post-deflection trajectory data are openly available by international agreement. Our model's prediction using these data is close to that of the Americans. We have it impacting with a smaller probability farther southwest, but still in China, still destructively close to Beijing. I suspect the Chinese prediction model has produced similar results."

"What about Lenin?"

"Sudař, our bomb remains in a parallel orbit with the asteroid, as yet undetected as far as we know. Our latest communication with Lenin, through our Pluton deep-space communications-antennae site at Yevpatoriya, has confirmed Lenin's track. All systems are fully functional. Thruster hydrazine is at 98 percent, more than sufficient to maintain its relative position. Or we can change its track again to match when the asteroid is deflected by its rocket thruster system. Or we can move the bomb closer."

The President pulled on his goatee, thoughtfully. "Crimea, Sevastopol, Yevpatoriya, and the antennae there remain firmly under our control."

"Sudař, another deflection is planned. This one may correct the earlier deflection error."

"What if it does not?"

"Sudař, we, or rather you, can publicly divulge the presence of the bomb and move it into position to deflect the asteroid. Lenin, and Russia, will help save the people of China."

The President's face morphed into one with a distant stare. He weighed the pros and cons of deflecting Nyame to save a large portion of China ... or not. Both nations had competing global interests, despite recent agreements of increased cooperation. He shook off the spell. "With only three years to go, will Lenin have sufficient thermonuclear energy to deflect the asteroid to miss the Earth?"

"Sudař, yes. But if we wait too long, it may not be sufficient, considering its mass."

"How do you know?"

"Sudař, we've been doing extensive nuclear detonation and velocity change simulations for asteroids in general, and for this asteroid in particular. Lenin's intense X-rays, gamma rays, and especially its neutrons will vaporize the facing surface and some of the solid sublayer. The super-heated vapor and ejecta will thrust outward from the irradiated side. The reaction force will deflect the asteroid.

"Enough for it to miss?"

"Sudař, yes, depending on when we detonate Lenin. But time is running out."

"Other considerations?"

"Sudař, yes there are many. The Jet Propulsion Laboratory, as agreed, has shared the measured composition, mass, shape, and rotational dynamics. It tumbles slowly. It is elongated. The face of the irradiated surface must be perpendicular to a line through the asteroid's center of mass. We will position Lenin accordingly, close, 30 meters from the surface, to control the area of the surface irradiated."

"Are there risks."

"Sudař, yes. Fissures. There could be deep fissures in the iron-nickel sublayer; we don't know. Vaporized material on the facing walls of a fissure could force the asteroid apart, and there could be more than one fissure."

"And …?"

"Sudař, the asteroid could be fractured into pieces, each almost as dangerous, impact points spread over a larger area, maybe even parts of Russia. Most of the pieces will miss, some will not. Each one could be like what happened over Chelyabinsk, or Tunguska, or worse; there could be many."

"Life has risks. Will you be ready, in case the next deflection is not enough to miss the Earth, or at least China, or our country?"

"Yes, Sudař. We will contact you immediately, as we have on all matters."

"Good, very good. If not needed to deflect the asteroid, Lenin, with its ablative nose cone, has other uses of which Vladimir would have approved. I, and the Russian people, do not take well to sanctions and economic threats. Ukraine had put us on the brink. The West must pay."

***

The NSA Director's style was point-blank. "Well, Adam, what the hell did you get out of that damn hidden meeting?"

"They're nervous, Sir. They couldn't tag the error on the trajectory model, nor the rocket firing algorithm. Lead physicists for these functions got their hackles up. Things got pretty heated."

"OK. So what caused the error?"

"The Sun, or so they think, or maybe hope."

"The solar flare the President mentioned?"

"You bet. I hope they're right. The next deflection operation has been delayed until they have confidence in the process and the models. But time's running out."

"Anything else?"

"A long stretch, to be sure, but an old fart suggested that somebody could've hacked into the rocket-firing command and control system. He cited a warning by Carl Sagan."

"Carl who?"

Adam hid his exasperation, "Carl Sagan, a famous astrophysicist who died over 30 years ago."

"Whatever. Is that even possible?" Pain shot through Adam's hip. He winced and hesitated while he massaged the old wound.

"You OK?"

"Yes. It's an old injury, a bullet wound from my CIA time in Saudi Arabia. The pain comes and goes. As for somebody else controlling the rockets on Nyame … not a chance … too many checks and balances to overcome. The entire place out there has more security than Fort Knox."

The old general leaned back in his big leather chair and looked up at the ceiling. "This deflection error may do what we are unwilling to do. Goddamn! The Chinese ambassador at the UN meeting seemed to suggest that we had something to do with aiming the asteroid at them. Things are still tense in the Straits of Taiwan." He leaned forward and looked at Adam directly in the eyes. "What's our next step?"

"Just wait and watch, Sir. When they decide on the next nudge, we'll run the model on Big Bertha, like we've been doing."

"Big Bertha?"

"That's our affectionate name for the most powerful computer we have."

"Fine, fine. Let me know when you have the results. I want to see them first."

"Yes, Sir."

***

They waited in the pick up line at Dulles. Within tinted windows, the passenger in the back seat looked through the windshield with powerful binoculars. Both he and the driver had large photographs on their laps; the faces of Lajos Vadja and Adam MacKellar. Days earlier, DeShawn Brown had transmitted the digital images to the Trinidad Crips along with their tasking. DeShawn's lieutenants had followed the cab carrying Lajos to LAX, then made the call to a basement in Washington's Trinidad neighborhood. The sleuth was on.

Lajos hailed a cab. They followed it down the toll road and into the heart of the U.S. capital to a pair of buildings on E Street. With his towed luggage, Lajos went into NASA headquarters. They found a place to park right across the street and waited, and waited. They discussed their tasking from the Grape Street Crips: follow, watch, report. They thought that Lajos would check into the hotel on the next block. He didn't. As he came out of the building, a black Mercedes SUV pulled up, a red-haired man in the driver's seat. That

251

face matched one of the photographs. Lajos opened the doors; the back door for his luggage, the front door for himself. The covert surveillance continued. They followed at a distance in cell phone contact with other cars of the Trinidad Crips. The task of following the Mercedes was handed off to others along the way, just in case the driver became suspicious of the same car following behind. Adam wasn't aware of it, or even suspicious, but should've been.

The crew that had followed Lajos from Dulles now followed Adam and Lajos to an upscale neighborhood. The Mercedes pulled into a driveway as a garage door opened. A special antenna in the Trinidad car captured the radio signal that triggered the garage door opener. That coded signal could come in handy later. These guys were good. Adam should've been more careful. They watched the garage door roll down, noted the address and time, and drove back to the Trinidad neighborhood. There, an encrypted report and photographs for the observed events from Dulles to Adam's home were emailed to DeShawn.

DeShawn touched numbers on his cell phone. Kayla answered.

Mugshot
[3 Years 16 Days before Impact]

Zhang-Wei stared blankly at his abacus, absentmindedly sliding beads back and forth. He was more than concerned, trying to absorb what Kayla had just told him about her self-initiated surveillance operation. "Why didn't you go to the FBI?"

"With what? My intuition? There's a security camera video of Lajos and that Adam MacKellar guy going into our Communications Room, and videos of Lajos later going into that same room alone. But that proves nothing. He has approved access."

"Kayla, they did a complete survey of all the equipment in there. What did they find?"

"Nothing. No seals were broken. I wish they'd had a camera in there. They didn't find a fuckin' thing."

"Kayla. You shouldn't use that language."

"So what? There *must* be something going on. Do you realize what's at stake?"

Zhang-Wei raised his eyebrows at her impertinence, "How can you ask that? Are you planning to do something on your own?"

"Maybe." She tossed a photograph on the desk of Adam and Lajos together, entering the Communications Room. As if dealing cards, this was followed by photographs of Adam and Lajos together in Washington, and entering the garage of a home in that city. "Lajos has good reason to visit NASA headquarters, considering all the work he's doing here. But someone that works at the National Security Agency? What the hell?"

"What are you thinking?"

"I don't know. I may fly back to Washington and check things out for myself."

"Kayla, please don't. We've got to figure out what went wrong."

Again, impertinence slipped out, "Zhang, I'm sure you can handle that all by yourself."

"They'll notice that you're not here. What should I say?"

"Tell them I'm very sick, congested with a high fever, recovering at home. They may even think another coronavirus variant has come from somewhere."

***

Kayla awoke early to check Tiger's automatic-fill water bowl and dry-cat-food dispenser, and to sift-out and fill his plastic box with fresh litter. She was slightly puzzled as the litter hadn't been disturbed overnight, no paw prints or paw-scooped mounds. Tiger appeared to be sleeping, not unusual considering his age. She went over to awaken him before she left. Kayla gently stroked his head, "Tiger. Tiger. Kitty, kitty." He didn't awake ... he had died in the night on his favorite little blanket on her bed. She thought of leaving him in the freezer until her return, but just couldn't do it. Shovel in hand, Kayla buried her beloved Tiger in the backyard properly, wrapped in his favorite blanket. Now, she was pressed for time to make her flight out of LAX. Tears trickled down her cheeks as she weaved through the morning traffic.

It was a long flight and a long time since Kayla had been to D.C. for the asteroid briefings at Homeland Security. She was thinking, lost in the drone of jet aircraft noise that filled the cabin. A lot had happened since her first drive up Mauna Kea to Keck II. A lot was on her mind, including Tiger, and the date and time of the next deflection. The IMCC had finally made the uplink decision.

It wasn't winter with jet stream turbulence, but they had to avoid thunderstorms over Kansas, and they, too, could stir up the air. She and DeShawn were jostled around, almost tipping glasses of white wine off their lowered tray tables. Business class was comfortable.

DeShawn could afford it. He was in his element, hard-fought-for and long-deserved in his mind. DeShawn had come a long way from the Projects on Grape Street and was thinking of what lay immediately ahead with his franchised operation.

The local Trinidad Crips leader met them when they came out of the concourse secure area. There were no introductions and no checked luggage. Darnell asked Kayla if he could carry her overnight case, as a gentleman would, and led them to short term parking. "You be stayin' at my place, extra bedroom upstairs." Kayla snapped her head towards Darnell, then at DeShawn. She'd figure something out, later.

They fit easily in the big Cadillac. Kayla was let into the back seat. There sat Jamal. He couldn't help but notice her beautiful face and the bullet scar on her cheek. He smiled, gave her a flirting wink, and opened his jacket to reveal a pistol in a shoulder holster. Testosterone was not in short supply in the Trinidad Crips. This certainly wasn't a drive to JPL.

Soon they were on the toll road at speed with a red sunset behind them. The conversation in the front seat was hard to hear, but easy to feel its weight. DeShawn was counseling Darnell. At last they weaved through the blocks in a northeast part of the city. A garage swallowed them up at the end of an alley behind old row housing. Window shades in the house had been pulled down. A round table awaited them in the kitchen. On it were two photographs, the faces of Lajos and Adam.

A Trinidad Crips lieutenant, Jamal, darted into another room and came back with two pistols and set them on the table: a 9-millimeter semi-automatic Glock 19 and a .45 Automatic Colt Pistol.

DeShawn spoke first. "This here be Kayla Williams. I think you know her. Well, she be a friend a mine. We grew up togetha' in Watts."

Darnell replied, "Yeah, we know who you be. We seen you on TV and in the papers. You be fuckin' famous, you and your asteroid. Let's get down t' business."

"It's not my asteroid. It belongs to all of us." Kayla stared at the hardware. "Do you think we'll need guns?"

DeShawn replied, "This be no picnic. We be ridin' dirty."

Darnell held up his cell phone. The video clip was of the front of Adam's house, with a black Mercedes SUV driving into the garage. He touched the hard-copy photographs. "DeShawn ordered we follow these two White folks. We seen two othas come to the place, driven by the same red-haired Whitey, same car. Somethin' important be happenin', maybe bad shit. It's all over the news. That asteroid be headin' fo' China. We don' need no college degree: has to be a connection with stuff goin' on in that house."

Kayla responded, "Yes, but I don't know what it is. We need to find out. And soon."

Darnell pointed to the calendar on the wall. "Need to find out, or stop 'em? I've heard, in one or two days, rockets on the asteroid will be fired t' change the path. I think you up against it, or DeShawn wouldn' be here."

Kayla didn't answer; her face did.

DeShawn warned, "Somethin' up, gettin' ready t' happen. Jamal, give Kayla some words and practice on the Glock."

"Kayla, that smaller one be yours. Go 'head. Pick it up."

Kayla picked up the Glock, rolled her right hand over and let it lay in her open palm. She moved her hand up and down slightly, trying to gauge its weight. Kayla drew the fingers of her left hand over its smooth black metal. It was a sensation as strong and exciting as when a boy in high school had first held her hand in the parking lot. Then reality swept over her, knowing it was lethal. She wrapped her hand around the grip, put her finger on the trigger, and lifted the Glock to where she could align the sights, aiming at a date on the wall calendar. Kayla placed the fingers of her other hand on her scar. From echoes of the past, she heard the shot that had caused her scar, and the rapid shots that had crumpled her father to the sidewalk.

Darnell instructed, "Cup your left hand around the grip and your right hand, like this. Helps steady your aim."

She tried it. She'd seen cops do this on TV and in the movies. Kayla turned to Darnell, "Do I *have* to carry this?"

He was firm. "If you comin' with us, yeah. You not just goin' 'long fo' the ride. You gotta have some real skin in this game."

Jamal added, "I be with you, and chamber a round when we get there. All you have t' do is point and pull the trigga', again and again."

DeShawn picked up the Colt like it was an old friend and examined it, then looked over the Glock. "No serial numbers. Good."

Jamal smiled. "Yeah, we got a micro-welda' in the basement and some fine tools. Used 'em to fill in the numbers, then polished the surface real smooth. Good job, you think? I made a ghoster, but it not be accurate. All the guns untraceable. Kayla, if you use the gun, drop it an' go. You do *not* want t' be caught carryin' it. They can connect the bullets with the gun they came from."

Kayla asked, "Where's the bathroom?"

"Gotta pee, huh? Best do that now. It's down the hall on the right. When done, we be goin' to the pistol range in the basement."

Jamal waited for her, then took her down the old wooden steps. Down there was a pistol range, a room wrapped in thick acoustic material. The Trinidad Crips needed training, and they got it in that room, part of their initiation.

Jamal came up the from the basement behind Kayla. He wore a big grin and announced, "She be a natural."

Darnell gave some final advice. "No round in the chamber, full magazine in the handle. My stakeout team jus' sent me a text. They all be in that house. Let's go."

***

Adam stood by the tunic with the red cross and held up his Montblanc pen as if it were a trophy. "Ian, Raphael, I got the numbers, the final numbers."

"*Mon ami*, will these drop Nyame in the middle of Beijing?"

"Maybe not dead center, but certainly much closer. The explosion shock wave will no doubt cover the city, followed by the devastating impact with the ground. It'll be very difficult to move people and entire industries in three years. That'll put a dent in their global plans! After this deflection, there won't be much liquid hydrogen left to do much deflecting, if Lajos is correct."

Ian added a bit of nervous realism. "Are there any suspicions at your Agency?"

"None, so far. My boss wanted to see the numbers when they rolled out. He was standing next to me when they did. He didn't know whether they were good numbers or not. He's an old war horse, demanding to see what numbers come out of the IMCC, as if he understood them. They'll be different, but by then it'll be too late, even if he suspects something."

"How about JPL?"

"Well …yes. Some old fart suggested the possibility of external control of the deflection system by somebody else."

"Has anyone done anything about that?"

"Lajos reported that a complete survey of the Communications Room had been done, and that nothing was found out of the ordinary."

"Our little yellow friend is still there?"

"Yes. I just pinged it to see if it was still functioning. It was, and is."

Adam inserted the flash memory chip adapter into the computer and brought up the formatted message to be sent to the yellow cable. He reached for the bottle of Louis XIII Black Pearl brandy that sat next to three crystal glasses. Raphael slapped his forehead. "*Merde!* I forgot! I brought a bottle of an even finer French brandy, a bottle of 1874 Louis XIII de Remy Martin. It is very rare, very fitting for this occasion, hand-carried on the flight. *S'il vous plait*, let me retrieve it from upstairs!"

Raphael opened the locked door and shot up the steps. Adam shouted, "Hurry!"

Raphael raced through the back of the barely lit garage, then through the back door of the house. He didn't see Kayla and her Crips team standing very still in a dark corner. The cellar door had been closed tight when they'd rolled the garage door up and down. The low grinding sounds hadn't been heard by Adam or his knights through the thick walls.

Guns were drawn. Jamal had chambered a round in Kayla's Glock and re-checked the clip before they entered the garage. DeShawn touched his lips with an extended forefinger and raised his open other hand, his signal to be absolutely quiet, then flashed a hand sign all except Kayla understood. He was in charge of this operation.

In less than a minute, Raphael raced back down the stairs, holding the bottle, and into the cellar. He pulled the door shut behind him … almost. Concentrating on the computer, Adam didn't notice.

DeShawn, Darnell, Jamal, and Kayla were soon at the bottom of the stairs, standing quietly outside. A sliver of light came through the edge of the frame and the unlatched door. They heard the toast. "To the future … to a new world order."

With the clink of the crystal glasses, DeShawn pushed the door open and burst in, his armed entourage following close behind. "Drop! To the floor, now, mothafuckas! Now!! On the floor, or your next breath be your last!"

Time became surreal, like that experienced by drivers in a car crash just before impact. Everything and everybody slowed way down in the scene in Kayla's mind. Adam immediately recognized Kayla. His brain also raced, also warping time. She raised her arm and gripped the Glock with both hands, straight out in his direction. "Kayla! Stop! You don't understand!"

She understood enough.

Standing next to the computer, Adam stood stone-still as he spoke, except for his right hand. He slid open the drawer just below his waist, reached in, and touched cold metal. At the very same time, he moved the forefinger of his left hand over the Enter key. He pushed it down as he pulled out his pistol with his right hand. Doing two things at once, under stress, the keystroke triggered his finger pull; Adam accidentally fired a shot into the table by his pen ... *Pop!*

DeShawn, Darnell, and Jamal swung their weapons from Ian and Raphael to Adam's direction. Kayla beat them to it. Her finger on the trigger reflexed, as if it had a mind of its own. *Pop! Pop! Pop!* From the Glock's recoil, her arm flinched up with each shot. Bullets impacted along a straight vertical line: the first through Adam's chest, the next tore through his throat, the last squarely through his forehead. Deep-red blood spattered onto the white tunic on its stand by the wall and onto the red cross of Saint George of the Knights

Templar. Before Adam's body hit the floor, the deflection numbers had embedded themselves into the yellow wire, there to await the uplink to Nyame.

The cellar door was wide open. DeShawn asked, "What you want us t' do with these two? Waste 'em?"

Still in the shock of killing another human being, up close, Kayla shouted, "No. No! We'll take them somewhere, back to Darnell's place."

She stepped over Adam's body to take a close-up look at the computer monitor. Her eyes widened. There they were, a list of times and durations, eight pairs of them, nicely coincident with the number of nuclear thermal rockets on Nyame, with the dates and times of the deflecting thrusts.

Darnell took control with an itchy trigger finger, "OK, you White fuckin' bastards. Stand up with your hands over your head. Hear me? Stand up!"

Ian and Raphael had been trained by their respective agencies for such an encounter. As Adam had learned in Riyadh, intelligence was a dangerous business. But without their weapons, Ian and Raphael could do only one thing: stand and raise their hands, palms forward to show they held nothing. They wanted to live to see the new world order.

As he did every night at this hour, Adam's next door neighbor was walking his German shepherd. Its big ears flexed in the direction of Adam's house. He started barking. He and his master heard the distinctive *Pop!,* followed by *Pop! Pop! Pop!* coming from the direction of the closed garage; this wasn't fireworks. Quick on the draw, out came his cell phone, followed by an immediate 911 call. The city's Emergency Communications Center was not busy that night. Not surprisingly, there just happened to be two police SUVs patrolling this wealthy neighborhood, two officers in each. Darnell's stakeout team casually drove off as police cars raced past them and down the street, sirens wailing, lights flashing. They screeched to a stop. The dog's master pointed as he told the cops what he'd just heard.

Six people were coming out the side door of the garage, two with their hands up, four looking suspicious. Now *they* were the recipients of "Down! Down! Down on the ground! Drop your weapons!" shouted one of the four officers crouched behind the police cruisers, now serving as bullet-proof barricades. The Crips were familiar with such circumstances, enough to realize that their odds were very low. They could count. Guns were dropped and hands were raised, matching those of Ian and Raphael. Except for Kayla ... she'd forgotten Jamal's admonition and still clutched the Glock, hanging down by her side. She squinted from the bright glare of a spotlight. From behind it came more instructions, "Drop the gun!! Now! Raise your hands!"

The radio crackled. Backup was requested. Two more cruisers showed up, their occupants ready for action, followed by a van used to hold arrested people. Guns drawn, two officers with flashlights made their way down the narrow cellar stairway, through the open doorway, and into the bloody room. More radio calls; an ambulance was on its way. The crime scene was busy.

A homicide detective arrived, pulled on thin, blue-latex gloves, and made her way to where Adam's still-warm body was found. She scanned the scene with her cell phone, taking a video of the gun on the table, the splintered bullet hole next to it, and Adam. The seasoned detective used a pencil to pick up the pistol by its trigger guard and dropped it into a plastic evidence bag. She spoke into her cell phone, the video recording icon still on, "Bullet lodged in table top, probably from this gun. Victim may have gotten off a round in attempted self-defense before being shot three times: chest, throat, forehead."

A white sheet covered what was left of Adam as he began his eternal sleep on the ambulance gurney; the order of his world had changed.

Being booked, finger-printed, and photographed by the police was a new experience for Kayla, as was the small holding cell. The intake staff didn't recognize Kayla Williams as anybody special, only that she was being held regarding a bloody homicide. The arresting officer filed his report after briefing the precinct chief directly. Homicide wasn't a new phenomenon in Washington, D.C.; but one in an upscale part of the city was, especially when the victim was found to be a high-ranking member of the National Security Agency. Another early-morning phone awakened the NSA Director, this one more in line with his military experience in the Mideast.

Each were interrogated in separate rooms. Kayla was coldly told that she had the right to an attorney and the right to remain silent. Not thinking clearly, she didn't wait. "I had to shoot him. He had a gun. He shot at me." Kayla followed up with her ace in the hole. "Do you know who I am?"

"Yes. You are one Kayla Williams, a resident of Pasadena, California."

"I'm also part of the team at the Jet Propulsion Laboratory for predicting and deflecting the asteroid Nyame."

They thought that she looked familiar, but the stress of having killed somebody at close range had somewhat changed her face, as if she'd aged 10 years and had not slept in nearly as long. In her mugshot, Kayla had that dear-in-the-headlights stare; her scar was obvious. One interrogator left the room and made a call to a special number, that of an investigative reporter for the *Washington Post*.

***

Zhang-Wei was worried, very worried. Kayla had called him just before she'd boarded her flight to Dulles, then ... nothing. Even though she'd said otherwise, he thought she'd return in time for the deflection transmission to Nyame. That communication, through the 70-meter antenna near Madrid, had been made. Adam's embedded clandestine numbers had been sent. The confirmation return message had been received. Members of IMCC, including Lajos, approved letting the on-asteroid countdown continue. The first nuclear thermal rocket had just fired, with more thrusts from the others to follow.

Nyame was close to the Earth, not in total orbital distance, but line-of-sight directly. Again, people with telescopes, especially the big ones, watched the night sky for the show: a slowly-winking, yellow star. The show was great and covered in the media, not for its eerie beauty, but to comfort the citizens of Beijing. They watched with considerable interest, and a few Russians did, as well. They would have to wait for post-nudge tracking to drive the ASA model to a new prediction.

Zhang-Wei was in his office, watching a replay of a special TV broadcast, proudly listening to the commentary. He jumped off his seat, startled. The banging on his office door was very loud and persistent. The stark face of NASA's Planetary Defense Officer was on the other side. He literally commanded, "Turn on Channel 2!" as he pushed his way in.

Zhang-Wei almost collapsed. There, filling the screen, was a mugshot of his best student.

Sequestered
[2 Years 305 Days before Impact]

The slit on the door was closed. Kayla finished up and flushed the cold, stainless steel toilet bowl mounted on the concrete wall of her small holding cell. She sat on the narrow metal-framed bed, thinking. Kayla had a lot to think about. A rap on the door broke her trance. The slit was opened, eyes looked in. "Dinner."

Kayla was hungry and was looking forward to her next meal, at least her body was. The detention officer opened the door. She was a big, no-nonsense woman. She set the plastic tray on the bed. It held meat loaf, mashed potatoes, gravy, sliced boiled carrots, a brownie, and a plastic bottle of water. The detention officer looked Kayla over. "Sister, what did you do? Been walking the streets?"

"No."

"Well, you could. You're fine."

"Do I have any visitors?"

"Not yet, honey. I'll check."

"Please do. Please." Kayla finished her meal. It wasn't too bad, she thought, if you're real hungry. An hour passed. She heard some conversation outside the door. The slit opened again. A different pair of eyes peered in.

"You've got visitors."

The head of lock-up came in. "Miss Williams, you get one phone call."

Two burly men escorted her to a stark room with bright lights, a table, and a chair. A push-button cradle telephone sat in front of her, a relic of an earlier era of law enforcement. Her escorts stood beside her; her call would not be private. It was also recorded.

Kayla quickly tapped out the number for Zhang-Wei's cell phone. He always had it with him, but its number was only known to a few.

There was an answer. "Zhang-Wei here."

"Zhang! Stop the rocket firings! Stop the rocket firings!"

Three other men wearing sunglasses and dark suits also walked in. They had bulges under their breast pockets. They didn't work for the Metropolitan Police Department. The phone was snatched from her hands and put back on its cradle; so much for due process. "Miss Williams, we're here to escort you to better accommodations while all this gets sorted out. A public defender will meet you there."

"Give me that! I haven't finished! It's critical!"

"I'm sure it is, Miss Williams, I'm sure it is."

***

Zhang-Wei sat across from a very upset Planetary Defense Officer who slammed the latest issue of the *Los Angeles Times* on the desk. The headline was not well received. "Scientist is Person of Interest in Brutal D.C. Murder." But it sold papers. Below Kayla's well-recognized face was her name, and the name of a very well-known institute: Caltech. The institute's president was not pleased. The article uncomfortably included the words asteroid, Nyame, Jet Propulsion Laboratory, NASA, international team, and Adam MacKellar. "OK, Zhang, what the hell's going on!?"

"I'm not sure, exactly, but Kayla was convinced that Adam MacKellar had somehow managed to corrupt the messages sent to the deflection system on Nyame."

"You do know Mister MacKellar is, or was, the Deputy Director of the National Security Agency?"

"I'm aware of that."

"Goddamn! This plays into the hands of the Chinese and their very public accusations. Is there any truth to her suspicions?"

Zhang-Wei was very uncomfortable, thinking that the targets of

Mao Zedong's Tiger Teams must have felt this way. But at least there was no execution squad waiting for him. "I don't know. Really. But she thought that MacKellar was in collusion with a key member of our team, Lajos Vadja."

"Lajos Vadja?!"

"Yes. But I think her evidence was circumstantial."

Just then, Zhang-Wei's small flip phone vibrated in his pocket, its number known only to members of his Solar System Dynamics group. He pulled it out and flipped it open. He raised his eyes when he saw 202, the D.C. area code. "Excuse me, Sir, this could be important. He pressed the answer button. "Zhang-Wei here."

He heard Kayla's frantic voice. "Zhang! Stop the rocket firings! Stop the rocket firings!"

"Kayla! How are you? Have you seen the papers!?"

The phone went dead.

"Who was that?"

"Kayla Williams. She said to stop the deflection. She sounded in a panic. Then her call was cut off."

They looked at each other, then both reflexively sprang up and literally ran into Mission Control, up to a specific console.

The specialist turned and looked up to see strained faces. "Yes?"

"What's the status of the deflection?"

"Command message was verified. Everything's proceeding as commanded. Four rockets have fired. We just received liquid hydrogen status on them."

"And …?"

"Their fuel is nearly exhausted. Only a few seconds of burn time remain on the ones reported."

Lajos saw the commotion and came over. "What's going on?"

"There's some concern with the deflection parameters."

Calm as cold granite, Lajos asked, "Why do you think that?"

The Planetary Defense Officer held back his newfound suspicions and replied, "Lajos, you were at the special meeting. Some asserted that the deflection system could be out of our control. We're just checking deflection status."

Lajos flashed back, "That's preposterous bullshit!" He walked off in a Hungarian huff.

They stepped away from the console. The Planetary Defense Officer whispered, "I'm going to have that bastard arrested. He knows something. I can smell it. The FBI will know how to handle this."

***

They stopped by her holding cell and waited in the hallway while Kayla used the stainless steel toilet, as they had strongly suggested. A back side door to the building was held open for them as they escorted her to a waiting sedan with dark-tinted windows. A driver was waiting. One of her escorts jumped in the front seat, the other two sat either side of her in the back. "Doctor Williams, we're afraid you'll have to wear this blindfold."

"What! Why?"

"Please don't ask. We have our orders. It looks like you're in a bit of trouble."

The big sedan rode smoothly. Nobody spoke. There were very few turns, and only the sound of an occasional passing car. Somebody up front turned on the radio and tuned in to a jazz station. A long three hours passed. Kayla began to sway side-to-side as the driver negotiated the curves of a state road that threaded through the mountains of Appalachia. A slow-down, a sharp turn, the tires growled over a graveled mountain road. Kayla couldn't see as they slowed and drove past armed sentries that waved them through, deep into the thick West Virginia woods. Finally, the car pulled to a stop next to a stout log cabin with shades pulled down over small windows.

Kayla was pulled out, led in, and set down on a long, deep, comfortable couch. Her blindfold was removed. Kayla found herself seated in front of a stone fireplace; flames flickered up, warmth radiated out. She gazed around at the rustic charm. A man and woman sat either side of her, their feet on a thick rug. The CIA had black sites for terrorist interrogations. Off any charts, this was what the FBI jokingly called a gray site on U.S. soil, for questioning a person of some notoriety, out of reach of the press.

"Miss Williams, I'm Agent Lawson. This is my partner, Agent Douglas. We're from the FBI office in Washington. Please relax. We just a have few questions for you."

"I had to shoot. He had a gun and fired."

"That's not why you're here." With that, Agent Lawson threw photographs on the low wood table in front of them. "Do you know this person?"

"Why, yes. That's Lajos Vadja. I took classes from him at Caltech. He's deeply involved with the asteroid deflection team at JPL."

"We understand from Doctor Zhang-Wei Huang that you suspected Mister Vadja of wrong-doing. That's why you're here and probably why Mister MacKellar is dead. Your Crips associates opened up to us."

"Yes, I had my suspicions, and still do, that Adam MacKellar had somehow managed to hack into the asteroid deflection control system."

"Is that why asteroid Nyame is now predicted to strike China?"

"Yes, I feel strongly about this. I wanted to intercede before the next uplink, which should have happened by now. I'm not sure if I called in time, or even if Adam MacKellar was able to corrupt the command message."

"They tell us that some of the rockets have been fired, and the remainder will be."

"Damn! Holy shit!! It's too late now. We'll have to track the new course and run the prediction model to see if Nyame will miss or hit."

"We're afraid you'll have to stay here until the prediction is known, maybe longer."

"Will I have to face criminal charges? It was self-defense! The prediction will be my defense. I was defending the Earth."

"You seem to be an honest person, Miss Williams. There's considerable concern that your suspicions will be spread around the world. Our President and NASA don't want people thinking that the asteroid may be under the control of some misguided person with an axe to grind."

***

Lajos sat stone-still, as if he'd been turned to salt. The *Los Angeles Times* article, and Kayla's face, shot fear through his cold Hungarian heart. He wasn't sure how or where, but he knew he had to make himself scarce. It didn't take long. He soon had unwanted help from men in dark suits and sunglasses who helped him pack. Blindfolded and handcuffed, he was rolled into the back of a van without rear windows. He had a fleeting thought that he might suffer the same fate as his grandfather back in Budapest. "Where in the hell are you taking me?"

"You'll find out when you get there."

A special unmarked aircraft descended into warm humid air; Lajos was aboard. His destination was not a tropical paradise: Guantanamo Bay on the southeast coast of Cuba. Terrorists held there had either died or been exchanged, but a few aging ones remained. Lajos would have company, which now included members of the Crips, one from Grape Street, others from the Trinidad section of Washington.

Ian and Raphael received special treatment in a special location. They were top intelligence specialists from friendly nations. They shared another log cabin at another gray site in Appalachia, incognito. Their story unfolded there, but would not be told.

The lid went on. The U. S. Government was well-practiced in handling disinformation. Suppressing information and freedom of speech was always a bit dicey, but this was a very special case. The Government had a secret as sensitive as Britain's ability to decrypt German messages during World War II: Nyame had been intentionally deflected to strike Beijing. The connection to the NSA cut like a razor, and had to buried. Very soon, there was a new NSA Director. There had already been naval brinksmanship in the Taiwan Strait. The citizens in and around Beijing were in an exacerbated panic, difficult to control with the CCP's mandatory plans for relocation. World wars had been triggered by less.

***

Weeks of intense post-deflection observations provided needed data for the ASA model running at both JPL and NSA. Despite Adam's death, the process still continued, now with FBI oversight. The results agreed. An emergency meeting in the White House Situation Room gathered the primary actors in the real drama of Nyame. The NASA Planetary Defense Officer had drafted the latest warning to be issued by the IMCC. The world and especially China were on a sharp edge. News releases had forecast when the next warning would be issued. Continued delays would arouse more suspicions and further lessen trust in deflection operations. Already, there'd been editorials and Internet posts that a nuclear bomb, or bombs, should have been selected as the Earth-saving deflection method. The intergovernmental members at the IMCC were kept in the dark. Messages of concern were leaking out back to their national leaders. Li Chen was especially frustrated. Finally, the U.S. President approved the warning, and the false rationale.

IMCC August 10, 2029 WARNING: PROBABLE ASTEROID EARTH IMPACT IN 1040 DAYS. The international intergovernmental team at the NASA Jet Propulsion Laboratory commanded nuclear thermal rocket thrusters on asteroid 2000 QW7 (Nyame) and again deflected its orbit. A solar flare disrupted the command data. With extensive post-deflection observations, Nyame is now predicted to impact close to Beijing, China, with a 76.8 percent probability on June 15, 2032, 22:23:13 Universal Coordinated Time. Other impact locations farther from this location and time are possible with less certainty. Evacuation plans should begin immediately for Beijing and for an area within 600 kilometers.

There was no mention that the liquid hydrogen aboard the quadrapods had been essentially exhausted.

Negotiation
[2 Years 301 Days before Impact]

An American cruiser of the carrier battle group was dead in the water at the southern end of the Taiwan Strait. It was taking on water through a gash in its hull, but pumps were keeping it afloat. Accusations and denials flooded the news. This followed reports of very low altitude, supersonic flybys of Chinese fighters. Sonic booms rattled the ship's bridge. Two war vessels had been on a collision course. Each hailed the other to stand off, to give way. Neither captain blinked. Hard rudder orders at the last minute weren't sufficient. Hulls ground against each other. Metal was punctured and peeled off.

The President's speech writer looked over the topics provided by his White House staff, NASA, and the Pentagon. In addition to the evacuation of the area around Beijing and Nyame's trajectory, he had to include solar flares and a damaged American cruiser in the Strait.

Draft finished, the speech-writer met with the President in the Oval Office. The words was edited and practiced. The final version was loaded on the teleprompter. The asteroid's name, Nyame, would be used in the verbal dialogue. He vowed to himself to project calm resolve, leadership, while sitting at the Resolute Desk. The camera was rolled in. This wasn't a press conference; no questions, no answers. The Administrator of NASA would hold a televised conference, but only after the President completed his address to the nation and to the world.

The familiar camera operator pointed to him. It was the signal that the President was live, on the air again.

"Good evening. We continue to work closely with our international partners as Nyame presents a grave risk to the people of China. They are being relocated to safe zones should Nyame strike near Beijing. We must face the hard truth. The United States stands ready to assist with the evacuation. The help of other nations will be needed. Flares on the Sun and their high-energy particles unfortunately corrupted the stored command data that had been beamed to Nyame. Nuclear rocket thrusters errantly deflected her to a trajectory with a most-likely impact near Beijing. The likelihood is not 100 percent, but it is high. This asteroid could completely miss the Earth. But the strike probability is high enough to take proactive action and evacuate the area. We have been in direct contact with the leadership of China regarding the accident during naval exercises in the Taiwan Strait. I have spoken to the President of China. I urge restraint as the people of China face this threat from space. Thank you, and God bless America." He hesitated, then unthinkingly ad-libbed, "… And may God bless the people of China."

The President's speech was shown on the big monitors on the wall in Mission Control at JPL. The dimly-lit room was packed. You could have heard a pin drop before the President came on the air. The collective mood was low. They had failed. Now all that was left, while critically important, was to predict Nyame's orbit, the date and time of Minimum Orbit Intersection Distance, the probability of that distance being zero, and the location on the Earth's surface where this would occur. Kayla Williams's splash in the news and Lajos Vadja's unexplained disappearance pulled at the fraying fabric of trust in the room. A frustrated controller at a desk position slapped his monitor and shouted, "What the hell is going on?!"

***

It had been four months since a city near Beijing had first been put in Nyame's crosshairs, and only two days since the crosshairs had moved close to the center of China's capital. Now was the time time to act. The President of the Russian Federation discussed the status of Lenin with his closest advisors from Roscosmos. Russia, Minsk, and even Moscow at first had been at some risk of a Nyame impact. Then the quadrapods arrived. The risk moved westward to the Pas-de-Calais. Now the risk had suspiciously shifted to China.

He was a pretty fair chess player and quite proud of the Grand Masters that Russia had produced. The Russian President weighed his options, his next move, and decided. Lenin was a major piece, maybe even a Queen. It would be moved.

The President of the Russian Federation boarded the plush near-supersonic Bombardier aircraft at Chkalovsky military airport near Moscow. His small security entourage came aboard, followed by the most important member of the secret delegation; his translator. There was ample room and a nice bed. He would arrive rested. Six hours later they touched down in the dark of night at Xijiao military airport near Beijing. A long Mercedes limousine with dark-tinted windows and no-nonsense guards awaited his arrival.

Armed motorcycle riders accompanied them to the Forbidden City, not the adjacent Imperial City which held the headquarters and buildings of the Chinese Communist Party. Along the way, the President noted many large buses and trucks scurrying about, despite the early hour. Nyame was being felt, but in the same dictated calm as had been used to lock down cities during the pandemic.

They were led through an intentionally-confusing labyrinth to a red door with a large, brass hànzì, which stood for Emperor. The escort opened the door and allowed only the Russian President and his translator to enter; Russian security had to wait outside. Like a bank vault door, it was shut, sealing them in. At a round rosewood table sat the President of the People's Republic of China. His face looked haggard, deep in thought about what his people faced in and around the ancient capital city. This was his private room for very secure meetings. Very few were allowed inside, let alone even knowing of its existence. A short, thin man sat next to him, his translator. He looked nervous, worried. Words and sentences in Russian and

Chinese were to flow back and forth. They had to be very accurate in their reception and understanding. The two translators would assist, and check each other when their translations were spoken as dialogue confirmation.

The Russian President quickly scanned and absorbed the special room. It was filled with history. Trappings of ancient Chinese dynasties adorned the walls and tables. There were latter-day icons, framed photographs of bushy-bearded Karl Marx and clean-shaven Mao Zedong, the room punctuated with the red and yellow National Flag of the People's Republic of China. Strangely, there was no photograph of the Chinese President himself. But he was sitting at the table; his photograph was unnecessary. He felt that his likeness should not share the honored space until after his death, and only if he proved himself worthy.

Nothing was said for a full minute. The two leaders just stared, each taking the visual measure of the other, despite their having met before on more than one occasion in more-public circumstances. The shape and sculpture of their faces confirmed an obvious divergence somewhere along a limb of the evolutionary tree. The Russian President reflected on current differences beyond bone structure and eye shape. China had ten times more people; Russia two times more land area and more than twice the length of coastline.

The Russian President spoke first, a matter-of-fact statement, "You have a problem with the asteroid."

The Chinese translator spoke, in Chinese. The Russian translator announced, in Chinese and then Russian, "That is correct." The translation cycle added time, but that provided more time to think before answering.

"Yes. I suspect the Americans." His staff had received encrypted messages from California, from Li Chen.

"I can help."

"What! By moving my people with aircraft and trucks? Ships on the river to the Bohai?"

"We can deflect the asteroid."

"How? My people have confirmed that the necessary fuel for the rockets has been used up. It is too late to launch kinetic impactors."

"With a hydrogen bomb, the most powerful ever."

The Chinese President grimaced, "We are not stupid! There is no time left to launch your bomb to join up with the asteroid." The translators' eyes widened.

"Do you think *we* are stupid?! From the very beginning, we did not trust the rocket deflection system. Our bomb is now close to the asteroid, in a parallel orbit. It was launched in time, years ago, its purpose falsified for the public."

Concern seemed to wash from his face. "Can you explode it to move the asteroid, to miss, to save my city, my people?"

"I can."

"When?"

"That depends."

"On what?"

"You."

"What do you want?" Concern returned to his face, sensing a different kind of negotiation, a Russian shakedown.

The pace of dialogue increased, taxing the translators' ability to keep up. Topics were far-ranging: mineral resources, territorial access, the fundamental underpinnings of economics, and geopolitical power. Some would be very difficult, but Beijing was in Nyame's crosshairs, more than enough motivation.

"You must put your requests in writing; a proposed agreement."

"No. Do you think *I* am stupid? That will never work. Memories will fade, despite what is on paper. Doing what is described will be delayed, indefinitely."

"Then what?"

"Money."

"Money? How much?"

The Russian President came prepared. From his suit pocket he pulled out a small folded slip of paper and pushed it across the table. "In Rubles." Beneath the very large number, also shown in equivalent Yuan, was a long set of digits and letters for secret communication links. A translator was not needed. "That is the amount, the account, communication and transfer information. When we have confirmation that the money has been transferred into our account, I personally will detonate the bomb."

The Chinese President's eyes widened at this astronomical level of blackmail. "And if I do not?"

"I will do nothing. I do not need to do anything. It is not Russia's problem that the asteroid is headed in your direction. The world does not know of our bomb in space."

The intensity of the Chinese glare was felt like a laser in the ensuing stare-down. Another very uncomfortable minute passed in absolute quiet. The translators felt uncomfortable, that they were witnessing a very historical decision that would change the order of the world, with either decision. Shattering the silence, the Chinese President replied, "I will need some time with the Central Committee."

"I must return. Do not wait too long."

The return trip unfolded. Soon the Russian President was asleep on the comfortable bed of the Bombardier 9500 as loose ends were tidied up back in Beijing.

The Chinese translator knew what came with the job. Breathe a word of anything discussed in private and you would be executed, along with your entire family, just in case you had passed government secrets to them. Such things had happened. The translator walked out of the Forbidden City. A car drove up alongside him and stopped abruptly. Like Ninjas of old, men dressed in black jumped out and stuffed him in the backseat. He was driven away, never to be seen again. He'd not had a chance to speak with anybody; his family was spared.

Detonation
[244 Days to Impact]

Good news was coupled with bad news in the Russian public communiqué. There hadn't been back-channel discussions or negotiations. The information was distributed in its rawest form. The Russian Federation reported that it had launched a huge hydrogen bomb into space and that the bomb was now near Nyame, able to deflect it with a single massive detonation. That was the good news. The bad news was that the Russians had secretly launched a nuclear weapon into space. World governments and their diplomatic actions exploded; but it was too late. Their reactions would have been even worse had it been revealed that the bomb was capped with an ablative reentry cone.

The President of the United States and the Administrator of NASA demanded that the IMCC team at JPL be a partner in the planning and detonation of the bomb. Astrophysicists at JPL, with the exception of Dimitri, publicly raised concern about the complexities of this deflection method, especially on a tumbling asteroid, and the risks of its fragmentation. The Russian President listened, then added more security around Roscosmos. He responded that Russia alone would be in command.

A hasty emergency meeting at the UN produced a similar result. Russia would not follow the recommendations of the Security Council. The requested emergency Defense Conference would not be held.

Communications continued and increased in intensity as Nyame closed the orbital distance to the Earth. Tension was taut, and tightened with each passing hour. The media became the mouthpieces for questions asked in secret, at the intergovernmental level. When would the bomb be detonated? Would there be fragmentation? What would be the new track? Would the pieces miss the Earth? The last two would be answered by Zhang-Wei and his team at JPL.

***

The President of the Russian Federation paced back and forth in the Roscosmos control room, waiting. His trusted Minister of Finance, a tough member of the old guard, was in the basement room at the Kremlin, waiting. A huge sum of money, the largest ever transferred, would be electronically deposited in a very secret international transfer account. It wasn't in Switzerland nor the Bahamas, but at an undisclosed location. This was brinksmanship at the highest level, a verbally-agreed *quid pro quo*. The President of the Russian Federation had his ace in the hole: Lenin.

Liquid hydrogen for the NTRs was almost exhausted; not enough remained to nudge Nyame with any consequence. But nuclear batteries and solar panels still provided power. Quadrapod cameras and communication systems still functioned. With the Russian revelation of Lenin, imagery was sent back to Earth of the approaching hydrogen bomb. The best close-up views were from a camera on a quadrapod at the girth of Nyame.

Thruster commands from Roscosmos nestled the bomb up close to Nyame's rotational axis, to within 30 meters of the surface. It was a beautiful deep-space ballet. The red square with a yellow star and yellow hammer and sickle stood out in the faint sunlight. It had been hand-painted, with honor, by a Russian artist who'd lived in the glory days of the Soviet Union. The flag of the Russian Federation was nowhere to be seen on the bomb-carrying spacecraft. The Communist flag had made a statement. It caused nearly as much discussion and coverage as the purpose of the bomb itself.

The red phone buzzed. The Minister of Finance quickly picked up the receiver for the special hotline. He answered sullenly, *"Nyet."*

The phone went dead, hung up at the other end. The President was impatient. This back-and-forth went through a few more cycles over the next hour.

Another phone, a purple one, made a rapid beeping tone. The Minister of Finance leapt for it. A long series of numbers and letters sounded like music to his ears. He quickly turned to the secure-banking digital communications system that made cryptocurrency security look like child's play. The long code was typed manually. It released the money into the very secret bank account of the Russian Federation … confirmed!

He picked up the red phone. It was answered immediately. The Minister spoke the hoped-for word, *"Da!"*

The command signal was activated by the President himself, as he had wanted. It was sent spaceward from the big antenna in Crimea. It arrived at Lenin's antenna. Physics played out in a micro-instant. A chemical explosive compressed the plutonium to critical mass. Fission produced very high temperature and pressure, igniting the same fusion that powered the Sun. As with the nuclear thermal rockets, nuclear reaction and hydrogen were combined; this time the energy resulted from the fusion of hydrogen's deuterium and tritium isotopes.

A small sun was born right next to Nyame, a temporary sun that massively emitted neutrons, along with intense X-rays and gamma rays. They irradiated the surface regolith and underlying iron-nickel. Instantly-vaporized matter was ejected, action-reaction, nudging Nyame.

The neutrons and radiation also reached into two deep fissures of the solid core that spoke of its molten formation. Nyame was not only nudged, it was fragmented into three pieces; two small, one large. There had been one asteroid that nearly struck Elcano; now there were three.

***

Their bodies glistened in the windowless log hut. The hot cast iron stove was fed with chopped wood stacked neatly outside. It reminded her of the banya of her youth in the logging camp in Eastern Siberia. He got up from the lone bench and walked over to feed the stove. It kept the banya very hot. She playfully swatted his bare buttock as he passed. Two bundles of leafed birch branches were soaking in the tepid water of a wooden bucket. She stood and spread a white towel over the bench. He returned and laid face down for the Russian banya ritual. Despite the modest temperature of the birch branches, they felt like searing hot irons as she beat his body, as if playing a kettledrum at the symphony. He flinched each time the soaked branches contacted his sensitive hot skin. He had never been into that kind of sex, but had become more than accustomed to her kind of Russian foreplay. She was next to feel the stimulating swats of the wet leafy branches.

Very much had happened since their overnight affair at Edwards Air Force Base, when she had brought in a Ruslan to pick up a quadrapod. At the bar, the phantom Russian bear had also arrived. Between shots of vodka, she had nudged against this American fighter pilot when they had crowded under the protective table, then later in bed.

Nyame had overshadowed everything since then, except their smoldering relationship, igniting when their flight paths crossed. Both had reached the rank of colonel. With typical Russian authority, she demanded; he relented. They sealed their commitment before God in a blue onion-domed Russian Orthodox Church near Arkhangelsk, then moved into their nearby old historic house on the coast. It came with a traditional banya, by the White Sea.

Retirement incomes weren't equal; but collectively, the world of coastal housing lay at their financial feet. They both liked the tranquility of water and thumbed through literature for sumptuous places in the Bahamas, Réunion, and Tahiti. They could've had a place on beautiful Kunming Lake in Beijing for free, but there would be nobody there to serve them. A very few stalwarts and fatalists remained in ghosted neighborhoods hundreds of kilometers in every direction from Tiananmen Square as Nyame approached.

Summer air flowed over their banya from the cool White Sea. The water's edge was close. They walked to the gravelly beach and dove in. The sudden change in temperature was shocking and stimulating. Farther back, at the edge of the woods, was their stout, squat log cabin made from the trees of the surrounding forest. It, too, reminded her of growing up in a Siberian logging camp, the main reason they'd purchased it.

As planned, as they did for each banya session, a metal pot with hot water sat over the red coals of a small fire pit. Small bags of herbal tea in a small bowl were on the round wicker table on the covered front porch. Next to the tea bags, a grooved wooden dipper was in a larger bowl filled with honey from hives in those same woods. They exchanged knowing glances and stood next to wicker chairs with padded cushions, awaiting another ritual. A Russian coin lay on the table. There had been arguments; now a coin was used to decide. In fighter-pilot-hormonal hurry, he always wanted tea and honey after, she before. He picked up the coin and flipped it into the air with his thumb. It bounced on the wicker and landed heads up. Tea with honey would have to wait. They entered the inner sanctum of the cabin. He slid the old wooden crossbar latch into place. The heavy wood door sealed them in, as it had others from the time of the tsars. As they finished their embrace, the massive nuclear bomb next to Nyame detonated.

***

In a blink, imagery of the bomb from the nearest quadrapod vanished from the monitors at JPL, but at a later time due to the speed of radio transmissions. Telescopes on the nighttime side of the Earth, and in space, were tracking Nyame when the unannounced detonation occurred. In greatly expanded views, a brief bright star appeared, then faded, especially dramatic in the infrared. Spectrographic data had sharp spikes. Subsequent data showed a hot, yet cooling, irradiated surface, or surfaces, as the evaporating fissures pushed Nyame apart into three segments.

Owing to Nyame's rotation, centrifugal forces interlaced with mutual gravitational attraction as the three masses separated. Of the two smaller fragments, one was about double the mass of the other.

Their iron-nickel cores became a binary asteroid around a common barycenter, it now on a trajectory different than the remaining much-larger piece. Rubble, from dust to stones to rocks, swirled around this center like bees around their hive. Tracking the cores, predicting, and warning became very complicated.

Two months of data from multiple telescopes were fed into the data maw of the ASA model, the Russian model at Roscosmos, and the model run by the China National Space Administration. The ASA model was used to convince the Administrator of NASA and the U.S. President to approve the resultant two-part warning without the involvement of the Russians and Chinese; the IMCC had also been fractured. This would be the first time the general public was informed of the nuclear detonation deflection.

> IMCC OCTOBER 15, 2031 WARNING: POSSIBLE ASTEROID EARTH IMPACT IN 244 DAYS. A massive hydrogen bomb has been detonated next to asteroid 2000 QW7 (Nyame) splitting it into three fragments. The larger fragment (Nyame I), will pass by the Earth 29,230 kilometers above Elkins, West Virginia, June 15, 2032, 08:52:43 Universal Coordinated Time; 04:52:43 Eastern Daylight Time, with a 0.003 percent probability of impacting the surface. Other closest point of approach locations and times are possible with less certainty. West Virginia evacuation is not recommended at this time. Monitor future warnings. The two smaller ones (Nyame II) are in close orbit around each other, a binary asteroid, predicted to impact the Leshukonsky District of the Arkhangelsk Oblast with a 12.8 percent probability June 15, 2032, 20:19:56 Universal Coordinated Time. Other impact locations and times are possible with less certainty. People in the Leshukonsky District should evacuate.

This agreed with the Russian and Chinese models, but with higher probabilities and different times for Nyame I and Nyame II. The Chinese President was relieved, the result of money well spent. Relocation operations for his people were halted and reversed.

Absolute authority turned the fate of millions on a dime.

The Russian President was not as relieved. Astrophysicists from Roscosmos nervously stood before him in the Kremlin, attempting to explain why the deflected asteroid had residuals, with a likelihood of impacting the surface of Russian territory in the far north. They tried to explain that this was very complicated, but that at least the possible impacts wouldn't be near Moscow. The boreal forest region was sparsely populated, including reindeer and some of the ancient Saami people to herd them. The area was warned, with some difficulty, but little aid was provided by the central government in Moscow. The Saami were pretty much on their own, as they'd always been. They and their reindeer would be on the move, some pulling sleds through the winter snow, as in the old days.

Zhang-Wei had closely examined the ASA model's trajectory forecast for Nyame II. The final angle of approach with respect to the Earth had changed. The pair of asteroids was forecast to cross the Leshukonsky region at a grazing angle, nearly tangent to the top of the atmosphere. Meteors had indeed skipped off the atmosphere before, like a tossed, flat stone over the surface of a smooth lake, but they were rare events. There had followed considerable discussion at JPL about this possibility. Zhang-Wei strongly advised not to make this part of the warnings. This had been one of the white-knuckled possibilities when the Apollo 13 astronauts steered their reentry vehicle to safely intersect the atmosphere at just the right angle, to not skip off into infinite oblivion.

The predicted track of Nyame II was from the east on a heading of 261 degrees, across the Leshukonsky region and Arkhangelsk. This would occur just after summer twilight and could provide quite a show if low enough to touch the atmosphere. If too low, it would be much more than just a show.

***

Kayla had reluctantly settled into a resigned routine in the cabin in the West Virginia woods. She'd actually become friends with her

285

FBI captors: Agent Tim Lawson and Agent Carol Douglas. Their beds in three separate bedrooms were comfortable. The couch by the cozy fireside welcomed them. There they discussed many things: her life in Watts, theirs in Portland and New York City, and what had led them to this place. They accompanied her, armed, on nearby trails for exercise to keep from becoming stir crazy. Together, they had become quite good cooks. Food stuffs and other living essentials were delivered periodically. Deliveries were done by various trucks, some rusty and old, so as to not arouse suspicions. Some hill people were curious about the cabin, seen when out hunting, but wisely decided to mind their own business.

Each delivery included a stack of issues of the *Washington Post*. Kayla was able to keep up with what was being released to the public about her now-fractured asteroid. After breakfast she read the latest warning and a headline. "Son of a bitch!!"

Agent Douglas asked, "What's wrong?"

"Fuckin' Russians! They somehow got a hydrogen bomb next to my asteroid. Lajos didn't trust them at the Defense Conference, even after. Neither did I."

Agent Lawson scanned the paper and added, "Isn't that better, now that some remote area has replaced Beijing as the most-likely place of impact?"

"Yeah, I suppose so. One piece of my asteroid, the largest, will pass almost right over us just before sunrise. If the weather's clear, we may be able to see it. It'll look like a moving star, with grazing sunlight from the east illuminating it. It may look quite bright, being much larger than satellites in low-Earth orbit which can be seen with the naked eye in the evening twilight, or the early morning just before dawn.

"Whatever. We have strict orders to keep you here until the asteroid either passes or strikes. Then you can come out and tell everything you know. We had lives, too, you know."

"Will there be a trial?"

"Don't know. From what you tell me, they may give you a medal."

"What about the others? Lajos Vadja and my Crips friends, the others in the room when I shot Adam MacKellar?"

"Can't say. Suspect they're being held incognito until Nyame does her thing, or not, in pieces."

Kayla looked over at Agent Douglas, then back at Agent Lawson. "Just why do you think Nyame is a her?

"Probably for the same reason hurricanes were given female names, for a time."

Kayla instructed, "For the people of Ghana, my people, Nyame is both male and female."

"Sorry. We'll just have to wait and see how *she* behaves."

Agent Douglas retorted, "Typical man."

Arkhangelsk
[27 Seconds before Impact]

Nervous months had passed for people in all walks of life, especially residents of Arkhangelsk and those in the forests of Leshukonsky. ASA integration time lessoned as the latest track data were ingested and modeled. Zhang-Wei and his team were busy. Pairs of warnings had been issued more frequently as model run times decreased; one for Nyame I, one for Nyame II. The President and his staff were immediately briefed by NSA and JPL, so they'd know official warning content before the rest of the world.

The accuracy of the predictions increased, the size of the probability ellipses shrank, but not to zero for Nyame II. After each run, the impact centroid of Nyame II kept shifting slightly westward; the time of closest point of approach became slightly later.

Nyame II would pass the Moon by a wide margin, but its gravitational effects were part of the model, being a more significant N-body.

The Russian President decided not to order the evacuation of Arkhangelsk, but to just keep the citizens informed. The decision to leave was theirs. A few did, almost all stayed. Some planned to be outside to watch, just in case there would be something to see.

On the last warning, the time of closest point of approach for Nyame II was predicted to occur at 23:21:17 Local Standard Time, above and just to the east of Arkhangelsk, June 15, 2032. The altitude was just above the Kármán line, the defined boundary between the Earth's atmosphere and the vacuum of space.

***

At her insistence, Kayla and her FBI captors hiked in the dark to a clearing in the woods atop a nearby hill. A flashlight lit the trail ahead. The early morning air was cool, the sky clear, stars twinkled. They waited there for 15 minutes. Kayla looked at her wristwatch; it was 52 minutes past the hour. She pointed to the east. "There it is!" The bright point of light moved across the sea of stars. Even the FBI agents were captivated while Nyame I traversed the sky and disappeared over the western horizon. Agent Douglas patted Kayla on the back.

Agent Lawson also was impressed. "That's something, that an asteroid's passage can be predicted with such accuracy."

The equations of the Adaptive Simulated Annealing model swirled in her mind. "Yes, we can … we have."

Agent Douglas shivered in the morning chill. "Well, let's head back down."

In about 12 hours, Kayla knew there'd be another show unseen by her, well over the eastern horizon ... or disaster. She turned back and faced east, in the general direction of Arkhangelsk. "Not yet. I need a moment."

***

The banya had been hot. He had put too much wood in the stove. After their cooling dip in the waters of the White Sea, he flipped the coin. It came up tails; he lost. In the twilight hours, they enjoyed herbal tea with honey on the porch looking to the northwest across the water, watching the Sun set. Bathrobes and blankets protected them from the cool evening wind.

They shifted their wicker chairs to look eastward. The local Russian newspaper *Pravda Severa* had been covering the story of two coupled asteroids that would pass overhead from the east. His skills in Russian still had not come up to speed; she had to translate it for him.

Twilight faded to black. The largest of the asteroid pair was in the lead. It felt the top of the atmosphere first and was heated to a glowing white-hot streak easily seen as it passed high overhead, then vanishing when it skipped back into space. They shouted, "Wow! *Vot eto da!!*" and clinked their cups of tea, then raised them toward the sky in tribute to the dramatic show.

They wondered about the second one. It arrived a few seconds later with nearly the same relative speed. The high atmosphere decelerated the smaller mass more than the first. It slowed further as it dove into denser air, dragged down by the lower atmosphere.

Its white-hot light caught their eyes. It was bright, grew brighter and larger, as if the Sun had risen. They were transfixed; minds raced, time slowed. They said nothing, heard nothing; the light from its air-friction-heated surface traveled much faster than its acoustic shock wave. It was coming straight at them, at their part of the coast of the White Sea near Arkhangelsk. The expanding glare was brighter than the Sun. There was no time to react; there was only time to stare in captivating wonder at what would end their lives in a flash, with cups of honeyed herbal tea in their fingers and a coin that came up tails.

Blinding light, a spreading and crushing shock wave, an enormous crater, a northward propagating tsunami, and very many sudden deaths and injuries marked the end of coupled events. They began with *Theoria Motus* in Watts, followed by the close encounter between 467317 (2000 QW7), Elcano, and Kayla Williams atop Mauna Kea. They ended with a dangerous, fractured Nyame.

More attention should have been given to the wisdom of Carl Sagan and Steven Ostro.

Robert Wright served 27 years in the United States Air Force as a meteorologist, officer and commander, followed by a decade working on the Washington, D.C. Beltway. He returned to his hometown of Portland, Oregon, took to writing, and has self-published: *You've Got Rocks*, an anthology of memoirs; *The Brass*, a history of Portland's world famous Horse Brass Pub; *3FTx - Timed Terror*, a mystery novel about the unique downing of an airliner. He lives in Portland with his wife.